Green Ivy Publishing
1 Lincoln Centre
18W140 Butterfield Road
Suite 1500
Oakbrook Terrace IL 60181-4843
www.greenivybooks.com

ISBN: 978-1-944680-74-9

Remember Me

Sins of the Father

By

Machell Hammond

After leaving New Orleans following a hurricane, Alisa Washington found herself all alone as she took refuge in Atlanta, where she wanted to put her life together after a bad breakup. She had met and worked for Ida Stanford, and decided to make Atlanta where she would finish her studies in physiology and land a job at the hospital, which would change her life forever. After Lisa's arrival, Ida suddenly became sick and was hospitalized, and that was the beginning of her nightmare.

When Ida became ill, Lisa met handsome Chris Weber. After finding out that she is pregnant, Lisa finds herself being stalked by darkness, a mysterious presence that follows her and threatens to take away her unborn child. This presence stalks her and seems to be determined to destroy both their lives.

Devin Jones, who decided that it was time for him to get his life together, went on a journey to meet the beautiful woman that he had bumped into at the mall but found himself involved in a car accident that left him with amnesia. He wakes to find a beautiful woman standing over his bedside. One night while in his hospital room, he witnessed an evil presence watching her.

Will he get his memory back in time to save the life of her and her unborn child, or would he lose them both to the dark presence that has threatened his family for centuries.

Chapter 1

"Will you sit down," Ida said, as Lisa paced the floor of the hospital room.

"I am sorry, Momma Ida, every time we come here I get nervous."

"Sit, honey, you are going to wear a hole in the floor."

Lisa took one last look out the door, "Where is that doctor," she asked?

"He will be here," Ida said, moving her sweater so Lisa could sit next to her. Ida looked her in the eye, "It's not over till it's over."

Lisa smiled, "You always say that, what does it mean?"

"It means I am not going anywhere until it is my time and not all the pacing in the world will change a thing."

Lisa smiled; she had been with Ida for over five years and now that her family had moved on from New Orleans, she had no idea what she would do if something happened to Ida because now she was all that Lisa has.

Ida placed her hand on her stomach. "It hurts, honey."

"I'll get someone to help, alright Momma?" Lisa jumped up fast and in a panic, but before she could get to the door, it opened. "Finally," she said in a low tone with an eye roll to show her disgust.

"Behave yourself!" Ida said to her in a soft, but caring voice; she know that Lisa worried about her all of the time, which is why she takes Ida on her errands with her, so that she would not be alone.

Dr. Robert Samuels entered the room with an ink pen in one hand and a clipboard in the other and was reading Ida's chart, "Stomach cramps and nausea," before he looked up and smiled at her. "Hello, beautiful."

Ida smiled so big you would question if she were sick at all. She stared at the doctor; she could not make him out. However, she could tell that there was something different about him, but she could not put her finger on it.

"Can you get on the table for me?" He lifted her hand to help her climb on the table, while Lisa stood biting her nails. Pressing his hand down on her abdominal area, "Does it hurt when I do this?" he asked, as he gently pushed.

She moaned, "Yes."

"You're pregnant," Dr. Samuels said in a joking voice.

Ida and Lisa both laughed at the same time, while Lisa waited for the doctor to diagnose the problem; she was hoping it was only gas, but she could see concern on his face. "There is a virus in the air, and it is causing a major panic in the community. It should only last about twenty-four hours. However, I would really like it if you spent the night in the hospital." He looked at Lisa in a way that he had never before—almost lustful—before turning back to Ida, "Because of your age, I would like to keep you here for observation."

Lisa sat straight up in her chair, as Dr. Samuels turned to her and said, "Do not panic, Ms. Washington, I will give her back to you tomorrow," as he reached out and touched her shoulder. After brief eye contact, he turned back to Ida, "I will get the admission papers ready for you."

"Thanks, doctor," Lisa said, when she noticed that there was something different about him. It was as if she was seeing him for the first time; his complexion was different: it was flawless. She thought to herself that his body from his hands to his face was the same exact color and he did not have a spot on him.

When she and Ida had appointments at the clinic, she had never noticed his caramel-colored skin and the perfect teeth. He was about six-foot-two, and the good doctor had dimples in both cheeks; with soft black hair, he looked like a young Phillip Michael Thomas from *Miami Vice*.

The doctor had a soft spot for Ida. Whenever Ida had an appointment at the hospital, she would ask about Dr. Samuels, so it was not long before he became her primary physician.

"He is cute, isn't he? Ida would say in a low voice to Lisa, as if the doctor could not hear her. Ida did not care; she thought Dr. Samuels was mysterious. He never said much to her, which she found strange, then he would call her beautiful. It was like he was a totally different person.

Lisa turned to Ida, breathing a sigh of relief. "Yes, he is. I had never really looked at him until tonight. I have been so busy with my sewing. I have not paid attention to anything." Not even the fact that her biological clock was ticking, which is why she made an appointment for tomorrow with her gynecologist to see if she was capable of conceiving a child. She tried to put the thought out of her mind, but it always comes back, front and center. What if she waited too late to have a child? What if she could have a child, she was not dating anyone, not even a prospect. In seven weeks, she would be forty-one years old.

"You need to pay attention, honey. The world is passing you by. You need to take chances, stop playing it so safe." Her frail hand lifted Lisa's chin. "It's okay if you fall down, get up and try again." Momma Ida could see the pain on the face of the woman she considered her daughter, the woman who had taken care of her, a woman who sacrificed her own personal happiness to make sure Ida had her independence so that she would be able to walk again and do things to help herself. She was Lisa's student and Lisa was hers; they became best friends.

She thought of her first time meeting Lisa and how dedicated she was to her. Ida fought back her own tears. She did not know what she would do if she lost her.

Five-and-a-half years ago, she was doing some work in her garden when her foot was caught in the hose in her yard and she turned and fell. She did not break any bones, but it was hard for her to get back on her feet.

The hospital would send nurses over to her home to give her a bath, and they would write up their daily reports; but they would not take her out on walks. They would complain that if they lifted her, they would hurt their own backs. So Ida would stay in bed all day. Finally, she called Judy to complain about the worker. Judy was Ida's caretaker. Judy moved from Jackson, Mississippi, to Atlanta, Georgia, to live with Ida after her grandmother could no longer care for her. After college Judy moved to Macon, Georgia, and married, but she returned years later to become Ida's caretaker. Judy lived with Ida for years after she was released from the Mental Hospital until she saved enough money to start her own business with her best friend, Ellen. Ellen and Judy were roommates who met in college. They would stop to visit and sometimes bring Ida food. But it was overwhelming trying to do both jobs, so Judy placed a help-wanted sign in her boutique window. Ida would tell Judy the hospital workers were there just to receive a paycheck and, if she wanted to get better, she would have to hire her own personal worker.

Judy notified the hospital that Momma Ida would no longer need their services. The doctors protested, telling her Momma Ida needed twenty-four-hour care and a lot of physical therapy. Ida could read their thoughts; they were wondering why she would waste her time, as she would not walk again without pain, so it was easier for her just to lay and rot in bed.

Lisa came along and changed her life. She would hold her and walk her all over the house, and massage her hip several times a day until her pain was gone. Lisa loved to cook her special Cajun food and let her soak in a hot bubble bath every day. They would even work in the garden together and she would not leave Ida's side. If she had to make deliveries, they would do it together.

People would call them beauty and the beast; men would stare at Lisa and Ida would ask them what in the hell they were looking at! Ida thought that, maybe, her being so needy kept Lisa from meeting her prince charming, which is why she did not object when Lisa came to her while she was sitting at the kitchen table having coffee to tell her she had found a house she loved.

"You are a good girl, sweetheart; you have a blessing coming," Momma Ida said with confidence, "real soon." Ida smiled, "Remember what I said to you when we first met?"

Lisa tried to think back, lifting her eyes to the sky. Her memory is not what it used to be, and she could see that her behavior was affecting Ida, so she tried to make her feel better, even if the conversation was upsetting to her, "No, remind me."

"Remember when I said to you, I will not leave this earth until we get you a good man, the man of your dreams?"

Lisa smiled, "Oh yeah, well, Momma, looks like you are going to be around for a very long time."

"Honey, God will bless you, wait and see, and you can mark my word on that." Ida thought back. She wondered what had gone wrong; she thought that Lisa would be dating by now, but it had not happened. "Somebody has a birthday coming up," Momma Ida said in almost a singing voice.

Lisa dropped her head in shame. Ida noticed it immediately—every year since she had known Lisa, on her birthday, she become depressed and withdrawn—she would work nonstop. Five years had gone by and nothing in her life had change; sure, she has a good, profitable business, but she was no closer to meeting a good man—or any man—at this point. She had grown tired of sleeping alone. Lisa laughed, even Judy gets more action than she and Judy was over sixty.

Every year Judy, Ellen and Momma Ida would throw her a party and invite all her friends, and everyone would have a date except the birthday girl.

"No party this year, Momma, please." Lisa stood to stretch her legs. She walked over to look out the window, and Momma Ida followed, placing her hand on her back, "We will make this the last one, honey; after this year, I will not ask for another."

Dr. Samuels entered the room with the paper for Momma Ida to sign. As he walked past Lisa, his arm slowly brushed against her body. It had been years since she felt the touch of a man and at that point, Lisa realized she made a good choice in getting a place to work and live. She loved Momma Ida, but she needed her own personal space. And she needed to start dating.

"Are you married, doctor?" Momma Ida asked after signing the admission papers.

"Divorced," Dr. Samuels said, as he glanced at Lisa and noticed she was watching the clock. "Somewhere to be, Ms. Washington?"

Lisa had been staring at the clock nearly in a daze. Something was not right. She could feel it; her thinking was off. She could not think when she was stressed, and tonight was really bad for her. Her head was spinning.

Lisa turned as if the doctor had poked her in the side, "No, not really." She then walked back to have a seat on the edge of Momma Ida's bed. She did not notice the doctor looking at her. She had a strange feeling something was going to happen—good or bad—something was going to happen.

Lisa thought she had been coming to the clinic since the doctor first started three years ago. He was quiet, as if he was shy; he did not make eye contact with her. Momma Ida thought he was cute and a good catch, and she would flirt with him and, slowly, he seemed to blossom from a caterpillar to a butterfly. He would say hello with a big smile, but that is as far as it went.

She turned and looked at the doctor, "Is everything okay, doctor?" Lisa asked.

Dr. Samuels noticed the worried look on her face. "She is fine; we just want to make sure it is just a stomach virus and nothing more."

She shook her head in an affirmative manner then stood and walked to the head of the bed, brushing past the doctor, to where Momma Ida was laying. She bent down to kiss her on the cheek. "I have to drive home and pack a change of clothing for you and feed my baby," she said with a sign of disgust. She had been in the hospital waiting room with Ida all evening and before that, making deliveries with Momma Ida, when suddenly, Ida started feeling sick and they drove straight to the hospital. She had not seen Claire all day. *How can I be a good mother to a child if I cannot be a good mother to a dog?* She thought once again. *Claire is home alone, sitting in the window, waiting for her mother to return.*

The doctor looked puzzled before saying, "Baby? I did not know you had a child."

"Yes, I have a little dog named Claire; she is a Shih Tzu," she said, while turning to pick up her purse.

Ida looked at the doctor. She could read people, and the doctor was interested in Lisa. She could tell, once again, that Lisa was not paying attention. She was always so preoccupied with something, so Ida thought she would help out. "Lisa is not married, either," Momma Ida said, while reaching her hand out to touch him, and giving him a *yes, she is available* look. She also went on to tell the doctor how good Lisa could cook. "Lisa makes some of the best food I have ever eaten, and I have traveled the world and eaten in some of the best restaurants, and she is by far the better cook—Cajun food, Italian food, and even Chinese." Ida's eyes closed, as if she were sniffing the aroma of hot gumbo on a cold day. Ida even pointed out to the doctor how beautiful and kind Lisa was to everybody. "A gentle soul, that is what she is, and she will be a good wife and mother."

The doctor looked at Lisa, as if seeing her for the first time and said, "You have a beautiful daughter." He then gave Ida's hand a gentle squeeze. Before turning to exit, he stopped suddenly, "Ms. Washington, if you are not in a hurry, I was just about to get a coffee, would you like to join me?"

Lisa was embarrassed. Ida practically begged the doctor to ask her out. She tried not to look so shocked. She knew Ida was not feeling well; however, she felt that her friend had gone too far. Before she could answer, Momma Ida said, "yes," firmly. She knew Ida meant well, but she did not want to appear desperate. She was more than capable of meeting someone on her own.

Lisa stopped and looked at her ailing friend and wondered if she was really ill, or if she was just looking for attention. She did not have an answer to that question, but the doctor was taking it seriously, so she had to do the same. She turned her attention back to the doctor and, after giving the offer a little consideration, said, "Thank you, doctor, coffee sounds really good right about now." She turned back to face Ida again, "Afterward I can drive home, shower, and pack a bag for you; besides, it takes forever for the front desk to get someone to bring you to your room, and I hate hospitals," Lisa said in a low voice.

Dr. Samuels was standing with the door open, waiting as Lisa walked through. He turned to Ida and said, "I will have the nurse bring you something to help you rest comfortably."

After feeding Claire and taking a hot shower, Lisa packed an overnight bag with a gown and slippers, just in case Ida felt better and wanted to walk around. She thought, with a smile, *today was not a total disaster; she got to spend time with a very handsome doctor, even if it was only to talk business.*

After leaving the room, she walked side-by-side with the doctor to a little lounge that had a coffee pot, a vending machine and three tables, each with two chairs.

Dr. Samuels poured two cups of coffee. "Cream and sugar, Ms. Washington?"

She smiled. "Dr. Samuels, please call me Lisa. Whenever someone calls me Mrs. Washington, it makes me feel old; Mrs. Washington is my mother's name."

They both smiled as the doctor handed her a cup of the hot coffee and stood while she took a sip; he wanted her approval, so she gave it, "This is good, thank you."

He then took his seat right in front of her. He looked like he wanted to read her mind or tell her something, so she sat silently and waited. "Let me get to the point; we have a shortage of staff in our physical therapy department. Dr. Winn and I noticed the excellent work you did with Mrs. Stanford and I was told by some of the staff you would be an asset to that department. You are also a licensed psychotherapist and God knows some of the patients could use a good listener and pep talk."

Pep talk, she thought. *No 'hey, baby, what are you doing later,' which used to be the line men used right before asking a woman out on a date.* It had been so long since she had been asked out, she did not know what lines men were using today, but one thing was for sure, this was not it.

"My schedule is pretty tight with my clothing and swim suit line . . ."

He stood to reheat his coffee and did not look at her before saying, "This is a great opportunity for you." He smiled. "It would be a life saver. You can broaden your horizons, be out there, meet new people, go places and do new things. Lisa, you are what we need," he turned and pulled another chair from one of the other tables so they sat side by side, as if he wanted her to read his mind . . . *Do not procrastinate.* "This could be a life-changing experience for you; do not let a great opportunity pass you by, it may not be there when you want it. I know you love Ida, and you think that you can help her, however . . ." He stopped and looked at her with sincerity, moving closer to her as she slowly backed up. "This offer will change your life, move you to another level in life."

She looked puzzled. The doctor was trying to tell her something and she began to feel uncomfortable. She looked at her phone for the time and said, "It's getting late, and I really have to get home and feed Claire and come back to be with Momma." She then stood to leave, but stopped and turned to the doctor. "However, I will print you a copy of my schedule and we will work from there."

He smiled, "That sounds good. I will look forward to working with you. We can start slow and see how that works out." He reached for her hand, but she declined his offer and walked away. She turned and looked at the doctor and thought about his last words . . . Somehow, she did not feel that he was talking about the work.

Dr. Samuels watched as Lisa walked away. He stood in the room for minutes; yet, he could still smell her perfume. He could still see her beautiful face and he wondered if he should practice what he preached about procrastinating. Should he have asked her out now so she could get to know him better, should he have told her he had filed for a divorce, though not yet final, and that his wife was playing hardball with him, that she was an adulterous bitch? He thought, no, he did not want her to run away; he knew that if he were not a free man, Lisa would never consider dating him. Besides, he did not want her to get the impression that he was the bad guy. He would wait and slowly woo her, let her fall in love with him, and then he would tell her everything. He had fallen in love with her; she was all he could think of, even now, the thought of making love to her was giving him an erection in his pants. He wanted to be with Lisa, only he wanted everything to be perfect—he wanted to be a free man when they started their new life together. Besides, he knew she wanted to have children. He remembered yesterday in the lounge listening to Lisa ask Dr. Young if she could fit her in for an appointment. She wanted to know if she would be able to have children.

🕉 🕉

Today is the day of glory for the organization called the Brotherhood; each member wore a black gown and a long black veil to cover his face. They were twelve strong and their mission was to please their father. These men had been trained from young boys to destroy their enemy. The Brotherhood stood and gave praise to the father they loved: "Tonight is the night he stood at the head of the table to settle a score with our enemy. We have eliminated the fraternizer and now, it is time to wage war on Eddie Jones."

Father stood and passed envelopes to the men with their wages, and the men received a bag that included the tool they would need to get the job done. "We are a few members short tonight; however, everyone is in place to do their jobs. We will cut out their bloody hearts . . . The sons and the father and all that they love will burn like the devils they are. There will be no chance to escape: the men of the Jones family will die one-by-one so that they can grieve the death of each other before we put them out of their misery."

They stood, played the organ, and sang the song of death they had written (*You will die and your heart will stop / and suddenly your eyes will pop.*) He pulled out the hat of death and passed it to his number-one. Will you do the honors, son?" He asked. Never had he been so pleased. Only the number-one got to pull from the hat, and he would make the one suffer that he picked. "Devin Jones, tonight you will die. Father said it was time to eliminate the past and start with the creator. Sister wants a child and she has been at the hospital, but tonight we will give her a job of love for her brothers."

"Sister is beautiful," one of the brothers said.

Father gloated. He was very proud of her. She was the apple of her father's eye, and later, they would all meet again at the place and toast their demise. Father went into his resting place and pulled out a picture, "I will do you proud, Mother, for I am not weak."

Father remembered when his mother knocked on the door of James Jones to ask for money to feed his son. "That is not my son," James had said. James threw water on them and told them to go away. They lived in one of his houses and later he put them out on the street with nowhere to go.

He remembered his mother and how she suffered pain at the hands of James Jones and how she was talked about around town. People called her a slut and other men used her as a bedmate and said she was 'damaged goods' and that her family would amount to nothing, but Father had proved them wrong. He was a creator of life and had profited abundantly, and now he was a pillar of the community; now he was called, 'Sir.' A tear rolled down his face. "I will avenge you, Mother, a mother for a mother," as he sang his favorite song by Barry White (*You're the First, the Last, My Everything*).

✑ ✑

Devin placed his clothing inside the duffle bag. He turned to look around to make sure he had packed everything. He looked at the nightstand next to his bed and picked up the paper that contained the address 24 Gilstrap Lane and a request for security at a wedding dress fashion show given by Cecil Dubois in honor of his daughter Darlene Dubois. Darlene was a woman that Eddie Jones, Devin's father, met at a club. Devin Jones was a private investigator who walked alongside his older brother

Jason Jones. He placed the address in his pocket but held the invitation in his hand. He looked around one last time before walking to the door.

He walked into the hall and turned and looked at the bedroom that no one entered anymore because it was the room that his mother died in. He walked down the stairs and pulled out his phone to call his brother Jason.

He stopped when he heard a voice coming from his father Eddie's office. "Are you sure you want to leave?" Eddie asked. Devin dropped his duffle bag on the floor and walked into Eddie's office. Eddie and his best friend Willie Williams always had a nightcap in Eddie's office. Eddie and Willie grew up together. After Willie's mother could no longer care for him, James Jones, Eddie's father, invited Willie to live with his family and the two men became like brothers. "Stay and let's talk about this," Eddie said. "I made a promise to your mother that I would look after you and your brother." Devin smirked because his father had no clue as to how destructive his behavior was. Devin handed Eddie the invitation. He wanted to confront Eddie about the invitation before he moved out.

Willie stood and walked over to the minibar to pour Devin a bourbon on the rocks. Willie handed it to Devin, but Devin said, "No thanks, Uncle Willie."

"I know you are not happy," Eddie said. "But we always worked things out." Eddie snapped his fingers because he had an idea. "Let's get Jason and the four of us go on vacation." Devin turned his head from side to side because his father did not understand. Eddie's idea of life was picking up women at the bar on weekends and inviting them back to his house for a night of sex; then afterwards he worked until he had the urge to be pleased again.

"You do not get it," Devin said. "This house is empty. There is no laughter or joy, and more so there is no trust and there is no love."

Devin sat in the chair next to Willie. Willie offered him a drink again, hoping he would loosen up and rethink his decision to leave. "No," Devin said.

Eddie read the invitation and looked at Devin. "You said there is no love in this house. If you marry Darlene, you could start a family."

Devin was baffled that his father would think he would marry a woman he despised so that he could do a hostile takeover of his company. "I am not one of your negotiating tools," Devin said. "I would never marry a woman that I do not love so that you can take over her father's company."

Eddie turned to Willie, who he knew agreed with Devin. Willie always took the side of Jason and Devin against him. "Talk to him, Willie," Eddie asked. "It would only take a year, and then you can have the marriage annulled," Eddie said. "Besides," Eddie said, "Darlene cares about you."

Devin stood because he was getting nowhere talking to his father. "Darlene doesn't care about anyone, not even her father," Devin said. "She is plotting with you against her own father."

Devin turned to exit the room; he stopped when Eddie asked, "Where will you be living?"

"I purchased a place but it need renovations, so I am staying with Jason until it is complete," Devin said.

Eddie stood and walked over to Devin. "I am sorry, son," Eddie said. "I will tell Darlene you are not interested in our business deal. Please stay."

Devin looked around the room. "Don't you understand, Eddie? This house is dead, it died when mom died. There is no glue to hold it together," Devin said and walked out.

Devin placed his bag in the car; he looked around one last time. He pulled out of the circular driveway and drove to the big gate. He listened to music and remembered he did not have a key to Jason's house, and pulled out his phone to call him.

Jason jumped out of the shower when he heard the phone ring; he answered, but he missed the call. He was taking Carolyn out to dinner. After years of living at home he decided it was time to work on his family. Carolyn had shown patience with him, allowing him to come and go as he pleased, but he knew he was hurting her. His father had never seen his grandson, and Devin had never met Carolyn or Lionel. Carolyn said she felt as if Jason was ashamed of her and Lionel because he never introduced her to his brother, who he was close to.

Jason looked at the phone, and it was Devin. He dialed Devin's phone, and he answered. Jason told Devin about the key under the flowerpot. "I am taking Carolyn to dinner, and I will come home later to show you around," Jason said. Devin sighed and Jason asked, "What happened with Eddie?" Devin told him about the invitation and how he needed to put distance between himself and Eddie. Devin was angry that his father thought so little of him that he would sell him to the highest bidder and now he wanted nothing to do with Eddie.

Jason hoped that Eddie would grow as he and Devin had, but Eddie was never going to change; it was his way or no way. "We both agreed to focus on getting our lives together," Jason said. "I am building a foundation with Carolyn, and you will meet the lady at the mall." Devin was frustrated because he was working a case that took longer than he expected. He hoped that he did not wait too long and she was seeing someone else..

Devin was about to speak when he drove around a curve and something was in the street. "What is that?" he asked. Someone was standing in the street wearing dark clothing and holding something in his hand. Devin was startled when someone else ran into the street from behind a tree to flag him down. Devin slammed on his breaks, but he was too late. He hit the person, and his car was suddenly on fire. The person wearing dark clothing had thrown something flammable on his car.

Jason listened. "What's happening?" Jason asked. He heard Devin yell out and the tires skid. "Devin!" Jason yelled. But the phone went dead.

❧ ❧

Chris Weber checked his watch because he did not want to be late for his meeting with his business partner, Shawn Davis. He pulled his car into the driveway. Chris got out of the car and ran up the stairs to his new apartment. He pulled out his phone to call his sister Constance to let her knew that he had arrived safely. Chris had moved to Atlanta from North Carolina to start his electronic business, and today he and Shawn were meeting to go over the details of their presentation at the college library. They were a new business and were competing with some of the biggest electronic specialists for a contract, and they had to give the best presentation to get the job.

Chris took a quick shower and stepped out and grabbed a towel to cover himself. He had not unpacked; he looked for a box marked CLOTHING, and one box in particular carried a picture of his family. He was feeling homesick because he would be alone for the next six weeks. Shawn was returning to North Carolina to move his wife Shannon to Atlanta, and his girlfriend Jonte had to finish the next six weeks of classes at the University of North Carolina before she could transfer to Atlanta University.

Chris thought of his parents. He wanted to make his father proud of him since he passed up on college and worked in retail to save money to·start his own business. His father always said, "You need a college degree to get a good job." His mother died when he was fifteen; she was born and raised in Kenya and moved to North Carolina when she met his father, who visited Kenya on spring vacation. Chris had his mother's dark brown skin color and her smile. He was five eleven and medium built. Chris dressed and looked at himself one last time in the mirror. He smiled in the mirror at his accomplishments: he owned his own business, and he was starting a new life in a new city. Chris walked out of the house and to his car, climbing in.

While in the car, Chris looked at his gas gauge and said, "Half full." He tapped the glass covering the dashboard with his finger to see if it moved down and it moved down a notch. The needle got stuck sometimes and if you tapped the glass it would stay in place or move down where it should be.

Chris arrived at the Tiki Bar where Shawn was waiting for him. Chris ordered a beer and sat across from Shawn. "We have to make rules," Shawn said. "If the merchandise is not picked up within thirty days we will sell the item to make up for cost of the repair." Chris did not like the idea of selling his customers' property. He remembered that his family fell on hard times when his mother was diagnosed with cancer. His father had to empty his savings account to pay the bills, and then they were living from paycheck to paycheck. However, he had to pay the rent and the cost of parts was coming from their business account.

"Okay," Chris said. Chris checked his watch and wanted to get home before dark. He paid the check and shook Shawn's hand. He stood and walked towards the door. He walked to his car and opened the car door and turned the ignition switch.

He drove down the highway. He looked at the gas needle because his car was slowing down. His gas needle was stuck on half full, and he had run out of gas. Chris made a mental note that he needed a new car. He had purchased an older model Chevrolet, and it did not have a fuel light. "Shit," he said. His sister ran errands and he did not keep track of the gas usage.

He tried to restart the car, but it would not start. He passed a gas station a mile back, and it was starting to get dark. He noticed a dark colored van parked on the other side of the highway. He stepped out of his car and walked to the back of the car. He smelled something burning and looked across where the van was parked and he could see a light. He stood behind his car and looked, and there were three people moving. He opened the trunk of his car to retrieve a gas can and a flashlight; he closed the trunk and looked again.

The three people were wearing black costumes, and they stood in sequence of large to small. One of them noticed his car and pointed in his direction. Chris ducked behind his car and peeped out to see the tallest one coming in his direction.

Chris backed into the bushes because he did not know if the men were hostile, but he did not want to take any chances; there were three of them and he was alone and it was getting dark. He started backing into the bushes so he would not be seen and to put distance between him and the man. He gripped the flashlight because it was the only weapon available to him. He looked down the highway, and there were no cars coming in his direction. He moved slowly to get a running start. Chris looked behind him and the tall man was catching up, but Chris stopped and now he could reach out and touch the man.

Chris noticed the man was much taller than he was and he was five foot and eleven inches tall and was looking up at him. The man placed his hand over his ear and Chris could hear him say, "Yes, Father, he will die." Chris started moving away again because he needed a running chance. The first car he saw he would run to for help.

Chris stopped and looked back to see if the man had moved, but he stood there waiting, with something in his hand. Chris looked around, and there was not another car in sight. One of the others joined the tall man, and they started chanting while the other one got back into the van. Chris looked down the highway, and he could see headlights. The two men started to dance, flapping their arms as if they were wings.

Chris hid in the bush, and one of them raised his hand up with something in it. "You will die," one of the said. Suddenly the car was passing and Chris made his move. He ran toward the car with his arms raised, crossing them side to side. Chris felt like his body was on fire as the car struck him.

ᗡ ᗡ

Ida paced her hospital room floor; she had realized that she had spoken too much to Dr. Samuels about Lisa. She wondered if Lisa was still with him. She liked the doctor, but she felt that there was something not right with him, and he would not want her around if he and Lisa decided to date. Ida knew men like Dr. Samuels; they would do what it takes to get a woman, and once they won them over, they would make their life a living hell. She knew Lisa deserved better than that. Ida wondered what she would do. Lisa was the only family she had now. Sure, Judy and Ellen visited, but she could not live without Lisa. Dr. Samuels was up to something.

Ida had asked Nurse Kandy for a soda, and after she drank the soda she burped and felt better. Ida only had gas, and yet the doctor admitted her overnight. Ida thought that he wanted to keep an eye on Lisa and tell her they were spending too much time together. Ida remembered him at the fashion show weeks ago and how he had stared at Lisa while she walked on the stage, and she had wondered why he was there. He sat right next to Ida, making her uncomfortable. However, Lisa paid him no attention, but Ida now knew that he had feelings for Lisa and wanted her for himself.

ᗡ ᗡ

Lisa returned to the hospital through the emergency entrance. Doc was right: it was a busy night. She was walking to the admission desk when she suddenly stopped, as she had a strange feeling something was going to happen. She could not put her finger on it, but something was not right. Her head was spinning, and all she could hear was a loud siren blasting and someone coming over the speaker: "Dr. Samuels to the emergency room. Dr. Samuels to the emergency room." She placed her hands over her ears before the person announced some kind of code blue or code green . . . She could not make it out.

Doctors were running toward the entrance of the hospital—it was what she thought to be chaos—the doctors were running toward the paramedics as they were wheeling someone in. She could not see clearly, but it looked to be a man. She stopped to look, but he was surrounded by doctors, nurses, and the paramedics . . . There was even a police officer. A hit-and-run victim, the police officer said. She could hear Dr. Samuels ask, "Sir, do you know where you are, sir? Do you know your name right now?"

Lisa started walking down the hall, but stopped when she got a pain in her stomach—not a physical pain—it was hard to explain. It was that feeling that something was wrong. First, the doctor's strange behavior; she had a feeling the doctor wanted to tell her something. Her heart started pumping fast, as if she was having a panic attack, and her mind quickly thought of Momma Ida. She started to run down the hall to the admission desk, but before she could get there, she could hear loud voices coming from the room where she had been earlier, the room where she last saw Momma Ida. She stopped and breathed a sigh of relief, as it was Momma Ida yelling, "I am hungry, goddamnit! I am not eating this crap." The nurse was explaining to her the doctor wanted her to eat light. "Then put it on a goddamn paper plate so it weighs less," Momma Ida said. Lisa laughed and walked through the door. Ida looked up at Lisa. "Look at the crap that was not food, but just a damn snack," Ida said. The nurse turned to Lisa for help because she was getting nowhere with Ida. "Blah-blah-blah-blah," Momma Ida mimicked, "I don't have to do a damn thing, but live until I die. You go and tell him that," Ida said.

"She will have it later," Lisa said to the nurse. "I will see to it."

As the nurse walked out she said, "She has to eat it tonight: doctor's orders." Lisa looked at the nurse and could tell she was not happy.

Lisa stood in silence, wondering whether this conversation was her fault. She prided herself in her cooking, and she and Ida ate the best of the best. She knew that food would not be the thing that would remove her friend from this world. "Thank you," Lisa said to the nurse, "I will take it from here." Lisa walked toward the chair.

"Your hands are pretty empty," Ida said in a sarcastic voice. While you were out on a date with the doctor, I was sitting here starving to death."

Lisa had that *'what are you talking about'* look on her face, when she realized she had left the overnight bag and the gumbo she and Ida would have for dinner in her car. She was still angry about Ida's behavior with the doctor earlier. She thought Momma Ida made her look desperate to the doctor. The doctor was nice, but she also thought there was something strange about him—she thought of Dr. Jekyll and Mr. Hyde.

Before she could talk, Momma Ida was on a roll; Lisa had never seen this side of her. She looked angry and concerned. First, she would not look at Lisa, then she turned very angrily and said, "The doctor must have really sweet-talked you. I have been sitting here for hours by myself, only to have these airhead nurses try to starve me."

Lisa pulled up a chair and sat in front of Ida, who was angry, but so was she. "First," she said in a stern voice, "it was not a date, it was a business proposition. Second, it lasted all of fifteen minutes. When the doctor said "coffee," he meant coffee, nothing personal, all business. Third, I drove all the way home and back in less than an hour, not hours, Momma, minutes.

Ida breathed a sigh of relief; the doctor would not take Lisa from her after all. "I am sorry, honey. I know you are looking forward to dating and getting married. I even know about your appointment."

Ida touched Lisa's hand sincerely. "I love you. I had three children, and if I were to have a fourth, it would be you." She then shook her head. "Dr. Samuels is not the one for you, trust me." Then she said it once again in a lower voice, "He is not the one; I know it and I feel it, and I know you know also. When it is right, you and I will know. I have a sixth sense about these things."

Lisa's eyes felt heavy as she was fighting back tears. She did not want Ida to see her cry, so she got up and walked out of the room.

Lisa stood at the admission desk. A nurse with braided red hair was on the phone with her back turned, but Lisa knew it was Carla Coleman, a friend and one of her customers. Carla was such a kind girl that Lisa called her Kandy. She was like a little sister to her. Carla turned and gave Lisa a smile and a '*give me one minute*' finger, so she looked around the hospital as if it was her first time being there. She looked at the chart on the wall of Rooms 200 through 210, and an arrow that pointed in their direction.

"Hey, girl, sorry about that." Carla had a big smile that faded . . . Something was on Lisa's mind because she looked stressed. "This place is crazy today." Carla gave Lisa a weak smile; she wondered if Lisa was concerned about Ida, which was why she looked so unhappy. "I gave Momma a soda, and she burped and she said she feels good now."

Lisa could not help but notice the new nurse that brought Momma the food; she had never seen her before at the hospital and wondered why she wanted Ida to eat Jell-O so badly. Carla turned to walk to Ida's room when she suddenly remembered that Doctor Samuels had offered her a job at the hospital: "By the way, congratulations."

Lisa's eyes stayed on the nurse as she paced back and forth, looking in their direction. "I see word travels fast around here." She had only been gone for a short duration and Kandy already knew about her job offer.

"Dr. Samuels said you would be helping us out here."

With a sigh, Lisa looked at Kandy, "I do not know how I am going to pull all of this off. I have orders piled up to the ceiling and have not had time to fill any of them. I need help."

Kandy looked at Lisa. "It is only one day to start and it will work itself out." Lisa looked as if she had a load on her shoulders. "Hey, girl, I am off tomorrow, why don't you get a bottle of wine and we'll get those orders filled; I will be at your beck-and-call, girl."

Lisa laughed. She loved Kandy and she knew she could count on her. Suddenly, she began to get that feeling again. "Kandy, can you keep an eye on Momma for me?" Lisa looked down the hall and saw the nurse again. "Kandy, who is that nurse?"

She looked and shook her head, "Lisa, I don't know but one thing I can tell you is that chick is strange."

Lisa walked back to Ida's room and flushed the food down the toilet. She told Ida that since she was feeling better she would bring back dinner for the both of them.

The phone started ringing. Lisa stood there while Kandy answered and she could hear a voice saying, "Second floor." The volume on the phone must have been up really high as Lisa could hear the other person say that the room for Mrs. Stanford was ready and that the room across would be ready for Mr. Weber. Ida's room was ready—it was the fourth floor, Room 410.

"Great," Lisa said, "I have to go to my car and grab her bags, Kandy." Lisa watched, as the nurse seemed to be walking back and forth. "Why is she pacing back and forth?" Kandy asked and seemed frightened all of a sudden, her demeanor had changed from bubbly to shaken.

"I will bring Ida up, and then I have to wait for the new admission."

Lisa thought of the man being wheeled into the emergency room, "Is that the hit-and-run?" Lisa asked.

Lisa looked sad when Kandy looked at Lisa. She knew something was bothering Lisa because she was not as cheerful as usual. Lisa always got depressed on her birthday and bounced back afterwards. Lisa always said that things would get better and she would put work aside and focus on her personal life.

"Yes," Kandy said. "I was at the desk when he was being brought in, and the police officer said it was a hit and run."

Lisa turned to walk away and Kandy yelled, "When Ida goes to sleep, if you want coffee, come to the lounge; I am here all night!"

Lisa stopped walking and turned and said, "So am I."

Lisa was walking down the hall when suddenly she got the feeling in her stomach again. She placed her hand on the wall and looked around to see if anyone was there, when she realized she was standing by the emergency room—the room where earlier the Weber guy was being placed. She did not know why, but suddenly she started walking in that direction. She thought she saw a woman in blue pointing at the room; however, it was just her imagination—no one was around. She started walking down the hall. There was dead silence and she felt as if she was in a trance as she walked to the room where she thought she saw the woman point. She looked in. Weber was lying there, his head was bandaged and he had an IV in his arm and a monitor with his heartbeat. She did not know what was drawing her; it was like a magnet to metal, as she was being pulled in, and she could not stop herself.

She entered the room slowly, trying to get a good look at his face to see if he was someone she knew. What was causing her to feel the butterflies in her stomach? She walked closer. She could not stop. She wanted to see him; she needed to see him. She did not understand. She did not know any Weber, but she had to see his face. She had been in the hospital many times, but had never felt anything this strong. She picked up his chart and the name read Christopher Weber. A face that, with all that he had gone through with the accident, was still recognizable. She could see that he was light-skinned with a sharp nose and thin lips. He was very handsome in every sense, a man that probably had romanced many women. He was truly blessed. He was muscled like a bouncer, which meant he had a gym membership somewhere, and there was a tattoo on his left shoulder. She could not tell what it was so she slowly pulled back his gown and the tattoo appeared to be a woman.

His eyes slowly opened, and they were a rich-brown. He was gorgeous, a man that took pride in his appearance. His hair was silky black and cut low, and his body, from what she could see, was a work of art. He moaned.

"Are you in pain?" she asked. His lips slowly trembled, as if he was trying to speak but could not; his hand slowly came out, as if he wanted her to hold it. She stood there staring. He lowered his hand and his lips trembled again. "I will get someone to help," but before she could walk away, his hand came out again and this time, she placed her hand in his. She then moved closer and said, "You're going to be alright." He gave her hand a small squeeze. "Hello, Mr. Weber, my name is Lisa," she said while slightly caressing his silky hair. "Can I do something for you?"

Chris licked his lips and mumble lowly. "Angel."

Lisa did not understand what he was saying, so she placed her ear closer to his lips.

Chris said again, "Are you an angel?"

She looked at him. "I am no angel, Mr. Weber," with a big smile, "I am no angel." Lisa could not believe her thoughts—she was attracted to him—she was imagining herself kissing and making love to him. It was comical that he would think that she was an angel. She looked him up and down. He had the body of a god. She smiled and shook her head. "No, sir, I am no angel." Lisa stood there, holding the hand of a man she had never seen before. She thought there was something familiar about him. She wondered where his family was and if the police had notified his loved ones to tell them about his accident. "Mr. Weber, can I notify your family? Are you married?"

Before she could ask another question, he said, "No family."

Someone was watching her; from the corner of her eye she could see someone standing in the doorway wearing all black. She looked up, but there was no one there. She then turned back to Chris and stroked his hair again and stared at him, and suddenly, she wanted to cry.

Dr. Samuels was walking past the emergency room door. He saw a man standing there, but when he turned to retrieve his charts and turned back, the man was gone. *Where did he go?* The doctor asked himself. *How could he move that fast?* The doctor then walked down the hall to see what was so intriguing. The man was looking at the new patient. A nurse was passing and the doctor asked her if she had seen a man wearing dark-colored clothing.

She said, "No," and the doctor thanked her anyway. He then stopped to look in on his new patient.

Before he entered the room, he could hear a female voice and noticed that someone else was there—a woman wearing a long white dress, a dress that covered the curves of her body to perfection. He stared at her for so long; her hair was pinned up and longs curls draped around her neck, as if she had pinned it up in a hurry and missed a few strands. She had a medium-brown complexion, lips not too thick, perfect for her face. This woman was stunning. It was Lisa. Before he said anything, he could hear her asking the stranger if she could notify his family for him. *She is an old soul, just like Ida said she was, someone who would help a total stranger, a person who is also a pet lover.* Lisa was special, and both he and Ida knew it. He had fallen in love with Lisa and now that she would be working at the hospital he would get to spend time with her, both business and personal.

Lisa had been coming to the hospital for years now, and from the first time he laid eyes on her he knew she was the woman for him. Although he was separated from his wife, he never asked her out because he knew she would not date a married man. He tried to make the marriage work, only to have his wife walk out on him and move into another man's home.

"You're going to put this man back on his feet," Dr. Samuels said as he entered the room.

She looked up. "How is he, doctor? He looks good for someone that has been through this type of trauma."

"He will be out of it for a while. It's the medicine . . . We had to give him something for pain, but he will recover."

She looked at the doctor, "He was a hit-and-run victim."

Dr. Samuels had that '*how do you know that*' look on his face, but he thought back and remembered she was standing there when the paramedics had brought Chris Weber through the emergency entrance. "That is the only explanation the cops can come up with, and he was found on the side of the road near his car, which had run out of gas," he said.

Lisa looked at Mr. Weber; he hardly looked like a guy that would run out of gas.

"The cops think that he was struck by a car while he was walking to a gas station."

Before the doctor could say anything else, she asked what his injuries were.

He could not read the expression on her face, and he became suspicious as to why she had taken such an interest in Chris Weber. "Do you know Mr. Weber, Ms. Washington?"

"No," she said, "I was just curious."

Dr. Samuels looked at Lisa suspiciously, and since she would be working with his recovery he decided to give her a list of Chris's injuries. "He has a mild concussion and a few cuts and bruises and swelling on the knee, probably an old injury, and there's a possibility of some memory loss, which we have no explanation for. None of his injuries are that serious."

The doctor was so focused on how beautiful Lisa was and how amazing she looked. He noticed Chris Weber holding her hand. The doctor slammed the clipboard in the slot. He looked at Lisa and this time it made her feel more uneasy, as if he wanted to call her a dirty name.

"Knock- knock," Kandy said before she walked in. She did not know what she had walked in on, but something was strange. Lisa was holding the patient's hand and the doctor seemed pissed about it. He was clenching his jaws, and his chest rose and fell as if he had been in a fight.

Samuels did not look at the nurse, but said, "Room 412, Ms. Coleman, please," as he kept his eyes on Lisa and Chris.

Kandy stood in the doorway. She, too, feared for Lisa, as she and the doctor stared at each other. The doctor's look was sinister, and Lisa's was fear. Chris looked at Doctor Samuels, and he, too, could tell that something was wrong. The doctor went from nice guy to angry in a snap of a finger.

Lisa began to shake in fear when she turned to Mr. Weber. "I will visit you later," she said before letting his hand go. She walked out to her car and retrieved the bags. On her way back, she walked down the hall to get to the elevator and realized she did not have those butterflies in her stomach.

Lisa knocked on Momma Ida's door. She was sitting in the wheelchair, as she did not want to go to bed without her bath. "Something smells good," Ida said.

Lisa smiled, "I can get into real trouble for this."

Ida grabbed the bag, as if she was getting a surprise and said, "The only trouble you are going to have is if you did not bring enough." She sniffed the bag and closed her eyes.

Lisa first helped Ida into the shower, as the room did not have a bathtub, and Momma Ida was not happy one bit. "What kind of a goddamn joint is this?" At home, she would enjoy her bubble bath at night. It relaxed her, and she slept like a baby afterward, but she was not at home and would have to make do with what was available. After the shower, the two women enjoyed their dinner. Lisa got up to rinse the bowls, and they decided to take a walk, a *tour de la hospital* Lisa said in a French accent.

"Sure, why not?" Ida said in her own voice.

Lisa pushed Ida to the opened door. Ida sat there and watched a young man being pushed into the hall in from the room across from hers. The nurse searched for the patient's file and walked to the nurse's station to retrieve it. Momma Ida looked at him. She stared, but she did not want to be obvious about it. He turned and looked at Ida, so she smiled and nodded, and the man gave her back a slight nod and smile. Ida stared at him again, and then she followed his eyes and noticed he was looking at Lisa.

After placing her purse behind a chair in the room, Lisa turned to see Chris. She walked to the back of Ida's chair, and pushed it out of the door. Momma Ida stood to get a closer look at Chris and looked at him, as if she was studying him. Ida had seen Chris before, once when she and Lisa were taking their weekend drive and Lisa had stopped to let Claire out to do her business.

Ida always asked Lisa to stop at the gate of a large house. It was a house that her husband James built for her and the family. James had died before the house was completed, and her son Eddie finished the construction and moved his wife and two sons in, leaving her out in the cold and forbidden from seeing her grandchildren.

Ida always watched the house and hoped that she would get to see her grandsons. She had only glanced at them once when they were boys. She had driven to the house to tell Eddie that she wanted to get married again, and Eddie said if she married another man then they were no longer family; that was when the boys walked outside to get into the limousine with their mother.

Ida remembered the first time she saw Chris, they were on their drive and Lisa stopped at the gate of the large house as they normally did. Lisa had placed Claire on her leash for a walk, while she waited in the car, when a red convertible pulled out of the gate. Lisa did not see the car or the driver, but Chris saw her. He watched as she squatted down and she swung her hair to the side, revealing her side profile. She was wearing black jeans and a white top, showing her washboard stomach. She was playing with Claire and picked up the dog toys. She had given her the last of her water before she stood and turned, placing the bottle in the trashcan behind her; Lisa turned to walk back to the car and looked at Chris before he drove away. However, Ida did notice he had vanity license plate, and it did not read Chris Weber. It read D Jones.

Ida recalled the second time was at the Keep Fitness fashion show, after all the models walked the runway; Lisa was introduced as the designer of the swimsuits. When Lisa's name was announced, everyone thought she was entering the stage the same as the models did, so all eyes were focused on that area, but Lisa entered from one of the department stores. As she walked out of the store, she walked straight into this man's arms. She held him to brace herself, as she was wearing eight-inch heels. Ida remembered Lisa complaining all week, "I am going to break my neck, Momma, they are too high," but she walked on the stage flawlessly. She looked perfect. Lisa looked him in the face; she even said something to him. Ida wondered why Lisa would say she did not remember. However, Ida remembered as if it was yesterday that he was with another man; yes, she remembered. Ida smiled. *Where have you been, handsome? We have been looking for you,* she said in silent thoughts.

He stared at Lisa as she stood there in her two-piece white bikini suit and a long white lace robe, a suit she hesitated to wear because she thought she would not look as pretty as the younger girls on stage. He watched as she and Lisa waved to each other, and Ida waved for him to come and sit with her, so he could meet Lisa when she walked off the stage. He started to walk toward Ida when the other man pointed to his watch, which made him stop and give Momma Ida the *'next time'* look as he walked away. Lisa smiled as she announced the address to her shop and her website; he stopped and looked at her one last time, and nodded at her before leaving the mall.

Ida remembered, not only did he notice her, but every other man did also. Every day after the fashion show, when she was on the town with Judy and Ellen, pretty much every man in town would ask her where her beautiful daughter was. She would reply, "At home minding her goddamn business," and suggested they mind their business and not ask questions about Lisa.

Lisa and Ida stood in the hall with Chris while the nurse was at the desk. Lisa noticed Momma Ida staring at Chris. She then looked at Chris. She had seen him before, she just did not recall where, she had been so preoccupied with her business and the stress of the doctor appointment she had with her best friend and gynecologist, Dr. Carolyn Young. She could not think straight, but she was sure that, in time, where she had seen Chris would come back to her. Lisa could not help but wonder if Momma Ida knew Chris Weber, or if he reminded her of her son, a man she never talked about?

Lisa looked around for the nurse because Chris was still waiting in the hall for her to return. Doctor Samuels was looking their way. Doctor Samuels did not say anything; he just looked at Lisa, and he looked angry that she was showing interest in Chris Weber.

Ida's frail fingers stroked Chris's cheek. Lisa turned and looked at her puzzled and she did not want Chris to feel uncomfortable, so she introduced them. "Momma Ida, this is Chris Weber, Chris this is Momma Ida. Chris was in an accident tonight." Ida was in shock, staring at Chris. Lisa was stunned; she did not know what Ida was thinking.

"Weber?" Ida said.

"Yes, Momma."

Ida snapped back, "How are you feeling, honey?" Ida smiled because she was sure the man lying in front of her was her grandson and finally she knew his name.

Chris did not answer, he watched the doctor stare at Lisa. The doctor is infatuated with her; he does not look happy at the attention I'm receiving from the beautiful lady I first thought was an angel. His body was aching, but Chris could tell the doctor was 'fantasy screwing' her; he had this sinister look on his face.

After licking his lips for moisture, he smiled, "I have been better."

"You are going to be fine," Ida said, as she sat down. "We are right across the hall. So, Lisa won't have far to go to check up on you. If anyone can get you back in shape, Lisa can."

Chris looked at Lisa again, "She is putting you to work."

Suddenly, everyone's heads jerked with astonishment. Dr. Samuels was having a meltdown right in the middle of the hall. He started screaming at the nurses, "Why is Mr. Weber still in the hall?"

Nurse Kandy ran from behind the desk and said, "We cannot find his chart."

He yelled, "That's because it is in my hand!" before slamming the clipboard on the floor. He then turned to Lisa with a look that had her shaking.

She was shocked at his behavior; she had never seen any doctor act so unprofessional in her life. Dr. Samuels scared her and she would no longer have any dealings with him, not business or personal, again.

He stormed past her, his shoulder hitting her and nearly knocking her to the floor. Momma Ida gasped and Chris lifted his body up to get into a sitting position while Nurse Kandy ran to Lisa's side to see if she was hurt. "Now I know why you said he has the Jekyll and Hyde complex. He has been looking at you funny all night. He is scaring me and you need to avoid him at any cost."

Lisa's heart was pumping fast. She was at a loss for words, but she did notice that Chris, too, looked angry at the way the doctor had acted. "I am fine," she said to everyone, as she pushed his shoulders back down.

Kandy smiled, "I will take you into your room, Mr. Weber." She looked at his muscles and asked, "Are you a body builder?" Kandy began to laugh, "Remember when we tried to lift weights," she asked Lisa, "and you could not move for a week?"

Chris smiled, revealing his perfect white teeth. "The two of you should have had a trainer, because you can get hurt if you do not know what you are doing."

Kandy touched his shoulder, and looked at Lisa and said, "He is solid as a rock," in amazement. Kandy pushed Chris to his room. She did not stare, but she thought that he would be perfect for Lisa. There was a kindness about him that he and Lisa both shared, and they would be good together.

"Are the two of you best friends?" he asked her.

She smiled because he was interested in Lisa and she could tell that Lisa liked him, so she said, "She is an amazing woman," as she sat in the chair. "I do not have any family," she explained to him. "My mother died when I was five and my father . . . I don't remember . . . He left me alone," Kandy sighed. "I met Lisa five and a half years ago and I have had a family ever since." She tried to explain that Lisa was like a big sister that acted like a mother. "She is so kind and non-judgmental," she said. She had suddenly forgotten that she was talking to Chris and not Lisa, "Now, Carolyn, she is judgmental; she can be a bitch sometimes,"

Chris laughed. He liked Kandy. She had a sweet disposition about her and he could tell she needed a mother figure in her life and Lisa filled that gap for her. He had met three of the women and wondered if there were any men around to take care of them.

"Lisa is single and she has not dated in several years," Kandy said to Chris in a 'do not tell that I said that' whisper. She now had his attention and she planned to keep it. "However,

Carolyn, on the other hand, says she has a man, but nobody has seen him." She had an expression that made him laugh.

Chris was amazed at how open she was with him; he could tell that Kandy wanted a family and she was very vulnerable. "How many years since Lisa has dated?" he asked.

Kandy rolled her eyes. "Oh baby, let me tell you," she said, "Lisa has only talked about one guy, but he was not nice, and she said he could not get it up, if you know what I mean."

Chris Laughed again and he suddenly felt a little pain.

"I will get you something for pain and, by the way, I am Kandy," she said.

Chris did not trust many people, but he liked Kandy, she had a certain innocence about her and he could see why Lisa was over-protective of her.

Kandy returned with pain medication. "These will not make you drowsy," they both looked up at Dr. Samuels when he passed in the hall. Kandy knew he was waiting for Lisa.

Dr. Samuels waited by Ida's door. Chris turned and looked out the door as Doctor Samuels talked to himself.

The doctor looked depressed and was mumbling to himself, "She is mine, she is mine."

He turned to Chris's room and looked at Chris, while Kandy's eyes went back and forth between the two men. Although there were no words said, she could tell there was a silent challenge. Dr. Samuels was saying Lisa was his.

Carla walked back to her nurse's station and she looked at the nurse that Lisa was concerned about. She had never seen her before. The nurse checked her watch and picked up Chris Weber's file. "Are you new?" Carla asked, while looking at her nametag. The nurse said nothing; she walked away and looked at her watch again. Carla wrote her name down . . . R. Klein.

She shivered and walked back to Chris's room, as she, for some reason, did not feel safe alone while the other nurses did their rounds.

Chapter 2

Sister paced her bedroom floor and said, "I am in love," as she looked at the picture she had taken of Chris Weber, "and he is mine," she said, but Father and the Brotherhood cannot find out she had stopped at the twenty-four-hour photo store to purchase her life-sized model photo of him. "Lisa is a whore and if she thinks she will get him, then she is mistaken, I will cut her heart out." Sister kissed her photo and smiled, she would get rid of Lisa once and for all. Sister watched as Lisa hovered over Chris like a slut. Sister will kill any woman that thinks they will have the man she has now fallen in love with. She smiled because she now had a secret, and she wondered if she should share it with Mother, but thought not because she is weak and she might tell Father.

"Sister, are you in?" Father was coming and if he knew she had fallen in love with the enemy, he would be angry.

"I did as I was asked." She noticed he was pacing the floor.

"Tonight was a victory for the family. We eliminated Devin Jones and now the others will suffer the loss," he laughed in a sinister way. "However, child . . ."

She waited patiently outside her bedroom door. She did not want him to know that she had gone down the road where the accident had happened and found the love of her life lying in the woods. She picked him up and carried him to her car and now she would please him.

"Brother got sloppy; he left a witness and on tomorrow, he will die also."

"No, Father," Sister cried. "He has amnesia and he will not remember."

"He is the enemy now, he saw us and can jeopardize the organization. Father was so focused on Sister, he did not notice Mother standing in the doorway with tears in her eyes. Devin Jones was dead and father would kill the rest of the Jones family.

Father looked at the women. They were weak; he had had such luck with the boys; however, he had no success with the women. "Tonight, your brothers will sperm the women they have chosen; soon one will lay the golden egg and the family will have riches beyond their imagination.

"I want a baby, Father," she smiled almost as sinister as he, rolling her eyes to her bedroom door. *And I will have one,* she thought.

Father was against the women in his family having babies, because they would not have the teaching that he had given to his boys, and he had become older and tired. "Simon will handle everything," he smiled and so did Mother and Sister because, if they showed their fear, then they would be punished for it. Their mission was to kill the Jones family, and that is what they would do. Simon was the leader. If they disobeyed, he was also their punisher.

❧ ❧

Ida and Lisa walked to a lounge where they sat and talked. When Lisa asked Ida why she felt such an attraction to Chris, Ida smiled and said, "I guess for the same reason you do." Lisa was confused as Ida continued, "You have been so wrapped up in work, Lisa, you have lost your memory. You have seen Chris before," Momma Ida said, "at the fashion show. You walked right into his arms."

Lisa rolled her eyes, she remembered him well. She tried to block his face out of her memory, but she could not. "I did not get a good look at his face, Momma; but I thought I'd walked into a brick wall. His chest was so broad and he had muscles out of this world, and he held me up to keep me from falling on my face. I just got a glance at him before the announcer announced me. I just know he had a body out of this world."

How could she tell Ida that she waited daily since seeing him that day, she waited for him to walk into her shop, but he did not? When he held her that day, it was all she could think of. She did not want him to let her go.

Ida laughed, "After the fashion show, you asked everyone if they saw the hunk you bumped into." They laughed. "Hell, you even offered Carolyn the other one, which you only saw from behind." Momma Ida then became serious; she, too, had waited for him ever since that day.

"He is the one," she said. "He is the one you are going to build your life with, wait and see, honey. I told you I have a sixth sense about these things and Chris Weber is the one for you. Remember what I said about Dr. Samuels, was I right?" Ida began to gloat; she never knew that Lisa thought the same of Dr. Samuels as she did. He was a man you did not want to make an enemy of, which is why she was always kind to him. Lisa nodded her head. "Don't get me wrong, honey, I like the doctor, but he has problems and I think tonight he showed it."

Lisa sat in front of Momma Ida, and she looked at her as she tried to explain to Ida the butterflies she felt that had led her to the room where Chris was lying in the bed. How could she not control herself, she was drawn to him. She looked at Ida, thinking she would say she was being silly, but instead, she was understanding and sincere with her, which was something she needed then. She had fallen for Chris the first time she laid eyes on him.

"Lisa, you have been in the hospital several times and never felt that way before, there is a higher power working here and it means for you to see Chris, to be with him in his time of need. Maybe Chris is the man for you."

Lisa turned her head, she was attracted to Chris; however, he did not feel anything for her. Lisa had hoped that one day he would come to her shop and they could have gotten to know each other, but he never came. After the fashion show she stayed in her shop later every night for week and Chris never came to see her, so she gave up hope of ever seeing him again. She thought that he had forgotten the address, but she was listed in the phone directory and he could have found her. Ida turned Lisa's face to have eye contact with her and told her, "He will fall in love with you."

Lisa felt closer to Momma Ida tonight; they have had heart-to-hearts before, but tonight it really meant a lot to her. "Do not forget, communication is what keeps a family strong—no dirty little secrets, anything that is done in the dark will find its way to the light, honey, honesty is the best policy.

Lisa held Momma Ida in her arms for what seemed like forever, she then stood to make the journey back to the room. Her mind was racing, she always prayed for a good man, someone to love her unconditionally, someone to be there for her when she needed him, she even wanted to have two children—a boy and a girl, in any order—and to be a wife and mother. If Chris was that man, she would not fight her feelings for him, she, for some reason, wanted to love him; even if Carolyn gave her bad news, she would fight for him.

Lisa couldn't wait to get back to the room. She wanted to see Chris and say goodnight to him before he fell asleep. She wondered if he would remember bumping into her one day. She and Ida started their walk, as she hoped she would not run into Dr. Samuels, but she walked right into him. She tried to avoid eye contact with him, but he grabbed her by the arm.

"Miss Washington, I wanted to apologize to you for my outburst earlier and stomping off the way that I did and bumping into you," the doctor went on to say he had been working nonstop, and he was just tired. She listened as he blamed the nurses for their incompetence while he looked at her with a big smile, a smile that made her think of a madman in the movies, the ones that smile and then stab you in the back. "Let me make it up to you," he said.

Ida sat in silence, while Lisa was shaking; there was something sinister about this man. "I accept your apology. No harm done," she replied, as she felt she should not make an enemy out of him, so she made light of the situation. "There is nothing to make up for." She checked his expression to see if he was becoming angry again. "I understand what you are going through and there is no need to apologize." She smiled. "You are just tired and you should go home and get some rest." She pushed Ida into the room. Before she walked in, she turned to see if Chris had fallen to sleep. He had not, so she put Ida to bed before walking over to see if she could help him with anything.

When Lisa walked in the room, she saw that Chris had removed the IV from his arm, so she asked, "What are you doing?"

Chris was sitting in bed and he turned when he heard Lisa walking in. "I want out of this place," he said. "I hate hospitals."

Chris smiled and replied, "I am blowing this joint, the hospital is for the sick and I am fine. I've had worse injuries playing football." He suddenly realized that the pain medication was beginning to wear off and the pain was resurfacing. He looked at the pills Carla had given him, and before placing them into his mouth, she handed him a glass of water.

She could tell that he was headstrong. But there was no way she could allow him to leave and be alone tonight. "Where will you go?"

He then looked at her, shook his head, and said, "I have no idea, but here is not where I want to be." Chris tried to stand, and Lisa rushed to help; she wrapped her arm around his waist to steady him. She looked at him with great concern, "Chris, it is too soon. Please, stay and get some rest and tomorrow you will see if you feel better."

He looked at her. Her eyes were begging him, so he took a deep breath and agreed. Lisa then helped him back into bed. "Are you hungry?" she asked. "I have some of my homemade gumbo," she said in a joking, but cajoling voice. His smile sent chills through her body. *I wonder if he remembers me.* She thought. In the movies, this would be the time for the characters to ignite a relationship that earned a kiss. This was real life, though, and things did not happen like that. "I will go to the lounge and warm it."

He agreed and before she left the room she turned and he said, "I will not move, I assure you that." She realized that he was in pain, again because he had refused stronger medicine from the doctor.

Lisa checked her phone and when she noticed the strange nurse was walking past her, Lisa gave her a smile and read her nametag . . . Nurse Klein. She turned to see if the nurse would go into Ida's room; instead, she went into Chris's room. Lisa could not help herself. She walked back to Chris's room and listened as the nurse tried and get Chris to take pills. Chris declined the medication. "It's the doctor's orders, Mr. Weber, that you take your medication," she said. Chris became angry: "You tell the doctor to take the fucking medicine himself," he said to the nurse. Storming out angrily, she turned and looked into Momma Ida's room. The nurse placed a smile on her face.

Lisa was getting that feeling again, and she wondered if Chris was causing her to feel what she was feeling. She felt so drawn to him. She than remembered what Momma Ida said, "There is a higher power working here, Honey. You will love him and he will love you." Lisa thought if love makes you feel this way, how do people take it? She also thought that, maybe it was because of the appointment she had with her best friend, Carolyn tomorrow, she would know if she was able to have children or not. Could that be what was causing her stomachache? What if she could not have children and Chris wanted to have them? Lisa had so much on her mind that she saw the tall dark figure again. She kept walking, feeling as if she were being watched; she looked around when she reached the lounge, placed the bowl in the microwave and turned on the power. Her head then snapped up . . . Someone was watching her. She started to turn when the bell sounded on the microwave. She just stood there; her instincts were kicking in that she was being watched. First, she thought of Dr. Samuels; maybe, it was him, but he had left the hospital for the night.

Lisa started to open the microwave when she heard someone say, "Got you!" She jumped, heart pounding, and she turned. It was Carolyn. "Girl, you jumped so hard, I jumped."

Lisa smiled with a sigh of relief. Someone was there, and it was Carolyn. Lisa rolled her eyes. "Cal, it has been a crazy night," she grabbed Carolyn and held her.

"Lisa, you are shaking!" Carolyn pulled the bowl from the microwave.

"Momma had a meltdown, and so did Dr. Samuels."

"Momma Ida, what else is new?" Carolyn laughed. She suddenly stopped when she could see the toll it was taking on Lisa. "There is a new nurse here. She tried to get her to eat Jell-O, and Momma went ballistic."

Carolyn laughed, "We know how Ida is, but what about the doctor?"

Lisa told her how the doctor screamed and threw his clipboard on the ground, and nearly knocked her over. "Carolyn, he had a meltdown."

"No meltdown," Carolyn said, "he is stressed." Carolyn then gave her the confidential voice. "He is going through a very nasty divorce." She looked at Lisa, "You know, it has been rumored that he caught his wife in bed with another man."

"Poor Dr. Samuels," Lisa said.

"And to make things even worse, she wants half of everything that he has worked for."

Lisa wondered what he could have done to make his wife leave and start sleeping with another man. She had a newfound sympathy for the man she said was a psycho.

"Carolyn, there is a new patient here named Chris Weber. He wanted to leave the hospital after Dr. Samuels's behavior. If what he did tonight is any inclination of how he is at home, then I understand why she would leave him; he scared me, Carolyn, and I don't scare easily."

Carolyn looked at the gumbo and said, "Momma is eating this late?" She was looking at Lisa in a suspicious way.

Lisa knew Carolyn all too well, and she knew that she could not talk to her about what she was feeling. "It is for Chris Weber, the new patient; I had to stop him from walking out of here tonight."

"So you decided to bribe him with gumbo," Carolyn knew that something was happening to Lisa. She was nervous about her test results and looking for a distraction.

Lisa then stopped and she took a deep breath, "I keep getting the butterflies in my stomach."

Carolyn removed the bowl from her hand as they walked to Chris's room. Carolyn stopped before walking in the door, "Girl, we have to talk; you are making yourself sick."

Lisa and Carolyn walked into Chris's room. Lisa did the introductions "Chris, this is my best friend, Dr. Carolyn Young," and she handed Chris the bowl of gumbo and a spoon.

Carolyn looked at Chris. "It is nice to meet you, Mr. Weber, but you need to get some rest."

Chris looked at Carolyn and he said, "It is nice to meet you too."

Lisa said to Chris, "I will be in the hall with Carolyn."

Lisa and Carolyn were standing in the hall when Lisa felt as if she was being attacked by her friend. "Girl, you are making yourself sick, get a grip on yourself; you are taking on entirely too much. You want to have a baby . . . Until you do that, you are taking on things that are out of you league."

"That has nothing to do with this," Lisa said.

Carolyn looked around to make sure no one was around before she took Lisa down memory lane. "Six months ago you were late with your period and you cried because you thought you were going through menopause. But that was a false alarm so you asked if you could start procedures to make conception easier. Every year around your birthday you get strange, but this year things are different because you want to start a family before it is too late," Carolyn said. "Do you remember your fashion show?" Carolyn asked. "It was three weeks ago and you compared yourself to twenty-year-old girls. 'She is thin, and my hips are too wide,' 'Do you think I am fat?'"

Carolyn continued. Carolyn reminded Lisa that one of the model's boyfriends was at the fashion show and Lisa had said, "I am prettier than her. What does he see in her?" Carolyn had left the fashion show before it started. She came to deliver flowers to Lisa for doing such a good job putting the event together.

"I know I can be blunt sometimes and my words seem harsh, but we are all the family each other has." Lisa became attached to Ida because of the bad blood between her and her mother, and now she was attaching herself to Chris because she was lonely and looking for male companionship.

"After the fashion show you got weirder. You cancelled lunch dates and dinner dates with both me and Kandy to stay in the shop late and work nonstop. Every year you said you were going to start dating, but you did not. You kept putting your career first. But this year you are not taking any more chances, so you see a handsome man and you are wondering if he finds you attractive."

Lisa knew exactly what Carolyn was saying—she wanted a baby and was falling fast for the first man that she met and that a man like Chris would not be interested in a woman like her. Lisa looked shocked, "What are you talking about, honey? "You are not Chris's mother."

"I can see something is not right with you, girl, you are developing very strong feelings for him and I can see why. However, you are out of your league."

Lisa continued to feel she was being attacked and now it was her turn to speak her mind, she was angry. "Carolyn you're so high and mighty, maybe I should be like you, a snotty bitch that puts down others to make herself feel better about her life; maybe he would fall for a woman like you." Lisa held up a finger: "Of course, you have a man that is like a thief in the night, so you say, and yet none of us have met him. Love is when two people work together and build a foundation together, and you would rather use your child and have occasional sex with his father. At least I am willing to go out of my league and try."

Carolyn, too, had become angry, "Alright, Lisa, at least I can have a child." She looked at Lisa's face and she knew she had hit below the belt.

"Yes, I want it all—the baby, the man, and the white picket fence—is anything wrong with that? Lisa started to walk away when she turned to Carolyn, "I don't want to be his mother; I am showing him kindness and trying to keep him from making a mistake he might regret. He is not well. He has amnesia, and right now he has nowhere to go." Lisa then got right in

Carolyn's face and said, "I am doing your goddamn job. If something happens to him, I do not want to feel I should have done something to stop it." Lisa looked around to see if they were drawing attention. Then she turned back to her friend and shook her head. She knew that Carolyn and Doctor Samuels were friends and wondered if he called Carolyn to tell her that she was taking interest in a new patient. "Did Dr. Samuels call you?" Carolyn was silent, "He did, didn't he? Oh, Carolyn, you should be ashamed of yourself," and she was.

She could not believe she was betraying Lisa as she was. Lisa was so kind and gentle and she was only looking out for the patient's best interest. Jason asked her not to say a word, but she was looking to see if Jason's brother Devin was admitted into the hospital. Jason and Carolyn had dated for many years and had a five-year-old son together. Carolyn checked the files, but Devin had not been admitted. Devin was coming to live with Jason a few days while his house was being renovated and to finally meet the woman that bumped into him at the mall. She was keeping a secret from Lisa, but she would prefer to have Lisa angry at her and not Jason.

"I am so sorry, Lisa, I did not mean to upset you." Carolyn could not believe her ears; she had never in the years that she had known Lisa heard her say any curse words.

Lisa held her hand up, "I am sorry, too, girl; it has been a hectic night. I have so much on my mind and it is driving me insane. I should not have said those things about your life, although I have said them to you before, but not out of anger."

They both laughed, "You are right, Lisa. One day I will fix my life, but first let's get you pregnant. Have you been taking the vitamins I gave you?"

"Yes, Doctor."

"Have you stopped taking the birth control?"

"Yes, Doctor."

"Is your period still regulated?"

"Yes, Doctor."

"You will be pregnant in no time."

"No," Lisa said, "let's get me a man first."

Ida finished her dinner. She was proud of Lisa. She did not call herself nosy, but she watched Lisa and Chris's every move. You do not stand a chance, Dr. Samuels. She smiled and called Ellen. "He is here," she said in excitement to Ellen. Ida met Ellen when Judy started college. Ellen studied with Judy after school and Judy's grades improved, so Ida hired her to tutor Judy for the rest of the school year. Ellen came from a strict family and an abusive father. Ida had to pay Ellen's father to allow Ellen to stay at her home on weekends to study with Judy. Everything went well until Ellen became pregnant and her father threw her out of the house. Ida liked Ellen because not only was she helping Judy stay in school, but her son Jimmy took a liking to her. After Jimmy's death Ellen lost her son and was placed in the same mental facility Ida was. One day when Judy went to the mental hospital to visit Ida, She discovered that Ellen was there also. Judy walked past a room, stopped to place her keys inside her handbag, and looked in one of the rooms to see Ellen in the hospital bed. Two weeks later Judy checked Ida and Ellen out of the hospital and they had been roommates ever since.

Ida jumped with excitement. "The man from the mall, the one Lisa walked into." Ellen laughed when Ida told her that Lisa was drawn to him and she was with him now. "She is on a roll," Ida laughed, telling Ellen that Chris seemed to recognize Lisa, but he had amnesia. She also talked of Dr. Samuels and how his plan had backfired on him. Ida thought of Carolyn and what she said to Lisa and she could see the pain on her face. She only hoped that her words would not stop Lisa from finding happiness. Ida hung up the phone when her door opened. Carolyn walked into her room. Ida looked across the hall and Lisa was going into Chris's room.

Lisa went to say goodnight to Chris. Are you guys okay?" Chris asked. He knew body language well. He learned it at the police academy and he overheard some of their conversation.

"Yeah," Lisa said and explained to Chris that she was disappointed as she and Carolyn had never had an argument.

"First, my compliments to the chef."

Lisa smiled. She got happier than a kid in a candy store whenever someone complimented her cooking. "Why thank you, sir, I am glad you enjoyed it."

The two of you have a strong connection, so you can agree to disagree and there is no harm done. The two of you fixed the issue before it became a problem and that is all that matters.

Lisa looked at Chris and said, "Thank you."

"For what?" he asked.

"For being a good listener and having a great response." She hoped he did not hear her and Carolyn talking, but she knew he did and he understood that they were like family and agreed to disagree. Carolyn always said what she felt without thinking of consequences to her or the person she was speaking with. But she always thought of others' feelings before she spoke.

He smiled, lifting her hand into his. "You're welcome."

They stared at each other and Lisa felt uncomfortable. If he kissed her, would she kiss him back? Would that make her a slut? Instead, she went into the bathroom to wash the bowl, hoping it would take her mind off wanting Chris to kiss her.

Lisa walked back into the room and was thrown by the next question Chris asked, and wondered how much of their conversation he had heard. "Are you pregnant?" The bowl shook on the plate and she nearly dropped it. He wanted her to confirm Kandy's story about her not seeing anyone, so he thought he would push her buttons.

"Oh gosh, no," she said.

"I am sorry. You look like you've seen a ghost," he said.

Those were not the words she had expected; she really felt uneasy, as she did not know what to say to him. She did not want him to think she had someone in her life, so she told the truth, "Well, Mr. Weber, in seven weeks I will be forty-one years old. I have no children and I have no man in my life. I want them both; however, I do not know if I can have a child. So, tomorrow I will find out if I can achieve both goals. She looked serious as she sat on his bed. "Who am I kidding? I don't know if I can do either." She looked at him and said, "I have not been on a date in years. I have worked and let life pass me by." Lisa thought she would feel strange talking to Chris, but she felt as if she had known him forever.

Chris felt badly because he knew he had hit a soft spot for Lisa and hurt her. He could see the pain in her eyes even though she was not looking directly at him, but he knew he hurt her. Kandy had answered his questions earlier, but he believed in honesty and Lisa was honest—she and Kandy said the same things and now he knew that he could trust Lisa.

He turned her face and looked her directly in the eyes, "You will do both and you will be perfect at it, trust me." His words brought a smile to her face because she did trust him, she did not know why, but she did. She wanted to lie next to him and curl up in his arms; she did not want to leave him, she felt as if she belonged with him.

"You should be the shrink, not me. Sometimes it gets hard to practice what you preach," she said to him.

"You're a psychotherapist?" he asked with a smile. "You're not reading me, are you?"

She smiled. "If I am, you are good, really good." She stood and started fluffing his pillows, and she than pushed his shoulders back so he would be comfortable. She opened her arms and hugged him and he did the same. "I am right across the hall. I will be in that chair; if you need me, just yell and I will come to you."

Lisa walked to the door, "Are you going to check yourself out of the hospital tomorrow?"

"I cannot stay here," he said, "I am a big boy and I will be fine."

She dropped her head because tomorrow would be the last time she will see him. "Will you wait for me before leaving? I want to make sure you get off to a good start."

He smiled and agreed to do so. He watched as Lisa disappeared into the room as Carla walked in to ask if he needed anything. He reluctantly agreed to take something stronger, but he knew that he could trust her and that she was a kind person.

"Did you see Carolyn; she is a piece of work, as I said."

He smiled at her and thought that Carolyn had gone too far as a friend, even if she was angry at the time, implying that Lisa would not be a mother.

Her heart was breaking, after tonight she would not see him again. She was not exactly honest with Ida when she said she barely got a good look at Chris. She did look at him and, for the first time in her life, she felt hope that there was someone for her. When she did not see him again, she lost hope. Now, though, he was here and he needed her. "You play it safe, Lisa. Take a chance and if you fall, get back up." She had heard her whole life and now she was faced with a dilemma—if she did nothing and he got hurt, she would not be able to deal with that, or if she helped and then walked away and wanted nothing to do with her, she would be crushed. She thought of what Carolyn said to her. "At least I can have a child," she said, as if she was telling her she had waited until too late to have a baby. Lisa tried to ignore that comment; she had to give it her all to keep from running and balling up in a corner. She wondered if Chris had heard her also, and if it would keep him from wanting her.

Lisa lay there, her mind full, and she was feeling that feeling in her stomach, that something was going to happen, as she said a silent prayer. *I have worshiped you and praised you,* a tear rolled down her face. *I have been a member of the 'Lonely Hearts Club' all my life, and I have not asked for much. I am asking now, just for a chance at happiness.* Lisa knew she could not hide her feelings. She wanted Chris; she closed her eyes and felt ashamed. How could she fall so easily? She had heard people say they fell in love at first sight, but she never thought it could happen to her. She looked at the sleeping Ida and she thought about what she said: "He is the one." She hoped Ida was as clairvoyant as she thinks, because she has fallen for Chris and she hoped that he would feel the same. He would leave the next day, and she had to find a way to get him to stay in the hospital.

Lisa lay on the chair in Ida's room that faced the door; she watched his room as tears rolled down her face. She lifted her head to see if Ida was awake, but Ida was sound asleep, so instead Lisa watched to see movement from across the hall and he, too, had fallen asleep. She could hear movement at the nurse's desk and wondered where Kandy was and if she was all right; something was wrong, and now she suddenly felt fear and loneliness.

She thought of the first time she had seen Chris, how he smiled at her and she did the same. She watched as he turned to exit the mall and she thought she would tell him where he could find her, but he never showed up. Every day at her shop she would look out of her window, hoping to see him and he never came. When she first laid eyes on him, she had hoped that one day she would find true love and he would be the one, and now he was here and she would lose him again.

She began to cry and just stared at the door when a dark figure appeared in the room near the door. It held out its arms, as if they were wings, and began to flap back and forth. It did a dance right in front of her. It pointed at her and it seemed to be pointing at Ida also, before it turned its attention to Chris and did its dance again. She wondered if someone was playing a joke on her, but it frightened her to say the least. She wondered if she was tired and her eyes were playing tricks on her, so she closed her eyes and opened them, and he was still there doing a dance. She wondered if she screamed if he would hurt her. And now she knew that her mind was not playing tricks on her; someone had been following her all night, and now he was standing at her door doing a ritual dance.

There was no sound; only a humming that was coming from it. The ghost made sounds and its voice was demonic: "I will kill you," it said, "I will kill you all!" It turned as if on wheels. She needed to breathe because she was holding her breath, careful not to move.

She wondered how it could be so tall when she suddenly realized the hospital was dead silent, there was no movement, only the sound of what was standing and staring at her. She suddenly thought of all of the movies she had watched. When a child had a nightmare, their parents would ask them to close their eyes and count to three before opening them again. She was not asleep, but thought she would give it a try.

Lisa closed her eyes. "God help me," she said before she started to count. One, two, three. She opened her eyes, and it was gone. She went to the door and it looked as if it had disappeared, then she walked back and lay down. She cried in silence at what she had witnessed and looked at the nurse's desk to see if Kandy was there. She wanted to walk out of the room, but she was afraid. So she walked back to the chair and thought that she would close the door, but she left it open because if it returned she would scream and she wanted someone to hear her.

Her mind drifted off to sleep. She opened her eyes to see a woman standing over her, wearing a blue dress with a pin on the lapel; Lisa could not move as the woman placed her hand on her and said, "Do not cry, child." Then she smiled at her. "This is your life," as her hands went across Lisa's eyes and she slowly closed them, but it was as if she was watching a movie of her life. She held a child with a pink blanket and looked out a window that was not familiar to her; she could hear voices, however, she did not see any faces. "Love him," she said, as she smiled and started to disappear, and Lisa opened her eyes. "Will he love me?" she asked, as the woman vanished.

Chapter 3

Lisa could not sleep. She tossed and turned all night; she blamed the chair, but it was not that. It was fear of her appointment with Carolyn and knowing today would be the last day she would see Chris. She hoped for the best, but prepared for the worst. She played both roles in her head: "I'm sorry, Lisa, you will not have children," and "Congratulations, you can be a mom."

She remembered when she first told Kandy and Carolyn she wanted to have children—they both thought she was crazy. "Why do you want to do that, girl? Once you have babies, you never get your shape back," or "That is a lifetime bill," which was funny because they both had a child and they looked pretty good to her.

She decided to get up and get started. It was six o'clock in the morning. If she showered, she would leave and go to Judy's shop and pick up the clothes she asked her to leave out for Chris. She had called Judy to ask her about her male clothes and she said she had all sizes of T-shirts and sweat pants. Lisa took a wild guess. Chris was tall—about six-three—and 240 pounds of muscle. She would never forget how Judy laughed, "Girl, you got you a good one; that's a sex machine." Lisa tried to explain, but Judy and her best friend Ellen were cracking jokes. "When you are done with him, let me take a shot at him," Judy said.

She took a shower and got dressed. She applied light makeup, which she always did if someone asked her out; she did not want to look the same. While looking in the mirror, she noticed the food cart was still in the room. She thought about what she saw and wondered why she was seeing a ghost, but she would place it all behind her and she and Momma would be gone in a few hours.

Doing one last check in the mirror, she wondered if she should have worn a dress instead of blue jeans, which made her hips and butt look big. She thanked God she had a twenty-nine-inch waist, which she was revealing.

When leaving the room, she closed Momma Ida's door. She even made the chair look like she was still there. She did not want the nurses to wake Ida before she got back.

Lisa drove to the shop and back in twenty-five minutes. Judy had left five different color sweat suits and large slippers and socks. She slid a check under the door and a thank you note for taking care of Claire.

When she returned to the hospital with three cups coffees and a buttery croissant with sausage and eggs, she realized she did not know if Chris liked coffee. She smiled; who was she kidding? Everyone likes coffee. Ida was sitting up in bed and Lisa handed her the coffee. "Black with one sugar, just the way you like your coffee. And your breakfast, madam." Lisa handed Ida a croissant with her coffee. Breakfast was not what Ida was accustomed to. Ida enjoyed bacon and eggs with fresh fruits. "I am planning a large lunch today," Lisa said, "so we are eating light."

Lisa wanted to tell Ida that she saw a ghost in the room, but she did not want to scare her. They were leaving in a few hours and she wanted to put it all behind her.

Ida noticed the bag of clothes. "What is all that?" she asked.

"They are for Chris. He's planning on checking himself out today."

Ida look concerned. "Can he do that?"

Lisa shook her head. "Yes, Momma, he can refuse medical treatment at any time."

"Honey, you can't let him wonder the street."

Lisa took a deep breath. "He is pretty headstrong, Momma, and you cannot make him do anything he does not want to."

"Talk to him," momma suggested.

Lisa lifted the coffees and croissant and said, "I will try." She removed one of the sweat suits from the bag along with the socks and slippers before going to Chris's room. Lisa checked her phone. She had one message from Kandy: "Leave your car key in Momma's room. I will stay with her until your appointment is over. Good luck." Lisa replied, "Okay," and told Momma her keys were in her purse for when Kandy arrived.

She took a deep breath before she walked in Chris's room. "I have something for you."

Chris smiled, "Good morning to you, too."

Lisa handed him the hot coffee with cream and sugar on the side, and his breakfast. She looked Chris in the eyes, "Okay, Mr. Weber, let me get to the point. You are leaving today, you have no idea where you are going, and I cannot stop you. But I can offer a solution . . ." Her heart was pounding as she did not know what she would do if he refused her, but she asked anyway. "Come home with me and let me get you back on your feet. I know you will not come back to the hospital for therapy, so let me give it to you at my home." She was talking so fast she had to get the words out before she lost the guts to ask.

Chris looked at her. "You are a beautiful person, both inside and out. I appreciate your kindness, but I do not want to be a bother to you."

"It would be no bother," she said while she sipped her coffee. "I purchased a three-bedroom home, an Arcadian style, on Gilstrap Lane. I loved living with Momma, but I need a place of my own somewhere I could have some alone time. I was starting a new business and the house was perfect. I use the upstairs part as a shop, so I am home all the time. Momma also has a home not far away, but now we are living at my house because I did not want to leave Momma alone. It would make me very happy, Chris. Besides, I can cook—you said it yourself—and we can work on your legs."

He smiled. He had perfect teeth, she thought. "If it will make you happy, I will do it. I will come home with you and I will let you fix my body and mind."

Lisa checked the time. "I have to go. I am late for my appointment." She was so excited that she kissed him without thinking. She turned to him and crossed her fingers, but before she walked out, she said, "The doctor will discharge Momma and when you are ready, I will meet you out front." She then handed him the sweat suit, slippers and socks. "It is a little chilly out. Do not leave without me, promise?"

He nodded, "Promise."

Lisa ran to Carolyn's office, "Sorry, girl."

"Momma?" Carolyn asked.

Lisa shook her head, "Don't ask." She thought it would be wise not to tell her friend she had invited a total stranger to live with her and Momma until he got back on track. Lisa sat in the chair.

"Okay," Carolyn said, "You know we ran several tests on you last month. Before that, we needed to get your period regulated. We are on track there today. I got those results back. Today, we will do a Pap test. Afterward, you can get Momma ready, and I will bring you the results."

Lisa got dressed. She noticed Carolyn sitting behind her desk. She placed both hands under her chin and looked at her. Lisa began to feel butterflies in her stomach again. She knew she had failed; she would not be a mother. Lisa walked back to Momma's room. She had tears in her eyes and was in a daze as she opened the door to find that Kandy had dressed Momma and she was ready to go home.

Kandy and Ida looked at Lisa and could see she had been crying.

"It's okay, honey, Momma said.

"You are amazing, Lisa, you can be a mother."

Lisa threw both hands up before walking out of the room, trying to control herself. She could see a doctor in Chris's room and heard Chris say, "Bring me my papers, I am out of here." Dr. Klein left the room, along with Nurse Jenny Amos.

Jenny looked at Lisa. "Are you okay, girl?"

She tried to smile, but instead she placed her hand over her mouth and nodded her head yes.

"Do you want to get some coffee? I have a fifteen-minute break coming up if you need someone to talk to."

Lisa grabbed her hand because if anyone would understand what she was going through, it would be Jenny. "No, Jen, I am fine." She placed her hand in Jenny's hand, which was twice her size. "I am fine."

Jen looked puzzled. "Is Ida doing well?"

Lisa was trying to stay together.

"Look, Lisa, when it is all over with, we will get together."

Lisa did not understand what she meant, but said okay.

"Oh, and by the way, Coretta and Cody are both doing fine."

"Those were the good old days," Lisa said. She, Jen and Coretta would go out to dinner and Jenny would tell her that Coretta and Cody were all the family she had for now.

Jenny pulled a picture from her pocket of Coretta and Cody, "This is for you." Lisa looked at the picture, and Jenny smiled. "He is getting big! He's twelve, thirteen? Oh, girl, you know my mind is not right."

"He is so handsome," Lisa admitted as she stared at the picture and then placed it in her pocket. "I will frame this as soon as I get home, and you tell Coretta that she has another family member that is interested in knowing that she and Cody are doing fine, and she should give me a call." Lisa watched as Jen walked away. She had never noticed she was such a tall woman and very flamboyant, and she always made hand gestures. Jen seemed to be a loner. She never talked of other friends or family, other than Coretta. She always wore a lot of makeup, and once, Lisa noticed that she had bruises on her face; yet, Jenny never talked about a man, just her sister Coretta.

Lisa walked into Chris's room. He, too, was dressed and was waiting for paperwork to sign. She sat on the bed next to him and she said nothing right away. He knew something was wrong. "What did the doctor say?" he asked.

Lisa began to cry. "Nothing."

"Then why are you so upset?" Chris turned to face her.

"I could tell something was wrong, she said she would have the results and let me know. She will come to Momma's room." She tried to explain the look on Carolyn's face to Chris and what she said last night.

Chris was taken aback by Carolyn's comment. He thought she had crossed the line in a friendship. He looked at her last night, she was angry, however. She had crossed the line and should never have said what she did last night.

Lisa smiled. "I did, too," she admitted.

"Babe, there are some things you can say that can be changed, and there are some things you can say that cannot be changed, if you know what I mean. Besides, maybe, she had a bad night. Maybe it means nothing. If something was wrong, I think she would have said it and offered a solution to you as a friend." He reached over and pulled a tissue from the box that was next to his bed and handed it to her to dry her eyes and said, "You will make it to the finish line."

Lisa sat next to him on the bed, "Promise?" She smiled because he accidently called her babe. *I am going to make you love me* she thought, while trying to be pleasant. She wanted to believe him. She even did her John Wayne voice. "We're about to blow this joint, baby."

He laughed, "That's my girl." He stood to walk out when Carolyn walked up.

"Hey, Cal, I am over here." Carolyn handed her some papers. "Just say it, Cal."

"Lisa, you have not dated or had sex in several years. Honey, you can carry a baby. When you are ready, we will start the procedures, all you need is some good loving, girl."

Lisa stooped down to the floor and felt her legs would not hold her. She placed her hands over her eyes, "Are you serious?"

"Yes, you are good and healthy. You passed every test. We will do an ovulation test when you are ready."

Lisa bounced up and hugged Carolyn then stopped suddenly when she noticed her friend's face. "Why are you so down?"

"Lionel was asking questions all night about his dad and I got to thinking about what you said, about Jason and my relationship, so I got no sleep," Carolyn said. "It is time that Jason and I work on our relationship. I am going to call it a day and I will give you time to get Momma settled, and then I will come over and let him visit his *Two Mommy*, I need a drink and some girl talk today," Carolyn said.

Lisa was happy. She'd get to practice being a mommy with Lionel. She sometimes babysat when Carolyn worked late, which is why Lionel started calling her Two Mommy. Lisa was happy to have Carolyn come to visit, but she did not know how to tell her that she had invited Chris to stay until he was feeling better. "Please, Cal, I will bake him some cookies and we can talk."

"You were right, I need to make things right. Stop living in fear."

Lisa was stung at the revelation Carolyn was having. "By the way, when do I get to meet Lionel's father?"

Carolyn thought, "We will do dinner. Does that sound good to you?"

"Yeah," Lisa said.

"You can cook," Carolyn said. "God knows I can't."

Chris watched as Lisa and Carolyn talked. He watched the expressions on Carolyn's face and thought *that cannot be good*, but Lisa was suddenly laughing and hugging her friend. She even turned to him and gave him the thumbs up. He smiled; he could see how much family meant to her. He thought about her. He watched as she tossed and turned all night. He was starting to feel something for her. He wanted to walk away, but he could not. He was starting to care a lot for Lisa and felt he needed to protect her from what he saw the night before.

Chris could not sleep, and when he looked across the hall, he saw something in the room watching Lisa. He did not believe in ghosts but it was wearing all black, like someone grieving at a funeral in the old movies. It wore a long, black dress and a long black veil covering its face. It was tall, too tall for most men. He was six-three, and it had to be over seven feet tall. It danced, flapping it hands as if they were wings. It looked like some kind of voodoo dance. And then it stopped and watched her again, before it turned to watch him.

He felt vulnerable, hardly able to walk with his knee being swollen, but he did not feel safe in the hospital. He turned his head for a second, and when he looked again it was gone. Lisa sat straight up and walked to the door to look down the hall. She then turned to look to see if he was awake, but he decided not to move since he was in too much pain to walk down the halls of the hospital looking for a madman or a ghost. When time came, he would ask her. There was something strange happening here in this hospital and he did not feel safe; he wanted to get Lisa and Ida far away.

Chris stood there watching Lisa. He thought she was very attractive and she had a nice body. He thought of how he could wrap his arms around her waist twice, and what it would be like to make love to her. He wanted to hold her and make her feel special. She was stunning and she would be his.

The nurse came with the papers and the wheelchair. "I can walk," he said.

"No, you can't," Jenny said, "I have to take you down."

Chris looked at her then sat in the chair.

"I will take these to the front desk, and I will be back." She said, after tapping him on the shoulder. "Behave yourself and I will be right back." Jenny pushed him into the hall where Carolyn and Lisa stood. Jenny looked at Lisa and gave her the *he's a hunk* look as she rolled her eyes. "Don't go anywhere. I mean it," she said to Chris. She then looked at Lisa and Carolyn and said, "Girl, he's a hot mess," she then pointed at Chris, "Remember, behave yourself." She widened her eyes.

Carolyn walked up to Chris. She turned as Kandy was rolling Ida from the room. "I will load up Ida for you and pull your truck to the front of the building, so that you could . . . " she then stopped. She knew Carolyn was not as opened-minded as she was, and she was judgmental, and sometimes got on her high horse. She was not one of Kandy's favorite people and the only reason she spoke to her was because of Lisa. When Lisa was ready to talk to Carolyn, she would. So, she pushed Ida away without saying a word to her.

Carolyn threw her hand up at Kandy, as if she were saying stop, as Chris watched. She then turned her attention back to him. "Mr. Weber," she said with hesitation, bending down to be eye to eye with him. "I know you can crush me with that arm, but I will speak my peace. I think it is a bad idea for you to be leaving the hospital. You need more medical attention." She went on to say that she would personally attend to him if he would stay.

Chris looked at her and smiled. "I will be okay, I am in very good hands," as he looked at Lisa.

Carolyn turned, then smiled also as she realized that he was talking about Lisa. "Besides," he said, "there is some weird stuff going on in here and I am better off out there where I can defend myself."

Lisa looked at him, could he have seen what she has, the dark figure? Carolyn stopped smiling; she had no idea what he was talking about. She remembered that one of her patients said you should not make an enemy of a doctor. They can mess you up and no one would ever know. She wondered if Dr. Samuels' temper caused Chris to feel unsafe. He did not look like a guy that spooked easily; he looked like he would take you on, big or small. She did not know what was going on, but she would find out.

When Jenny returned to push Chris out, Carolyn decided that she would do the honors. "It's okay, nurse, I will take him down," she said.

Jenny looked disappointed, but she stood in front of Chris, "Don't let me have to come out there and get you. Take care of yourself." She hugged him. "And be good, big guy," pinching his cheek.

Lisa was smiling, shaking her head. She had never seen such a display of affection. Jen meant well, but this time, she was overdoing it; she even turned to Lisa and Carolyn and said,

"Chris is a big man. He could handle pain. But if it gets to be unbearable, come back and see Doctor Winn." Chris nodded, but Jenny knew he would not return. She had seen it many times before; when patients leave the hospital in pain they would not return. Instead they would buy drug store pain medication.

"Girl, he is hard headed," she said as she placed her hand on her hips. "Girl, do you know he wanted to walk himself out?"

They both laughed after Jen walked away. But they knew that Chris would leave the hospital and he would not return again.

Chris asked if he could get out of this place.

Carolyn laughed, "Now I know why you do not feel safe here." Carolyn had her back to the elevator door. She was going to back Chris in when she heard a scream from Lisa. Chris jumped up and turned around; he noticed that the elevator door had opened, but there was no elevator. He then grabbed Carolyn, and picked her up before she could back up and fall into the shaft.

Everything happened fast. People came running when they heard Lisa scream, Jenny and the other nurses ran, asking what happened. "Carolyn almost fell down the elevator shaft!" Lisa said, holding her chest.

Jen looked in the elevator and started praising God that Carolyn had not fallen. She fell to her knees. "Girl, God sent you and angel. Oh Lord, praise God," she did a shake and jerk of her body, "in the name of Jesus."

"I am fine," Carolyn said. She looked at Chris and wrapped her arms around him. "Thank you so much," she said with tears in her eyes. Shaken, she began to think of Jason and Lionel and all that Lisa had said to her. "If you'd not acted fast, I would not be able to kiss my son good night tonight."

Lisa was at her side, hands shaking. Chris looked at them and said, "Let's get out of here."

Carolyn pushed Chris out of the hospital. She looked at him, concerned for his well-being. "Where will you go?"

Kandy got out of the driver seat. "I will see you at the house." When she noticed the look on everyone's faces, Carolyn hands were trembling and she looked scared. Lisa looked nervous and could not wait to get into the car. They all looked as if they had seen a ghost. "What is going on?"

"Carolyn almost fell down the elevator shaft," Lisa said. "Chris grabbed her before she stepped backwards."

Carolyn had tears in her eyes. "We will talk later, Kandy, when we get home."

Lisa opened the passenger door for Chris and helped him into the truck. Carolyn stood there, "Where will you take him?" she asked.

"I will take him home to my home," and before Carolyn could say anything, Lisa hugged her. "I will see you and Lionel later."

Chris sat in the family room of the house. He looked around and noticed that Lisa and Ida had not been there long. Lisa was in the kitchen where she still had boxes that read KITCHEN on them and FRAGILE. Ida decided to go to her room and watch television. She wanted Lisa to get Chris settled, make him feel comfortable. When they walked into the door of the two-story Arcadian house, Ida gave Chris a small tour of the facilities— she showed him his room and where he could find everything. She joked that she had to unpack the boxes. That's how she would know where to find things. "Lisa has to ask me where things are around here and this is her house."

Chris sat in Ida's room after she got into bed. He looked at the picture of the two men that sat next to her bed. "Those are my boys," she smiled. "One is gone." She lowered her head. "And one . . . " She did not say any more. She smiled and she thanked him for acting fast on Carolyn's behalf. "Carolyn is like a daughter to me and I could not bear losing her." She showed him pictures of herself, Carolyn and little Lionel. Ida placed her little hand on the side of Chris's face. "Don't rush getting better. I'm going to love having you around." They laughed and Chris gave her hand a light kiss.

Lisa entered the room with a tray of food, "Hungry, Momma?" she asked.

"Hell yeah, the food in the hospital smelled funny, so I put that crap in the garbage can. The big girl brought it in."

Lisa shook her head. Momma, that's Jenny," she said and he set the tray in front of Ida.

"That is a really big girl. She's over six feet tall and broad shoulders." Ida inhaled the aroma of the food Lisa placed in front of her. "Now this is how food should smell," Ida said.

Lisa had prepared brunch for her and Chris also; she looked at Chris and asked If he would like to have brunch in the bedroom, or would he sit at the kitchen table with her.

He looked at Ida's tray: there was a lot of food on the plate. Chris decided to have brunch with Lisa at the kitchen table. He wanted to get to know her; she talked and he listened. He wanted to share his life with her; he told her he was once a policeman. But right now, he could say so little, but she understood.

Lisa showed Chris where he could take a bath or shower. "I have one of the whirlpool Jacuzzi tubs that will help massage your knee." Before they arrived home, she had stopped and purchased underwear and other things he would need to be comfortable. She ran a hot bath for him while he unpacked the items they had purchased from the store. He felt bad that Lisa would be on the sofa because he would be sleeping in her bed. He was feeling guilty now as he watched her bend over the tub to check the water temperature. She then turned on the Jacuzzi and placed some Epson salt in the water.

Chris walked in the bathroom wearing his robe, which he took off right in front of her, revealing his naked body. She felt like a child, not knowing what to do. She did not want him to think that she was afraid of his body, so she tried not to stare. But she could not help herself. His body was beautiful. He was the perfect specimen of a man, and he was not ashamed to show her. He even had a nice-sized manhood, as she called it.

Lisa pulled back the covers for Chris after his bath. "Let me take the sofa," he said.

Lisa looked at him and noticed he was wearing only the pants of his pajama set and not the shirt. She wanted to ask him about the tattoo, but she knew he could not answer due to his amnesia. She would save it for later. She tapped the bed, "This is better for you, honey, you have to be able to straighten your knee. On the sofa, you will not be able to do that. Besides, I work upstairs pretty late sometimes, and I do not want to disturb you. Trust me, this is better for you." Lisa knew he was feeling guilty, "If I feel any discomfort, I will come and lay right here," she said as she patted the other side of the bed.

"Promise?" he asked, and she said, "Promise."

She tucked him into bed. She almost kissed him, but she didn't. It felt strange having a man in her bed whom she could not touch. Before leaving, she placed a tray of grapes, cheese, and crackers, and a drink, next to the bed. "I will be in the office," she said, handing him the remote control to the television.

"Judy, they are home!" Ellen ran through the store excited. He came home with Lisa and Ida." Ellen started to cry. "It is finally happening. I cannot believe this," she said as she reached over and rubbed the box. "I know you had something to do with this," she said to the box. "Thank you, my time, too, is running out."

Judy watched Ellen; she always carried that box every time they traveled to Lisa's house and now she was talking to it, "Damn fool," she mumbled.

"Ellen, you are losing it, girl; now you are talking to boxes." Ellen laughed; it was surprising to Judy, as she had not seen Ellen laugh in their entire friendship. She would smile, sometimes, with her head down.

"Judy, don't you understand? Everything is finally happening. Lisa can get pregnant and Chris is living at the house with Lisa and Ida until his knee gets better," Ellen said.

Judy smiled, she had given up hope that Chris would ever find his way to them and now; they could one day have their lives back intact. Ellen would be with her son and she could make a life for herself.

Ellen began to cry. "It is not fair to come so far and lose in the end."

"Ellen, you will not die." Judy wanted to sound enthusiastic. "You will be with your son and he will take care of you. Girl, you are this close to holding him. Remember what Lady Clem said? Lisa will put you in the arms of your son and now she has begun the process. Chris is living at the house and, come Friday, you will be close to Chris and show him you are an amazing person, and he will fall in love with you, and never want to let you go."

Ellen smiled, "I hope you are right, Judy, because he is coming for me soon." Ellen looked around. She feared being alone. She remembered the first time she saw it—she was watching it watch her son—and it pointed at him and its voice sent chills down her spine. She would always stand outside of the gate, watch her son play ball with his brother and laugh when he did.

Two weeks ago when Ellen was in bed, she looked up. It told her that her time was up, that she had to die. "Please," she begged, "I have lived in misery for all of my life, and if you can grant me one dying wish . . . "

It spoke to her, "What?" Its voice made her cry.

"Let me hold my son one last time," she begged. "Please, it is all that I want to do." She smiled and cried at the same time, and it felt pity for her, because Ellen only wanted to see a son that did not know she existed and would not accept her as a mother. She wanted him to know that she did not abandon him, that he was taken from her. The more Ellen humiliated herself, the more it would make killing her easier. It said nothing and walked away.

It backed away and said, "Granted, and then you will die." It returned daily to remind her that she would die.

She listened as it tortured her, "Why me?" she asked. "I have done nothing wrong."

"You were a friend of my enemy and for that you must die."

Chapter 4

Lisa and Kandy worked for hours, processing orders and packing boxes, and they decided to call it quits for the evening. Kandy explained to Lisa her son was at a sleepover, and she was in no hurry to go home to an empty house. Lisa poured two glasses of wine. She asked Kandy to stay for dinner, and she accepted the offer. Lisa thought there was something on Kandy's mind. "What's wrong, Kandy?"

"I don't know if you noticed, but there was some weird stuff happening at the hospital last night."

Lisa stopped and took a sip of wine, she wanted someone else to say it first; she did not want to be the crazy one, if she was wrong. She handed Kandy a glass of wine and she took a sip before she started chopping onions and green peppers for dinner.

"Someone was making weird sounds all night and when we went to check it out. No one was there, and Lisa, I could see a shadow of something moving in the hall, but when I walked around to see what it was, there was nothing there. I thought I was losing my mind last night, Lisa. I did not want to be there. I would have rather been at the club. I saw something." She looked at Lisa, "Kandy, the club was not the life for you," Lisa said with love in her voice to her friend. "One day, you will be grateful that you only did it a few weeks and now you have a good life, and you are making good, honest money; you did the right thing to stop and return to school."

She thought back to when Kandy asked her to come to the club to watch her perform. She thought she would see her friend sing a song. Instead, Kandy was a stripper. She would never forget the expression on Carolyn's face as they both watched Kandy remove her clothes.

They were in shock; however, Jenny and Coretta came in and saved the day. They ordered drinks and they all cheered Kandy on. Jenny even got on stage and did a dance before she was asked to get off the stage or to take it off. After that night, they had girl's night out and brought Momma Ida when they returned the following week.

However, that was the end of Kandy and Carolyn's friendship. She has never judged Kandy and tells everyone that Kandy is her little sister, but Carolyn thought it to be degrading of Kandy to take her clothes off in public for money, so Kandy stopped and went back to school and became a Registered Nurse.

Lisa did not want to reveal what she had seen that night. She thought it was a ghost or a monster, but now she knew that something was there and it was not her imagination.

Lisa admitted to Kandy that something was strange at the hospital. "I would have sworn that someone or something wearing all black was in the hall doing weird stuff. But what frightened me was that it came into Ida's room."

"Lisa, am I crazy? I have never seen anything like that before. I have heard hospital stories about the angel of death, but I've never seen it before."

"You are not crazy, Kay because I saw it, too. I could not scream or move, all I could do was lay there as it danced. And now I know that it was there. After the incident with Carolyn, maybe we cheated death, thanks to Chris."

Kandy was stirring the pot when the doorbell rang. Lisa went to open the door. "Hey," Lisa said when she saw Carolyn standing there with Lionel.

"Something smells good," Carolyn said as she handed Lisa several gift bags and removed her jacket.

Lisa kissed Lionel. "Guess what Two Mommy has?"

Lionel laughed and answered, "Cookies!"

Carolyn looked in the kitchen and saw that Kandy was there. She knew she was wrong for the way she had been treating her and she needed to make it right.

Lisa held up the enormous bag. "What is this?"

Carolyn smiled, "It is for Chris. I am not here to judge, I am happy someone cared enough to help him. You are amazing, Lisa; besides, if he gets out of line, I think all three, make that four of us can take him."

Lisa smiled.

"This guy is a saint; he has not even looked at me. He is grateful. "Do you want to do the honors or should I?" Carolyn pointed to the kitchen and asked if Lisa and Lionel would do the honors of presenting Chris with his gifts.

Lisa walked Lionel into the bedroom to meet Chris, while Carolyn went into the kitchen. She walked behind Kandy, placed her arms around her, "I love you."

Kandy rolled her eyes, which were filled with tears, "I love you, too."

"I mean it, Kandy, you do not have one sister, you have two. I really am sorry for not understanding what you were going through."

Kandy cried, "I do not know what I would have done if Lisa would have turned her back on me," as tears rolled down her face. "I would have had no one."

Carolyn cried also, "I know that feeling, honey. I only have my son, that is certain; I was a single parent for a while when finally Jason and I started being parents to Lionel."

Carolyn wiped her eyes, "I guess that is the tie that binds—I have Lionel, you have Justin, and Lisa has Ida—all together we have each other.

Both women looked up. They did not know Chris was standing there. "If this keeps up, I am going to get spoiled," Chris said All three ladies laughed. "Being in the company of three beautiful women can do it."

Lisa pulled out a chair for Chris to sit, but before he did, Carolyn gave him a hug. "Lionel, come over here," Carolyn said. "You can watch television later; Mommy wants you to meet someone."

Chris looked at Lionel and smiled while his mother introduced him as her angel. "Mommy could have been hurt today and this man helped her. You can call him Uncle, okay, honey?"

Kandy was looking in the kitchen drawer. "Lisa, get me something to break his other leg. We have to keep him around." Everyone laughed.

When Momma Ida came out to see what all of the racket in the kitchen was, she put on her special dress. She wanted to show who the 'hot girl' was in the house. Chris was laughing and talking when the doorbell rang. Lisa walked over and opened the door; it was Judy and Ellen, and they had Lisa's pride and joy, Claire.

Claire was wearing a pink dress and pink ribbons in her hair. Lisa took Claire, as she wiggled her body. "Did you miss Mommy?" Lisa walked into the kitchen and introduced Chris to Judy and Ellen, and her little dog, Claire. Lisa was impressed with Claire; she did not bark or growl at Chris. Claire liked him and so did she. "I am going to shower and change into something more comfortable before dinner."

Lisa touched Chris's shoulder and asked, "Can I get you something before I go?" He looked up at her and smiled. "I am fine. Go and take your shower."

Ida joked, "I will take care of him."

"And, so will I," Judy laughed, before pouring Chris another glass of wine.

Everyone turned to look at Lisa when she entered the kitchen. She was wearing a long sleeved red dress, which fit her curves perfectly. She looked like she should be on the cover of a magazine and everyone noticed the way Chris looked at her when she walked into the kitchen. Lisa was not only attracted to Chris, he was also attracted to her. The atmosphere was amazing in the kitchen. Lisa poured everyone a glass of wine before dinner while Lionel watched television.

Judy and Ellen were all over Chris, and he seemed to like the attention. He looked happy. He looked like he belonged there, as if he had known everyone his whole life. After dinner, Momma asked Judy and Ellen if they wanted to watch a movie she had ordered on pay-per-view. Judy asked Ida what kind of movie and she became dramatic as she described the movie she had watched the night before.

"I don't want nothing scary Ida, I have to drive home, and Ellen isn't any help. She's always hearing noises and seeing things."

Momma Ida said it was a documentary called *Deep Throat*. Chris laughed and shook his head while Kandy dropped a plate she was placing in the cabinet. Carolyn asked the Lord to have mercy as Momma Ida described what she thought the movie was about. "It's about a little girl who might have throat cancer."

Lisa threw up her hands and asked Ida if she wanted her to order another movie. "I am fine and we will enjoy the movie I ordered, if I can find my glasses." Ida was proud of her selection. She could not tell what she was watching, but they did not have to know that, so she would watch the movie with Judy and Ellen. "Chris, if you would like to watch the movie with us, just walk on in," Momma said.

Carolyn and Kandy were walking to their cars parked in Lisa's driveway. Carolyn noticed a black truck parked across the street. She stared at it and it scared her because now that she and Jason were living together, and after the elevator malfunctioned, she thought that Eddie Jones would send someone to hurt her. Eddie had had his son's life planned and would do whatever it took to get what he wanted. Eddie hated her, and when she went to his home to tell Jason she was carrying his child, Eddie had his men throw her out of his house and told her if she returned she would regret it. She began to shake and wondered if Eddie had sent someone to hurt her. "Kandy, let's do a sleepover at my house," since Justin was at a sleepover tonight and Jason was out of town with his father, and she did not want to be alone. Jason had not been the same since he last talked to his brother, and now he and his father were looking for him.

Kandy, too, noticed the truck. She said nothing to Carolyn about the hospital but asked, "Do you know who that is?" She could tell that someone was in the truck because cigarette smoke was drifting out of the driver's window. She could see the smoke coming through a small crack in the window.

Carolyn said no. Carolyn started walking backward when Chris opened the door to the house and asked if everything was alright. They had been outside for a few minutes and now they were walking back to the house. Carolyn turned to him, and when Chris walked out of the house. The truck engine started, and the three of them watched as it rolled away.

"Is everything okay?" he asked.

She pulled herself together and replied, "Yes, Chris, we are fine."

The two ladies got into their cars and drove away. Chris walked back into the house. Lisa was putting away leftover food in the refrigerator. Suddenly, they heard Ellen say, "Oh my God, would you look at that?"

Lisa and Chris laughed. "Do you think they are going to be okay watching that kind of movie?"

Lisa laughed, "The question is, will you be okay with them watching that kind of movie?"

"Let's go in the bedroom," she said. She wished he were hers, as she would love to make love to him, lie in his arms and kiss him all night as he slept.

Lisa applied cream and a compress to Chris's knee, and he watched as she worked on him. He noticed she was a very dedicated woman, one who would take care of her man. She was a good woman, and he was looking forward to a future with her.

"How does that feel?" she asked. When he did not answer, she looked at him. "Does it feel better?"

He shook his head, "It feels much better."

Lisa walked to the sofa in the bedroom. Since Judy and Ellen were staying the night and took the sofa in the family room, she would share a room with Chris.

"I can sleep on the sofa," offered Chris.

Lisa removed her robe, revealing a two-piece lace red pajama set. The top was short, showing all of her midsection and the pants were see-through, showing her red thong underwear. "This is my spot. I sleep here many a night when I am too tired to get into bed. I am good here.

Lisa could not sleep; she could see someone watching her through the window and it looked like the same thing she saw at the hospital. She wanted to scream but remembered what the voodoo priestess Anna Gore said. "A ghost gets its power from fear, and if you acknowledge one then it could attach itself to you." If it was a ghost then it would leave her alone, or if someone was trying to frighten her she would need proof. She did not want to cause a scene, so she watched the figure watch her. *It followed me* she thought. *How is that possible?* It held out its arms as if it was inviting her into them. She wanted to wake Chris, but she did not because if it vanished before Chris could see it he would think that she was crazy. She needed proof that she was being stalked before she went to the police. Both she and Kandy had seen something, but without proof they would not be taken seriously. First thing in the morning she will have a security system installed.

She climbed off the sofa and curled up her body at the bottom of her king-sized bed and stared at the window until she fell asleep.

$$\mathcal{O}\ \mathcal{O}$$

Lisa waited on hold while the man at the security company give her a time that they would send someone out to install her security system. She breathed a sigh of relief that she would not have to wait weeks before getting cameras placed around her home; when he said before noon, she smiled. Now she would find out if she was going crazy or if someone was watching her.

"Good morning," Lisa said to Chris, as she walked into the bedroom with a newspaper and a tray holding coffee, eggs and bacon, cut fruit, biscuits, two bowls of cheese grits. Chris looked at the food, "Wow, this looks really good." He had not eaten homemade food since he left home for college. Lisa loved to cook. She talked about the culinary classes she attended in New Orleans and hoped that one day she would open her own restaurant.

Chris went into the bathroom to clean up, and staring at him, Lisa noticed he did not sleep with a shirt. She thought she would sleep in his shirt one night after he made love to her and that thought brought a smile to her face.

Lisa picked up the newspaper. There was a write up about a missing man. But before she could read the article, Chris interrupted her, exiting the bathroom: "How did you sleep last night?"

Lisa placed the paper aside and looked at him with a grin on her face. "Sorry about last night." She chose her words very carefully. She did not want Chris to think she was a psycho, so she said, "Claire wanted to sleep on the sofa and she kept jumping on me, so I gave in and crawled into the bed." She wanted to confide in him about what she witnessed at the hospital, but she did not know what to say. "Chris, I saw a ghost." It sounded crazy, so she kept quiet until she got proof. She quickly changed the subject. "You're in a good mood this morning."

Chris turned and looked her in the eye, "Last night felt good," he said. I felt you trusted me and that meant a lot to me."

Lisa gently stroked his face, "I do trust you, Chris." She wanted him to kiss her and she would surely kiss him back.

Judy and Ellen knocked at the bedroom door. "Good morning the both of them said as they walked in with big smiles on their faces. Lisa walked into the bathroom to get dressed to work out at the gym.

Ellen sat next to Chris on the bed. As she looked at him, her eyes held questions for him that she could not ask. Chris felt she wanted to say something to him or ask him question, but she did not, she just stared at him. She touched him as if she felt it was forbidden to do so. There was something sad in her eyes. Chris remembered at dinner she was kind and she wanted to serve him; there was something sad about her, and later he would ask Lisa. "Chris, honey, we are leaving," Ellen said as she patted his hand. He pushed the tray aside and he hugged her and gave her a soft kiss on her cheek.

"I am so happy you are here. Lisa will take good care of you, she will cure you or kill you," Judy said.

Lisa commented from the door, "Hey, I heard that," and everyone laughed.

Lisa walked out and hugged both women before they left for The E and J Boutique. "By the way, Lisa, we are almost out of merchandise. Everything is selling so fast this time of the year," Judy said.

"I will have Constance bring over the boxes I have packed with the invoices," she said to Judy.

Lisa could not help but notice how Ellen was watching Chris. She looked as if she wanted to divulge some information to him, but decided to keep it to herself. Chris also noticed Ellen's expression and he asked Lisa why Ellen's eyes were so sad. What could have caused her so much pain?

Lisa could only think of one thing and that was Ellen's son; she did not know the details of her son—if he had passed away or if he had been taken from her. "Ellen had a son," Lisa began, "and when he was a child, something went wrong. She only said he was gone," and Lisa sighed. "Ellen was placed in a mental hospital. Chris, I have known her for a while now, and I can see only pain and a mother who loved her son. Something is not right with the whole situation, and I feel that Judy has something to do with it. She seems to have a guilt complex. I have not had much time to look into it, but when you are better, maybe you could look into it." She knew he would need more information, though. She was happy that Chris had remembered that he was once a cop.

❧ ❧

Judy and Ellen walked to Judy's car. Ellen could barely keep herself together. They sat inside the car several minutes before Ellen asked, "Do you think Lisa and Chris will fall in love?"

Judy shook her head. She wanted to say something to make Ellen feel better. "They are attracted to each other. Let's just hope that it's enough. Let's hope Lisa will open herself up. After her last relationship, she did not date and she had some pretty good prospects. We have to motivate her, give them some alone time. We will take Ida for the weekend so they can get to know each other."

Ellen sighed, "That's easier said than done; you know how over-protective Lisa is of Ida—she barely let's Ida out of her sight. And, what about Chris's memory loss? What if I confide in him and he doesn't believe me? We get them to fall in love and one day he will leave, her and God forbid, if she gets pregnant in the process." Ellen wiped her eyes.

Judy looked out the window at the house. She thought if Lisa became pregnant, that would be a good thing; they would forever connect.

Ellen was shocked at Judy, "But he will be gone and she will have to raise a child on her own. That does not seem fair, maybe, for a little while.

"He is a good man, he seems to be a protector; he will not leave Lisa or his child. Remember Lisa is very smart, she will make sure she and Chris care for each other before she becomes intimate with him. We just have to make sure Chris stays put and Lisa is the key to him doing just that."

"I saw them walking in the mall. I felt so much joy," Ellen recalled, "I saw the two of them staring at Lisa; they stopped and watched as she stood there. I then got hope that I would be able to tell my son that I am his mother and I love him and that I had not abandoned him. I can only imagine what his father has told him about me."

Ellen cried. "I will see and hold my baby, Judy," she said with a smile of tears. "I will hold my son before I leave this earth, and he will know why I was not around. Lisa will help him to understand that, but first, I have to get the guts to tell her." Ellen stared into blank space. Lisa is the glue to putting this family back on the right track. I knew it from the first time I saw her. I knew there was something special about her."

"Lady Clem described her to a tee. She said she would be attractive. She would have a certain innocence about her, and she would have a heart of gold. Now that she is here with him, I know it will not be easy for her, but I need her to understand. We will talk to her soon. Remember, she is opening an office at the hospital." Judy smiled. "Lisa loves and cares for us both. She is a mother hen and will understand. Unlike Carolyn, she will not judge us. She will try to help. Lisa will vindicate you. She will get him to understand that it was not your fault. Lisa is the key to putting you in the arms of your son. Remember what Lady Clem said: she will put you in the arms of your son." Ellen cried again, "Lady Clem also said she would suffer at the hands of a madman. We will have to make him understand; if we say nothing, we will lose her forever."

Judy did not understand what Lady Clem meant when she'd said, "Chris is no madman." Judy said, "Maybe, it is not Chris. Lisa is starting her new practice. Only time will tell what it all means; nevertheless, things are starting to happen now and we have to be prepared. Like it or not, all of our lives will change and there is nothing we can do about it."

They drove into town before Judy said, "Lisa's birthday party . . . We have to have a heart-to-heart with Lisa before that day. Meanwhile, that will be our excuse for getting Ida out of the house. We can make it a theme party—come as a celebrity party—that is how we will get Ida out of the house. We will make our costumes and Chris's." Judy was excited now. She has lived her life under a rock and now she will come out and get some air.

Ellen wanted to be optimistic, "Lisa is the key, Ellen, just wait and see."

"What about Carolyn? She can be a real snob, sometimes." Ellen remembered the day when she and Ida were preparing some baked goods for the charity event and Ida told her that Lionel's father's name was Jason Jones. She'd cried because her grandson's mother thought she was not good enough to be with him. When she would bring Lionel over for Friday dinner, she would pull Lionel away when Ellen would try to touch him.

"Carolyn does not know you are Jason's mother; maybe she will have a change of heart."

Ellen shook her head, "No, she'll talk down about me to Jason and he will hate me."

"Lisa and Chris will not allow that to happen. Chris likes you a lot, Ellen, and he will defend you to Jason. You have to have faith," Judy said, "right now, Carolyn is not one of Chris's favorite people. He thinks Carolyn is trying to come between him and Lisa. If Carolyn says anything bad about you, Chris will stop her."

Ellen smiled, "I hope you are right, Judy. I am running out of time, you have to talk to Chris and tell him that someone is still playing Halloween jokes and see if he reacts." Ellen shook her head. "No, because he will want to know if you have seen it also, and we both know you are a bad liar."

Jason would soon be around, and she would not be able to talk to him or touch him; however, she did touch Chris. She wondered if they both wore the same cologne, she felt more comfortable talking to his brother who had amnesia. She could only hope that her instincts were right. Jason and Chris were close and they trusted each other. They both seemed to go in the same direction, and if Chris accepted her, then Jason would also, regardless of what Carolyn had to say.

"Talk to Chris. Tell him everything now, Ellen. This secret is driving you crazy," Judy said. "You are not the only one that has lost someone you loved!"

Ellen watched as Judy snapped at her. "All my life I have been abused. I lost the man I loved and my unborn child at the same time, I married a man I did not love only to have him cheat on me." She raised her hand, "how about that? So, please, do not tell me about pain." Judy realized she had been hard on Ellen. "You now have the opportunity to change your life, even if Jason does not accept you. At least he will know why you were not in his life."

Judy had never admitted the role she played in Ellen's life. She and Ellen were friends. They talked every day and after Jason was born, she was the one who told Eddie, Jason's father, where Ellen was and that she was offered a recording contract. It was better to be on Eddie's good side and, if you lied to him, he would make you pay just like his father had, so she told him everything, even about Ellen, and that she was singing at the club. Eddie had blackballed her and Ida from his life since he had married, and did not want his wife to find out about his dirty little secrets.

She knew that Eddie would do whatever it took to stop her, but she had no idea how far he would go. However, Eddie stole Jason and Ellen had been put into a mental hospital and she had felt guilty ever since. *Like it or not, things are about to happen and there is nothing we can do about it, because they have already started, just as Lady Clem had said.*

❧ ❧

"Jason, where are you?" Carolyn was frantic; she finally had him to herself and suddenly he had run off and he did not say a word to her. He'd received a phone call after they made love and had to leave all of the sudden.

Jason traced Devin's steps from that night; he could see skid marks in the street and the charred remains of clothing. He turned to see if someone was watching him. He looked and there was no one, but he felt as if he were being watched. He followed the skid marks and came up on a canal behind the trees. He felt someone touch his shoulder and quickly turned to find his Uncle Willie behind him. Willie shook his head, "Devin cannot be in there; he was an excellent driver and would have bailed out long before he hit the water."

Jason eyes were watery. "Then why hasn't he contacted us? Devin and I touch base every day, we call and check in, but I have not heard from him since that night and I had a family contact me about a missing person." He contacted his father to let him know his findings, and asked if he could get someone to dredge the canal as soon as possible, as he needed closure and the sooner the better. He could only think of the last words he heard Devin say, "What in the fuck is that?" Before he heard the crash and the phone went dead, and now he could be standing in the spot where his brother was last.

"I let you down," he said, as he pounded the steering wheel of his car. He wondered what his brother had seen that could have caused him to lose control of his car and what the crashing sound was that he heard?

He looked at his phone to see that Carolyn was trying to reach him. *Not now, Carolyn,* he thought as he placed the phone on the seat. If it were not for his brother, he would not be sitting here today.

Jason remembered when Carolyn first told him that he was a father. He walked into his office, where Devin was looking over files. Jason handed Devin a picture of baby Lionel and said, "I am a father."

"Who is the mother?" Devin asked.

"Carolyn Young," Jason answered.

Devin stood and walked over to the mini fridge and pulled out a cola and poured them both a cup. They toasted to fatherhood.

"Next time we will toast you," Jason said.

"Not now," Devin smiled, "we have a lot of work to do, but soon I will meet the woman that I will want to spend my life with." He thought of Connie Haymond, a woman he had dated for only a month, and later was found dead. He was a suspect in her murder because he was the last to see her alive. Also Stephanie Walker, a woman that Jason had dated. They both died the same way and, luckily, he had been out of town when she was found dead and cut open.

Devin had decided to finish the paperwork, when he received a call from Carolyn, telling him that his son was running a fever and asking if he would pick up a prescription at the drug store. When he got to his car, someone fired a shot, hitting him in the shoulder. He went down and when he looked up, he could see someone wearing all black coming toward him. First, he thought he had blacked out because what he was seeing was something in a horror movie; someone was walking toward him with a long black veil covering his face. He reached for his gun, when suddenly he heard another shot and it was Devin; he had shot the person, who went down, but managed to get up and run, and get into a truck before Devin could exit the building.

ᗧ ᗧᗜ

Jason jumped out of his car to have a second look at the skid marks. He spotted what looked like arms in the bushes, so he pulled out his gun and started walking toward the sight, and pulled back the branches when he saw mannequins. There were several of them, some of them had on wigs and clothing. He turned suddenly to see a woman looking at him, but she drove away before he could get a good look at her.

ᗧ ᗧ

Eddie was in disbelief. He had talked to Jason and was informed that Devin was missing. Jason said, "Something happened to Devin as he exited the interstate the night he was coming to live with me." Jason tracked down Devin's last whereabouts and found skid marks that led into a lake. Eddie called the family physician, Leonard Pendergrass, to meet him at the scene. If the diver found anything, he wanted to be there. Eddie ordered his workers to search the area just in case Devin was lying in the woods hurt; Leonard would be there to help him.

Eddie closed the door to his office and cried. His father always said a grown man was not supposed to cry. "This cannot be happening," Eddie said, out loud, to himself. A father is not supposed to bury his children. Eddie sat and cried with his face in his hands. Eddie remembered his and Devin's last conversation and wondered if his son forgave him or did he die hating him.

Eddie looked up when he heard a knock on his door. Leonard Pendergrass walked in. Leonard looked like an old college professor with his wire rim glasses. "I came right over," Leonard said.

Eddie stood and shook his hand. "They are dredging the lake and I hired diver," Eddie said.

Leonard sat in a chair across from Eddie. "They will not find Devin in the lake because he is a trained professional," Leonard said.

Eddie and Leonard turned and looked when Mark knocked on the door.

"I pulled the car to the front of the house," Mark said.

"Thank you, Mark," Eddie said.

Eddie and Leonard stood to walk out the door. Leonard touched Eddie's shoulder and said, "Everything is going to be all right. Devin probably took a vacation somewhere."

Eddie looked at Leonard and said, "I hope you are right."

They arrived at the site, where Jason stood and waited. One of the divers found a car under the water. Eddie and Leonard got out of his limousine and walked over and stood by Jason.

"They found a car," Jason said.

The divers hooked the car up to a crane and it was lifted out of the water. Eddie closed his eyes and grabbed his chest; it was Devin's car, and the driver's side door was open. He held out all hope that Devin had gotten out of the car. Ben, one of Eddie's security guards, walked over to tell Eddie, "They have searched for miles and have found no signs of Devin, only parts from mannequins."

"Keep searching," Eddie said.

Eddie listened as one of the divers yelled, "We found something." Jason and Eddie walked closer to get a better view as a body was lifted into the grassy area.

"Oh God," Eddie said. "What is that? That is not my son."

Leonard walked over to examine the body; it was burned beyond recognition and the bloating made it impossible to identify. Leonard checked for Devin's tattoo, but the body was in such a bad condition that he had to get it on the examining table. Leonard walked back over to Eddie with tears in his eyes.

"We are going to need Devin's dental records," Leonard said. "But that is not Devin. It can't be.

Chapter 5

Five years ago

The day was beautiful. It was the calm before the storm. The weatherman interrupted the radio broadcast for an important message about a hurricane that was heading towards New Orleans. Lisa had left her job at the Get Fitness Center. Lisa worked in the physical therapy department. She was a student at Tulane University and studied psychology and worked on weekend as a home health care provider. Running from the hurricane was not an option for her because it was normally wind and rain and in a few hours the sun would be shinning. She would take refuge in another state only to find that leaving home was in vain and very costly.

She went shopping for food and water to prepare for the storm. She picked up flashlights and batteries just in case they lost power.

After Hurricane Katrina, Lisa was watching the news; all of the streets were flooded as there had been a breach in the levees. The *News Reporter* announced that there were people on roofs and there were bodies of people floating in certain areas. She sat with a patient, Mrs. Robinson, who awaited her son to come and remove her from the madness.

"Where will you go, Lisa?" The older lady asked with concern.

"I have no idea, right now," Lisa replied. "My sister and mother have headed to Atlanta, and maybe that will be the direction I will head." She knew they did not get alone, so she would need a place of her own.

"Good, dear, that is where we are headed, so you and Claire can follow. If you would like, you can stay with us until this is all over." Lisa was happy to know she did not have to be alone, but she needed some time to work on herself and thought she would get some studying done. She would let her family know that she was fine and start a new chapter in her life.

WELCOME TO ATLANTA, she read on a sign, and breathed a sigh of relief. She had been driving for twenty-four hours in bumper-to-bumper traffic and had noticed that she needed gas. She decided to take the next exit. She had her navigation system ready and the address of the Robinson family, if she needed it. She wanted to see what was in Atlanta. She tried to book a room, but none was available. She pulled into the gas station for gas and coffee.

She sat in the car, sipping her coffee when sudden she felt the need to cry. She was now alone. She did not want to spend the next couple of weeks arguing with her family, but she did not want to be alone. Her eyes were brimming with tears so she started to look for something to wipe her face. She exited the car just to have a look around and placed Claire in her bag, so she would not be left alone inside of the car. She looked across the street where there was a little clothing store that had a HELP WANTED sign in the window. She did not know why, but she wanted to answer the ad. She wanted to stay busy while she waited for the word that the city of New Orleans had reopened.

Lisa drove her truck in front of the store. She walked inside where there were two women; it was a small boutique and Lisa thought they could use an upgrade in fashion. One of the women came out to greet her. Lisa smiled and one woman looked at her, as if she were sizing her up. She felt uncomfortable, but putting her pride aside, she asked about the HELP WANTED sign inside of the window. The other woman walked from behind the counter, "Are you from New Orleans?" She said yes. The ladies were playing tag team on her—one would ask a question, then the other; however, both women were pleasant and slowly everyone felt comfortable enough for them to offer her a second cup of coffee, which she accepted.

"My name is Alisa Washington." She extended her hand.

"Hello, can I call you Lisa?" Judy asked.

"Yes," Lisa said, "everyone does.

"I am Judy and this is my best friend, Ellen. We are the owners of E and J Fashion." Judy smiled, "If you do not mind me asking, what was your employment in New Orleans?"

She had worked in retail when she was younger, but she hoped her little experience would be enough for her to get the job. "I did home health care while going to college to get my degree in physiology. I have one year to go."

Ellen walked from behind the counter. "Honey, you are perfect for the job. However, you will only be in town for a short period of time."

"Atlanta is beautiful, and I could see myself making a life here," said Lisa.

"Great," Judy said. "You are the one."

Judy walked to the phone and made a phone call while Ellen told her what job she would be doing. We have a friend Ida Stanford, who is in her eighties. She is very independent, but a few months ago she fell in the garden and now she is having trouble getting around." Lisa watched Ellen talk; Ellen never made eye contact with Lisa; she looked around as if she were looking for someone and never made eye contact. "Ida needs twenty-four-hour care. Judy and I and are here all day, and we just cannot take care of her."

Judy came back from her telephone call and joined in: "Ida has complained about the other helper the hospital sent over. She thought that she should hire her own personal help. Do you have a place to stay?"

"I just arrived," Lisa said.

"That's good because it is a live-in position."

Lisa looked in the direction of the door because the dog was in the car. "I have a shih tzu dog," Lisa said. Judy walked back to the phone to call Ida to inform her about the dog. Lisa looked around while Judy talked to Ida and Ellen started fixing the clothing on the clothes hangers properly.

"The dog is fine," Judy said. "I do not have a problem with the dog as long as it is friendly and you clean up behind it."

Lisa lifted her eyes to the sky; she and Claire would not have to sleep in the car tonight.

"We will pay what you ask. Money is no problem."

Judy looked at Lisa again, "You will do well with Ida and I hope you decide to stay and finish school here. There is a college not far from here, as well as the hospital."

Judy handed Lisa a piece of paper with Ida's address and written directions as to how to get to Ida's house. "She will be expecting you. Ellen and I will come this weekend and show you around town."

☙ ☙

Lisa followed the directions and found the house with no problem. Along the way, she noticed many newly renovated homes. She looked at Claire. "This could become home for you and Mommy before kissing Claire and placing her in her bag." Lisa rang the doorbell and waited; she heard a voice asking her to come in. Ida was sitting in front of the television when Lisa entered the house. "Hello, Miss Ida," she said, and she walked in to get a closer look at Ida. She noticed Ida was very thin and frail looking. Lisa's heart melted because she also noticed the house was in disarray. Lisa looked at Ida, who seemed embarrassed that she had not been able to do any housework since her fall. Surely, Judy and Ellen stopped over to visit sometimes. But the shop kept them very busy.

"Hello, honey," Ida said. "Have a seat, if you can find a place." Lisa smiled and the two of them looked at each other.

"Judy said you were very pretty and she was right," Ida said. "You know I have to keep up my image around here," while giving Lisa's hand a squeeze.

Ida began to show Lisa the house. Lisa thought Ida must have been looking at her old pictures, as they were all lying on the table. She would look at some of them later, after Ida was cleaned up and put to bed. Ida showed Lisa the bedroom she would be occupying. Lisa pushed Ida in her wheelchair into the bedroom that she slept in every night. Lisa thought she would start her cleaning in this room while she fixed Ida lunch. Lisa checked the fridge and cabinet, and she made a list of things she would have to purchase at the grocery store. "Miss Ida, we have to go to the grocery store, I saw one as I was coming in."

She put Ida and Claire into the car and Ida decided to stay in the car while she shopped. Ida inhaled the fresh air; it had been months since she had been outside of her home. "Thank you, Lisa," she said when Claire laid her head on her lap. She smiled because she had been starting to give up, and now there was hope.

Ida sat at the table having lunch. She was disappointed that Lisa did not join her, but she knew that Lisa wanted to get things clean in case Judy and Ellen stopped over for a visit.

Lisa was folding laundry and looking at some of the photos. She especially liked one in particular; it was a picture of Ida and her children—two young men. "Wow," she said, "how handsome they are." One of her sons looked very happy. He was laughing, while the other look preoccupied. There were even pictures of Ida and Judy at a young age, which she thought was strange because there was such a big age difference between them. But they were friends, even then.

Lisa looked at pictures of Ida and her husband. She looked at the gleam in Ida's eyes, compared to the eyes she looked at when she entered the house. Ida was laughing in one of the pictures and she looked to be so happy. She finished the laundry and the back of the house. She looked around and noticed all of the beautiful things Ida had, and now she was pleased because everything was clean and in place.

She walked into the kitchen where Ida was sitting. Ida had eaten all of the lunch and she thought for such a small person, Ida had a big appetite. She had piled her plate, thinking that she would nibble until Lisa cleaned the rest of the house; however, that was not the case. She stopped and wondered if Ida had not eaten for a while.

"That was delicious, honey. Where did you learn to fry chicken like that?"

Lisa loved when someone complimented her cooking; she had taken classes and learned how to season food for taste. "I am from New Orleans and we are known for our food." Lisa placed her hands on Ida's shoulders. "You wait. I am going to prepare you food that will have you dancing on the ceiling."

Ida sat in the bathtub. "Stay and talk, honey. It's late. We will not get any visitors at this time of night," Ida laughed, "unless you are expecting a gentleman caller."

Lisa laughed also, "No, Mrs. Ida, I guess it is just the two of us." Lisa realized she had not had a gentleman caller in years; since her last relationship went bad, she decided to go back to school and make a life for herself while she still had time. Lisa made coffee and she and Ida talked for hours. Lisa asked Ida about the pictures on the table, and suddenly she had a sad look on her face.

"You have trusting eyes," Ida said to Lisa, "and that says a lot. You also have a good heart, honey, I can tell. Mark my words: one day you will be a good mother and wife. You have a blessing coming, trust me," Ida said while patting her on the hand.

She told Ida how bad her last relationship was. Ida said, "That is because he was not the one. Every relationship has its ups and downs, but when it gets physical, it is time to leave. I was married to my husband for over twenty years. We had two boys and a girl," Ida said with passion, ". . . And he had a short fuse. Sometimes, he would yell at me, but he never laid a hand on me, not even when I provoked him," she said with a smile. He would just say, 'Ida, get control of yourself,' which, by the way, teed me off," she laughed. "Then, one day, he was gone," she said, as a tear rolled down her face and Lisa handed her a Kleenex. "We were having a party for one of the kids and he picked up my son from the school campus. They were going to ride home together and they never made it home. They were involved in an accident." Ida looked away, "I am not sure what happened. It was a one-car accident. The police said they were burnt to death," Ida dried her eyes. "Lately, they have been on my mind, so I went through some old pictures to keep their faces in my head."

The tables were suddenly turned, Ida now handed Lisa the box of Kleenex. "I am so sorry, Mrs. Ida."

"Mrs. Is my momma's name, honey, call me Momma or Momma Ida," she smiled.

"Okay, Momma." Lisa asked Momma if the two handsome gentlemen were her children.

She smiled. "Yes, she looked at the picture in her hand and pointed. "That is Jimmy. He was the baby. He died with his father." And then she pointed to the other man in the photo. "That is Eddie. The oldest boy is Eddie. He has a family now, I think," Ida said. "I am not sure, after James. Passed, he left home. I think, somehow, he blamed me for the death of his father and brother. He was the apple of his father's eye. No father could be prouder of his son than James was of Eddie. James would say,

Eddie was a hardcore businessman. He took over the family business and places money into accounts for me, but he never comes and visits. I have not seen him in over thirty years. I tried to call him when I learned he had children, but he said he was busy and I never seen my grandsons."

Lisa then realized how lonely Ida was. She sat all day looking at pictures and she sometimes would get a visit from Judy and Ellen.

Lisa looked at the clock: it was 11:30. "Wow, time really flies."

Ida looked and she was surprised, also. She was normally in bed by eight o'clock.

"Get out of the chair; you are going to walk to your bedroom tonight."

Ida looked at her; she had been sitting for so long, she did not know if she could. Lisa lifted her up. "Don't hurt yourself, honey," Ida said, her legs wobbled for a minute.

"Just stand for a while to get a feel for balance while I hold you."

Slowly, Ida's legs started to move while Lisa walked behind her with her hands out. Ida walked slowly, but she walked into her bedroom. Lisa massaged her legs with muscle relaxing cream for several minutes.

Ida watched her and was very impressed with her new employee. "You have very beautiful gowns in your closet; you must have been the belle of the ball," and it brought a smile to Ida's face, to have someone interested in her life.

"I was a seamstress. I could make anything, girl," Ida said with pride. There was a glow in her. "I used to make my husband's suits and all my gowns and dresses. If you could envision it, I could sew it."

Lisa was impressed; she had always wanted to learn to sew and make beautiful things. She could do a little, but Ida was a pro. "Will you teach me how to sew? I could be your protégé," she said with a smile.

Ida loved the idea. "Tomorrow we will go and get some material and start your first lesson." Ida was happy because she would have her second outing and the best thing was Lisa did not mind taking her.

Lisa gave Ida a hug and tucked her in for the night. Lisa put away the dishes and looked at the pictures and wondered what kind of man would turn on his mother in her time of need. She studied the face of Eddie Jones. "Why would you abandon your mother like you did?" And then she thought, *money*.

Ida awoke to the smell of coffee and bacon. Lisa walked into her bedroom. "Wake up, sleepy head."

Ida waited for her wheelchair, but Lisa said no, she would walk to the kitchen table and have breakfast and she did. Ida ate enough for ten people. Ida took a bath and Lisa fixed her hair in one of the latest hairstyles. "We are going out for the day." Lisa got Claire and dressed her, and the three of them went for a ride.

Ida was happy; she had not been out in months. She asked if they could stop at a friend's house. She did not want to go inside, but she just wanted to see if they were home. Lisa placed the address in her navigation system. They arrived at one of the biggest houses Lisa has ever seen. The house sat off the road behind locked gates. Lisa and Ida sat there for a few minutes and watched the house. Lisa noticed people coming out of the house, and she also noticed Ida's face—it was happy and sad.

"There is lots of money in this place," she said to get Ida's attention.

Ida laughed, "Yeah, they are pretty well off." Ida watched as someone pulled out of the gate. Lisa could not tell if it was a man or woman. Claire wanted to play, so her attention was on her.

Lisa and Ida continued their sewing class. They had sewn so many pieces there was no place to put them. Judy asked if she could put some in her store to sell on commission. Lisa agreed as she would soon start her classes and could use the extra money.

Lisa called the bank. She had received her bank statement because she'd had too much money on the statement. She had not made a deposit into her bank account, other than the sales of some items she had posted on her web site. However, Judy would take the sales from the store straight to the bank, so she was not aware of her balance. The teller checked her statement and told her that she was getting direct deposit from a Jones, Incorporated. Lisa realized Momma's son was paying for her care and he was very generous about it, at least, he was willing to pay for good help since he was not willing to help himself. Lisa asked Momma Ida about Jones, Incorporated and she explained that it was her husband's company. She'd given an employee document to her attorney and they made her deposits for her.

Lisa thought it was too much, but Momma said it was not enough for all she did for her. "I can walk through my house again. I have also gained twenty pounds and I eat the best food I have ever tasted in my life," Momma said. It is the least Eddie could do, considering he will not come and say hello to his own mother," Ida said with anger. "As a matter of fact, honey, I think you deserve a raise; he and his family enjoy my husband's money why can't we?"

Ida had an appointment at the hospital. There were new employees there so Lisa waited in Room 3 with Ida. She'd never leave Momma unattended. "Mrs. Ida, hello, my name is Carla Coleman; may I check your blood pressure?" Carla checked Ida's blood pressure, as she stared at Lisa. "I love that dress you are wearing and you really smell good."

Lisa smiled, "Thank you, I make my own clothes. I also have a clothing line I started."

"No wonder you look so good," Carla said.

"I started a web site, but I'm thinking about opening a shop because the demand is so high. Right now, though, I have a few more months in school before I could consider anything."

Carla asked, "Can you use any help?" She did not want to say that she had recently given birth to her son, and she was a single parent and could use the extra money to help with daycare.

Lisa gave Carla her phone number and address. "Give me a call and we will work something out."

Carla walked out the room and a doctor named Carolyn Young walked in.

"Hello, Mrs. Ida, my name is Dr. Carolyn Young and I will be your physician today." Ida just looked at her; she seemed so young, so Dr. Young decided to appeal to Lisa. "Some of the physicians have moved to other hospitals," she laughed and some left for California to pursue a music career."

Lisa laughed, "You go to school all of those years and you decide to become a musician . . . Wow!" Lisa said.

Carolyn noticed Lisa's accent and asked, "Are you from here?"

Lisa wondered why people thought she was proper when she was in other states, but when she said she was from New Orleans, they assumed she would have come from California. "No, I am from New Orleans."

Carolyn stopped, "You're kidding, right? I lived there for years. I attended Xavier University." The two of them high-fived each other.

"I attended Tulane before the storm, and now I'm at one of the local colleges getting my degree."

"Lisa, I have only been back in Atlanta for a few months and it is only me and my son; if you would like to have coffee sometime, I could use a girl's day or night out." Carolyn looked at her appointment book. "There is a coffee shop across the street, if you and Mrs. Ida are available . . ."

"Coffee sound good, Carolyn, but I could use a glass of wine later. I have been here for a few months also. I have not been out in years, so I could use some conversation. Momma, will you come and have a glass of wine with us? I accepted thinking that we both could use a night out on the town."

Ida admired Lisa and she wanted to make sure that Lisa was happy. The time she and Lisa spent together was great. She knew, however, that Lisa needed her time to get to know people and meet a guy, and she did not want to be a burden to her. Lisa needed to spend time with people her own age, she needed Lisa to stay, and she hoped someone would sweep her off of her feet.

Carolyn walked into Ida's house and was very impressed. "It is beautiful here." She looked around and Ida was sitting at the table.

"You girls enjoy your night out," Momma said.

Carolyn looked at her. "You are not coming?"

Ida was shocked because Lisa asked her to join them and said, "You youngsters don't know how to have a good time, and the two of you will bore me."

As Momma got up and did a little dance, Lisa threw up both of her hands and said, "You get dressed, you are coming with us."

Ida was happy. She could not recall the last time she had been out on the town. She was especially happy when the bartender asked her for an identification card. Momma blushed and the three of them laughed and talked. They learned that Carolyn had a one-year-old son.

"You look amazing," Lisa said. Lisa toasted Carolyn for not letting a child hold her back. "I want to have two children one day," Lisa said. "Right now, I don't even have a date and no time for one." She explained, "I wanted to be established, just in case things do not work out, because I have friends back home that are taking a lot of crap because they have children and they feel they cannot make it on their own."

Carolyn looked into her drink. "I know that feeling," Carolyn said, "because I am a single parent. His name is Jason Jones, so if you run into anyone with that name, he is off limits." She said it with a smile, but Lisa felt she was serious. "We are together and we are not together. What does that mean? We get together and you know, make love," she explained.

Carolyn looked at Ida, who was flirting with a young man sitting next to her; she could clearly hear Ida tell the man she was twenty-two years old.

Lisa laughed and shook her head at Ida, then turned her attention back to Carolyn. "It was just recently that he had found out about Lionel. Apparently, his brother, Devin, saw me and realized I was pregnant and he told Jason, who came looking for me."

Lisa looked surprised. "Why didn't you tell him?"

"Jason comes and goes," Carolyn said. "We were together several times when I got back from New Orleans and when I found out I was pregnant, he was not around. I moved, of course, now I am settled and he is in his son's life." Carolyn ordered another glass of wine, and it was clear that she was not happy and probably was not telling the whole story. But a friend in need is a friend that listens.

"Jason's father hates me; he is a really controlling man, a real asshole . . . Eddie." Ida stopped, she did not say anything, and she just listened. "He once had someone following me to make sure that I did not contact Jason. When Jason and I first met, I knew I was not the kind of girl he dated—I was poor and he was rich. I often wonder if he asked me out to spite his father. If Eddie did not like you, he could make your life miserable."

Carolyn did not take a breath. Lisa thought she needed to get this weight off her chest, so she just shook her head.

"I knew I was causing a problem with Jason and his father; he left home and he didn't speak to him for a while, not because of me, but because he did not want his father to try to control him. Before I left for school, I had a very bad confrontation with Eddie and I have just returned. He does not know he has a grandchild."

"Carolyn, sometimes with age comes wisdom. Jason has stood his ground with his father, and it is obvious he cares about you, or else he would not have looked for you. Stay with him, Carolyn, love him, show him stability, and let him stay in his child's life. This will work itself out. Give it some time."

Lisa invited Kandy and Carolyn for dinner. Lisa wanted to invite them both to her graduation party next week. "You done it, honey," Ida said, she was so proud of Lisa.

"I am not leaving, Momma, if that is what you are thinking. I just needed to do something with my life."

"You're stalling, Lisa."

"I am not. When Mr. Right comes along, I will know . . . Right, momma? You said so yourself."

Ida laughed, "Do not use my words against me." The two of them stood there. For the last two years she and Lisa had become very close. Ida referred to Lisa as her daughter to everyone. "Before I leave this earth, I will make sure you have the perfect man for you, mark my words, honey, you are a blessing and you will get one." Ida placed one hand on Lisa's cheek.

"I love you, Momma," Lisa said and Ida gave her love back to Lisa.

✑ ✑

Every week, the gang would get together for weekend dinner—the eight of them. Lisa would make dinner and Carolyn would bring wine and Lionel, and Kandy would bring dessert and her son named Justin. Carolyn walked over with gift for everyone, "Lionel is having a birthday party."

Lisa accepted the invitation. She thought she would finally meet Lionel's father, but each year she would ask if Jason would be there, and Carolyn would say he comes like a thief in the night, makes love to her, and by morning, he is gone. She wondered if Lisa was judging her.

"Carolyn, you have to allow some growth and then give him an ultimatum. I know that there are missing pieces in every puzzle. But communication is the key to a healthy relationship, and if Jason cannot attend the party, then you should plan something for the three of you because Jason has to know that Lionel needs to be with his father and needs him to be a part of his life."

Chapter 6

"If you were a guy, would you date me?" Lisa asked Kandy and Carolyn as they sat at the Starbuck's coffee shop.

Carolyn threw up her hands, "Girl, where on earth is this coming from?"

"Ladies, it has been over a month and Chris has not even tried to kiss me, not even a touch." Lisa looked hurt. "We work side-by-side in the office, we work out together, and I have even slept in bed with him."

Carolyn was stung; she could not believe that Lisa was throwing herself at Chris like that, "Hold up, you have been sleeping with him?" Carolyn asked, with a frown on her face. It was time to get through to Lisa, who thinks that men want a good woman, that men want eye-candy. While Lisa was attractive, she lacked certain qualification—her skin was too tan and while she was a size seven, men wanted a size one. "Lisa, you are so naïve, you think that you can nurse him back to health and spoon-feed him and be a loving and caring woman and that will do; but, you are wrong. First of all, Chris looks like he should be on the cover of a magazine and when men look like that, you are not what they are looking for; you are getting him back on his feet, so he can get what he really wants and that is not you." Carolyn was on a roll. "I can tell you what disqualified you. Men like Chris like eye candy—young and thin women—which, by the way, women pay doctors for the body that you have, and Chris is light complexioned and he is probably looking for the same."

Lisa was so hurt she could not say a word. "Wow, Carolyn, you talk about a kick in the self-esteem . . . I hope you never have to give your son a pep-talk."

And, once again, Carolyn said, "At least I am a mother and I will tell my son what is true, not what he wants to hear."

Kandy looked at Carolyn. She had that I-am-better-than-you attitude. Carolyn was judging Lisa just as she had judged Kandy when she broke up with Justin and started dating other men. She wished Lisa would stand her ground with her today.

Lisa had her hand under her chin, and Carolyn and Kandy could see the pain on Lisa's face.

"Lisa, I am sorry; I did not mean to sound judgmental or hurtful. As a friend, though, I don't want to see you make a fool of yourself."

Lisa looked around. She had barely slept because someone watches her at night. "Carolyn, I do not care what you think because there are no angels at this table, okay? It is just that I know someone is watching me." Lisa threw up her hands and knew that she would sound crazy. "I swear, Claire starts to growl and barks at the window. I looked and I could see someone through my window, watching me. I was laying on the sofa in the family room. First, there was nothing there, but when I turned off the light, I could see its shadow. I know you think I am desperate, but this is not an excuse to get into bed with Chris. I am an adult and if that is what I choose to do, I can. But it's not like that. I've just been so scared." Lisa thought Carolyn would say she just wants to be close to Chris, but to her surprise, she did not.

"Why haven't you gone to the police?" Carolyn asked.

"Because when I check the surveillance camera there is nothing there," Lisa said.

"Do you think it is the man in the truck?" she asked.

"What truck?" Lisa asked. She was surprised; she knew nothing of a man in a truck.

"Kandy and I both saw him, Lisa; he sits out there every night, smoking cigarettes. When I work late, I pass on your street and that truck is there. First, I thought that Jason's father was having me followed, but he sat in front of your house every night."

Carolyn was concerned, "Have you talked to Chris about this?"

Lisa shook her head, "No, I do not want him to think I am crazy. When we were in the hospital, I know this is going to sound crazy, but something or someone was watching me; it stood in the door wearing all black like it was grieving, but it danced."

Kandy looked at Carolyn, "I saw it, too and it scared me so badly."

"I did not want to say anything, hoping it was a joke, but it followed me home and I'm scared. I do not know what I would do if Chris was not there," a tear rolled down her face. "I know that he will probably soon leave, and I think it will come in then. I think it has not come inside to get me because it knows Chris is there. I am not making this up."

Carolyn rolled her eyes, "Lisa, you have been under a lot of stress lately. Maybe, your mind is playing tricks on you."

"Do not fucking say that. But I hope you are right because it is something that you would not want to see. I try to scream but I can't, and knowing my friends will think that I am crazy and want attention doesn't help," Lisa said.

Carolyn's eyes opened wide, Lisa was serious, she was truly afraid. "Just in case you are not, I will get Jason to look into it."

Carolyn's words were eating at Lisa's soul. Her whole life, she was told that she was not good enough and now her best friend thought so.

"That would be nice, thanks, Cal." Lisa then changed the subject. "The two of you are not getting off that easy." Kandy and Carolyn looked at each other. "Well, would you do me or not?"

Kandy said "yeah," but Carolyn needed the question repeated. "Are we talking long term or a one-night-stand?" Lisa looked at her. "I am picky, I mean you are okay, but long term . . . I don't know."

"Ouch," Lisa said. She knew that Carolyn thought that if Chris were with her, it would be a one-night-stand.

"I think you are a good catch, Lisa, you're a good cook, you're attractive, you do it all; any man would be happy to have you."

"You are so naïve," Carolyn said to Kandy, "who knows what a man wants? They do not know what they want. You can do all those things and it still sometimes is not good enough. They will have you at home cooking and cleaning, while they find some young thing to bang.

"Lisa, Chris is a good guy. He just does not want to use you. Have you ever thought that Chris is just not interested in having a relationship with you?" Carolyn knew that she was hurting Lisa, but they were friends, and she needed to be honest with her. "You think that you can seduce him. You need to stop, honey. He is not interested. Chris has amnesia; one day, you could walk into your house and he will not be there. One day, he might not know you exist and you would have crossed the line with him.

Lisa lowered her head and said, "All the time and I know one day he will be gone, which is why I have to find out what is going on. Carolyn, we are doing dinner Friday, maybe Jason could come with you and I hire him since he is always working."

Lisa stood to leave, but Kandy stopped her. "Sit down, Lisa, I have something to say." Lisa looked puzzled. "I have been trying to speak and, as usual, no one is listening."

"I am sorry, Kandy, I just got caught up in the moment."

"Yes, Lisa, I know. And you are about to ruin your life, so listen to me. I know I am young; I have been promiscuous in my time, which is how I know what I am saying. Chris cares a lot for you. You are special to him. I know this because of the way he looks at you. Chris is not crazy; he knows he will never find a package like you. You are sexy, maybe a little rusty, girl, if you know what I mean. He knows you do not sleep around, and you are beautiful, both inside and out. Not to count, girlfriend, you can cook, and most of all, how good you are to him and for him. What you did for him, no young thin package would do and he knows that. When he makes love to you, he will be making love to you, not having sex with you. Right now, he is trying to get his mind right; he wants to make sure when he moves forward with you, he can go straight and not have to wonder what he has left behind. Chris is going to love you, just like you love him," Kandy made sure she stressed her last words. "Have patience, Lisa, your life will begin soon with Chris."

Lisa tried to act natural, but Carolyn had a point—she used to work in a uniform and no man ever looked at her. When a young girl came around with half of her butt crack out they paid attention. "Thanks, Kandy, your words mean a lot to me and, by the way, I know sometimes you think I am not paying attention to you and that your opinion does not matter to me, but it does. You really mean a lot to me and I think you are wise beyond your years. You may have done things in your life, but you know when to stop and work on becoming a better person."

Carolyn knew that last remark was directed towards her. Lisa always told her to check herself, that her attitude would get her into trouble. Carolyn also got the last remark Lisa made about Jason working and retaining him. "Lisa, you can keep your money; Jason will be happy to help you pro bono. Jason and I have more money than we would ever spend, but he is now grieving the loss of his brother. His brother Devin has been missing for several weeks, which by the way, is why I have not invited him over for Friday dinner. Last week, they pulled his car out of the canal and, later, they found his body after dredging the canal."

Lisa sat down. She remembered seeing the picture in the newspaper of a car being lifted out of the canal. "I am so sorry to hear that, Cal; please ask him to come over for dinner and be with friends." Lisa was saddened by the news; she felt petty and selfish.

Carolyn now had both ladies' attention, "He has been so preoccupied lately. Jason does not know how to grieve. Lately, he has been like a jack rabbit."

Lisa knew that Carolyn was being sarcastic now, letting her know she was making lots of love to Jason, while Chris had not touch her.

"He comes home every day wanting to make love. He says it take his mind off of his problems."

"Girl, you must be worn out," Kandy said with a laugh.

"We make love, Kandy, which is something you know nothing about. We love each other."

"Oh," Kandy said, "he was not screwing you this much before he started grieving."

Carolyn sat straight up, "Listen, Boo, Jason and I have known each other for years, not weeks."

Lisa also knew this was directed toward her.

"From the first day we met, we were attracted to each other."

Kandy sat straight up. "So, you screwed him the first day you met him, and you call me a slut."

"We made love, if you want to know, and it was good because years later we are still together."

"You got pregnant, slut," Kandy said with anger.

Lisa tried to stop things before it got out of hand. She was proud of Kandy, but the two of them were going at each other and she did not want them to get to the point of no return.

Carolyn tried to pick up where she had ended. "Jason lost his best friend; he said they were very close. They were half-brothers."

"How long had he been missing? Lisa asked.

"The same night Chris was admitted in the hospital, which is why I came to the hospital that night. I checked to see if a Devin had been admitted, but he was not, so I had to give him the bad news." Carolyn gloated, even in this situation. "We had just made love when Devin called. The two of them were talking on the phone when Jason heard the commotion. Now you know why I was so tired the next morning doing your examination and why I decided to fight for my man," Carolyn looked at Lisa. "Life is short; it is true what they say: 'You can be here today and gone in a blink of an eye.'"

Carolyn stood straight up, "Jason and I will see you tomorrow for dinner."

Lisa knew Carolyn was milking it, so she suggested that they wait and talk about her stalker later.

"No, do tomorrow what you should have already done, Lisa; I will talk to Jason about the stalker tonight and you can fill him in tomorrow."

Kandy and Lisa watched as Carolyn drove away. "Oh, my God, Kandy, that is so sad."

Kandy looked depressed. "I know what it feels like to lose your best friend, Lisa. I lost my mother and I don't remember my father."

Lisa looked at Kandy. She never asked her how her mother died, so now she did.

"I do not know," said Kandy. "I was told by my Aunt Tina that she committed suicide. They say she cut her wrists after setting the house on fire. I was not there; I spent the night at Aunt Tina's house. My mother wanted to surprise Daddy with a special dinner."

Lisa looked at Kandy, "That does not sound like a woman who is about to commit suicide." Lisa made a note to look into Kandy's mother's death; she would call Detective Milo later. "Honey, why don't you remember your father?"

Kandy suddenly looked depressed. "After my mother's death, he moved and left me behind. Why did he leave me, Lisa?" Kandy said with tears in her eyes.

"Honey, things are not always as they seem. Do you have any pictures of your mother?" she asked. Kandy looked at Lisa, "I would like to put a face to her."

"I will ask my aunt; she has a yearbook with Mother's senior photo and I will bring it to dinner tomorrow."

Lisa thought to ask Jason to look into the death of Kandy's mother, but knowing about his brother, she would not burden him, she would do so herself. Maybe she and Chris could do this together. Lisa felt depressed and wanted to be alone. "Kandy, I am going to go home and go to bed," she said. "It will be alright, just wait and see." Lisa turned quickly; she was falling apart in front of Kandy as they walked to their cars.

"Jason, honey, are you home? Carolyn threw her purse on the sofa. She walked to the computer where Jason was working. She picked up a picture of a young man—dark brown complexion with light brown eyes; he had a low haircut. Carolyn thought he had a beautiful smile. His teeth were white, and he was handsome.

Jason walked behind her. He placed his arms around her, and she jumped with horror. "Oh, my God, Jason, you scared the crap out of me."

Jason kissed her and said, "You are so jumpy today."

Carolyn sighed, "It's Lisa."

Jason tried to recall which of Carolyn friends Lisa was. "Baby, I don't remember her."

Carolyn pulled out a picture of herself, Kandy, and Lisa. "She is the one on the end."

Jason looked at the picture. Now he remembered her. He tried not to stare or let it slip that Lisa was a very attractive woman because he knew Carolyn would take it in the wrong way.

"First," Carolyn said, "tomorrow night, we are invited to dinner at her house. I will not take no for an answer, Jason, my friends think you are a ghost. Second, Lisa is in trouble, babe. She is my best friend, and she is such a loving person but she trusts people too fast." Jason just sat and listened; he had never seen Carolyn show such concern. Normally, she would say if you make your bed, you should lie in it.

"That night, when we went to the hospital, a man by the name of Christopher Weber was admitted into the hospital; he was a hit and run victim. Lisa said she was drawn to him for some reason." Carolyn sighed again. "Honey, she is falling for this guy, he has amnesia, and I am afraid for her.

"Jason, she is now seeing things. Lisa was as close to perfect as you can get. She is a wonderful person and this Chris Weber is running her crazy."

Jason did not know what to say. He could not tell Carolyn that the family of Christopher Weber had hired Jason to find him, he had been missing for over a month, and that his brother Devin might be responsible for Chris's accident. Chris Weber's car was found a few feet from where his brother's car went into the canal. The next morning when he checked the hospital, he was told he had checked himself out of the hospital and they did not have an address to where he had gone. Jason had to get all of the facts. How did Lisa meet Chris Weber?

Carolyn sat next to him, "The night when you and I went to the hospital to see if Devin had been admitted, she was there with Momma Ida. Lisa said she was getting this strange feeling in her stomach, which led her to the emergency room where Chris Weber was being treated.

She brought Chris home and nursed him back to health— she cooked for him, she fed him breakfast in bed, she has fallen for him, and now she is losing her mind."

He had often heard Carolyn say, "Lisa needs a man, baby, she is strong and she needs a good piece, if you know what I mean. Since I've known her, Lisa hasn't dated at all, and that has been over five years, which is why she is vulnerable to Chris."

Jason tried to make Carolyn feel better. "Cal, if this guy was up to no good, he would have shown himself by now."

"Jason, Lisa is seeing a seven-foot ghost!" Jason laughed, *she really does need a good man*, he thought. "Yeah," Carolyn said, "she said she's been seeing some ghost wearing a long black dress with a long black veil covering its face. And, to make things weirder, he does this voodoo dance and watches her through the window of her house. She said she first saw it that night in the hospital and that it followed her home and now she is afraid."

Jason suddenly stopped laughing, "A long black veil?" He repeated.

"Jason, I am telling you, she is losing it."

Jason then asked if Chris Weber had seen this ghost. Carolyn could not answer that question. "Chris is a macho man," she said, "if he has seen anything, he has not said a word or he would probably beat the hell out of it. However, Kandy said she had seen it also."

"Who is Kandy?" he asked. Carolyn pointed at the picture, "She is the one in the middle on the picture," she said.

"Cal, if Kandy and Lisa both say they are seeing the same thing, what makes you think Lisa is going crazy?"

"Honey, Kandy and Lisa are very close, and Lisa does not have children and she treats Kandy like her child, and to keep Lisa from looking silly. Then she would say anything, because Chris has no interest in Lisa, and she does not want her to feel bad."

"What makes you think Weber has no interest in Lisa?"

"He has not made a pass at her. When she sees this monster, she runs and jumps into bed with him and, babe, he is gorgeous he looks like a movie star, and I told Lisa today that she was not good enough, he probably wants someone young and sexy."

Carolyn stood, "Today while having coffee, Lisa wanted to know if Kandy and I thought she was attractive. Lisa sees this ghost, she runs into the bedroom and jumps into bed with Chris, and he has not tried to hit on her. You will meet all of them tomorrow for dinner and you can judge for yourself." Carolyn said, and before Jason could say a word, "Honey, I need you to tell me if my friend is crazy and also I need you to take a look at Chris."

He picked up the picture again and looked at Lisa; he thought back to minutes before his mother died. Her last words were about how the devil wearing the black veil had come for her, while his father thought she had committed suicide because she was lonely. He later was shot by someone wearing the same thing. He looked at Lisa's picture. "Why you?" he asked. "What did Devin and Chris see on the road that night?" Did this person kill Devin and leave Chris to die on the side of the road? He looked at the picture again and wondered what Lisa's role in all of this was, why she was now a target and more so, why Chris had not made a pass at her. She is beautiful and attractive and has a very sex body. He needed Chris to answer questions because he may be the one that has put Lisa's life in danger. Whoever killed Devin that night, could now be after him because he witnessed what happened that night.

Lisa woke up in the morning feeling hurt. She thought Chris was disappointed with her and did not want to see her. She went into the bathroom to shower and noticed Chris was not in bed. She walked out of the bathroom wearing only her robe. She lay in the spot where he slept at night; she thought of last night.

Chris had prepared dinner and after her shower, she walked into the kitchen and he had the table set with candles in the candle holders. Chris pulled out her chair and they had dinner alone. Chris had taken Ida a tray to her room so that they would be alone. After dinner they sat and talked, and Chris stood and walked over to her and she stood and he kissed her. Chris pulled Lisa into his arms and he kissed her with passion, their bodies were as one. He held her so close in his arms, she felt guarded and protected. She welcome him, she kissed him back. They were in each other's arms for what seemed like forever before he lifted her and carried her over to the sofa and laid her down very gently, and then he kissed her again. She knew what he wanted and she wanted to give it to him. He removed her dress; she was not wearing anything under it.

She reclined and watched as he removed his pants and shirt. He looked at her and kissed her again—first her lips, then her breast—he adjusted her body for entrance and he pushed, but she did not receive him, he lay on top of her with her legs spread. He did a slow and gentle swirl on top of her and she did the same beneath him. She wanted to feel him inside of her so badly. She opened her legs wider and he tried entrance again, but he could not. They could hear her room door open, so Chris quickly dressed and so did she. He looked at her and kissed her on the cheek. "I am going to bed," he said.

Lisa was disappointed when Momma came out of her bedroom to bring her dinner plate to the kitchen; they could hear her bedroom door open, so Chris went to bed and she stayed up to work.

🖋 🖋

She was sitting at the kitchen table looking over the police reports she had obtained on her three new patients. She pulled out one, in particular. It made her laugh. She had seen mug shots of people smiling, some even crying, but Mr. W. Williams was laughing and flipping the bird at the same time. Chris came out of the bedroom to get something to drink. They had been packing boxes to send over to Judy's shop when she started to talk to him about Jason's brother. "His name was Devin and he had an accident in his car the same night you were brought in." Lisa did not know where everything had taken place or whether it was just a coincidence that he was hit by a hit and run driver the same night Devin had his accident. She did not pressure him for an answer or ask what kind of car had hit him. She just informed Chris that Jason would be coming to dinner, and they would fix something special to try to take his mind off his problems.

Chris smiled. If anyone could make Jason feel better, it would be the people in the house because there was so much love here. He had never been in the presence of people that loved and looked out for each other the way that they all did, and Jason would welcome it with open arms the way that he did.

Lisa had awakened in the morning and Chris had gone. She wanted him to hold her and tell her everything would be all right. Lisa called his cell phone and realized he did not have it with him. She got dressed. She wanted to see him before she went to the office. She walked through the house and there was no Chris. Her eyes were full of tears when Chris opened the door. She started packing her briefcase; she did not want him to see her crying like a baby. She walked into the next room and got herself together before she spoke to him.

Lisa walked into the bathroom where Chris was taking a bath—he lay there with his eyes closed while the bubbles from the Jacuzzi massaged him. She did not know what to say. "Honey, I am leaving," she said. "I will be home around noon," she smiled. "I have a very special dinner planned for tonight, so I will stop at the grocery store before I get home."

Chris opened his eyes; he stood, and grabbed a towel. He walked up to Lisa and placed in arms around her; he held her and kissed her again with the same passion. I have a very special night planned for you, as well," he said to her.

Lisa wanted him. "I have a few minutes before I have to be at the office."

Chris smiled, "I need more than a few minutes. It will probably take me a few minute to get you warmed up." He kissed her again and whispered, "Tonight."

Lisa sat in her car, thinking of what her night would be like with Chris. She was getting out of her car when Kandy pulled up next to Lisa in her car. "Lisa, I have something for you," she said. Kandy got out of her car and walked over to Lisa and opened her mother's high school yearbook to show Lisa exactly which picture was of her mother.

They started walking toward the hospital entrance, when Lisa stopped and looked at the picture and said, "Kandy, you look a lot like your mother."

"Do you think she did it, Lisa?" she asked. "Please, be honest with me."

"Kandy, I am gathering up information, however, I need a little help. I would like your permission to let me and Chris do a little research tonight. I will let him know what I have and maybe, he can gather more information, and we will keep you posted."

Kandy was puzzled. "I thought Jason was the detective."

"Yes, he is, but right now, he has a lot to contend with. Chris is starting to remember things he has been sharing a lot with me. Did you know he was a police officer?" She said with joy because now she knew more about him.

Lisa walked to her office door. She was carrying Kandy's mother's yearbook. "Ms. Washington, she heard a voice say." Lisa turned to see a man that she recognized. He was very well groomed and dressed to perfection. It was Mr. W. Williams. Lisa looked him up and down. She was feeling good and hoped her thoughts were not written on her face: *tonight she will become Chris woman in a true sense.*

"How can I help you, sir?" She smiled and thought of his mug shot. She knew very well who this man was, but she wanted to size him up a little bit more.

"I am your first," the man said with humor. Lisa smiled and said, "You are Willie Williams?"

"At your service, madam."

Lisa thought of Mr. W. Williams' mug shot again and how he was a very pleasant man. She could tell by looking at him that he was the kind of man that took no crap from anyone. He was a man that demanded respect, and if you did not give it to him, you would have to pay a price that you did not want to pay. However, she was getting good vibes from him, he reminded her of the late Robin Harris from Mo Better Blues, only in sense of humor. He was an older, very attractive man that had taken very good care of himself and smelled of the best fragrance money could buy. "Mr. Williams, you are dapper. I feel underdressed looking at you."

He smiled, revealing a set of perfect teeth. "I like you, Doc. You and I are going to get along fine," he said, placing her hand through his arm. They both walked into her office, where she placed the yearbook on her desk. She placed a bookmark on the page where Kandy said her mother's picture was.

"Where do you want to start Mr. Williams?"

"First of all, Doc, we can start here," he said. "I told the judge in court to go fuck himself. He was not pleased with that, so he told me to get my goddamn head examined. That is why I am here. I do not need a shrink. Nevertheless, I could use a friend of sorts."

Lisa smiled, "Okay, Mr. Williams, if that is the way you want it."

He then said, "If I share my life with you, then you will share yours with me. That way, it is not one-sided in here."

Lisa looked puzzled. She had never had any of her patients ask her to do that before and it was probably unethical, but something was telling her that she should get to know him and he was a man she would want on her side in a crisis.

"If you like, Doc, you can start small. I will start where you want me to," he lifted his head, "agreed?"

Lisa was mesmerized by him, so she agreed to his terms. She felt he was trustworthy.

He lifted the yearbook off her desk and said, "How about we start here?" He remembered Atlanta High School very well. He attended for only his senior year and when he was a graduated, he would play Basketball on the court and hung out. Later, his boss was given a contract to do repairs and to build another section on the building. "This high school is where I met my wife and this would have been the year that she graduated." With a little anger on his face he said, "Are you researching me, Doc?"

Lisa was stunned. She had no idea. "No, sir," she began to explain, "it's just a coincidence I assure you, a friend, or should I say my little sister from another mother, attended Atlanta High. I am from New Orleans and I was doing some research for her."

"I am sorry, Doc," he said, "it's just that my wife, or should I say, late wife, committed suicide twenty years ago and seeing that yearbook really hits home. I met her after I was betrayed by the woman that I thought that I would spend the rest of my life with, and it turned out that she betrayed me, too."

Lisa took the book from his hand and placed it in her desk. She was curious about his wife and needed to know more about her. It has to be a coincidence his wife and Kandy's mother both committed suicide twenty years ago.

"How about we start there? Maybe, we can get you some closure."

"There is no closure. She killed herself and my daughter Nibble . . ."

"Nibble?" She said.

"Yes, that is what I called her. She used to nibble at her food like a little mouse, so I called her Nibble," he said, before standing and walking to the window. There was a lot of love and pain involved. Talking about her brought tears to his eyes. He was a strong and powerful man, and it would take a lot of pain to bring him to tears. He did not look at her. He just stared out the window. She could tell he was in pain. "What would make a woman kill herself and her child?" he asked.

Lisa did not know how to answer his question. "I am sorry, Mr. Williams, I cannot answer that question. I have no information about what went on, so I cannot speculate as to how she may have felt at that time."

He then turned and walked back to look her in the eye. She felt a little intimidated because he wanted answers and she did not have any to give him. What was your wife's name, Mr. Williams, if you don't mind me asking?"

He looked away and replied, "Elmira."

Lisa sat up straight in her seat; she wanted to be eye-to-eye with him before she asked, "How did your wife die?"

He turned his face away from her again. "She sliced open her wrist," he said with anger. "She was smoking a cigarette that set the house afire and my daughter was asleep in the next room."

Mr. William resented his wife for killing herself and taking little Nibble with her. His love for his wife became hate. He was a good provider and could not understand why she was unhappy; therefore, he only mourned the loss of Nibble.

The bell rang and he stood up as if in a trance for the last hour. As he stood, he fixed his jacket, business as usual for him. There was a lot of pain and she would do what she could to give him closure.

"Doc, do you work on Saturdays? I would like to get this over as soon as possible. It's an hourly thing, if you get what I mean."

She wanted to make him smile before leaving, "For you, I will work nonstop."

He smiled with his perfect teeth, "I like you, Doc, and we are going to get along just fine."

Lisa packed her briefcase. She wanted to look through Kandy's mother's yearbook before everyone gathered for dinner that night. Before they walked out the door, he placed her hand through his arm again. "You, sir, are a perfect gentleman, and I would come to work on Sunday if I got to stand next to the best dressed man of all times," she said with a big smile.

"I like you, Doc," he said again. "There is something really special about you. May I walk you to your car?"

She smiled, "Yes, that would be nice."

"What the hell is that?" he asked.

Lisa looked, then she stopped and dropped everything; there it was, standing there in the parking lot. Her heart started pounding; today, it pointed at her.

"He looks too damn big for Halloween, don't you think, Doc?" He watched as the color drained from her face and she was gasping for breath. "Are you alright, doc?"

She had to get control of herself. He looked at her, then he looked for it again, but it was gone. "Yes, I almost forgot it was getting close to Halloween; he is a bit old, don't you think?" she asked.

"I have seen everything, Doc, and nothing surprises me anymore."

Mr. Williams saw it. She almost smiled, if it picked on him, then it would surely have met its match. Then she wondered why it showed itself to Mr. Williams; it stood there and it did not move or hide. It allowed itself to be seen by someone other than her. She looked at Mr. Williams. He reminded her of Chris—strong and fearless, as if nothing gets to him. She wanted to feel that, however, she was falling apart. Carolyn's words were haunting her and she was coming apart. She wondered if she made love to Chris, whether he would leave her for a younger, prettier woman. She wanted to cry her eyes out, but she did not want to be unprofessional.

🕭 🕭

"Hello, my name is Lisa Washington. I am here to see Detective Milo."

"Hello, Dr. Washington, Detective Milo is expecting you. She is out on a call, though, and asked if you would wait for her."

Lisa looked at the officer's nametag. "I will be sitting over there," she pointed to a seat by the window. "Thank you very much, Officer Given." Lisa sat by the window and reached into her briefcase. She wanted to do some reading on Kandy's mother. She turned to the picture that Kandy circled in the yearbook. She looked at Kandy's mother who was an attractive woman. She hardly looked like a person who would commit suicide, but then again, she could have had psychological problems that she could not share with her husband in fear that he would leave. "I know how you feel," she mumbled. If she told Chris that she was seeing dead people and a ghost, then he would pack his bags and head for the hills. She looked to see what Kandy's mother's name was—Elmira Coleman. Lisa studied her picture for a while; she was attractive with a medium-brown complexion and shoulder-length hair. "Kandy has her mother eyes."

Lisa sat back in the chair and closed her eyes; she could not think straight. She thought what might have happened to her if Mr. Williams had not walked her to her car. She knew she had to talk to Chris about this thing, as it has now shown up on her job and pointed its finger at her. She was afraid about whether or not Chris would think that she was crazy because Carolyn thought she was loony, and she was using this thing as an excuse to get into bed with Chris, however, Mr. Williams saw it also . . . Someone else besides she and Kandy had seen it.

She sat up straight in her seat and began turning pages in her tablet. She began reading the notes she had taken from her session with Mr. Williams. Elmira Coleman . . . Oh, my God . . . She then turned to the notes she had taken when she and Kandy had talked over coffee. 'I was at Aunt Tina's house and Mommy wanted to surprise Daddy with dinner.' *It was no suicide,* she thought. *Someone killed Kandy's mother, and Mr. Williams is Kandy's father.*

Lisa heard someone call her name. She looked up and it was Detective Susan Milo. She had known her for two years. They met while working on a murder case and since then, they had become close friends.

"Lisa," she said, "you look good."

"Oh my, Susan," she smiled, "you do also."

The two of them embraced each other and immediately, Susan knew that something was wrong. The detective looked at Lisa. She had known her for two years and knew something was on her mind, and it was heavy.

"I looked up the cases you asked me about." They walked to her office and she pulled out several folders, "But first, you have to tell me why you are asking. Besides, honey, you look like you have seen a ghost."

Lisa tried to smile, but she knew she had to have a good reason for asking her friend for help and she had never kept secrets before, but lately, it was all she could do. "Well, Susan, I have a client who came to me. She has had problems and one of them is the death of her mother. After listening to her, I came to the conclusion her mother did not commit suicide twenty years ago."

The detective sighed, "Have a seat, girl, because you are opening up a can of worms. Between you and me," she said, "twenty years ago, there was an epidemic of these so-called suicides." The detective then passed her the folder, "Both wrists were slashed so deeply, it nearly severed the bone."

Lisa's face was of shock, "How could that be?"

"Exactly," Detective Milo said, "when you asked, I checked, and not only was Elmira Coleman murdered, there was also an Asia Jones, who had both wrists slashed also, only the killer was interrupted when a family member knocked on the door and he did not get to burn the body."

Lisa looked puzzled. She began looking at the pictures and noticed what looked like a large doll that had been burned. Elmira Coleman was burned after her wrists were slashed. How could they rule it was a suicide? There is no way she could have slashed both of her wrists and then burn herself."

"I do not have an answer for that question." Susan looked to see who the investigators on the cases were. There were no names.

"What about Asia Jones? You said the job was not finished . . . What does that mean?"

The detective stood to pour coffee. "Asia Jones was not burned. Apparently, the killer was interrupted. She was found in her bathtub with gasoline poured over her; she was still alive when her son knocked on her door. She had lost too much blood; she died before she got to the hospital. Did the killer slash both of her wrists also?"

"Yes," detective Milo said, "and there were others."

Lisa read the list and went through each file with shock. There was a Melissa J. Thomas, and several others that fit the same profile. It was what looked like a ritual killing because some of the women had both wrists slashed and they were cut open in the mid-section of their bodies. She checked the dates and found that Melissa Thomas was killed forty years ago.

"Susan, would you do me one more favor, will you pull the files of a Jimmy and James Jones?"

The detective looked at her suspiciously, "Why, Lisa; is that the family you are working for?"

She took a deep breath. She did not want to say anything about seeing the ghost of Asia Jones. She thought, however, there could be a connection. "Momma Ida's son and husband died by fire also. Maybe Asia Jones is a relative." Lisa checked her watch. She had to get to the grocery store. She stood, "Is that it? We will do dinner next week."

"No can do," Susan said, "I am going to visit my daughter next week." She laughed and pulled out an ultra-sound picture.

Lisa jumped up and down and said, "I am going to be an aunt."

"I will get those files for you, but Lisa, be careful, and if you find something, let me know. I will talk to Henderson about reopening the cases." The detective started to walk away. Then she stopped and pointed out to Lisa that Asia Jones told her family something about a ghost wearing all black that came for her before she passed away.

Lisa's mouth dropped open. Could it be that Asia was trying to warn her that it was coming, but she did not understand? Why me? She wondered. She knew nothing of the Jones family, and then she thought of Momma Ida.

Lisa looked at a picture of Asia Jones again; she looked like a china doll. She was a beautiful woman. She asked if she could take the files back to the office with her as she wanted to look at them more closely.

"That's against the rules, but I'll give you a day to copy them and pick them up tomorrow."

Before Lisa walked out the door, something that Mr. Williams said hit her—his boss had a contract with the school where he had met Elmira. "Do you know if Elmira Coleman and Asia Jones knew each other?"

"I have no idea. But I'll ask around; there are some detectives here that were around at that time. I'll see what I can gather for you and we'll discuss it over dinner when I get back."

Detective Milo walked Lisa out and into the parking lot. When Lisa looked around, there it was standing there and pointing at her again. She followed its finger, but this time it was pointing at Susan. Lisa turned back to Susan and said, "Look behind you." Susan turned around and looked, but there was nothing there. Lisa told Susan what she saw. "It wore a black veil and a long black robe" and that she first saw it when Ida was ill at the hospital. She then told Susan that it followed her home and watched her through the window. Lisa described it to Susan and told her that she first saw the ghost of Asia Jones before the dark figure appeared in Ida's room.

Lisa sat at her desk, looking through Elmira Coleman's file. There was no mention of finding a child in the fire, just Elmira Coleman. She wondered what made Mr. Williams think Kandy was dead. Lisa read the fine print—a mother and her unborn child were burned to death. Lisa had tears in her eyes. Someone killed her while she was pregnant with his child. She was preparing dinner to tell him he was going to be a father for a second time. Mr. Williams had lost a child, but not the one he thought.

Lisa arrived home with tons of grocery bags. "Hi, honey," Momma Ida said when Lisa held onto her for dear life. "Wow," Ida said, "you really missed me. Chris is lifting weights in the workout room, like he needs more muscles. Also, Judy and Ellen are picking me up in a minute and we are going to do some baking for dinner tonight. Besides, it will give you and Chris some time alone. What's wrong, honey?"

Lisa tried to look normal since she did not want Ida to worry about her, plus, she could use some quality time with Chris—someone who would understand what she was going through. "I'm fine, Momma. I did not realize what going to the office would be like. When I worked at home, I worked at my own pace. But it's a dog-eat-dog world out there."

Ida started to unload the bags. "You will be alright. Just get some rest and do not make a big deal out of tonight." She laughed, "We finally get to meet Mr. Jason. Hell, I was beginning to think he was a figment of Carolyn's imagination."

Lisa laughed, "Now she brags on him he's like a jack rabbit." Lisa mimicked Carolyn. She missed the old days when she and Ida talked about everything. "Just tell them to go to hell is what she would tell Lisa to say to someone who said something ugly to her."

Judy and Ellen walked in the door, carrying bags of food. Ellen wanted to bake some of her sweet potato pie and Judy wanted to bake her chocolate cake and pecan pies. Lisa wanted something different, so she decided to bake her bananas foster cheesecake. She wanted dinner, short but sweet, Shrimp Tasso with cheese grits; but Judy and Ellen wanted much more and they had the pots and aluminum pans to show it, which made Lisa decide to do Shrimp Creole also because she would not be defeated in the kitchen.

Chris walked into the kitchen while Lisa was taking her cheesecake out of the oven. "Something smells good," she smiled, "and tastes good," she said. She hoped he would not come into the kitchen because she didn't need that type of a distraction. She had so much going on inside of her head, it felt like it was going to explode. She would, though, ask his advice on how to reunite the father and daughter.

Chris sat at the counter in the kitchen and said, "A penny for your thoughts."

Lisa sighed, "Where do I start?" She began to tell him about the well-dressed man without saying his name and told him she knew his daughter that he thinks died but she is alive.

Chris offered her some advice, "Before you say anything, you have to be sure," he said. "If you are wrong, you will put salt into both cuts."

"Okay, I will triple check."

He stood and walked behind her, placed his arms around her, and she closed her eyes and leaned back into him. "You feel so good," she said to him.

He then turned her around so that they could be face-to-face. He kissed her and slid his tongue into her mouth, and she welcomed it. He held her so close she could feel his erection. He lifted her and carried her into the bedroom. He started undressing himself. While she lay on her back and watched, he laid his naked body on top of her. Before he started undressing her, he lay on her doing swirls of his hip and opened her legs, and then he stood and opened the drawer next to the bed. She thought he would pull out a condom, but instead, he pulled out a tube of lubricant. He massaged himself and then he massaged some between her legs. Just the touch of his hand between her legs made her back arch, so he lay on top of her again. He took her breast into his mouth, then he kissed her lips before working his tongue to her neck. Their bodies were two, yet, they moved as one. He tried to enter her and her back arched again as she spread her legs wider. Then he pushed harder to get inside of her, when finally, her body opened and he penetrated her. She let out the breath she had been holding and moaned now that he was inside of her and she could feel every inch of him. His hips swirled in circles as he pushed deeper. She moaned as he suddenly moved up and down with gentleness.

Lisa could not believe she was finally making love to the man she had come to love. Her body ached, but she enjoyed every thrust of his hips. She looked at him to see if he was enjoying her body, as she was enjoying his. She wanted to please him; she wanted him to want her again. Suddenly, she gripped his shoulders and cried out, his body tense, and he pushed deeper inside her, careful not to let one drop of the liquid gold he was placing inside of her spill. He moaned and squeezed her tighter and kissed her passionately before he pushed inside of her for the last time.

◑ ◑

"Lady Clem, this is Momma Ida," Ellen made the introduction.

Ida was skeptical about meeting a psychic, but Judy and Ellen swore by it. "Ida, she will tell you things about your life that you will not believe," Ellen said.

"She is a skeptic," Lady Clem started.

Ida mumbled, "Bullshit, you can see that on my face."

"She loves you with a passion, you are the mother she did not have, but she will suffer; he must remember her before it is too late."

"Chris has amnesia; she knows, but he is getting it back." Ida got angry and chided, "Stop talking in riddles, who will hurt her?"

They will take her baby . . ."

"What are you talking about?" Ida said, "She doesn't have a baby."

"One unborn child will die." Lady Clem flipped a card and turned to Judy, "You resent her, but she will bring to you what you have lost and adore so much, for you are the sister she never had." She closed her eyes.

"This is bullshit," Ida said.

"Oh, Ellen," Lady Clem clapped her hands, "tonight is your night."

Ellen smiled, "But what about Lisa? He will not remember her and she will suffer for loving him."

"He wants her and will order the death of her unborn child," Lady Clem said, "and he will make her suffer."

"Who?" Ida shouted. "Who will hurt her?"

Lady Clem looked at her, "You will see, you wanted her to put your family together and she will, but her pain will be abundant."

❧ ❧

Chris and Lisa lay side-by-side, breathing hard. Looking for validation, she wanted to lie in his arms. She knew she had not been active in her life; she needed to know if he was happy. "A penny for your thoughts," she said.

He said nothing, he was breathing hard with his eyes closed. Claire began to bark at the window. Lisa's focus was on Chris. She wondered what he was thinking. Claire started to bark and growl at the window.

"Will you shut her up?" He said in an angry voice.

Lisa said nothing, but she stepped out of bed to chastise Claire for her behavior. She looked at the window and it was staring at her, and she jumped back into bed. Chris was frustrated, "What is going on with the two of you?"

Lisa reached over to grab her robe. "There is someone at the window," Lisa said.

Chris got out of bed and looked out the window. He got dressed and said, "Stay here." Chris walked out the room and went out the front door. Lisa looked out the window and Chris was looking around the side of the house.

Chris stopped at the side gate that led to the backyard. The gate was open and Lisa always kept it closed. Chris walked around the house and walked to the opposite end of the yard, and the gate was opened. The gate led to the street and the stairs to Lisa's shop. He looked around and there was a dark colored van and other cars parked on the street.

Chris stood and looked around before walking back into the house. Before he walked back into the bedroom, he checked Lisa's office and the security camera Lisa had installed. He checked the footage and nothing was on the video. Chris walked back into the bedroom. His back ached because he had pulled a muscle while lifting weights in the home gym in Lisa's house.

Chris stood in pain and looked towards the window. Lisa sat on the bed waiting for him to reveal his findings, which she already knew by the look on his face. "Did you leave the gates open?" Chris asked.

Lisa said, "No."

"The gates were opened," Chris said. "But I did not see anyone out there. I also checked the video footage and there was nothing." Chris sucked in the air because he was in pain. He walked past Lisa and went into the bathroom to clean up and take pain medication.

Chris walked out the bedroom and laid across the bed. Lisa grabbed Claire and walked into the bathroom. She had hoped that he would say that he believed that someone was there but ran away before he got there, but she could not explain why the video camera had not picked up her stalker.

She was now believing she was going crazy and Kandy was trying to protect her feelings, but she knew better because Kandy said she saw it first. Could she and Kandy imagine the same thing? Then she thought of Mr. Williams, who pointed it out to her. Was someone playing a joke on her? This started happening to her when she met Chris. Then she thought of David.

She felt sick as she thought of her ex-boyfriend David. He was a good provider. Although he often traveled, he always brought her very expensive gifts, and in return, she would prepare very special meals for him. He always wanted her to stay in shape, so she joined the gym and would work out diligently. However, when they got into bed, David could not perform with her. He would tell her trying to get inside of her was like trying to walk through a brick wall, so he gave up trying. Instead, he would get frustrated and hit her.

And then there were times when David would look at her as she watched television. He would pull her hair and drag her through the house. She even recalled him kicking her in her stomach several times. "You are dead weight, Lisa. You will never be a wife or mother. No man is ever going to want you. They will kill themselves trying to screw you. You had better hope you keep that body . . . If they get inside of you, that would be all they would want from you.

She turned to her friends for understanding when she decided to leave him. They would ask her what she expected. "Girl, it is like buying a new car that you can't drive."

Lisa thought of all the times she allowed David to beat her because she felt guilty, and now she and Chris had made love. Lisa stood in the bathroom, looking at herself in the mirror. She would not give up on their relationship. The next time Chris made love to her, she would make him proud. She would make him want her again. No matter what it took, she would give it her all.

Claire began to growl at the bathroom window. Lisa stood frozen, she knew that whenever Claire barked and growled, it was because she was trying to tell Lisa the stalker was there, watching her. She jumped and turned to run. Instead, she knocked over the mirror on the vanity, causing it to break. She looked at the window again and it was gone.

Chris opened the bathroom door, as Lisa was picking up the glass. "What is going on in here?" he asked. He could see Lisa was upset. He looked around. Nothing was there. He noticed that her hand was bleeding, and he bent over and grabbed her hand to stop her from cutting herself any further. He placed her hand in the sink when he realized his actions were bad. He should have told her about pulling a muscle; instead he made love to her and turned his back on her. He showed her no affection even after finding out her last relationship ended badly.

He thought of his father and how he treated women. He never wanted to be like his father. He thought of the time his father had brought home a woman he had met in a bar. After his father had sex with the woman, he started beating her. Chris heard the woman screaming, he entered his father's bedroom, and he was kicking her in her face and stomach. He said it was because she was a whore and she tried to take his jewelry.

Chris had pulled a muscle while working out in the gym; he knew he should have waited until later before making love to Lisa, instead he reacted harshly toward her. Lisa checked her hand; she had only a small cut so she placed a bandage on her finger. She hoped Chris did not think she was being childish and that she was cutting herself in order to get attention. She wondered if her ex-boyfriend was stalking her. *I am going crazy just as Carolyn said*, she thought, and she started to cry. *Why is this happening to me?*

She stepped into the shower; she needed to have a good cry and she did not want anyone to see her. After what happened today, she could not tell Chris about it because he would not believe her. She thought of Elmira and could understand why she never said anything to her husband. She drew her knees into her chest because, if she did not say anything, then it would kill her just as it did Elmira.

"What is all of this?" Chris laughed. "After dinner we will all have to go to the gym."

She opened the oven door and the aroma consumed him and took him back to when he was a kid. On Christmas his mother would cook and bake, and the house was decorated while he and his brother played and opened gifts. He walked behind Lisa and placed his arms around her, when she turned and placed a sample of food in his mouth. "I am so sorry about my behavior, I pulled a muscle earlier and I know I should have waited to make love to you, however, I could not control myself."

"I accept your apology and I am sorry for Claire and my behavior also. When Claire started barking I knocked over the mirror, and tried to pick it up too quickly. I should have got the broom." She gave a little laugh, "That was not smart on my behalf." She kissed him this time and said, "I can do this all day" as he lifted her.

"So can I, but you have pots on the stove, and I took a muscle relaxer and can use a nap before dinner." She handed him a sandwich she had prepared for him when the doorbell rang. He walked into the bedroom with Claire behind him and Lisa answered the door.

"Hey, baby girl, as usual I brought wine this time because I know that Ellen and Judy will have all of our teeth rotten before the day is over. Would you care for a glass?" Normally, Kandy would accept, but today she could not. "I wanted to see if you needed any help with dinner, so I decided to stop over early."

Lisa could hear Claire barking, her heart began to race. She asked Kandy to wait while she went to see what Claire's problem was.

"Did you get all of the boxes packed?" Kandy asked.

"No," Lisa said.

Kandy looked at her watch and said, "I have time and I can pack some boxes for you if you would like."

"That would be great," Lisa said. "I will meet you upstairs."

Lisa walked into the bedroom and saw Chris teasing Claire with food. Claire was happy, jumping up and down and standing on her two little legs, waiting for Chris to reward her. She walked into the bedroom and sat next to Chris on the bed when he gave Claire a treat and then turned his attention to her. He was still wearing his robe and she could see he was not wearing anything under it. He looked at her and then he laid her on the bed and kissed her passionately. She knew this time she would please him.

Chris entered her and a moan came from him, and she wondered if he had pulled his muscle again, but he hadn't. The look on his face showed that he was in ecstasy and the pleasure was overwhelming. When she started to move her hips and allow him entrance and exit, she was spread wide and she moved with such intensity that the headboard knocked against the wall. His eyes were closed, but his lips were moving as he moaned and said, "Oh yeah, baby . . . Yeah . . . That's it . . . Oh . . . That feels so good, baby."

He moved with a swirl and small thrusts inside of her as she also moaned. She looked at his face and she knew she was pleasing him. He moaned and shouted, "Oh, baby, that feels so good," he then lifted her hips as he rose on his knees. He knew she wanted to please him, so he took advantage. Her shoulders were pinned to the bed, but her hips were lifted and he thrust his hips in and out, his eyes were rolled back and he swirled, and so did she. He lifted her hips again. "That feels so good." He moaned before his body tensed and he went deeper and deeper before she moaned also, as they both sang the song of pleasure. Chris lowered Lisa's hips and lay between her spread legs. She massaged his shoulder muscle as he did his last swirl on top of her.

Chris walked into the family room and Kandy was coming downstairs to wait for Lisa. Kandy looked at him and saw he was wearing a pair of sweat pants and he smelled of fresh soap.

"Where is Lisa?" Kandy asked.

"She will be out in a minute," Chris said.

"Can I talk to you?" Kandy asked. She looked at him in need of advice.

"Hello, Kay, I did not know that you were here," he said after he looked back at the bedroom door.

"Chris, can I talk to you?" she asked.

He walked over and sat next to her. "What's up, Kay?"

"Chris, I am pregnant."

He did not know how to react, having never heard those words before, so he listened.

"I want to have an abortion."

"Does the father know?"

She lowered her head and replied, "No, I only found out today and he is out of town again," which was not true. She had met Kevin and she did not know much about him, so she did not know how he would feel about becoming a father. Chris had looked at her like a little sister. From the day he laid eyes on her, he knew she was naïve.

"Kandy, you have to tell him. You have to be fair_because it's his baby, too."

A tear rolled down her cheek. Before he could ask why she wanted to have an abortion, she started to talk. "I already have a child. I do not want to be a single mother of two children. It's hard now to find a good man with no children—one may be accepted, but to have two children with two different fathers, it is next to impossible. Chris, I've made many mistakes in my short life, and I do not want to make another.

"Carolyn commented to Lisa today that you would not want her, and that you will soon leave and get a younger, sexier woman. When I saw the look on Lisa's face, the pain Carolyn's words had caused, I knew what I would have to deal with for as long as I lived, and I cannot do that. Carolyn thinks that Lisa and I will not find the love she has found with Jason," then she laughed. "You know, Jason is like a jack rabbit."

Chris smiled, "What if he wants the baby, Kay? Would you consider keeping it? He knows about your son and, if it bothered him, then he would have never taken it to the next level."

Kandy kept her head low, "I don't know." She raised he head and asked, "Would you accept someone with two children?"

Chris knew his answer to that question would make Kandy's decision for her so he thought carefully. Kandy rephrased the question, "If Lisa had another child besides Claire, would you be with her?"

Chris smiled and said, "If I loved her, I could accept her child, Claire included."

"If Lisa was pregnant, would you be angry, would you leave her? Would you hit her?" Kandy's pain was on overload and she was asking from experience. Lisa had talked about how Kandy's son's father treated her, how Kandy would have black eyes every other week.

"Kandy, you can't think that all men would react the same; maybe, this time it will be different."

He had not answered her question, though, so she asked again, "If Lisa were pregnant, would you want the baby? Would you love her and let her have the baby?" Kandy asked with tears in her eyes.

Chris wanted to console her, but he was at a loss. "Kay, this is not about Lisa or me; you have to do what you think is right, not what Carolyn thinks or anyone else. Carolyn sometimes forgets where she came from and she says things because she is insecure. When she is in pain, she wants others to feel it." He pulled Kandy into his arms and held her; he knew she needed a shoulder to cry on and he would lend her his. He looked up to see Lisa standing there. He did not answer Kandy's questions; he did not know how he would feel about becoming a father. She turned and walked back into the bedroom, silently.

"Kandy, I am so sorry. I forgot you were here."

Lisa was embarrassed.

"How long has this been going on?" She was excited for Lisa; she knew how Lisa cared for Chris and now she had taken the next step with him. Kandy started to mock her, "Kandy, he don't find me attractive. Kandy, he won't touch me. Girl, you almost killed him, Lisa. I swear he made more noise than you," she joked, "and now I need pain medication," when she lifted the bottle of wine. Girl, it will go away in a minute. I will never forget my first time; it was in the back seat of a car," she said, "and that was painful itself because you know that I do not work out."

"Kandy, is everything okay? I saw you talking to Chris."

Kandy knew she had to say something, so she talked about the thing in black. Have you seen it again, Lisa? Because I swear I saw it last night at the hospital."

Lisa's hands began to shake as she told Kandy about Claire barking and it was in the window. Kandy jumped when she heard Chris's voice.

Chris was listening to their conversation, "What are you talking about?" he asked. Lisa could see he was upset. Chris always talked to her about honesty, trust and communication, and now he knew she has been keeping a secret from him.

"Someone has been watching us and you decided not to tell me about it?" He shook his head and walked back into the bedroom.

"Go after him, Lisa, and tell him everything. He feels like you do not trust him and now he is hurt."

She walked into the bedroom. Chris was getting dressed she knew he was leaving her and she had to stop him. "It is not trust, honey, it's fear," she said as she walked to him. "I am afraid if I tell you something, it could jar your memory. One night we will go to bed, and the next morning, you will wake and not know who I am. I am afraid that when you get your memory back, you will not remember me." Lisa squatted down on her knees between Chris's legs and he sat on the bed. Her eyes were stained with tears. "It is a bad feeling, baby, to have something out there that frightens you and also have something inside your home you are also afraid of." A tear rolled down her cheek. "Whatever happens, Chris, please promise me that you will remember me, okay?"

He could see the pain in Lisa's eyes. He stood her straight up then placed his arms around her waist. He put his face into her mid-section before looking up at her. "You have brought me so much joy. I have never felt the love and support in my life that I have felt since I have been here. This house is full of laughter and so much love. There is also a lot of pain, but you work through it all together as a family. I feel like I am a part of something beautiful when I am with you." Chris looked Lisa in the eyes. "Baby, you complete me and one thing I know is I could never forget the best thing that has ever happened to me. I am a man now and I want a woman. If I wanted a young girl, I would be with one." He smiled. "I dated them in high school. Lisa, you are beautiful and sexy and have a heart that sometimes people will take advantage of. I am your other half, and now we are both complete." Lisa smiled and wondered what Carolyn would say if she could hear his words.

Lisa began to tell Chris all the times she had seen her stalker. She told him when Claire barked and growled at the window, it was to let them know that someone was watching them. Recently she discovered several pieces of lingerie missing.

Chris looked at her puzzled; he also had had clothing missing. He wanted to blame Claire. He thought she was hiding things. "I did not want you to leave because you think I'm crazy."

Chris sat on the bed. He knew Lisa cared for him, and he felt like a hypocrite because he also saw something at the hospital and never said anything. He never knew that someone had followed them home. He wrapped his arms around her and kissed her forehead. "I need you to trust me. I need you to be able to talk to me about anything, no matter how big or small you may think it is." He lifted her chin. "I need you to understand that we are in this together and that we have to work at things together."

She kissed his lips softly and said, "No more secrets. I will tell you everything." She sealed it with a kiss.

Chris smiled, "Now that's my girl."

Before Lisa walked out of the bedroom, and knowing that Chris was a policeman, she handed him the files on the new client she had received. "I get the feeling whoever is stalking me will reveal himself to me. Most psychos want you to know who they are. They get a kick out of watching their prey suffer."

"I am going to check the cameras around your building," he said when she gave him the files on Elmira Coleman and told him the story surrounding her death, and also those for Asia Jones. She did not know why, but she felt her stalker would strike soon—He will reveal himself to her.

Chris grabbed Lisa by the arm, "From here on out, I will take you to work and pick you up. I do not want any of you out there alone, especially after dark." Claire jumped on the bed and Chris began playing with her. "So you are the little protector, girl." Claire wagged her tail in excitement.

Lisa asked him to look at W. Williams. "Your new boyfriend," he joked.

"I like him a lot, and I have to find a way to tell him that his wife did not commit suicide. We have been having lunch instead of therapy sessions. He is an amazing man," she said, "and he is also Kandy's father. I double-checked. He is her father. He said he'll come by next week and bring a friend, but I need to come clean with him. He has suffered long enough and so has Kandy."

She walked to the door and stopped. Something was on her mind and it was heavy. "Lisa, what did we just talk about? Babe, you can talk to me about anything."

She sighed, "Have you ever seen someone that was not there?"

He looked at her, thinking the stress was getting to her.

She pulled out a picture of Asia Jones. "I saw her at the hospital that night when you were admitted." She shook her head and continued, "I know I sound crazy, but she was wearing a powder-blue dress, and she had a gold pin on her clothing."

He pulled her into his arms. "I believe you and yes, I have seen things that were not there."

She bumped him with her hip, "You are not a good liar." She kissed him and left the room.

Chapter 7

Jason watched the house he had grown up in. He sighed and took a deep breath. Every day he checked his phone and prayed for a miracle. He had not received one—not one phone call or text from his brother. He had to accept the fact that his brother was dead and he would not talk to him again. He walked into the home of his father. "Hello, Dad," he said with a tired voice.

Eddie was happy to see him, since he did not come to the home that often. "Son, it is good to see you." When he embraced Jason, his son was like stone. Eddie had alienated his sons. They did not approve of his of lifestyle. Eddie Jones was a hard-core businessman. He took no lip from anyone. He had also been under investigation several times concerning his shady business deals, which had brought embarrassment to his family.

Eddie Jones made J. R. Ewing look like a church boy. In business, you name it, Eddie Jones had done it. His motto was, *you get nowhere in this world if people think you are weak.* He ruled his home and business with an iron fist. "What can I do for you, Jason?"

"I need your help," Jason said.

Eddie was pleased. Jason had never in his adult life asked him for anything. Jason looked at the picture of him and Devin on his father's desk. "I miss him too, son. This house is so empty without the two of you. Jason, please come home," Eddie said.

Jason looked shocked. He had never in his life heard his father say "please" to anyone.

"I need to talk to you about a few things." First, Jason took out a picture and gave it to Eddie. He looked at the picture and said, "Well, son, I don't know how you are going to dispute this one, however, I will do what I can."

Jason smiled. He knew Lionel looked just as he did when he was a boy. "No, Dad, that is a picture of your grandson. His name is Lionel, and his mother is Carolyn."

Eddie remembered Carolyn. "How old is he, son?"

"Lionel is five, soon to be six, and Carolyn, she is good, Dad. She's a doctor."

Eddie looked at him. "I knew she had spunk, all she needed was a push in the right direction." Jason did not question his father about that comment.

"Tonight I will be having dinner with Carolyn's friends; one of them is her friend Lisa who is a psychotherapist."

Eddie began to snap his fingers because that name rang a bell. First, Willie said he was ordered to see a shrink, and he got drunk one night and dreamed of his late wife, who asked him to help Lisa. But he left out that part. Jason knew he had to say very little to his father, he knew if he said too much, his father would take matters into his own hands. "She has been caring for a man by the name of Chris Weber."

Eddie shook his head, "The name does not ring a bell to me."

"Dad, Chris Weber was the man Devin hit with his car before he went into the canal."

"That son of a bitch will not get a penny from me," Eddie said. "He should not have been on the goddamn road, so you tell him I will see him in hell before I give him anything."

Jason tried to stop him and wondered if he should go any further. But he could not stop now. "Dad, he is not asking for money. Carolyn's friend Lisa has been seeing some guy wearing a long black veil and long black dress. She saw it the night Devin was killed. Dad, I think Devin and Chris Weber saw it also."

Eddie poured himself a drink. "What makes you think that?" As his late wife's picture flashed in front of his face and the memory of the night she died when she said that the devil in black came for her.

"The last thing I heard Devin say before his phone went dead was, 'what in the hell is that?' I think Chris Weber was spooked by this thing and maybe ran into the street where Devin hit him. Have you spoken to the Weber guy?"

"I will do so tonight. Dad, I need you to do me a favor."

"Anything, son."

Jason looked him in the eye and said, "Please let me handle this. Whoever this person is in the black veil, I want to catch him."

"You think this guy is responsible for your brother's death. Son, I loved your mother; the three of you were all I could think of every day. Asia was unhappy. She was lonely, and maybe this girl Lisa is lonely. Also, I realized too late she needed more of me than I was giving, which is why she took her own life. She cut her wrists and your brother could never forgive me for it. I had to do something because Devin was grieving to the point that he was losing control, so I thought I could help," Eddie said

"You messed with his head, Dad. He barely remembered his own mother. You took Asia away from him."

Eddie stood because he was hearing her voice and he tried to drown it out with alcohol. I don't apologize for my actions, Jason. He was suffering badly. He found his mother in the bathtub, bleeding to death. Her last words were haunting: 'The ghost in the black veil came,' is what she said before taking her last breath." Eddie sipped his drink and he could hear her voice again, 'Help Lisa.' "He was leaving that night. He said there was no life in this house anymore."

"I know." Jason turned as his eyes were filling. "He was coming to stay with me a few weeks. He wanted to . . . " Jason stopped, he had said too much already. "Dad, let me check into Chris Weber. I will find out what happened, what he and Devin saw on the road that night."

Jason started to walk to the door. "There is one problem . . ."

Eddie said, "Son, if you need some muscle, I can have the team rounded up for you."

"No, nothing like that. Chris Weber has amnesia, he may not remember too much."

"Bring that son of a bitch here, and I will make him remember."

"Let me handle this and I will keep you posted," Jason walked away. He took a deep breath and hoped his father could not see that he was keeping something from him; he did not dare tell his father that the woman his brother was hoping to meet was the same woman Chris Weber was now sharing a bed with.

✺ ✺

Kandy opened the door and Momma Ida, Ellen, and Judy walked in. "Is he here, yet?" Ellen asked, as she was excited to see him. "Child, Carolyn better look out because she got competition in here," Kandy said, giving Judy a high-five. "Ellen, you look great," Kandy said.

Judy smiled. She had never over the years seen so much joy in Ellen as she had seen today. The doorbell rang, it was Carolyn and she was alone. Ellen's smile quickly faded, as she looked at Judy with disappointment. Ellen turned to walk into the kitchen when she heard a man's voice. Ellen turned around slowly and looked at Jason. It had been over forty years since she had been face-to-face with him without a gate to separate them. She wanted to touch him, but she didn't. When Carolyn started introducing Jason to everyone, she also pointed out to him that everyone thought he was a figment of her imagination. "Are you all satisfied?" She said with sarcasm in her voice.

Ellen smiled, and before she could extend her hand, Chris walked into the room. Kandy was excited. She had never seen such beauty in men as she was witnessing now, so she pulled out her camera to take pictures. "Oh, my God, you guys are so handsome," she said. "I have to get pictures so I can brag when I go to work tomorrow."

Everyone was laughing at her. Carolyn introduced Jason to Chris. "This is the man I told you about," she said. "He is the one that saved my life."

Jason and Chris locked hands, and Kandy snapped a picture. Jason could not take his eyes off Chris; they were both bodybuilders, however, Chris was bigger. Kandy then asked if they would take a picture with her. "If anybody messes with me, I can say, 'look at my big brothers.'" Kandy could not help but notice how the two men were sizing each other up. Jason was wearing navy blue pants and a light blue shirt that revealed his muscular chest, and Chris was wearing black pants and a red shirt that revealed his chest.

Kandy was still taking pictures when Ida stepped in. "Girl, I know what you mean." Ida walked between the two men and said, "Take one of us and if anyone asks, I was at the strip club." It was almost more than she could bear. She was standing in the middle of the room belonging to her grandson, who she was never supposed to meet in life. She remembered when she asked Eddie if she could meet them. He said, "Not in this life."

Chris and Jason both laughed at Ida when Judy saw the sadness in Ellen's eyes; she wanted to take a picture but she would not ask.

Lisa walked into the room and everyone, including Jason, stopped and watched as she came in wearing a red dress with lace running through both sides. Carolyn looked from Jason to Lisa and wanted to make a snooty comment but knew Jason would not tolerate bad behavior. "Hello, you must be Jason," Lisa said as she embraced him. She offered him a drink and said, "Jason, please make yourself at home."

Kandy was excited; she wanted to take more pictures of her and the two men. "Girl, I am in hunk heaven and when Jenny sees these pictures, she is going to flip."

Lisa snapped several pictures of Kandy before asking Kandy to let someone else take pictures with Jason and Chris besides her. "Ellen, you look amazing. Get in there, girl, and take a picture with Jason and Chris. Besides, the guys could use some eye candy of their own."

"Oh no," Ida said, "I already took mine and that is all the eye candy they can handle." Laughter overtook the room. Ellen was so excited she stood between the two men, but before Lisa snapped the picture, she walked over and placed Jason's arm around her and placed Ellen's hand on Jason's chest. She pushed Chris closer to her, leaned Ellen's head on Jason's chest, and said, "Say cheese. Ellen, before you walk away, let's get one with each of the guys." Ellen was excited and posed with Jason where she leaned her head on his chest, and she did the same with Chris.

Ellen and Lisa walked into the kitchen to check on dinner, and Chris followed with Lisa holding his hand. "Can you give me your opinion on dinner?" she asked. She wanted him to taste each dish she had prepared, which he did, giving his approval. "Everything is great, baby," he said and gave Lisa a kiss on the cheek.

Jason noticed that something small and wearing a red dress was scratching at Chris's leg. He had heard of people dressing their pets like children, but he had never actually seen it before.

"Claire, stop, you are going to get hair on Chris's pants, honey," Lisa said to her.

Jason watched as the man called Chris Weber was treated like a king. He watched as he would taste each dish and Lisa stood there and awaited his approval, which he gave with a kiss. If you were on the outside looking in, you would think they were one big happy family. Carolyn was wrong about Lisa and Chris. There was something between them and it was strong. Jason noticed Chris. It was almost as if he was gloating and throwing Lisa in his face. Jason looked as he held her in a corner of the house and kissed her. Something had happened between the two of them, and he wanted her to know and to mind her own business.

Everyone sat at the dinner table—each man was seated at the end of the table. Jason had never seen so much food. He had ten different dishes in front of him. He and Chris laughed when they placed salads in front of the both of them. "Do you all eat like this all of the time?" he asked.

"Oh yes," Ida said braggingly, "Lisa is an excellent cook and she is not afraid to show it. Don't waste your time with that green crap, the real stuff in coming." She smiled at him, "It is really good having the both of you here."

He smiled also and said, "It is good it be here," when he noticed what looked like a tear in Ida's eyes as he looked at Chris.

Carolyn quickly changed the subject. Ida would not dote on Lisa in front of her man. First, Lisa came out of her bedroom dressed like a slut, and now Ida is praising her, not in front of her man, she thought. "Chris, your legs should be healed by now and there are plenty of jobs in the newspaper today," she said with a smirk and a looked at Lisa.

Before Chris could answer her, Lisa stepped in, "Mind your goddamn business; he will move at his own pace, not yours."

Judy and Ellen's eyes widened as they had never heard Lisa raise her voice and never had she said a bad word.

"Chris, what do you do for a living?" Jason asked. He needed answers, and if Carolyn kept talking, then Chris might leave Lisa out of guilt. He gave her a hard look after her last comment before Lisa stepped in to defend him. He smiled and held her hand. He needed to know what happened that night and he needed to get Chris to let his guard down.

"I was a cop, and then I moved on," but he did not say to what. Jason looked and Carolyn gave him the 'I told you so' look. "And what about yourself?"

"I am a private investigator," he said.

Chris took a sip of his drink. He knew he was being drilled. He looked Jason in the eyes and asked, "Had any action lately?"

Jason smiled, "Well, I am working on a case right now and I could really use some help."

Chris thought Carolyn had asked Jason to hire him to get him away from Lisa. "I am working on something myself, maybe we can help each other." Both men nodded in agreement. He needed to know if Lisa had mentioned the man in black and if that is what he was talking about.

Judy and Ellen looked at each other when Ida asked Jason if he wanted to watch a movie with her. "Oh, honey," she smiled, "I have been watching some good ones lately, and I could use better company then these two. Ellen covered her face and watched between her fingers. Judy said, 'Oh Lord,' throughout the whole movie. I have been watching these pay-per-views and tonight there is one about a doctor. Carolyn, you can watch, too. We can watch it out here if you would like," Momma said.

"Sure, Momma, what's it called, *Dr. Lust?*" Jason smiled.

Chris laughed and Kandy rolled her eyes; Carolyn looked at Lisa, "I see you have not fixed that problem, yet."

Ellen and Judy thought it sounded interesting and they asked Ida what the movie was about. Momma Ida got frustrated because she had to answer the same questions all the time and Ellen and Judy would stay and watch the movie. Throughout the movie, they were saying "Oh, my God."

Lisa placed her forehead on Ida's, "You are a mess, girlfriend."

Both men watched the display of affection Lisa showed to Ida. Lisa is from New Orleans he was told by Carolyn, and thought he would look into the background of Ida to find out if there was any other connection to the thing in black, besides what was sitting in front of him. The person was now stalking Lisa because of Chris.

Lisa started to pick up the dishes when Kandy asked Jason, "Will you be attending the *Come as Your Favorite Entertainer* party?" Carolyn answered for him, "Yes, he will, but I have no idea what or who we will be."

Jason smiled at Kandy and thought the name suited her; she was a sweet girl and very pleasant to be around, and she also called Chris her big brother. He doted on her also like a protector. I did not know anything about the party when Carolyn started to explain when Lisa went into the other room.

"Chris and I will be Ike and Tina Turner and we have watched the movie dozens of times," Momma Ida said when Chris started saying, "Tina," in his Ike voice and Momma Ida said, "Oh, Ike," in her Tina voice and they both started singing "rolling on the river," when Ellen excused herself from the table and returned with a birthday cake for Lisa.

"Happy birthday, Lisa," everyone entered the family room where there were gifts waiting for her. "You wanted small," Ida said as she gave Lisa her gift. *This would have been a good year to have a party* she thought *because now she has a man and would not sit alone.*

After opening all of her gifts, including the Coach purse from Jenny, she called to thank her. "Hey, Jenny, this is Lisa. I am sorry that you are not feeling well and if there is something that I can do, all you have to do is call me. I miss you so much."

"Me, too," Kandy yelled from across the room.

"I am calling to thank you for the gift, and I wish you would have come to dinner tonight and let us take care of you. I love you, Jenny. Call me, okay, because we miss you and tonight I know you would have had a good time," while Kandy yelled, "I love you, Jen," into the phone. Lisa hung up and said, "I hate leaving messages, but I will thank her in person when I see her."

Lisa asked if everyone else was ready for the party. She had no idea what celebrity she would dress up as. "Jenny will be Marilyn Monroe; I have her dress upstairs in my shop," Lisa said.

"I hope she is drama free. Everywhere Jen goes, she is a drama queen," Kandy said. "We were at the nail shop and she started fussing at little Minh Lee. She said she was having morning sickness."

Lisa and Carolyn laughed. "Remember when we went to fight Justin because he had hit Kandy, Carolyn said and Jenny took out her mace and sprayed herself instead of Justin?" Everyone laughed. "Poor Jen thought she would be blind." Kandy was embarrassed so she changed the subject.

"Has anyone noticed that Jenny always wears gloves?" Kandy said. "We were at the nail shop and I went to pick out nail polish. She removed her gloves and I saw that her thumb was deformed."

Lisa looked at her, "What do you mean?"

"It looked like part of it was missing."

Lisa started to think. Now she knew why Jen always wore gloves. Lisa remembered when Jen asked her to make her a dress for the party. Jenny came over for a fitting for her dress and never removed her gloves. First she thought Jen was imitating a famous celebrity but now she knew different.

Lisa said in a singsong voice that she had been listening to old music and came up with the idea that she and Kandy and Carolyn could dress as the Supremes.

"Ellen, you and Jason could be Tammy Terrell and Marvin Gaye, since we have Ike and Tina already. Ellen is an excellent seamstress. She can put your outfit together in days."

Ellen smiled. This would be the best thing that could happen to her if Lisa could convince Jason to do it. This is more than Lady Clem could have imagined, however. Jason had not said yes, yet.

"What do we have to do?" he asked.

"You can put on a show. You and Ellen can sing, *Ain't Nothing Like the Real Thing*; or, you guys can be Ashford and Simpson and sing *High Rise*."

Kandy said she loved that song, it was a nice dance song and they would get the crowd going.

Jason laughed, "We have only one problem." Everyone looked in his direction. "Everything sounds like fun, but I can't sing," he said.

"Ellen is a pro," Chris said, "and she'll carry you; she has the most beautiful voice," he said. "She is not only beautiful, but she can sing."

Chris asked Ellen why she never pursued a singing career. He always heard her singing in the kitchen and thought she had great talent.

Ellen was happy. She had felt like a loser her whole life. She admired Chris and Lisa, but now her life was over. She only hoped Chris could get Jason to forgive her. Ellen blushed. "You are so sweet, Chris." She looked away. She would not open up a can of worms and have Judy hate her, so she said nothing of her singing contract.

"While everyone is here, ladies, I do not want any of you out alone. Travel in pairs. Judy and Ellen, be careful at the shop; if you see any suspicious characters hanging around, call the police or call me. Also Kandy, Lisa, and Carolyn, you should try to work out some kind of car pool. If you cannot work it into your schedule, then you can call me and I will come and pick you up."

Everyone sat quietly and listened to him. "Is something wrong, Chris?" Judy asked.

"No, Judy, there are some weirdoes out there and we all should be careful."

"I agree with him," Lisa said.

"Of course you do," Carolyn said in a nasty voice. "This time of the year you cannot be too careful. There are some strange things happening. People are doing anything to get by."

Lisa had purchased cell phones for Judy and Ellen because she knew they would not buy them for themselves. They were the only two women she knew that did not travel with a cell phone.

"Why in the hell would I want to carry a phone all day? The only person I talk to is Ellen, and she's usually in the other room. But if Chris thinks we need to have a cellphone, then we will keep it," Judy said.

"I have a cellphone and they come in handy. Last night I called Lisa to bring me a glass of water to my room," Ida said.

Jason laughed at Ida. He observed there were no other men in the house, only Chris, and now he understood Carolyn's behavior. Carolyn did not dislike Chris but she was afraid of losing her friendship with Lisa.

Carolyn included, and he needed a reason to come around and now he had it. Jason squeezed Ellen's hand. "How about it, Tammy or Valerie? Can we do this?"

Ellen laughed, "Yes, Nick or Marvin, we can. I can get your measurements and be done in a few days. We have time. We can even do rehearsal from Friday until the day of the party."

After dinner, Kandy, Judy and Ellen decided to spend the night at Lisa's place. "What's in the box?" Kandy asked Ellen. "You always carry it with you."

Ellen smiled. "I do not know," she said. "I am holding it for an old friend."

Devin looked at it. He remembered his mother had a similar box that she called her "time capsule."

✑ ✑

"Well, what do you think of Chris and Lisa?" Carolyn asked Jason. "I think he will not be getting his memory back any time soon. The guy is treated like a king."

"Yes, he is," Carolyn said. "Do you know, she serves him breakfast in bed every morning, and did you see that they were both wearing something red, including Claire?"

Jason looked at Carolyn. "You should take lessons from Lisa on the breakfast in bed, give it a try."

"Seriously, honey, I do not want Lisa to get hurt."

"Cal, he is very smart and perceptive; he has a cop mentality. He suspected that you are having him checked out. Tonight he made a statement without saying a word. He let me know that he can take care of Lisa and their relationship is their own business. They are together and it is not a dirty little secret."

Carolyn sighed, "And how dare she talk to me like that, 'He will find a job when he is ready.' She enjoys taking care of him. She thinks her doting over him will keep him with her."

Carolyn shook her head in disgust. "You think they are having sex? I knew she was using this thing in black to get close to him, and he has fallen for it. She always purchases sexy lingerie and until she met Chris, the only thing that has seen her parade around in it is Claire."

Jason laughed, "That is a plus for Lisa. He knows she is not the kind of girl that sleeps around." Jason stopped at the red light. His patience was getting thin with Carolyn, so he knew he had to be firm with her. "Carolyn, yes, Lisa and Chris's relationship has become physical; yes, they both care for each other a lot; and yes, if you try to interfere, you will lose your friend. Carolyn, she is happy and so is he. She showed tonight she will not let you come between the two of them."

"Jason, what if Lisa gets pregnant? Lisa thinks she cannot get pregnant without help." Jason looked puzzled and she continued, "She has been taking prenatal vitamins, and she stopped taking her birth controls months ago. She thinks she needs medical help, but she doesn't; all she needs is sperm."

Jason was beginning to understand. "What you are saying is you have your friend thinking she can't have a child unless you perform some kind of in vitro procedure on her, when she can get pregnant on her own. Now that she and Chris are sleeping together, you are upset."

Carolyn dropped her head in shame. She wanted to appear bigger and have something to throw in Lisa's face when she did become pregnant. She had the words all picked out, "You would not be having a child if it were not for me." Now, she wondered if she should say something to Lisa.

"Stay out of it, Carolyn. If you start talking now, she will resent you, especially if something goes wrong. You have done enough; you should have been honest from the beginning because she trusted you."

Carolyn looked at Jason. She knew she had gone too far, however, she needed to know he was not upset with her. She reached out and touched his hand. He turned and gave her a soft kiss.

"He is a good guy, Cal, and if you start talking about babies and all that, Lisa may feel you're deliberately trying to sabotage her relationship with Devin."

She looked at Jason. "Are you alright?"

He did not believe he had let Devin's name slip out of his mouth. "I am sorry, babe. It has been a long day, and I miss hanging out with my brother. That's all."

Carolyn was getting ready for bed. She stared in the mirror. She always wanted another child, but she did not know how Jason would feel about it. She would talk to Jason first, before she stopped taking her birth control, so there will be no secrets between them on her behalf.

Jason always asked her not to keep any secrets from him, which was why she told him about her deceptive words to Lisa, telling Lisa that she could carry a baby but needed help getting pregnant, which was why Carolyn placed her on prenatal vitamins. She knew Lisa would forgive her because Lisa was the forgiving type. She was a little jealous of Lisa, she admitted, because whenever one of the others had a problem they turned to Lisa and not her. Lisa took especially good care of Ellen and Kandy, which was why Carolyn did not talk to Ellen much. Ellen spent most of her life in a mental hospital and now she acted crazy, and Lisa always embraced her and told her that she loved her. Ellen would smile and tell Lisa that she was good and she was special. Ellen was strange to her, and that was why Carolyn kept Lionel away from her. She and Kandy bumped heads all of the time. Kandy said that Carolyn was jealous of Lisa and did not let anyone meet Jason because Lisa got all of the attention from men, and Carolyn thought that because she was a doctor men would fall at her feet. Lisa was the glue that kept them all together and the one that started the Friday dinners. Lisa looked out for everyone, including Carolyn and if you needed anything, and if Lisa had it, she would give it to you.

When Carolyn felt bad and needed someone to talk to about Jason, she always turned to Lisa. She and Jason had an on-again-off -again relationship. Jason was attending a friend's graduation in New Orleans when they met again. She was graduating also. They reunited and spent time together after several nights of passion, Jason asked her to come back to Atlanta with him and she said no. Six weeks later she found out that she was pregnant. When she tried to locate Jason after finding out that she was pregnant, she could not find him; he had returned to Atlanta and he was no longer living at his father's house. She worked in New Orleans to save money and applied for a job at the Atlanta General Hospital. After giving birth to Lionel, she returned to Atlanta and started working at the hospital.

When she returned to Atlanta she found Jason by luck. She was at a red light and he pulled up next to her. Before she could get his attention, the light changed and he drove away. She followed him to a house. Later that night she returned and Jason's car was parked in the driveway. She pulled out Lionel's picture from her handbag and then placed it back inside for safe keeping before she exited the car. She walked up the driveway and up to the front door. The door was opened and she could hear Jason talking to someone. She heard a woman's voice and turned and walked back to her car. She opened the door and sat inside, and her heart started to pound. When she turned eighteen, she met Jason at a friend's party. They dated, and Jason was her first true love and the only man she ever loved. Jason treated her well and stood by her while her mother went to a drug rehabilitation center. She started to depend on him until Eddie sent him off to college in another state. They talked every other day and she found out she was pregnant and did not want to tell him over the phone. Jason said he was returning home over the weekend and for her to meet him at his father's house.

When she knocked at the door, Eddie greeted her with his dirty comments.

"Why are you here?" Eddie asked. "Jason's plans changed and he will not be returning home this week." Eddie looked at her as if she was trash. "You are not Jason's type," Eddie said. Eddie threw her an envelope with money to bribe her, but she did not take it. "Jason is seeing someone else and he asked me to give you money and send you away." Eddie was brutal with his words. "Has it ever dawned on you, Ms. Young, that he never brought you home to dinner and you never met any of his family members, present company included? I know who you are because Jason told me you were coming and asked me to give you money and send you away," Eddie said.

"Take the money, Ms. Young, and go away and get a life," Eddie said, and she did. She had an abortion and moved to New Orleans and started medical school. Five years later, she ran into Jason at Xavier College and he said he had been trying to contact her. She told him about his father and what he said to her, and Jason said, "I never would have asked my father to treat you like that." From then on there was tension between him and Eddie.

She sat outside Jason's house, thinking about their past together; she had never mentioned the abortion to him. Carolyn suddenly became angry as her mother's words started to play inside of her head. "He is rich and could have any woman he wants. Why would he want you?" She stayed outside to rehearse what she would say to Jason. She tried to control her anger when she went back to knock on the door, but she remembered the door was unlocked. She walked inside and the house was quiet. She heard voices coming from a room in the back of the house and walked toward the moans. She had opened the door slowly to see Jason making love to another woman.

Carolyn snapped out of her thoughts and placed the past behind her. She and Jason were together now and he was a good father to Lionel. She walked out of the bathroom and Jason was lying in bed, staring at the ceiling. She loved him, and the past months they had grown close and he had been a good man to her and a good father, but she needed to know that she and Lionel were his first priority. She wanted him to lay his brother to rest because he had been obsessed with Devin's death. He was working all of the time now and she wanted to have him all to herself. Lisa could talk to Susan Milo about her stalker, but Carolyn would not allow Jason to take away valuable family time from her. She had shared Jason before but not again.

She climbed into bed with Jason and wrapped his arms around her. "I know you are not happy with me because of what I did to Lisa, and I know that you want to help her," Carolyn said. "But I need you, and Lionel needs you. Let Chris take care of Lisa," she said. Jason looked at her because after all the years that passed, Eddie's words still haunt her. When Eddie said that he did not care for Carolyn, it hurt her. Now she was a successful doctor, and now she was a woman that said the first thing that came to her mind, even if it hurt someone's feelings.

"I am going to spend more time at home," Jason said.

Carolyn smiled and kissed him. Finally she had her family together.

"I love you," Carolyn said.

Jason kissed her again and she sat upright to remove her gown.

"Make love to me," she said to him. After their conversation, she needed to know that he forgave her, even if Lisa would not. He was not in the mood tonight, but if he rejected her, she would think Chris Weber was not the only person that was interested in Lisa. Jason reached up and picked up Carolyn, and laying her down gently, he kissed her with passion before rolling on top of her. After making love to Carolyn, Jason held her in his arms and thought of dinner at Lisa's. Lisa was in trouble. She thought that what she was seeing was in her imagination, but it was real. Jason looked at Carolyn, and she was sleeping.

Jason climbed out of bed. Carolyn was sound asleep. He needed to think about the Weber family and his father. Jason sighed. He could not believe he had grieved for his brother for weeks, and tonight, he had sat and eaten dinner with a ghost. The man everyone thinks is Chris Weber is actually his brother Devin Jones. His father had buried the wrong man, and if he told his father that Devin was alive, he would have a fit and take his frustration out on Lisa; he would make her life a living hell. Devin and his father would go to war, but Lisa would still get hurt. There is no way Eddie Jones would allow Devin to stay with Lisa, even if he had to run her kicking and screaming back to New Orleans. How would he tell his father Devin is living and is happier than he has ever been in his life with the woman he came to meet? He did not find her. Instead, she had found him and saved his life in the process.

Jason thought of the night he was shot and Devin wounded him, and now someone or something is out there, and it is trying to destroy their family. Devin led it to Lisa and he needs to protect her because it will kill her, just as it did the other women in their lives. Lisa was not supposed to meet and fall in love with him. When Eddie finds out that Devin is alive, then he will take Devin away from Lisa and leave her to protect herself. Jason could not believe Carolyn had made the situation even worse by letting Lisa think she could not get pregnant. Lisa is naïve. She probably has never had real sex. The last guy she dated beat the crap out of her. He only wanted a piece of eye candy, which was her justification for what she had done.

Jason shook his head. Devin is one lucky son-of-a-gun. The first time he saw Lisa, he joked that she could be his sister-in-law. He was ready to get his life on the right track and living with his father was not the right way—it was a revolving door of women that he knew he did not want a future with. He had seen Lisa at the mall and was attracted to her. He thought there was something good about her.

The evening was dancing in Jason's head. He paced the floor. He had to find out from the Weber family if their brother was a cop or attending law school. He could not help but think Devin was trying to tell him something. Could two men collide and both have the same career? Jason could not wait, he dialed Constance Weber; he had to know. But one thing for sure is that he would be able to give the family closure.

Chris Weber was only twenty-five and he was no student, he had graduated high school and began a small electronics company. Jason was confused as to if Devin was trying to tell him he did not have amnesia. He would not wrack his brain any further. He needed answers and would get them from Devin the next day.

⚬ ⚬

Ellen waited patiently for Jason's arrival, "He said he would come and be measured early this morning because he had a busy day," Ellen said to Judy. Every time the door opened, Ellen would jump.

"Ellen, you are going to make yourself crazy if you do not stop."

Ellen was happy, "Judy, it was just as Lady Clem said, however, it is more than I could have imagine. Jason and I will spend time together. He will get to know me and I will tell him that I am his mother."

Judy wanted to be optimistic for her friend, because she felt responsible for Eddie putting Ellen in the mental hospital. She told Eddie that Ellen was leaving and taking his Jason. "What if Jason does not accept you? God knows Carolyn will not help the situation. She thinks she is all high and mighty, and Ellen, he seems to care for her. And here is Lionel . . . He will not jeopardize his family for you and I do not believe Carolyn will accept you as Jason's mother."

Ellen lowered her head, "I am okay, Judy, I will not be around much longer. I begged the man in black to let me live long enough to see my son and touch him and after the show, I will have done that and he will come and take me."

Judy threw up her hands, "There you go again with that crap." She got in her face. "If you keep this up, then Jason will think that you are crazy for sure, and he would have you committed, regardless of what Lisa might say. Honey, there is no man in black."

The door to the store opened. It was Jason. Ellen was so proud. She stared at him, wanting so badly to hold him. Instead, she smiled and asked him to follow her. She took his measurements. She was so close to him, she could smell the shampoo in his hair. She knew he was pushed for time so she hurried, "All done." She was so nervous she could not speak. She turned to go into another room to show him the material she had picked out for his suit.

Jason looked at Ellen's pictures. He noticed one of her holding a baby—she had a big smile. She looked so happy then. Now, the eyes of the woman measuring him were full of pain and sorrow. He wondered if she had lost her child. What could have caused her so much pain?

Ellen walked Jason to the door. She wanted to say something to him, but she did not know what to say. Jason stopped and turned to face her. "Do you like hamburgers?" she asked.

He smiled, "I used to live on hamburgers. It was my favorite meal until my brother said I was going to turn into one, he bought me a book for my birthday about the kid that ate so many hamburgers, he started to look like one."

She was at a loss for words again when she noticed her enemy watching the two of them. He followed her eyes because he saw fear in them and he looked also and only saw a shadow. When he turned back to her she said, "Jason, Chris said people are doing bad things this time of the year. The two of you should watch each other's back, okay?" Jason agreed and kissed Ellen on the cheek before leaving the store. He looked up again and there was nothing.

Ellen watched as Jason walked to his car. She cried uncontrollably. Judy tried to comfort her. "I need more time with my son, Judy, just a little more time to get the courage to talk to Jason. He will come back for me soon, I can feel it."

"Tonight we will stay at Lisa's and we will talk to Chris," Judy said.

Judy called Lisa to see if Chris had left for work. Ellen was losing it again; first she thought it was Eddie's fault, however, now she knew differently. She has carried the burden for years because she felt responsible for Ellen's condition. Every day she would go to the hospital and take care of her, she even signed her out of the hospital and signed documents saying she would be responsible for her care, which caused her marriage to fall apart.

"You are at the goddamn hospital every day," her husband, Winston, would say to her. "You need to be a wife to me," and her favorite was, "If I can't get love from you, then I will get it somewhere else," which he did. He fathered a child with another woman and left her. Ellen was losing it, and she was not planning to go through that hell with her again. Her life flashed in front of her, and she started to yell at Ellen. "I cannot live like this," she said as she began to throw things. "This is not my fault and I will not go through this shit with you again. Ellen, you need to go back to the hospital because, this time, you have really lost it and I cannot go through this again."

Ellen's eyes grew big. "No, Judy, I will not speak of it again," she begged. "Please do not call the hospital. I just want to be with my son, and that's all."

"Don't worry, Ellen, because we both know that precious Lisa will not let them commit you; she would take care of you, and then I will be all alone." She was angry and continued, "You will cause Chris to leave Lisa, just as Winston did me, and all that Lady Clem predicted will be entirely your fault."

Ellen did not tell Judy that he watched her and Jason while they stood at the door. Did he see it also? She wondered.

She went to her room to lie down, and all she could do was cry when he spoke, "I came for you, but I will not take you. At least not today." He laughed. "Because his presence in her life is causing you more pain than death, so I will let you suffer longer. When she cried out louder and begged him to kill her now, because Jason would never accept her because he thought that she abandoned him, he did not say a word because watching Ellen suffer was giving him pleasure. He turned and walked away.

ᘛ ᘛ

Lisa made her bed. She thought about Chris all night, how he kissed her when they were driving Kandy home. "What do you guys think about Jason?"

Kandy said, "He's cute." Then a puzzled look came to her face, "I wonder how he met Carolyn's snobby ass. He seems so down to earth." She kissed both Lisa and Chris's cheek. "Love really must be blind." She laughed.

"That's right, Kandy. I could live in a one-room shack, as long as I am with the one that I love," Lisa said.

Chris looked at her and he knew Lisa was the one for him, as she was willing to accept him with nothing. "You can live in a one-room shack with me, baby."

"Yes, I can," she said to him. Then he kissed her.

❧ ❧

She remembered the look on his face, *wherever he goes I will follow*, she thought before her phone rang. Judy thought Ellen was going crazy, again, but she did not say why. Lisa knew that it had something to do with the black entity that had been following them around. She just had no idea as to why she and Ellen were seeing it, and no one else. Kandy saw it, but only because she was there when it presented itself to her in the hospital. Lisa thought of the other nurse on duty that night. When Lisa set out to find out who she was, no one remembered her. She wondered if she might have seen it that night also, and decided not to work at the hospital anymore. She remembered her nametag read KLEIN; she was the nurse that brought Momma Ida her tray and when she asked the other nurses, they said there was a new employee who had decided to switch to another hospital. Her name was not Klein.

Lisa asked Judy if she and Ellen would pack a bag and move in with her and Chris for a while. She knew she could not mention it to Judy, so she used the excuse that Chris would be working late night and she could use some company.

"Donna, can you file these papers?" Lisa turned when she could hear a woman calling a man named James. "James, wait." She said. Lisa looked but there was no James there, only Dr. Samuels and the janitor with the nametag, AL, who had been working at the hospital for a few weeks now.

Two weeks ago she had been walking to her office. "Hello, Ms. Washington," he said, which was when she noticed his nametag read AL.

"Hello, Mr. Al," she replied. "Is it Allen or Albert?"

"No," he said. "If I told you, I would have to kill you," and for some reason, she felt he was not joking. "I guess I will have to kill someone to get a plate of your food." He had a serious look on his face, but she knew he was talking about the lunch she and Mr. Williams had during his sessions.

She stepped back, not wanting Al to see her. She did not like him and did not wish to be in his company. She was now complete and happy. She could not help but notice the woman calling out "James." She was sure that Doctor Samuels was James. She sat in Lisa's lobby to catch her breath. Lisa walked over to see if she could help her.

"May I help you?" She said to the older woman who was looking for James.

"Yes," she said. "Do you work here?" she asked.

"Yes," Lisa said. "My office is over there." She turned around and pointed.

"I am Maxine Turner and I have to get my paperwork to Dr. Johnson so that I can get my bloodwork done."

Lisa smiled at her because she was confused. "My secretary will take it for you. You are confused. That is Doctor Samuels, not Doctor Johnson," Lisa said.

Ms. Turner looked upset and thought that Lisa thought she was senile. "I know Doctor Johnson from a boy and he was my physician in Macon many years ago before he transferred here. He just ignored me," she said. "I have known him since he was a boy and they get successful and forget where they came from." Mrs. Turner whispered in a low voice, pointing in the direction of the janitor. "Those boys were nothing but trouble. I lived next door to them for years. The whole family was strange, and there were a lot of them. Even the father was weird. He was a medium-height man, about five-foot ten and, sometimes he would be at least eight feet tall, which made Lisa think about the tall person in the hospital that night.

The older woman sat down, "Honey, I am too tired to walk down the hall and chase the doctor." She handed Lisa her files, and Lisa read her full name.

"Mrs. Turner, Maxine," she read, "I can have my secretary take these for you," she said.

Mrs. Turner looked at her, "You have a glow about you, honey."

"I assure you, Mrs. Turner, I will get the papers to the proper department. She looked and she thought that she saw Dr. Samuels, which made her feel uncomfortable. She handed the files to her secretary and walked into her office to call Chris. She did not tell him what had happened with Mrs. Turner mistaking Doctor Samuels for another doctor.

Chapter 8

Jason was sitting, drumming his fingers on his desk. When Devin walked in, he did not say a word; he pulled up a chair, faced Jason and said, "You have nothing to say to your baby brother."

Jason jumped up and embraced Devin so fast, "I do not know if I should hug you or kick your ass. Man, you really had me going last night. I wanted to kick your ass and hug you at the same time, the way they all doted on you. I thought Lisa was going to spoon-feed you and Ida, Chris this and Chris that. Has Carolyn always had that mouth on her?" he asked. "She is a work in progress, which is why I did not say anything to her about you."

Devin got out of the chair and walked over to his desk; he pulled out his .357 Magnum and an envelope full of cash. "I tried to give you a signal, but little Kandy was watching our every move."

Jason had many questions: "What in the hell is going on, Devin? How did you become Chris Weber?"

"Something strange happened on the road that night and I knew I was the target. The cops thought I was Chris Weber, so until I got myself together, I used his name."

Jason was pissed, "You should have called me, Devin."

"I could not take that chance, Jason; besides, I knew that you would be around soon enough and I needed to get my body back in check. So I kept a low key."

"The same person that shot you that day, tried to kill me that night, and if we were seen together, they would have figured out that I was Devin and not Chris."

Jason understood what Devin was doing, but there were others involved now. "Does Lisa know who you really are?"

Devin took a deep breath. "She knows who I am. I have told her everything about me, except my name. He sighed, "I did not expect things to go this far. I thought I could wake up one morning, and I could tell her I was really Devin Jones, but time has not permitted me to do so. Jason, the person that tried to kill me that night has now started to focus his attention on her. She has seen someone several times; not only her, but Kandy also and sometimes I think Ellen has seen it, too. She comes over and she does not want to go home and she seems to be scared out of her mind."

Jason got up to make coffee, "What do you know about Ellen?"

"Lisa said she had a son, but she is not sure what happened to him; she thinks he was taken from her because she was in a mental institution. So if she has seen anything, she will not say a word."

Jason looked at Devin, "Man, Ellen is not crazy and she never has been; maybe, she has been seeing this thing and someone had her committed."

"You are right and I think that she saw it today. I thought I saw a shadow of something black and the look on her face when she asked that we take care of each other, as if she does not plan to be around."

Devin read a text from Lisa and smiled. "Ellen and Judy will be staying at the house." Jason laughed, "How do you two have any privacy with so many people around?"

Devin stood and walked to the coffee pot. "These women are amazing; they respect each other and Lisa and I have all of the privacy we need. Lisa is a woman, and she does not care who knows if we make love whenever we please. We sometimes have our own candlelight dinner and it is respected—no one gets in our way." He remembered his first night at the house. "Everyone was so warm and kind and loving. They looked out for each other and they welcomed me with open arms, as if they were waiting for me and I found out why." He now had Jason's undivided attention, "Ida is Dad's mother."

"Lisa has the paperwork on my mother's death," Devin said. "She also has the paperwork on other deaths, including Elmira Coleman. There is a connection here; we just have to find out what it is."

Devin's phone rang. It was Lisa. "Hey, babe, how is it going? I am working my fingers to the bone," he said with laughter.

"Hey, don't work too hard. You know what they say, 'All work and no play . . . '"

"What are you doing for lunch? There is this place I would like to take you."

Jason smiled, realizing that Devin was talking about the hotel across the street from the office building.

With a smile in her voice, Lisa said, "Do we actually get to eat food?"

"No, baby, we don't."

"Great," Lisa said, "I will see you for lunch."

❧ ❧

Lisa was excited, she was having a noon fling with the man she had fallen in love with. They checked into the hotel as Mr. And Mrs. Johnson. They could not keep their hands off each other. Devin ordered food to be sent up a half hour later. Devin kissed Lisa passionately.

"Why, Mr. Johnson, are you goofing off on your first day of work?"

They barely got into the room and Lisa was undressed. She was happy. She loved the patience he had with her, and he always took his time, making love to her slowly so she could get as much enjoyment from him as he did with her.

Lisa drove back to her office. She was disappointed. She wanted to hear Chris say he loved her because she had fallen in love with him. Should she say it first and see if he feels the same or should she wait? She wanted to build a life with him and, maybe they could have a baby, his baby. Lisa smiled and rubbed her stomach. She would love to have his baby.

🐚 🐚

"Is it serious with you and Lisa?" Jason asked Devin. "Do you care about her or are you just having a good time? Devin, I have to tell you, Lisa is in love with you."

Devin smiled, "Yes, I know she cares about me and I care about her. I feel good when I am with her. Lisa is what I have been looking for all my life. I have been with many women and I felt nothing. When I am with her, I feel everything—love and passion and pleasure beyond my wildest dreams, and she is the most caring woman I have ever met. She is warm and loving, not to forget beautiful and sexy as hell."

Jason did not want to bring up the accident; nevertheless, he had to know what happened on the road that night. He had to give the Weber family some closure. What did he and Chris Weber see that night? Did they both see this person on the road and who killed Chris Weber? His body was burned, which is why they could not identify his remains.

"I had just exited the interstate. It was dark, but I could see through the headlights. When I came around the curve, I could see someone standing in the middle of the road, wearing all black. I slammed on the brakes and out of the blue, Chris Weber ran into the road. He must have seen this person and hid, waiting until a car passed to run for help. All of a sudden, the person threw fire at my car; I lost control, and hit both him and Chris Weber. The car was on fire, I jumped out, looked back, and the person was gone before I lost consciousness.

Lisa was sitting at her desk in her office, waiting for her last client of the day. She needed to get home soon. Dinner plans had changed: instead of Friday dinner, they would have Thursday dinner. Friday was the day of the big party and everyone was planning to attend. She sat there and looked in her diary. It had been six weeks since she and Chris had become intimate. Chris was now working with Jason and he enjoyed catching the bad guys.

Lisa had a flashback to the first day she had met Chris. It was the same day Carolyn had said she could carry a baby. She went through her calendar and noticed she had not marked her period date. She started to count back, but did not remember having her period. She remembered having one when Chris first moved in with her, but the next month she did not have a period. Lisa thought she had been under so much stress, wondering if Chris would forget her and leave, maybe, she had thrown her cycle off track. She made a note to see Dr. Winn soon; she did not want anything to interfere with her plans to have a child when she and Chris decided the time was right.

She looked at the wall where Chris had installed a camera. She thought she should put up a sign warning her clients that they were being taped, but she had not gotten around to it. Chris had also installed cameras around the house. Since he had been working, he felt more comfortable knowing that he could watch the house from his computer at work and she could watch from her office.

"Ms. Washington," a voice said from the door.

Lisa looked up and stood to greet her last client. She then glanced at the file for his name. "Mr. Samos, how are you?" She said, extending her hand.

Lenny Samos walked in. He was an attractive man and as she looked at him, there was something familiar about him. She looked at the button on her computer; she wanted to make sure her session was being recorded. She needed to look at him again without being obvious.

Lenny Samos wasted no time, he started talking and he did not stop. She thought he had rehearsed his words and wanted to make sure he did not forget anything. He talked about his youth—how his family was a disgrace to him, how abusive his father was to him and did not want him to live his life. What struck her as odd is that he talked about fire—he felt that he was on fire. Could it be a metaphor he was using? She did not know. One thing for sure is she felt uncomfortable with him. The bell rang, but Lisa could not move for a while; this guy was making her sick. "Same time next week, Mr. Samos."

He looked at her. Lisa extended her hand and noticed that he was wearing gloves and that once again, he did not shake her hand. She walked him to the door and gave him an assignment to write down all the things he remembered as a child. They would discuss it in their next session.

She packed her computer and police reports in her briefcase. Her head was spinning. There was something strange about Lenny Samos. He claimed to have amnesia, which she found strange, considering he talked about his family. Her head started to spin, she felt dizzy, and wanted to get home as soon as possible.

Her instincts were normally right. Lenny Samos scared her and she was getting that feeling in her stomach again, but this time she felt dizzy.

Lisa finally felt better after some time and was preparing to leave when Dr. Samuels walked into her office carrying a gift. "I bet you thought I forgot," he said to her.

She smiled. "Please leave," she mumbled. "Dr. Samuels, my birthday was weeks ago."

"It's never too late, is it?" He said, smiling like a hyena. "I wanted to do something special for you, and this is what I came up with."

"Thank you," she said. She turned to grab her things, but he moved closer to her and she turned to face him.

He looked into her eyes and said, "I can make you a very happy woman." Before she could move away he kissed her. She was totally off guard and she pushed back from him. He was so close to her that she could smell the peppermint gum on his breath.

"I love you, Lisa," he said. "You need someone to love and protect you and I am the one to do it." He got down on one knee and then pulled a small box from his pocket. "Lisa Washington, will you many me? I promise, I will take good care of you and make sure no harm comes to you."

Lisa was speechless. She did not see any of this coming. She was truly scared, what did he mean she needed protection?

"Dr. Samuels," she said. "You are amazing," he smiled, "but I cannot marry you. I do not know you." Lisa looked up. She hoped Chris was not watching.

She was confused, her head turned as someone was knocking on her door; it was Detective Milo. "Hello, Lisa, do you have a minute? I thought I would take you out to lunch." Susan felt uncomfortable. She wondered if she had interrupted something because Lisa had an unsettled look on her face. She was relieved someone had entered the room, but before Dr. Samuels exited, he asked Lisa it give his proposal some consideration. She said nothing. She was shock and felt as though she had been holding her breath and could finally breathe again. She ran into Susan's arms and decided to come clean about it all—something was wrong and she needed as much help as she could get.

Lisa and Susan Milo walked out to her car together. She wanted to get home because her stomach was doing flip-flops. "Sorry, honey, I did not come to take you to lunch. It seemed like you needed to be bailed out. However, I do have a few questions for you."

Lisa stopped and looked around. She had not seen it and hoped that it would not catch her off guard.

"What do you know about Dr. Samuels?" she asked.

"He is crazy, Susan, that is what I know. That was him in my office," she said when she felt dizzy again, and she stopped to catch her breath. "Susan, I do not know him well. In the years that I have known him, he has said maybe twenty words to me, and a minute ago, he proposed to me with a ring on bended knee, saying he could protect me."

Susan noticed Lisa was shaking. "Slow down, Lisa. You're going too fast."

"I have seen it, Susan; it has been terrorizing me and I am not the only one." Susan listened as Lisa described it to her and how it watched her and who all had seen it, besides her.

"Has Chris seen it also?"

She took a deep breath, "I think so, because he is so over protective of us all, but he is a big man and he does not fear it, as I do. It has been a weird day. I had a patient that claims to have amnesia, but he remembered how much he hated his family. His name was Lenny Samos or, maybe Leonard Samos. Can you fax me at home what you have on him?"

"Do you know where Dr. Samuels was last week?"

Lisa stopped. "At a convention in New York," she said, "several doctors went."

Susan knew Lisa's next question, so she spared her the words. If she did not think so earlier, she now knew Lisa was in trouble. "Dr. Samuels's wife, Patricia Samuels, was found dead."

Lisa's eyes opened wide.

"Lisa, she died in the same manner as Asia Jones and Elmira Coleman—both wrists slashed and she was burned afterwards."

Lisa grabbed her stomach and bent over.

"I am driving you home, Lisa; we can talk on the way."

"He is involved, Susan, and I know it, and Chris thinks so, too. A patient said that Doctor Samuels was trouble. Maxine Turner said that there were several siblings, but she did not call him by that name, but she knew his face. Maxine Turner knows Doctor Robert Samuels by a different name. She called him Doctor James Johnson."

"We have trouble, Father. That old bitch recognized me, and I know that it's just a matter of time before Lisa puts two and two together."

"Stay calm, son, we will take care of it."

Devin and Jason were going through the files of his mother. They also noticed she had files on James Eddie Jones and Jimmy Jones and several others. Jason looked at the file Lisa had on Stephanie Walker; he wondered why she had all of the files. "We have to talk to Lisa," he said. "Maybe she can help us out. "If there is a connection here, maybe she can point us in the right direction."

They turned to see Kandy and Jenny walking through the door. Devin helped Kandy carry in the boxes she was carrying and Jason helped Jenny. Kandy was standing when suddenly they heard scratching and growling. It was Claire running and charging at Jenny. Jenny screamed and ran circles around Kandy. She and Claire were doing ring around the rosy around Kandy. Jenny screamed, "Get this vicious beast away from me."

Devin and Jason ran out to see what all the commotion was. They could see Jenny running circles around Kandy and Claire was the reason why. "Claire, stop!" Devin yelled and she did. Kandy bent down and picked her up; Claire looked at Jenny and started growling again. Kandy took her into the bedroom when Jenny's body starting shaking as if she had the Holy Ghost in her before she passed out.

"Lord, help me," Jen said. "The little vicious beast." Jen's body began to shake again. "Oh, Kandy, she was trying to make a snack out of me." Jen tried to stand, but she passed out again. Kandy stood there looking at Jen, shaking her head, while Devin and Jason were bent over in silent laughter in the kitchen.

Lisa walked in and she could see that there was something wrong with Jenny; she rushed to her side. "What happened to Jen?

"Lisa, is that you, girl? I was attacked," Jen said, placing her hand on her heart. "Girl, it was awful; I feared for my life." Jenny's body started to shake again. "Lisa, I was attacked," she said, "Chris came to my rescue," Jen said, as she blew Chris a kiss.

Lisa could not believe someone had come into her home and attacked her friend; she felt dizzy again, it was all too much for her. She looked back at Chris and Jason, and noticed that they were not concerned about Jenny's attack, they were actually laughing.

Chris poured Jenny a glass of water. "Jen, have something to drink; it may relax you," he said.

Jenny took a sip of water before telling Lisa how she was viciously attacked and how she had run for her life.

Did you see who attacked you? Lisa said, concerned.

"Yes, I did," Jenny said, "it was that beast Claire. Lisa, she was going to eat me alive, if Chris had not come along and rescued me, I would not be sitting here. Chris, you are my hero," she said as she praised the Lord.

Lisa was outraged at Claire. She never behaved badly toward anyone. "Jenny, I am so sorry. Chris will put Claire in a time-out for what she did to you. Jen grabbed Lisa and embraced her. "Lisa, you are so good to me. Girl, you are sweeter than cotton candy, and that phone message you left for me brought tears to my eyes. And, Chris, I love you," she said, waving her hand at him. Kandy had motioned for Chris and Jason to help her get the other boxes out of the car.

"Jenny came to pick up her dress," Kandy said to Lisa. She needed a distraction; if Lisa saw the boxes, she would know that the party tomorrow night was actually a late surprise birthday party.

Lisa and Jenny were in her office, "Here we go, Jenny or should I say Marilyn; you are going to be so beautiful. It was then she noticed that Jen was wearing gloves. She did not ask any question. Her head was spinning.

"Lisa, I need to talk to you," Jenny said. "You are the only person in the world that I trust."

Lisa embraced her. "Jen, you can talk to me about anything, I love you, Jenny and I enjoy the time we spend together."

Jenny had a tear in her eye, "Not today, okay, but soon we will talk." There was a sadness in Jen today. She was not her bubbly self.

"Jen, if you need me, then I'm here for you—both me and Chris because he likes you a lot."

Jenny bounced back, "Girl, how much does he like me? Because I like him, too. Lisa, the two of you are good together and I'm going to dance at your wedding."

Today the ladies decided to have lunch at Lisa's house to talk about the party and make sure every one of them would have a designated driver.

Lisa and Jenny were sitting in the kitchen, waiting for Carolyn to arrive. Kandy, Chris and Jason walked from the front of the house. Lisa thought something was strange, but did not say anything. Chris kissed her, "We are leaving."

She jumped up and held on to him, "You're not staying for lunch, babe, we have lots of food." She tried to entice him she did not want to be alone.

"I know," he said, as he patted his stomach. Jason and I had our share of it. We have to get back to the office."

Something was bothering her and when he got back to his office, he would check the footage and find out why. Jen looked at Jason, she had not noticed him before Claire had attacked her. She extended her hand so that Jason could kiss it, but he did not. He noticed that Jenny's hands were almost bigger than his.

"Hello, I'm Jenny," she said. Jen grabbed her chest and said, "The Lord has blessed me with sight," while she raised her eyes in thanks to God. Jenny started to flirt with Jason.

"I will scratch your eyes out, Jen," Carolyn said when she entered the house.

"You cannot blame a girl for trying."

Carolyn kissed Jason with passion; she was sending a signal to everyone in the room that Jason was with her and hers alone.

"Excuse me," Jenny said, as her body jerked twice, "can't blame a girl for trying."

After lunch, Jenny had an announcement to make. She hit the fork on the crystal glass. "You ladies are all the family I really have, and you know I have been feeling badly the last couple of days." Jen started getting emotional. "Yes, I have a good man; praise the Lord, 'cause a good man is hard to find. Leonard will bend over backwards for me and I will do the same for him, if you know what I mean."

She reached over and high fived Carolyn, "You go, Jenny."

"I mean, sisters, I am so happy to have you all in my life." She then handed everyone a gift bag, containing a pregnancy test and a blue and pink rattle. "Ladies, I am pregnant."

Carolyn and Lisa looked at each other, while Kandy sat with her mouth open. "Jenny, that is great; how far along are you?"

Jenny sighed, "I am not sure, I took a home pregnancy test and it was positive. I will see the Dr. Samuels tomorrow. "I know this is a lot to ask, but I need a partner in crime. Will you all take a test also, I need to know if the test is accurate."

Kandy refused to take the test, Carolyn said she had her cycle two days ago, so no, she was not pregnant, and Lisa agreed with Kandy—she was not pregnant and did not need a test to tell her. "Jenny, we will support you in any way that we can, but getting pregnant is not easy for some of us," Lisa said. "Some of us have to go through a process. My advice to you is to see the doctor tomorrow and take it from there."

"Well," she said, "I know for sure because Dr. Samuels congratulated me. Remember, when we all took the drug test, you know when we pee-peed in the cup? Well, mine said that I was pregnant."

Ellen was preparing dinner in Lisa's kitchen; she wanted to do the cooking today since Lisa did not feel well. She wanted to make something special for Jason. She opened the kitchen drawer to get a towel and saw the pregnancy test; Ellen smiled and called Judy to come see. "Do you think Lisa is pregnant?"

Judy placed her hand over her mouth, "Ellen, I don't know."

"Oh my, Judy, do you think Chris will be happy?"

Chris walked in the front door, and Ellen quickly put the test back in the drawer; she did not want to make Chris think she was a snoop. And, if Lisa were pregnant, they would make the announcement when they were ready.

"Hello, Chris," she said when she walked up to him and kissed him on the cheek.

Chris looked around. "Where is Lisa?" he asked.

He did not look happy to see Ellen in the kitchen, cooking. "She is in the bedroom lying down. She has a headache and wanted to get some rest before dinner."

Chris did not say a word. He washed his hands, opened the drawer and saw the test. Ellen walked away. He was not looking happy at all, as a matter of fact, he looked furious. Chris took the test into the bedroom to confront Lisa.

Ellen was so scared for her; she hoped Chris would not hurt her. She had seen that kind of anger before and it had left her lying on the street in her own blood when Eddie found out she was pregnant. "Judy, he is so angry, do you think he will hit her?"

Judy shook her head, "I don't know, Ellen. What should we do? Lady Clem said if we do nothing, she would get hurt."

Chris entered the bedroom where Lisa was lying awake, "Hey, honey, how was your day?"

Chris said nothing. He threw the test on the bed, "What the hell is that?" Chris was not upset about the pregnancy test, but he was furious about the video from Lisa's office. Dr. Samuels kissed her, and she said nothing about it earlier. When Lisa came home, she looked as if she had seen a ghost, but she said nothing of what had happened.

Lisa could see the fire in his eyes, and she knew she had to explain.

"That was in a gift bag from Jenny," she said. "After lunch today, Jen announced that she is pregnant."

Chris looked at Lisa, "Are you kidding? Why would she give you a pregnancy test kit?

"Babe, she gave all of us a pregnancy test kits. Her excuse was she wanted to see if they were accurate and she needed a partner in crime. She said a random drug test that we all had to take confirmed that she was pregnant."

Chris shook his head. "That does not make any sense, Lisa."

"I know. That's what I was thinking. Jen is weird and over dramatic, but her explanation for wanting all of us to take a test is crazy. Chris, something is wrong. Today was strange." He looked at her. "I have a new client and I need you to take a look at him when you have time. He scared me, and that is why I was shaking today. I got this weird feeling . . . There was something about him. Chris, I have seen many patients and I can tell you this guy made my flesh crawl. It was like I was seeing a ghost, I literally felt nauseous after his visit. I know I sound silly, but I feel like I am being set up; something is going to happen and until we figure out who is who, it is going to be bad."

Chris pulled Lisa into his arms. He had all but forgotten about the doctor's kiss. He knew he needed to work on the issues with his temper. Lisa was in pain, and all he could do was think about his own selfish needs. He and Jason agreed they had to work on their temper. All their lives they had watched their father rule his home with an iron fist. As a child, he watched his mother cower in a corner because she feared his father's wrath, and as an adult, he had had to stop his father from attacking many women he would invite to his home. One of those women was a woman whose name he would never forget . . . How she begged God to help her as he beat her because he may have fathered a child with her. That night he and Jason had agreed to get their act together and never raise their hand to a woman. He sometimes got frustrated and raised his voice, but he was working on being a better man than his father.

He had wondered why nothing had come of that night; neither he nor his father had ever seen her again and today he learned why—the same night his father attacked Betty was the same night someone had burned her to death—she had both wrists slashed and her belly was cut open, revealing the small fetus inside of her. Every woman the Jones men had touched and may have fathered children with have all died by fire, and the only thing that may be keeping Lisa alive is that the killer thinks he is Chris Weber.

Lisa was special. She trusted him, and he would do anything in his power to protect her. Someone was out there killing every woman his family touched and she was now beginning to feel his presence because it watched as they made love.

Lisa hoped that Chris would not misunderstand because she barely knew Doctor Samuels, but she promised that she would not keep a secret.

She walked over and looked into Chris's eyes and said, "Dr. Samuels proposed to me."

He knew the doctor was fucked up in the head, however, he could not believe what he was hearing. He could see the video, but he could not hear what was happening; something was interfering with the equipment. And now he knew why there was a time difference in the equipment when Lisa was seeing her stalker. He had not noticed, but the clock at the top of the camera showed a thirty-minute discrepancy.

"I thought you barely knew him."

"I was shaking all over," Lisa said. "He even tried to kiss me. Chris, I am afraid of Dr. Samuels, he said I needed someone to love and protect me and he was the person to do it."

Chris was burning up. "As of Monday, I will take you to work and pick you up. I need to make my presence known to Dr. Samuels. If anyone is going to love and protect you, it will be me."

Lisa was happy. Chris did not say he loved her, but at least she knew that he cared. He kissed her head like a father kissing a child, "How long before dinner?"

"About an hour," she said. She was hoping that he would have time to sit and catch up with her before dinner.

"I need to get into the attic." He checked the wires and realized right away that someone was hacking into their system.

Lisa wanted to tell him she had not seen her period, but he was angered at the fact that Dr. Samuels had propositioned her and she picked up the test he'd thrown on the bed. Would he be happy or would he hit her like Kandy's son's father did her when she told him she was pregnant. *Pregnant*, she thought. *Could she be or was it just stress?* She decided it would be in her best interest to keep her mouth closed and make an appointment with Dr. Winn.

Lisa entered the kitchen, "Ellen, something smells real good." Ellen hugged Lisa for dear life, "Are you okay? Chris was so angry when he came home."

"Yes, I know," Lisa said. She explained to Ellen what Chris had seen. Ellen always avoided Dr. Samuels; he reminded her of the one of the doctors at the mental hospital, but they kept her full of drugs. She did not like him and made no secret about it.

"Has anyone been in the house today?" Chris asked Lisa.

"No, not today."

He was concerned, "Someone has run extra wires to the security system and it is going to take a while before I can trace it to whom."

Lisa did not understand. "What does that mean?"

"It means, baby, someone may be watching us."

Lisa got nervous.

"Don't worry; I disconnected the wires. Jason and I will check it out; we will work here instead of the office. Someone has been here; we will use the office upstairs."

Lisa smiled, knowing she should be worried, but he made her feel safe.

He turned his attention to Ellen, who was preparing dinner. He could tell Ellen had had a hard life and he did not want her to feel uncomfortable. He could see the fear in her eyes. He knew abuse when he saw it, and Ellen had been abused.

"I am sorry for the way I acted when I first walked in the house," Chris said. "You are a loving and kind woman." Chris was recalling when Lisa was away at work, how Ellen and Judy would come over and Ellen would prepare lunch for him. And when his knee was aching, Ellen would put ice in a ziplock bag for him to place on his knee. Chris kissed Ellen on the cheek.

Lisa smiled because of the affection Chris was showing to Ellen. Ever since she met Ellen she had never dated. She had been put away for so long, and for the first time Ellen seemed to be at peace and she cared about Chris. "We love you, Ellen," Lisa said.

"You are the best," Lisa said. "And thanks for preparing dinner." Ellen smiled. No one besides Lisa had ever said kind words to her, and she did not want to cry because if she did, Judy would have her sent back to the hospital.

"Do you promise?" Ellen said as she lowered her head.

Lisa turned to Chris. "Yes," Chris said.

"That means a lot coming from you," Ellen said. "Because Lisa loves everyone."

"I do, Ellen, and you should live with me and Lisa," she smiled, "here, anywhere," he said. "Wherever we go, you will go with us."

She was truly happy. "No one has ever wanted me," and her words almost made him cry.

"Ellen, if there is something bothering you, then you can tell me."

She was about to speak when she looked at Judy coming into the room, and she turned away. He looked at Judy and then back to Ellen, and realized that Ellen feared Judy.

At the dinner table, Kandy could not wait to hear everyone's opinion on Jenny's announcement. "Did you guys hear about Jenny?" Chris knew what Kandy was talking about, although everyone else was in the dark. "Jenny said she is pregnant," Jason laughed and some of his drink spilled from his mouth. "She gave all of us a pregnancy test kit," Kandy said.

Jason did not know what the magic age was for women to stop having children. He had once read an article on a woman in her seventies having a baby, but he had never thought he would see one. "Isn't she a little too old to get pregnant? Besides . . ." he decided not to finish his statement.

"Jenny is an exception to the rules," Carolyn said, "She was in Dr. Samuels's office today. According to Dr. Samuels, Jenny is pregnant."

Lisa excused herself from the table. She needed a minute to think. If Jenny is pregnant, something is wrong. Dr. Samuels was up to something and she wondered what. She did not have time to worry about it now, but why would Jen want them all to take a pregnancy test? Lisa was puzzled; she could not help but wonder if Dr. Samuels and Jenny knew each other and were plotting something. She said nothing when she returned to the table she knew Carolyn would defend Dr. Samuels's diagnosis, so she said nothing. According to Carolyn, there was a doctor's oath like a policeman's oath: you do not stab your brother in medicine in the back, but she felt that this was not the case. Carolyn defended Dr. Samuels all of the time. She wondered if Carolyn and Dr. Samuels had dated before she reunited with Jason.

"He is a brilliant doctor," she said, "he saved my life. Lisa, you remember that day when he and I went for coffee and all of the sudden I was bent over in pain? Well, he carried me back to the hospital and preformed a surgery on me. I had to get my appendix removed, and he had me on my feet in no time. He even took care of me. He would not let anyone else near me. He is a friend, indeed," she said, "so if you guys don't mind, I would like it if you would not call him names. Everybody has their bad days. He was having problems in his marriage and he still kept his head up."

Lisa remembered, she asked Carolyn if she thought that Dr. Samuels had done something to cause her harm, and she said, "Absolutely not." She found it strange that one minute she was perfectly fine and the next minute she was in severe pain. She never pushed the issue or brought it up again. She asked if Momma Ida could see a different doctor, but whenever they had appointment, the only doctor available was Dr. Samuels. So she would cancel the appointment.

"Lisa, you are not being fair, you just pulled Ida from him and I know that it hurt his feelings. Every day he would ask about Ida and I would have to lie and tell him you are busy and that is why she missed the appointment." Carolyn could be very headstrong. Jason listened and wondered how much stress her and Lisa's relationship could handle. If Lisa found out about her deception about having a child, would she forgive her or kick her to the curb?

"Carolyn, I understand your loyalty to Dr. Samuels, but you understand this, I am not putting Momma's life in the hands of that madman." Ellen and Judy looked at Ida with a smile, and Judy knew that Lisa was the true little sister she would never have. "There is something not right with him and I know it: there is something sinister about him." Lisa put up her finger, not allowing Carolyn to say a word. "If you like him, I am fine with that, but I will not compromise Momma's health for you or anyone else."

"What is your problem with him?" Carolyn yelled. Jason wanted to step in, but Chris stopped him.

"For one, he makes false diagnoses. He told Momma she was sick and she was not. And, telling Jenny she is pregnant is another. Something is not right and I do not know how you cannot see that. What he is up to, I do not know, but Dr. Samuels is an impostor. When Momma was in the hospital, he and the nurses were huddled in a corner looking strangely. They watched the door and tried to force medication and food down everyone's throat."

"She is right," Kandy said. "That nurse was crazy. One minute she was pleasant and the next minute she was looking like she wanted to kill someone. She scared me so bad, I stayed in Chris's room for hours. And she was at the elevator that day when Momma and I were going down. Lisa looked shocked because she did not recall seeing the nurse. I gave Momma a knife," Kandy said.

"Are you sure she was there?" Lisa asked. "Because we were so focused on Jenny that none of us were paying attention."

"She was there, I know," Kandy said. "I took out my pepper spray for that bitch, and she was watching you all."

Chapter 9

Kandy stood at the front desk. She was dressed as Cindy Birdsong of the Supremes, while Jenny entered dressed as Marilyn Monroe. Jenny decided to do a performance in the doctor's lounge to get Kandy's approval. "Does she know," Jenny asked, "I am so excited. Lisa will be so surprised. She thought we had forgotten about her birthday, and tonight we will give her the surprise of her life."

"Keep it down, Jen, we do not want Lisa to walk in and hear you. She has no idea this party is for her. We had to get Chris to take her out after she wrapped up for the day. We got her to come back to the office by telling her she had forgotten about an appointment she had this evening, which is why we are getting dressed here in the hospital." Kandy even told Jen how they planned an emergency phone call from Ida, which would be why Lisa would return home and everyone would yell surprise.

Everything was going according to plan. Ida had called Lisa just in time and now the Supremes were on their way to Lisa's house. Lisa parked in her driveway. Suddenly, everyone had an excuse to get out of the car. They walked inside and everyone yelled, "Surprise!" Lisa was truly shocked; she'd had no idea and nearly jumped out of her skin. Everyone started singing "Happy Late Birthday" to her, and then the entertainment began.

Lisa was stunned. They hired photographers and everything looked amazing. There was so much food cooked, there was no place to put it. They even had servers for the food. Lisa and everyone laughed as Momma Ida and Chris performed "Rolling on the River." Ida was in rare form. She did her Tina Turner impression to a tee and so did Chris. The two of them had watched *What's Love Got to Do With It* for days, and they were amazing. However, the highlight of the night was Ellen—

her Tammy Terrell was magnificent. She looked and sounded better than they had ever seen. She stood next to Jason with her arm around him, and they were the perfect Tammy and Marvin impersonators. The ladies screamed for Marvin and Tammy to do an encore, and then there was applause with a standing ovation, voting them the best performance of the night.

Jenny did her Marilyn Monroe, and everyone cheered her on, which is why her performance lasted three times longer than any other. Jenny loved the attention of the captive audience. She even let her dress blow in the air.

The party was over and everyone had left for the night. Chris asked Ellen and Judy to stay the night. He was tired and did not want to leave the house.

Jason and Carolyn stayed over for coffee. Jason had one drink too many and he needed time and food in his system. Kandy was waiting on her ride. She had to work the morning shift at the hospital, so she declined Chris's invitation to spend the night. Lisa knew that there was more to Kandy's story than she was saying. She had seen Kandy engulfed in conversation that seemed to be overwhelming to her, and she got the feeling that Justin's father was the reason why.

"Kay, I really wish that you would stay," Chris said, "and let me take you to work in the morning."

She wrapped her arms around him, "You worry too much. I'm going straight home to bed."

Lisa walked into the kitchen. She was starving. The servers were starting to pack up the food, and she wanted a plate before everything was put away.

"Chris, before I leave, I just wanted to say thank you," Kandy said. "I took your advice and I talked to Kevin. He's excited about everything." Kandy was careful not to say "baby."

Jason sat and watched as his brother gloated, "I told you, baby girl, communication is the key, and to answer your questions . . . No, I would not want Lisa to have an abortion, and yes I would love her and support her."

She smiled. "Why didn't you answer when I asked?"

He took a sip of water. "Because I knew you would make your decision to talk to Kevin according to my answer, and you needed to do what you felt in your heart was the right thing."

Kandy looked outside. Her ride was there, waiting to pick her up. Lisa ran from the kitchen. She wanted to see if Justin Sr. Was Kandy's ride. He was not, so Lisa embraced her. She did not want her to leave, "Are you sure you can't stay, Kandy?"

Kandy smiled, "No, Momma, I can't, but I'll see you in the morning."

Ellen walked into the room where Chris and Jason were sitting; she know her time was getting short and she hoped she could hold Jason just one more time before he came for her. "Jason, I just wanted to thank you for an amazing time."

Chris laughed, "That is probably the first time in his life he has heard a beautiful woman say that. They had an amazing time with him, Ellen."

Jason laughed, too; he stood and pulled Ellen into his arms and he kissed her cheeks. "You have an amazing voice, I just stood there while you sang."

Ellen cheered, "We won!" She wanted to say more, but he was not prepared to hear what she said next. "If I don't see you again, I just want you to know how wonderful it was spending time with you."

Jason and Chris looked at each other, "Ellen, remember what I said, I want you here with us," and he kissed her goodnight. Ellen walked away and went into her bedroom. "We have to keep an eye on Ellen," Jason said, "I think you were right, someone is scaring her."

Lisa soaked in a hot bath; she wanted to be prepared for Chris when he entered the room. She had received lingerie for her birthday and wanted to put it to good use. Before Chris went into the bedroom, he checked in on Ellen. Everyone was sound asleep. He then checked the video of the house, both inside and out. Seeing nothing strange, he went to the bedroom.

❧ ❧

Kandy and her cousin arrived at her home. Her son Justin was spending the night with a neighbor, and she wanted to sleep late in her own bed. She enjoyed being with Lisa and Chris; yet, she needed some time to think about what she wanted to say to Kevin. "I want to keep the baby," she thought would sound too selfish. "Can we keep the baby?" It sounded as if she were asking permission. Before she could think anymore, someone had knocked at her door. She knew her cousin would not be back so soon after dropping her off at home. Kandy looked through the peephole, she stopped and backed up; she could not believe that Justin had come to her house, even when she told him not to do so earlier.

Justin started knocking on the door harder, "I know you're in there, Kandy. I saw your cousin walk down the street to the card game." Justin started knocking harder. She opened the door, she did not want him to cause a scene and wake the neighbors with his loud voice.

Justin walked in, "Hey, baby, I just want to talk to you, that's all. He was up to something because he was using his sweet voice, which now had no effect on her.

"What do you want, Justin?"

He looked at her, "Who in the hell are you supposed to be?"

She removed her wig and started walking toward the kitchen.

"I want you back, baby; I want to be in my son's life."

She looked at him and he looked sincere, but he had sung this song so many times before, and she was not falling for it. He started caressing her face, "Please stop or leave." She did not want to look at him. She had fallen for these lines and ended up with a black eye.

"I love you, Kandy, and I am willing to do what you ask."

She shook her head no. He could tell that he was getting to her, so he decided to work his magic. He kissed her, pressing his body into hers. She did not fight. It had been weeks since she had made love and to have someone touch her like he was made her feel the heat stirring inside of her.

"Justin, stop," she said. "Please leave; I do not want to do this with you again."

He wanted to win her back, so he went a step further, raising her dress. She was not wearing underwear, so he pushed his erection into her and started kissing her.

She said no again in a low tone. She wanted him so badly, but she had told herself that she would not allow him to hurt her again. "Justin, please leave," she asked, because if he did not leave soon, she would do something she would regret.

He unzipped his pants, revealing his erect penis. "I love you, baby, and I know that I will never find another woman like you," he said before lifting her and inserting his penis inside of her. He started pushing deep into her, she moaned and he pushed deeper again.

When she came to her senses, she could not believe she had let him enter her. She felt guilty and ashamed. She thought of Kevin and their unborn child. She was now confused, did she just cheat on Kevin? She did not want Justin back. She cared for

Kevin. Was she really a whore, which is what Carolyn would think of her? She walked to the door and opened it so that he could leave.

"Don't do this to me," Justin said. "We can work things out." Kandy held the door open and asked him to leave. Justin pulled up his pants and walked out to his car. He opened the car door and climbed inside. He sat alone in his car thinking *Kandy had stood her ground. She had never reacted like she had tonight.* He had taken her money, and he had even slapped her around a few times, and she had always let him back into her bed. Tonight, she made it clear she wanted nothing to do with him. He looked up as Kandy was putting trash in the trashcan. He wanted to shoot her the bird, but she seemed to be in a trance. He did a double take, there was something behind her—it was tall. He just stared at it. When she walked inside, she never looked around to notice the person in black behind her.

Kandy walked into her kitchen, she wanted to call Chris and ask if what happened with her and Justin was forgivable in Kevin's heart. The word slut kept popping into her head, which she had been called many times before; she knew Lisa would say she did not cheat, only because she would not want to hurt her feelings. However, Chris would tell her the truth. Kandy started crying when someone tapped her on the shoulder. She turned slowly, but before she could see who it was, she was hit so hard, her legs went from under her. She screamed and she was picked up and hit again. She had lost her senses; she was being attacked, and she started screaming again, louder. She was being kicked in her stomach and her head was beaten against the wall until it left a hole in the wall. She was thrown on the floor until she could scream no longer. She was going to die; Justin was going to kill her, as her screams were being ignored by her neighbors because they had heard them before.

⟳ ⟳

Chris stood in the bedroom doorway. He was pleased Lisa was wearing sexy lingerie and she wanted to do a dance for him. He was tired out of his mind, but Lisa had his full attention. He sat on the sofa and she did her sexy dance for him, wearing a red sexy lace teddy. She unrobed as she swirled her hip and rolled her belly like a belly dancer. She rolled and grinded on him until he could take no more. He rose to the occasion and she sat on him and swirled on top of him. He lifted her and carried her to the bed, where he made his entrance. Her phone rang several times, but there was no answering. He had to finish what she had started. She rolled him over, now she was on top. She rode him to the heights before he decided to end it. He was on top and pushing in and out deeply, when they both yelled out at the same time. She grinned until every drop had entered her. They were panting for breath, neither could move for minutes.

"You're going to kill me," he said. "I can't get enough of you."

They both got up to take a shower when Lisa's phone rang again. This time, she answered. It was Carolyn, "What in the hell are you doing?" Before Lisa could answer, Carolyn starting yelling, "I have been trying to call you for an hour."

"Carolyn, its two in the morning."

"Yeah, right," Carolyn said, she wanted Lisa to feel guilty for sleeping with Chris and she knew exactly what button to push. "While you are screwing Chris, someone just beat Kandy almost to death. She is in the emergency room," she said, before hanging up the phone.

Lisa started screaming and crying for Chris. He ran from the bathroom and saw no one. "Someone just beat up Kandy. Carolyn said it was bad."

☙ ☙

Lisa and Chris arrived at the hospital and two police officers were there to get a statement from Kandy. She said nothing. Lisa looked at Kandy, but she did not recognize her. She placed her hand over her mouth; she could not believe what she was seeing—her face was swollen and black-and-blue. Kandy reached for her, which surprised her, because it looked as if her eyes were closed.

Kandy would not say a word unless her family was there. She wanted to feel protected and Jason and Chris made her feel that way. They both stood next to her as she told them what had happened. She was shaking as if she were freezing. She was in a lot of pain, both physical and mental.

Kandy began to talk. "Justin had come over," she started, "and I asked him to leave. I went to take the trash out, and he tapped me on the shoulder and started beating me."

"Did you see Mr. Royal hit you, Ms. Coleman?"

"No," she said. "It all happened so fast."

"Are you going to arrest him?" Carolyn asked. "Because he has hit her before."

"We are not here for prior incidents, Dr. Young. Mr. Royal and Ms. Coleman's stories have some similarity. However, he said he did not touch her."

Jason looked at Devin. They knew that cops, even in this type of situation, were playing good cop-bad cop. One gave a cleaner version of what had happened, while the other gave the full X-rated details of the story.

"Justin will say anything to save his ass," Carolyn pointed out to the policeman.

"Not this time, Ms. Young, Officer Johnson said. "There were two other witnesses to his story and they both saw someone wearing a long black veil run from Ms. Coleman's home. Ms.

Coleman, you were a stripper. Do you think you may have a secret admirer out there?"

"I knew it!" Carolyn yelled. "Kandy's creditability was being put to the test. The police officers see her as trash, and have no intention of helping her. They'd rather take the word of a snake like Justin. That is Dr. Young to you, and also this is Dr. Washington, and that is Nurse Coleman to you, sir," Carolyn said so sarcastically that Devin and Jason had to smile. They wanted Kandy to be taken seriously and not as someone who has put herself in harm's way.

Lisa also could see what was happening, that the police officer had no intention of helping Kandy. "I'll call Detective Milo," she said.

"Susan Milo?" The officer asked.

"Yes, she is a very good friend of mine and she will get to the bottom of this. Officer Johnson, Kandy is an independent woman," Lisa said. "A few years ago, she wanted to purchase a home for her and her son, and she was a little short on money. Instead of asking for a handout, she took a job at the club. She only worked there for two weeks. She wanted to make things perfectly clear that Kandy was not a loose woman. "Kandy is a nurse here at the hospital," she said with conviction. "So, whatever Justin said, he said only to make himself feel better because she wants nothing else to do with his sorry ass."

Carolyn was so angry she demanded to know what Justin said.

Officer Johnson gestured for Jason and Devin to walk outside the room with him. Jason and Devin went to the academy with Scotty Johnson and worked murder cases with him before leaving the force to start their private investigation company.

"Talk to me, Scotty," Jason said. "What did Justin say?"

"Okay," Scotty said. "I wanted to spare Ms. Coleman anymore embarrassment. Mr. Royal said he talked to Ms. Coleman earlier, asking if he could come over and talk about their son. She said no, but he did so anyway. He waited until her roommate left to go to the card game two doors down before knocking on the door. First, she asked him to leave, but he did not, so she let him in. He then went on to say she was wearing some tight dress from the sixties. He asked her to take him back. She said no, so he tried sexual persuasion; he dropped his pants and raised her dress, and started romancing her. These are not his exact words, if you know what I mean. She asked him to leave, which he did, but he waited in the car because he had a hard-on, when he saw her come out of the house with a garbage bag. He also said she looked like she was in a trance, because she never saw the person behind her. She went inside. The person wearing the black veil followed her. Later, he heard her screaming, to which he grabbed his gun and ran to the door to find that it was locked. He looked through the front window to see that the person was kicking her in her stomach. He kicked in the front door, and the person was chanting while holding up a blade and a glass with a rag inside. The person looked up at him when he yelled for him to stop. While Justin was holding the gun on the man he could smell the gasoline, to which he announced to the man in the black veil, 'Motherfucker you will burn too.' He did not discharge his weapon because the person was standing over Kandy. Then the man ran toward the side door and that is when he called the police."

Jason said, "He knew the layout of the house."

"Yes," Scotty said, "and the front door was damaged, which corroborated his story."

Kandy began to cry. She knew Justin would say anything to make her look bad. Chris and Jason will no longer have any respect for her. They would probably suggest that Lisa and Carolyn sever their ties with her. She could accept not seeing

Carolyn, but Lisa was her only real family. The two weeks she worked at the club would haunt her for the rest of her life.

"You are going to be fine, Kandy," Lisa said. She knew Kandy needed protection and she knew just the person to call. It was time Kandy met her father. Mr. Williams had a team of security, and she and Kandy needed more protection than Jason and Chris could provide. She had often referred to the person as "it," but now someone had started to physically harm them. Today it was Kandy; tomorrow, it may be her.

Dr. Winn entered the room, and it was not good news. There was something he wanted to say, she could tell by the look on his face. "Kandy, we are getting a room ready for you."

She became paranoid and frantic. "No, I can't stay here." She began to scream. "No, Dr. Winn, I can't stay here, he will come back for me; please let me go. He tried to calm her.

"Kandy, I will be right at the desk. I can see everyone that comes and goes."

She started yelling for Lisa, who had stepped out to make a phone call. She ran to her side.

"We have to sedate her, Lisa, before she goes into shock."

Lisa held her hand, "Kay, you have to calm down and listen." Lisa continued, "Chris is here and Jason and Carolyn also, and you know that I am not going anywhere. The same people you see now will be here when you awake."

She stopped and became calm, and allowed Dr. Winn to put the needle into her arm; she reached for Chris who lay right next to her. "I messed up. I was so tired, I let my guard down. I am not a bad girl." She said in a whisper to Chris, "Did I cheat? I am so sorry, everything happened so fast. Did I cheat?"

This time, his words were like gold to her, as her mental state it was at risk. "No, baby girl, you did not. What you did was brave. You stopped a situation before it went too far, and you let Justin know you will not take his abuse anymore." He looked up at Jason because Kandy should be thankful that Justin had not left, or she would be dead.

Dr. Winn stayed until Kandy drifted off to sleep. "How could this have happened?" He said in a low voice to Chris and Jason, "these ladies are like family to me. Lisa and Carolyn took me under their wings when I first started working at the hospital. They would invite me to Friday dinner because I had no family here. They are like my big sisters. And Kandy, she is the little sister I never had. "I tried," he said to Jason and Devin and they could see the pain and guilt in his eyes, "but I could not save Kandy's baby."

Both men could see pain on his face. "Doc, you did everything you could do and I know Kandy is happy that you saved her life. She can have more children, but to lose her would have been unbearable for us all and we owe that to you."

Mr. Williams returned Lisa's phone call minutes after she had dialed him. "Sorry, I missed your call, Lisa, but I was kind of into something."

Lisa was trying to choose her words. She knew this was not something she could say over the phone. "Mr. Williams, will you meet me in my office? I have something very important to talk with you about."

"Is everything okay, Lisa?"

"Yes and no," she said. "If you could just give me a few minutes of your time?"

"I will see you in an hour."

Willie arrived at Lisa's office and she was sitting there all alone; he could tell she had been crying. "Lisa," he said, as he walked into the room. She ran into his arms. She knew she was being unprofessional. But she was in no mood to think of ethics.

"Did someone do something to you, Doc? I will take care of it, just tell me who."

Lisa shook her head no. She needed to pull herself together. She offered him coffee as they sat at the round table in her office. She had to talk to him tonight or Kandy would die at the hands of a madman. Lisa knew she had to keep control of the situation and get him to listen to her every word. "Mr. Williams, remember when you said that I was like a daughter to you?"

Willie did not know where the doctor was going with this, but he decided to play along. "Yes, I recall we were eating gumbo and I said that. Doc, I meant it, you are family to me."

"Then you trust me, right?"

He nodded his head yes, although he found it hard to trust anyone these days; but he did trust her, there was something about her that said he should.

Lisa pulled a picture out of her briefcase, along with the file she had on him and his family. She handed him the picture. He looked at it and he still did not know where she was going with this. But she had his attention.

"Mr. Williams, the young lady in the middle . . . I call her Kandy, because she is so sweet. She is my little sister, the one I told you about. She is the one I told you I was investigating the death of her mother."

He nodded his head. He remembered that day very well. It was the day he thought of the death of his wife and that night drank so much he passed out.

"Mr. Williams, is your daughter's name Carla Coleman?"

He lifted the picture again. Before lowering it, his finger released it as it fell to the floor.

"Tonight, someone beat her pretty badly. Someone wearing a black costume with a long black veil."

His voice was cracked, "Is she dead?"

"No," she said as she pulled out a picture of a little boy and handed it to him, "this is her son, Justin. His father had come in while the attack was taking place. The attacker had a scalpel and a jar filled with gasoline." He said nothing, but she could tell that he knew what she was going to say, "Mr. Williams, Kandy is Nibble, your daughter."

"No, Doc, the police said my wife and child both died in the fire."

She shook her head and pulled out Kandy's paper and read it to him, "Mommy was preparing dinner for Daddy. She was playing Otis Redding songs all day. She dropped me off at Aunt Tina's to spend the night."

His eyes watered. He knew the doctor had worked hard and done her job well. "Elmira's sister's name was Katina and everyone called her Tina. Tina hated me," he said, "she thought I was a thug and did not want Elmira with me, but for her to destroy my life like that and take my child away from me . . . He thought for a minute. "She must hate me; my little girl will hate me for the rest of my life."

"No," Lisa said, "I have been preparing her for this day, especially when I read the police report. She knew that something went wrong and that you did not abandon her. Mr. Williams, she understands and right now she needs you more than ever." It was time to vindicate Elmira; all these years, he resented his wife for taking her own life, but today he will learn different. "Mr. Williams, your wife did not commit suicide; she was killed by the same person that attacked your daughter."

He stood and paced the floor, eyes full of tears. He did not want anyone to see the pain he was in. "Doc, I hated her; I cursed her, a woman I loved more than life itself. I hated the mention of her name, and now you tell me that all the law enforcement and lawyers I hired had fucking stiffed me." He was now angry and she knew that whoever it was, they would have hell to pay. "Why would they tell me my wife and child were dead?"

She touched his hand because she needed to keep him under control. "Mr. Williams, Kandy needs you. We both need you, please help me." He stopped and looked at her. "I know the pain you are in. I will not keep anything from you, but I need you to keep control." He shook his head and sat next to her. "The reason the police officers said your wife and child died was because Elmira was pregnant, and so was Kandy until tonight. She miscarried the baby. The attacker had kicked her in the stomach. He did not want the baby to survive under any circumstances. Did your wife ever say anything about seeing someone wearing all black?"

"Yes," he said. "She was scared out of her mind. She would look out the window and see the person staring at the house. She said he even pointed at her as she watched him. I didn't take any chances, Doc. I had security with her all of the time. We thought it was over, maybe an isolated incident. She started feeling comfortable, then a week later she was gone."

Lisa pulled out files of several people who died the same way. He looked at the files and he knew them all—Asia Jones, Betty Jackson—he even knew of the others, but never made any connection.

"We let our guards down, Mr. Williams."

"Doc, stop calling me Mr. Williams. Now that you and I are on a first name basis, you can even call me Poppy. I always wanted another daughter and to get two in the same night, kind of makes up for some of the hell I have been through." Willie was stunned at how sharp Lisa was; he had hired investigator and they all said the same thing: *your wife committed suicide.* She talked to her friends about a man in black and they said she was probably depressed. He had heard it all. They were wrong and he would collect all that was owed to him.

Lisa talked about how her first time seeing her stalker was when she first met Chris and Ida was ill and admitted into the hospital for observation. "Chris was the victim of a hit and run and both Kandy and I had seen someone doing some kind of dance in the hall. After that, someone followed me home and watched me through the window, and Kandy said that she saw someone outside of her home."

Willie thought the sins of the father had been passed to the children; this was not Carla's fight, it was his. "Lisa, you said you let your guard down, what did you mean?"

"When Chris found out about this person, he would not let any of us out of his sight, he would follow us from the hospital and Kandy would stay at my house. Chris said, maybe, he showed himself to people he had a beef with. Carolyn, who is also a friend, has never seen anyone, and Chris…" Lisa sighed. "I think he has because when Kandy and I told him, he did not think we were crazy. He just jumped into protective mode. He would drive her to the hospital and pick her up. She was never alone and tonight we thought she was with her roommate." Lisa looked at her watch: it was six in the morning. "Kandy will be up soon; maybe you and I can sit with her together."

Willie shook his head and said, "Okay."

Lisa and Willie watched as Jason, Carla, and Chris slept. Willie stared and asked her, "Which one do you say is your boyfriend?"

"Chris is the one laying with Carla. I guess you can tell they are very close, Poppy; he has been amazing to us both. If he was not here, maybe, this would have happened a long time ago to us both."

Willie looked at Chris. He knew that Lisa was very smart. But she had not made a connection as to why, after meeting Chris, all of this had started happening. The man she knew as Chris Weber was actually his nephew Devin Jones and until he got his memory back, she was in a lot of danger. Every one of the murdered women's files she has was connected to the Jones men.

Devin watched as Lisa and the man he knew as Uncle Willie watched him sleep; he wondered if he would tell her who he really was. He knew now that it was time for him to come clean. They were all being stalked by this person, and if they were going to survive, there could be no secret between them.

A nurse entered the room; Devin and Jason were on their feet so fast, the nurse nearly dropped the tray. "Sorry, Nurse Klein," Jason said, "but you can take that back." Carolyn walked in with a bag of food. She and two others nurses had walked across the street to get breakfast for everyone.

"Lisa is cheating on you," Carolyn said, as she pointed to her standing in the hall with Willie."

"Jason, you let one get by," he said. "We didn't frisk her," as Jason began to pat Carolyn down.

Lisa and Willie walked in while the nurse was leaving the room. Lisa looked at her; she was the nurse on duty at the hospital that night when Ida and Chris were there. Lisa said nothing, but she would look for her later and ask her what she saw that night.

Willie could not keep his eyes off Devin. He and his best friend had buried him months ago. The body pulled from the water was burned and had been in the water for several days, making it impossible to identify. They thought it was Devin because Devin's car was dredged from the water and the driver's side door was open. Jason said Devin was sharp and he could not believe he would let someone get a jump on him, and now he saw that he was right. They were both standing there in front of him right now. He would not tell Lisa who Devin was for now. He would wait until he found out what was going on.

Lisa and Willie walked into the room. Lisa kissed Chris and pulled Willie close so she could introduce him to everyone. "My God, you look amazing," Carolyn said to Willie. "If you look like that this time in the morning, there's no wonder Lisa has been talking about you. Every week after your visit, she is talking about her Mr. Williams."

Willie kissed Carolyn on the cheek. Jason noticed she had blushed as his uncle turned his attention to him. He could see he had questions, but it was not the time to answer them.

"She will be out for a while," Devin said. "Dr. Winn said it was better that she rest. She had to have surgery, but everything went well."

Willie nodded his head before Lisa explained to everyone why he was there. "Carolyn, we now have an amazing man in our life. Willie is Kandy's father."

Jason looked at Kandy, "Is that Nibble?" He remembered her; he and Devin had to babysit her for punishment from their father. She could not have been more than fifteen months old then and now she was at least twenty-five. He had wondered why this person had attacked her, why he wanted to take away her baby, and now standing before him was the reason why. Any father of Kandy's is a father of mine," Carolyn said.

"No, he is my poppy," Lisa said.

Carolyn gasped, "Mine, too."

Lisa mumbled, "Mine," under her breathe.

"Ladies," Devin said, "You all can share him."

Willie stood with his arm around Carolyn and Lisa, as they watched Kandy sleep.

Devin and Jason drove back to their office to go over the files. "Kandy is Willie's daughter, which means that they had to know that. We are looking for a family member or someone that was very close to the family because they know all of us." Devin looked at the computer. He wanted to make sure that Lisa was not alone. "Thanks to Uncle Willie, none of the women will be without security. It is good having him in our corner, which means now we should be able to focus on the files."

Carolyn felt like royalty. She has had a shadow all day, thanks to Willie; he did not want any of them left alone. She sat at her desk doing paperwork, and she got this feeling she was being watched. She looked through the glass in her office to see her bodyguard was reading a newspaper. She felt uneasy with everything that had happened with Kandy. She turned and looked out of the window. She scanned the ground with her eyes and then she saw someone. She stared. She was not losing her mind. She really did see someone watching her, wearing a long black robe from some kind of an old horror film. She could not see his face because he was wearing a veil. *Is that what Kandy had to face that night?* She began to shake.

Jason and Devin were at the office, their desks covered with files. "Man, I feel like we are beating a dead horse. The answer is here, but we can't put all of this together. We need answers," Devin said. "Lisa has all of these files. We have to find out why and where she was going with all of this."

Jason looked at the monitor to see their uncle walking into the building. "Did you see the way they doted on him? He looks amazing," Devin mimicked Carolyn's voice.

Willie walked in and did not say hello. He got straight to the point. "Who in the hell are you?" he asked.

Devin smiled, "Okay, Uncle Willie, you got me."

Willie shook his head, "Then why in the hell does Lisa think you are someone by the name of Chris Weber?"

Devin explained to his uncle everything that had happened on the road, as well as the events in the hospital, which was where Kandy and Lisa had first seen it.

"Do you think it followed you?"

"I do not know. It has only watched us up until now."

"Why did it attack my child?" Willie was furious.

"Because she was pregnant, Uncle Willie," Devin said.

Willie was confused. "Why? Don't want us to procreate? I do not understand. Carolyn has a child for you, Jason, and Kandy has a son. Why was she attacked now?"

"Because their focus was on Devin and me. They did not know about Lionel because I did not allow them to see me with Carolyn and she gave birth to Lionel in New Orleans, and they probably thought that Kandy was dead, just as you did."

Devin was deep in thought. "We are missing something here because I believe that Ellen has been stalked by someone before I arrived. It knew that Kandy was your daughter, or someone found out; this is about making you suffer, Uncle Willie. Someone knew Kandy was your daughter and someone wanted Lisa to reunite the two of you." He thought about what Lisa had said, she felt like she was a part of something sinister and she was. Lisa was the key to all of this. "This is not a one-man operation," Devin said. "Someone is giving the orders and others are carrying out the orders. They could work in the medical field or law enforcement."

Devin played out a scenario for Willie and Jason but first asked Willie how he became a client of Lisa's. "The judge ordered me to talk to a psychiatrist and one of the officer's recommended her," Willie said.

"Just as I thought," Devin said. "They sent you to Lisa for a reason. They have been watching Lisa and they have been listening to her sessions. They knew I was Devin Jones and not Chris Weber and that I worked in law enforcement. Lisa and Susan Milo had been investigating the death of Elmira, and someone knew that she would put together that you were Kandy's father. They put Kandy back into your life in order for you to relive her death, but she is still alive." He lowered his head, "but she would not have been if Justin had left. They messed up and they will try again, or move to the next one on the list. It is about dividing and conquering. This family has lots of secrets they will use to drive a wedge between us, and then they can pick us off one at a time; Uncle Willie, they know personal things about us all and they are using the information. Someone wanted us to suffer by watching each other die."

"I think Dr. Samuels is a part of this," Devin said. "He proposed to Lisa, telling her she needed protection and he could protect her. I think, just like with us, there are secrets among them. Whoever is calling the shots has his own reason for revenge on you and my father. Dr. Samuels thought he could win Lisa over, but he did not and now she, too, is fair game."

"Uncle Willie, we have to get everyone together under one roof, open up the communication lines. No secrets because they are going to get us all killed," Devin patted the files. "Lisa has the answer right here, we just have to figure it out, no more distraction we have to stay focused."

Jason looked at Devin; he noticed he did not mention Eddie. "Devin, Dad does not know you are alive and he is a key part of this all." He nodded his head. He would do anything to save Lisa, so he gave Jason his approval to talk to Eddie.

❧ ❧

"How is Kandy?"

Lisa yawned, "She is fine, Momma, but she lost her baby."

Ida sat down and tried to remember what the woman had said about an unborn child dying. Lisa pulled out a picture and handed it to Judy. "That is Willie Williams and I call him Poppy." Judy's eyes closed. "He will be coming around to make sure we are safe; he is Kandy's father."

Ellen looked at the picture; she remembered him, he was her angel.

"Chris wants us all to stay here together and there will be twenty-four-hour security teams around until he and Jason can find out who attacked Kandy."

Judy looked at Ellen; she was shock. She thought Ellen had truly lost her mind. She still did not believe in ghosts or men in black veils. Ellen had talked to Lisa and told her that she was going to send her back to the mental hospital and now Lisa was buying into Ellen's delusions.

"I have seen it myself," Lisa said. "It has been watching me and Chris since we left the hospital, and maybe Chris has also. This person is dangerous and we have to be extremely careful."

Lisa walked into the bedroom for a nap. "Something is not right," Ida said, "why would Chris want to hurt Lisa and his baby? He seemed to want to protect us all, why would he hurt her?"

"He will not remember her, Ida, that's why. You are so concerned about Lisa, but you didn't listen," scolded Judy.

"Well, one thing that I know for sure is that you resent her and she loves you, Judy. You fucked up your life and you want to blame everyone for it," Ida threw the picture of Willie at Judy. "Now she has given you what you have worshipped all your life."

Ellen was curious, she said, "They will make her suffer and I do not think she was talking about Chris. She said Lisa will suffer for loving Chris." Tears rolled down her face, "Chris will forget Lisa and he will come for her, too."

"You are crazy, Ellen. We should have you committed. Someone is playing a joke on you and Lisa."

Ellen lowered her head. "Well, I guess the damn joke is on Kandy, lying in the hospital fighting for her life."

Eddie sat at his computer. For the last two weeks he had been having trouble with his surveillance cameras. Eddie called his computer specialist, J.T., who had been working for an hour to get the system back up and working ."Sir, I think you should look at this." Mark and J.T. scanned through the memory of Eddie's computer. "Someone has hacked into the system." Two weeks ago Eddie's surveillance camera went out and Jeffrey Electronic Company came to repair the camera because J.T was working at one of his office buildings and was not available. Everything worked well until the computer screen shut off and restarted, and then he was looking at someone's bedroom with a little dog.

"Can you rewind the camera back two weeks ago?" Eddie asked.

"Yes," J.T. said. He clicked on the icon and that asked his destination. J.T. typed in two weeks.

Eddie looked at the screen. There was nothing at first, and then someone walked into view and stared up at the camera. The person held up a picture and then burned it. He could not hear anything, but he could see enough. The person walked out of view of the camera.

Eddie looked at the screen again and saw Devin. He was in disbelief; his son was alive and well, and now he was feeling betrayed that his son would let him mourn him, and was living with a slut and fucking her, thinking nothing of the pain he had caused him.

Eddie excused the security team when he heard one of his men say that the woman was setting a trap for Devin, that she knew who he was, and it was all about money. "I bet you five thousand dollars that she would become pregnant and try and get money from the boss."

Eddie could say nothing; he just sat and stared at the computer, he watched Devin and a woman make love. She was wearing a red teddy and did a seductive dance for him, as he sat and watched. They made love and he watched as his son moaned in pleasure as he made love to this woman. He was angry he had been betrayed. He had not talked to Jason in weeks before leaving town on a business trip. Jason had some explaining to do, to let him think that Devin was dead was unacceptable, and to have him fucking some bitch was unforgivable. He had big plans for Devin, a corporate takeover, and if that bitch thought she would keep him, she had another thing coming.

He looked up and there was Willie, "Come and take a look at this," Eddie said. "It's Devin," he laughed, "my son is alive."

Willie said nothing and that was surprising to him. He and Willie took pride in his boys, especially when he had lost his daughter in a fire. "She is living and breathing, Eddie, my little girl is alive."

Eddie went to pour Willie a drink, but he declined. "I have to meet Lisa in a while and I do not want her to think I am a drunk," Willie said. Willie talked about the hospital and all that had happened, "Devin was there," Willie said, "and Jason. Elmira and Asia were both murdered by the same person and he tried to kill Devin that night and ended up killing a man named Chris Weber instead, who Devin has lived as since the accident."

Eddie's blood began to boil, "Who is this Lisa?" He said as the voices started in his head again, "Help her. Help Lisa."

Willie smiled, "She is the psychotherapist I have been seeing and she was the one that brought me and my daughter back together." Willie looked at the computer, "Eddie, this girl is special to me and I, under no circumstances, want her to get hurt. I would like for you to meet her and listen to what she has to say. You may not be interested, but I intend to find out who killed my wife. She can point us in the right direction."

Jason walked into his father's office; Eddie was so preoccupied with what he was watching, he did not hear him come in. "Eddie," Jason said he looked up to see him standing there.

"Son, just the person I wanted to see," Eddie said. "I was wondering if you could take a look at something for me." Jason walked to the computer and saw Devin and Lisa making love. "I watched over and over again from beginning to end, not bad for a dead guy wouldn't you say?"

Jason looked stunned; how could this be happening? Who was sending this to Eddie? But he knew why, Devin was right, it is about divide and conquer and most of all distraction. Whoever sent the video to his father knew he would be pissed and that he would interfere with Devin. Lisa would be fair game; they would use Eddie to get to her.

"You son-of-a-bitch!" Eddie yelled. "You could have said something to me." He was yelling so loud his security team ran into the room. "And who is that bitch he is fucking? I will see her in hell if she thinks she is going to have Devin, and if she thinks that she is going to bribe me with a brat, then she has another think coming."

"Dad, get a grip on yourself and I will explain," Jason said. He knew that they were not being fair to Eddie. He had grieved for Devin for months, and to find out he was alive, in his eyes, was a betrayal and unforgivable.

Eddie sat and listened to Jason; he was in disbelief. "Devin was in danger from some son- of-a-bitch wearing a black robe, not to mention that his wife, Asia, was murdered in his own home. Someone had walked into his home and killed her. He did not believe it, he had security all over his home," Jason was trying to cover his ass because he knew he had crossed the line.

Before Eddie could say anything, Willie stepped in. "He's telling the truth," he said while pouring himself a drink. "Eddie, I have seen it with my own eyes. I watched this person wearing a black costume pointing at Lisa. Both of our children are alive and they are being haunted by a ghost of our past. Whoever this is, he is trying to erase any existence of us both."

Eddie did not believe any of it. Willie had defended the boys since they were born and now, he stood in front of him with this crock of bullshit. He was not buying any of it. "Jason, you tell your brother, if he does not get his ass here to see me, I will come and see him and I can assure you it will not be pretty."

Devin walked in, from the front entrance. He had hoped that Jason and Willie would be able to explain to Eddie what had happened with the accident, and he would stay away from him and Lisa until he and Jason found out who was trying to kill them. "You wanted me to see you, Dad, and here I am."

Eddie looked at him, "Is that really you, son?" Eddie wrapped his arms around Devin, whose heart was so cold he would not embrace his father. He resented him.

"Stay out of this, Dad, I am not asking you, I am telling you. I have a life, a beautiful life, and I will not let you ruin it." He looked at the monitor and watched his last night with Lisa before Kandy was attacked. "There is an impostor in your security team and everything you do, they know what is going on, and they have access to this house." He stared his father down. "You know how I know this, Dad, because I am looking at it. Someone had to have sat at this computer and wired this house to send this to you.

"Do you know what is going on, Dad? Why someone would connect you to my home? Well, I will run it down to you. Whoever this person is, they know you well. They know that the only thing you care about is control. This person knows you are a control freak and a money hungry son-of-a-bitch that has no intention on helping us find out who he is. If you are not part of the solution, you are part of the problem. If you are not going to help us, then stay the fuck away.

"That night in the hospital, I laid in that cold-ass bed, and I could feel that I was being watched. I felt helpless and confused; and for a while, I had no idea who I was and what would happen to me. But these amazing women . . ." He pulled out a picture of Ida and Judy and Ellen, "especially this one," showing a picture of Lisa, "took me in and brought me back to reality. Do you know who they are, Dad? Jason watched Eddie's expression. "I told you that there was no laughter and no joy in this house, but with them, I had it all. They were one big happy family and they welcomed me with opened arms." He pushed the picture of Lisa in Eddie's face. "Never in my life has a woman treated me as she does and I brought a fucking monster into her life."

Devin realized that Eddie did not acknowledge Ida as his mother; he just said nothing. He had kicked her to the curb and thought nothing of her.

"Do you know what happened, Dad?" He showed a picture of Kandy. "She is the sweetest girl I ever met and she lost her mother, just as I did. She is Uncle Willie's daughter and it almost killed her. She was beaten badly. It took out a scalpel to slash her wrists and cut her open." He showed him pictures of women they had known.

Eddie showed no emotions.

"Dad, this is Betty."

He looked. "No, it can't be," he said.

Devin hoped that he had reached him because the women that he loved so much had met the same fate, and it was destroying him.

"When Betty left that night, they took her from the gate, Dad, right under our noses and took her across the street; they cut her open and burned her just as they were going to do to Kandy and to the mother of your grandson, in just a matter of time.

"Let me help," Eddie said. "If someone is out there hunting my family, I want to help. Bring everyone here, where there is security. I know I have crossed the line on many occasions, but I did what I thought was right. Please, son, let me help, and we will find out together who is who around here."

"There are several of us; you need to have J.T. have surveillance cameras put in every room. Whoever this is, they know this place inside and out, which is how Mom was killed. He walked out without being noticed. We also need to check out your security team, all except J.T. We all know that he is clean, but everyone else could be a part of this because I have a feeling that there is more than one."

𝒪 𝒪

"Dr. Bryant, just the person I wanted to see."

"Eddie, I was surprised to be kidnapped at gun point by your goons."

"Have a seat, Bob. I need your help, your expertise, you might say." Eddie pulled an envelope out of his desk and handed it to Dr. Bryant.

"What's going on, Eddie? I thought we were finished doing business a long time ago. I kept my end of the bargain and so should you."

"I need you to hypnotize my son, and I will not take no for an answer. The envelope I handed you contains ten thousand dollars and when the job is over and I get what I want, I will give you another ten thousand. After that, we will not have to see each other again."

"What if I say no? It could cause irreversible damage to your son."

Eddie looked at Bob. "I will not take no for an answer."

Mark escorted the doctor out and said, "You do what the boss asks you to or I will personally take care of you myself."

Dr. Bryant returned to his office and poured himself a drink. "You're what got me in trouble in the first place. He talked to the glass filled with alcohol as he talked to another person"

There was a knock at his door; he looked up to find an older, well-dressed man standing in front of him. "Dr. Bryant, I am Dr. Klein." The older man talked funny to him, almost as if he were trying to impersonate Barry White. "I know you are a busy man, but I will get to the point. You and I both have an enemy by the name of Eddie Jones and I understand he has asked a favor of you."

Dr. Bryant looked at the older man and thought that there was something odd about him—something that scared him more than Eddie Jones.

The man reached in his pocket and Dr. Bryant began to duck. He pulled out an envelope, "This contains fifty thousand dollars. You are to do what he has asked of you, but you will make it irreversible. Devin is never to remember Lisa," he said.

I am making another pact with the devil, he thought, but this time he knew he would not live if he refused. "I will do what you ask. But can you tell me why?"

The man's voice suddenly changed; it was softer before going back to his Barry White voice. "She carries his bastard and she should pay. They all will pay." Then he stood and walked out of the room.

Dr. Bryant sat there frozen. He listened as the man had a conversation with a woman waiting for him in the lounge. He could not move. Devin had ruined this man's daughter's life also . . . And Lisa would pay. He could hear her beg him not to hurt Devin because she loved him, as her father yelled for her to shut up.

He had never thought that anyone could put fear in him as this man had. There was something unusual about him, and his voice was outrageous. He looked out of the window and watched as the man pointed at his office; he stood back, so he would not be seen. The other man was big. Bob looked again. He was the man who had attacked Jason in the bar because his girlfriend looked at him. He would never forget his voice. It was almost rehearsed as in a horror movie.

However, Jason was not afraid. "The bigger they are, the harder they fall," he said as he knocked out the man.

Eddie bragged, "That's my boy," and ordered a round of drinks for the house, and now he was out for revenge on Devin.

He picked up the phone to call Eddie, but instead called the airline for a plane ticket. He would do what he was asked, but he would not hurt another human being. He would leave a note to tell Willie what Devin must do to regain his memory after he was away and safe.

He placed the phone on the receiver. He could hear footsteps approaching, so he hid in the closet. If it was the big guy, he would die, he could feel it. He was in trouble. He stood silent and watched as the big man went through his desk, pulled out his bottle of bourbon and placed it in his pocket.

He waited for the doctor to return, but jumped when someone knocked at the door, "Bob, are you here?" It was Willie.

The man pulled out a scalpel and went into another room. Dr. Bryant laughed, "You will need something bigger than that," Willie carried a gun and he could hit a dime on a pig. Suddenly, there was quiet; the man was no longer waiting for him. After Willie left, he did also.

The doctor grabbed the phone quickly. "Willie, come back," he said as his eyes moved, but nothing else. He was paralyzed with fear, "but be careful," he said with a low voice into the phone receiver, "he is here somewhere."

Chapter 10

Lisa was exhausted; every morning she was up at six in the morning. Today, though, she had slept until nine, and her back ached from sleeping on the sofa sleeper. Chris had tossed and turned all night, too. She hoped they did not keep everyone up all night because they were both restless. Especially Kandy, who had been released from the hospital before she could talk to her about her father.

Claire looked like a stuffed animal lying on the bed with Kandy. "Girl, Claire is a hot mess," she laughed. "You know, you and Chris made so much noise, she started rubbing her hair to cover her ears." It was good to see that after all she had been through, she still had her sense of humor.

Lisa handed her a cup of coffee. "Can we talk, Kay?"

"Lisa . . ." She held up her hands, "I know what you are going to say; it's about Poppy, right, that he is my father," she pushed back her hair.

"How did you know?"

"You guys always underestimate me. I was listening when you introduced him to everyone in the hospital room as my father." Now she smiled and lowered her head. "We are not alone. He will not let anything bad happen to us. Both he and Chris will take good care of us."

Chris knocked on the door and kissed Lisa good morning.

"You all don't stop." Kandy said. "Give it a rest," when he wrapped his arms around her and whispered, "It's not your fault, just so you know." She started to feel sad because she had not talked to Kevin. He had not called her; she checked her phone daily and he should have been back in town days ago. However, he had never called. "I need to put my words together for Kevin, and I needed some alone time, but . . ." Now she threw up her hands, "he never called and I have nothing to tell him."

Lisa carried a tray of food to Jason and Chris. There was frustration written all over their faces. "Jason, I am sorry to hear about your brother," she said. "There has been so much going on, that I never got to say anything. I know it is no consolation, but you have now gained sisters and, later, I can tell you about the guy I have fallen for." Jason smiled and looked at his brother. Something was strange; the two of them seemed close and preoccupied.

"What's wrong, babe?" she asked Chris. He had been acting strange for a few days now.

"Lisa, we have everything right here and we just can't see what the hell is right in front of us. There is a starting point to this, but where?" Lisa pulled out the file that read JIMMY AND JAMES JONES. "Here is your start."

"James and Jimmy Jones were burned," Lisa said, trying to get her point across. She was no detective, but it seemed more than logical to start at the beginning. "Whoever is out there did not start ten or fifteen years ago. They have been out there for a long time. Before they were burned, they were shot at close range in the chest." Lisa pulled out a piece of paper and continued. "They were shot with a gun registered to James Jones Sr. Guys, he was shot with his own gun. According to Momma Ida, he was a big man, and he trusted only one or two people, so how would someone get the ups on the two of them, take James's gun, and shoot the both of them? How did they know he had a gun?"

Jason and Devin looked at each other, "Someone else was in the car with them."

Lisa then pointed out the date the murder took place. She pulled out a file on Melissa S. Thomas's death—same date, two years later. "Look at how she died, though. Both wrists slashed and burned, same as Elmira Coleman and Asia Jones." She then pulled out files on seven other women. We have to find the connection between these files. Their wrists were slashed, stomachs were cut open, and they were burned. I talked with Detective Milo. Asia Jones had gas poured on her, which means they were interrupted before they could finish her off.

James Sr.'s son is James Eddie Jones Jr., who was the husband of Asia Jones, right? I think the grudge against the family came right after the death of the father and son. But some of the files were in between, some were before Asia's death, and some after. For all we know, it could be a family member." Lisa handed over the file of Patricia Samuels, "She was killed the same way, both wrists slashed and she was burned."

"That is what they were going to do to Kandy," Devin said, as he looked at the files of four of the women he dated in the past, and three of Jason's. They cut open the stomachs to see if they were pregnant."

"It is not a family member," Jason said, "but it is someone that knows the family very well." He did not know if Lisa had made the connection between Asia Jones and Elisabeth Jones Stanford. "Momma Ida is my grandmother," Jason said, "and Eddie Jones is my father."

She smiled, "Do you live in the big house on Sweet Tea Court? Momma and I would sit outside of that house for years. She wanted to see her grandsons because your father would not let her be a part of your lives, and now she has to mourn the loss of a grandson that she never met but has loved from a distance his whole life."

The men were both impressed with Lisa. They were so personally involved, they could not see anything. It was time for her to know the truth about him. Keeping a secret from her was clouding his judgment. He did not know how she would react, so he just said it. "Lisa, I have something to tell you," he sighed. "My name is not Chris Weber. Its Devin Jones."

Her jaw dropped. "You have your memory back, honey. That is great!" Before Devin said anything else, Jason shook his head. It was better that she did not know he knew he was Devin from the beginning and he never had amnesia.

"Everything started coming back to me when you gave me the file on my mother—Asia Jones was my mother. I was the one who found her that night, and on the road, I saw the person that killed her."

She walked up to him and kissed him. He had his memory back and he did, as she asked, he did not forget her.

"The files of the other women were women we dated or my father dated. They are taking away our ability to procreate."

She walked into his arms. Her body was shaking. She had not seen her period and now she was afraid she would end up like the others.

"He is a coward," Jason said. "They shoot men and then burn them, but women . . . They cut their wrists to make it look like suicide. That is the key—someone committed suicide and they blamed James Sr. For it, a women Devin said and now they are killing women in the same manner as she died.

"Momma Ida has a daughter no one has seen. Maybe she has a grudge against her brother and is taking it out on his family. Momma never talks about her. She has only acknowledged her once since I have known her. Maybe she is the missing link here. Maybe she married a psycho who feels that Ida abandoned her daughter."

"How does it feel to have your memory back?" Kandy asked Devin. "Oh my God, now that explains everything . . . The way Jason looked at you when he first walked into the house.

I thought the two of you were going to start arm wrestling; it freaked me out."

Devin laughed as he held Kandy. "Welcome back, baby girl, you are one of the most amazing people I have ever met."

"He is right, Kay. Most people would be hiding in a corner somewhere, but you came back stronger than ever. I will take a page from your book. It would have been easy for me to tell someone they were a survivor and should not let someone make them live in fear. But it's not that easy."

Kandy smiled. "I feel safe when I am with you guys, and now I have my father to look after me. He explained everything to me. How could Aunt Tina do something like that, take away the only family I had left? She did not want me. She tolerated me, but she did not want me. I will never speak to her again."

"What do you think happened with your father and his sister?"

"I don't know," Devin said. "My father has never mentioned a sister to us, only a brother, who we know died."

Lisa and Devin went through Ida's photographs, and there were no pictures of her daughter, only James and Jimmy. There were a few of Judy and the two men, however. Devin pulled out a photo of the Jones family. This photo included another man standing in a family photo who was shorter than the others and wore glasses.

"Who is this?" he asked her.

She shook her head. She had never seen that picture before and there were others with the same man. Devin placed it in his pocket. He wanted to ask his father about the man. He then pulled out a photo of his father, who had to be about six years old, and there was his brother Jimmy, opening Christmas gifts. There was a girl. It was Judy and she had to be at least eight. She was there in her nightgown, while the boys were in their pajamas.

"I think we can rule out the sister theory." Devin handed Lisa the picture of the family. She does not exist in any of the photos. If Ida has a daughter, she was long gone before my father came along." He looked at the picture again.

"Has your father ever talked about Judy?"

Devin sifted through more pictures. "Yes, he said that his cousin came to live with them when she was little."

"His cousin," Lisa repeated.

Devin stopped and looked at her. "He said his mother's sister died and her daughter moved in with the family, and they were pretty close growing up. Poor Judy, she must have been really young when her mother died. It must have been hard for her to live in the shadow of the Jones boys."

Lisa handed Devin a picture where Jimmy and James were laughing and having a good time, while Judy was in the background. "She looked sad in a sense, which is why when I first met her, she asked if I would be a caretaker for her friend, not her aunt. She resented Ida."

Devin shook his head. "Why would Ida give up her child in order to raise someone else's child?" Lisa knew she and Devin were thinking the same thing—it was not her husband's child.

"We have to find out where Judy and Ellen fit into all of this also." He had a feeling about them both. There was a connection, but he had to make sure his thinking was right. "The two of them have been best friends for a long time, Judy was married before, and both Ellen and Ida had been in the mental hospital. Judy said her husband was cheating on her, and he left her for another woman. The two of them became each other's shoulder to cry on. Ellen was messed-up about losing her son, and Judy had lost her husband, in a sense. She dated other men, but Ellen could not get past her loss."

He tapped his finger on the desk. "Both Ellen and Ida were in the same mental hospital?"

"Yes," she said. "Judy said that she had no idea that Ellen was there, but when she went to visit Ida, she saw Ellen."

He wrote down on a piece of paper that he wanted to know who had Ida and Ellen committed. Devin wondered if Ellen's son was taken or did he die? He needed to find out; her being friends to Ida and Judy could be what had put her life in jeopardy. He looked at a photo of Judy and Ida together; he did not say a word, but he was deep in thought. There is not one picture of Ida's daughter. He wondered if Judy was Ida's daughter. He remembered his father saying his cousin Judy came to live with his family when Ida's sister was ill. Then he thought that Ellen might be Ida's daughter and wrote a note of where he and Jason would start their investigation.

Lisa pulled out a picture of Jimmy Jones. "Look at him," she said, unable to take her eyes off of him. "He is perfect. His eyes are grey, and they fit his complexion perfectly. And he has long wavy hair," she said. "He is beautiful, but there is a sadness." Her stomach began to get that feeling again.

Devin took the picture and looked at it. "I will hold on to this for a while, I would like to get Jason's opinion on something." He kissed her. "No more distractions, baby, you have just opened up my eyes." He sighed, "because of secrets, we could have lost Kandy. So, as of now, there will be no more, and I now have all of the information that I need to put an end to all of this." He took one of the family pictures of the short man, *I have to find out who you are* he thought.

Claire ran into the room and scratched at Devin's leg. Chris Weber or Devin Jones, it made no difference to Claire. "She loves you," Lisa said. "Claire has a vet appointment coming soon."

Lisa smiled. She had no secrets from Devin now. Should she tell him she had not had her period, or should she wait until after her appointment, which both she and Claire had on the same day?

Devin pulled Lisa into his arms. "Claire loves me, and what about her mother?" As he planted a kiss on her lips. He lifted her onto the desk, opening her legs, and pressed his body into her, so close she could feel his erection.

Lisa kissed him softly. "Oh yes, Mr. Jones, Claire's mother loves you also."

"And I love . . ." before he could finish his statement, his body went limp.

"Baby, you are heavy," she said.

He moaned.

"Devin, what's wrong?"

He reached behind his back, something was stuck in his back and he was beginning to feel tired.

Lisa looked up to see there were two men; they were not wearing robes or hoods, she could see them perfectly. "Why are you here?" she asked. She felt uneasy and knew who was behind this. "Please don't take him," she begged. She looked into the eyes of the smallest one.

"Mark, maybe we can tell the boss we could not find him."

However, the larger of the two was not having it. "The boss sent us for him and, J.T., you are an asshole."

"You can't have him." She held onto him. She tried fighting for him. She screamed, "Devin, wake up!" She tried, but she could no longer hold him, when Ellen and Judy and Ida entered the room.

Momma Ida had a broom stick. "Leave him alone."

"You bitch, get your ass out of here. We are just following orders," Mark said.

"When Ellen joined in to help Lisa get Devin out of the hands of the man Mark, she was slapped so hard she flew over Lisa's desk sending pictures flying to the floor. Lisa was then shoved so hard, she went into the wall head first, putting a hole in it the size of a basketball.

Ellen got to her feet, but Lisa did not move at all. J.T. knelt to check her pulse. "If Lisa dies, Devin will come after us, blood for blood," he said to Mark.

"Fuck Devin!" he yelled. "I am not afraid of him."

"This is not right," J.T. said when Skeet ran into the room.

"What is taking so long?" When he looked at Lisa, "What happened to her?" He checked her pulse. Lisa was breathing, but she was not moving.

Judy ran to the phone to call Jason.

"You two are a bunch of pussies, fuck her!" Mark screamed. "She is a whore and fuck Devin, too" he yelled as he carried him to the car.

"Jason, please come," Judy said, "two of your father's employees have come and taken Devin, and Lisa is hurt pretty badly."

Willie and Kandy arrived back at Lisa's house. Willie thought that Eddie was sending security to watch over the woman when he saw Eddie's chauffeur Mark pulling away from the curb at Lisa's house.

Kandy and Willie walked in; they could hear the commotion upstairs. Willie was wondering why the women would leave the front door wide open for anyone to walk in.

"Call the ambulance," Willie said as he checked for a pulse. "How long has she been out," he asked, "and where is Devin?"

"Two of Eddie's people came and took him away. He was out cold," Judy said. They walked in the door when his back was turned. He and Lisa were looking at pictures and they shot him with a tranquilizer dart."

Devin was right, Willie thought, *they keep letting their guards down and there are consequences to pay.* He had been so busy talking Eddie out of his plans, he did not think to have any of his men look after the house and let Devin know what his father's plans were for him, and now Lisa was paying the price for their incompetence.

Jason ran up the stairs. Lisa was lying on the floor with a lump on her head. "What the fuck happened?" He shouted, looking at Willie.

Lisa started to moan in pain. "My head hurts," she said as she tried to get up but could not. She leaned her head against the wall and it began to feel numb. She had blacked out earlier, but now it was all coming back to her. She grabbed her stomach and began to cry. She would not see Devin again before finding out if she were carrying his child. Now she felt empty.

"Don't move, Lisa," Ellen said. "You might have a concussion."

Jason knelt beside her and said, "You are going to be fine," when he noticed she had her hand on her stomach, "he thought of Carolyn's deception when she said to Lisa that she would need a medical procedure to have a child.

"They took him," she said, and then she became quiet again.

Jason looked at Ellen for the first time since he had entered the house. She had blood dripping from one side of her face, and that one side of her face was swelling. She had been so concerned with Lisa; she had not realized that she, too, needed to see a doctor. Jason watched as Ellen's eyes pleaded with Lisa, as if her life depended on her survival.

ꙮ ꙮ

"Lisa has a concussion, we need to keep her here for observation because . . . " Dr. Winn paused, "Lisa's pregnant," he said to Willie and Jason. "She had a bad fall and we need to make sure there is no internal bleeding."

"Will she lose the baby?" Willie asked.

"As far as I can tell, she went head first into the wall, which softened her fall when she went down. If everything is good, I will release her tomorrow. She is awake and she wants out today, but I need her to stay here one night."

"What about Ellen?" Jason asked.

"Her injuries are much milder, she will be release today."

"Thanks, Doc."

"I'll bring Ellen to you when we are done with her."

"We are screwed. Devin called me and said that he thinks he knows who is behind all of this and, if Eddie goes and does something stupid, then we have to start from the beginning and time is not on our side. This person is now becoming physical, and he is out for blood."

Willie walked to the door and looked out. He hated hospitals and had never stepped a foot into one, but this place had become his second home, lately. "Your father called Bob Bryant right after he talked to Cecil Dubois."

"Darlene's father?" Jason asked as Willie shook his head.

"He wants Devin to marry Darlene, and Bob is there to program him to do so, and that means that Lisa and her unborn child are dead."

Jason was angry, "Let him fuck himself, Uncle Willie. I am so tired of trying to keep the peace with the two of them. I finally got Devin to forgive him and he turns around and does something like this." Jason was outraged.

Ellen walked into the room, she knew instantly something was wrong. "How is Lisa?" she asked.

They wondered if they should reveal her condition, but they knew that it was secrets that were destroying them. "Lisa's pregnant and she has to stay overnight."

Ellen's mouth opened. She was happy and sad at the same time. "They will take the baby," she said in a low voice. The two men looked at each other. She and Judy wanted Lisa to have Devin's baby, but now he is gone what will they do. "Eddie will not let Lisa keep Devin's baby." *Could this be what Lady Clem was talking about?* "I will stay with her, if you want me to."

"No," Willie said, "you need to rest in a bed; she will be fine. I will stay with her tonight and bring her home in the morning and I will have someone stay at the house with you ladies."

Jason and Ellen made their way back to Lisa's house. Jason could tell that something was on Ellen's mind; she wanted to talk to him. "Ellen, I know all of you care a lot for Devin and you feel comfortable with him, and I know he feels the same, he cares a lot for all of you. But he is not the only man in your lives. I am here and you will find that I am more understanding than you know. If there is something I need to know, please talk to me."

Ellen knew it was time she could tell him her side of the story, and hope that he would understand. She would now tell him she was his mother and that Lady Clem said they would take Lisa's baby.

"I had just turned nineteen and started classes at the community college." She needed him to know that she was not some loose woman, chasing men. Eddie was the only man she had ever loved.

Before she could say another word, Carolyn started beating on the truck window. "What the hell happened and where is Lisa?"

Jason started trying to calm her down, "Let's go inside."

Ellen's eyes welled up. She had lost her opportunity. Carolyn wanted to occupy all of Jason's time, Devin was gone now, and Lisa would be vulnerable. Carolyn wanted to fight and she was winning; she would never let her have a moment with her son.

"What happened to Lisa?" Carolyn asked. She looked over Ellen as if she were not there.

"Lisa and Ellen are both fine. Eddie sent two of his men for Devin, and Lisa and Ellen tried to stop them, and they both ended up in the hospital."

"They were not the only ones to get hurt," Ida said. "I hit one of them assholes with that broom and he yelled like a little girl. And if I'd had my cane, I would have knocked him the fuck out," she said, "There would have been some sad singing and all night coffee drinking."

Jason laughed, "Which is probably what pissed him off."

"Devin . . ." She said. "Jason, what are you talking about, honey, are you okay?"

"Yes, Carolyn, I am fine." Jason was going to have to deal with a guilt trip from her. Still, there could be no more secrets. "I cannot explain now. Before any more damage is done, I have to go and see Eddie." He kissed her and said, "We will talk later."

Christian and Ben walked in. "How is Lisa?" They both like her and remembered how much she talked when they were having lunch with her. They had guarded many people. However, none of them would prepare lunch and talk with them as much as she did.

Ellen thought of the man Mark and how he called Lisa a whore. "Jason, before you leave, there is something about that Mark guy that works for your father . . . When Ida joined in. "He had so much anger that if the other men would not have been there, then Devin would have been in trouble. He hates your brother with a passion."

Jason listened as everyone talked about Mark and his actions and begged him to be careful. "He is up to no good," Ida said, "trust me, honey, I know these things."

He looked at Christian who said, "I told you from the beginning there was something fishy about him."

Jason nodded his head. "We will take care of Mark, but first, I have to stop Eddie from making a fool out of himself."

"Ellen, I have not forgotten you," he placed a kiss on her cheek. "Christian, make sure nothing happen to my girls," he said before he walked out. He now knew why Devin loved them all so much. They were so loving to each other and to the ones they love. Devin said he felt like he was where he belonged and now Jason had the same feeling. He had the missing pieces of his life. He thought of what Ellen was saying . . . They would take her baby . . . And what she wanted to tell him before Carolyn interrupted.

Dr. Bryant worked his magic with Devin, and then Eddie walked in. He needed to test the waters before the doctor was allowed to leave. Dr. Bryant snapped his fingers three times and Devin did not respond. "What you all gave him has not worn off. He should be awake by now."

Devin opened his eyes; he sat up and said, "Dad, you have any aspirin? I have a headache."

"Maybe Lisa could bring some," Eddie said.

"Who is Lisa?" He said.

Eddie smiled; however, he was not quite convinced. "Hang around, Doc. I'm not done, yet."

"Whatever you say, Eddie; I will just pour myself a drink."

Over the next hours, Eddie said Lisa's name several times because he needed to make sure that the doctor's hypnosis worked. Eddie called Ida and Ellen and, at no time, did Devin respond. He even became hostile and asked if he was losing his mind; he did not remember any of them.

"Where is Devin, Dad?"

"Hey, Jason, I was just about to call you," Devin said.

"Lisa is in the hospital."

Devin looked confused, "Who is this Lisa and do I know her?"

"Devin, the girl from the fashion show."

Jason had thrown a curve ball. Eddie had no idea that Devin had seen her before he became Chris Weber.

"What happened to her?"

Jason threw up his hands. He was tired, his brain was on overload, and this psycho doctor his father hired was drunk. "In forty-eight hours it will all be over." He had an idea what that meant, and he could only hope.

"Jason, I am coming with you. I can't find my car and, since you are here, I still want to take you up on your offer."

Jason himself now was confused. Devin came downstairs with a duffle bag and then he remembered he and Devin had talked about him staying at his place until the home he had purchased was ready.

Before Devin walked out he said, "I will be back in a day or two to pick up my other things."

Eddie nodded his head; he had work to do if he was going to get Devin to marry Darlene in a week.

Dr. Bryant was beckoned back into the Jones estate, "What can I do for you, my lord?"

"When Devin returns in two days, you will need to reprogram him; he is to marry Darlene in a week."

The doctor nodded in agreement. Now, Mr. Jones, if you could be so kind as to get one of your goons to give me a ride, I would be so grateful. The doctor was happy. *In two days, you asshole, I will be on a beach somewhere*, he thought as he rushed home to pack. He hoped Eddie would not have him watched. He did what he was asked, he removed Chris Weber from Devin's memory and bought himself time when he told Eddie that he could only do one thing at a time, and that one request might interfere with the other.

He was home free. At least he thought so, when he looked up and saw Willie, who pulled out a canteen of vodka. "Don't you guys have anything better to do than to harass little ol' me?" Dr. Bryant looked at Willie, "I did what I was asked," and his hands began to shake.

"You did Eddie's job and now you are going to do a job for me; you are going to tell me how to reverse this memory loss thing you did to Devin."

Dr. Bryant pulled out a bottle of water. "You're playing on a different team. Devin got this Lisa girl pregnant, and this guy wants to kill her, and Eddie is going to let him so he can keep his hands clean. He wants to remove her from his life." Willie said nothing. "That's it," Dr. Bryant said. "Eddie knew she was pregnant, and he is going to let this psycho kill her. He was having a guilty conscience and now another innocent woman will suffer for what he has done. Eddie has never taught his sons how to be humble; they have never apologized for anything.

They would break young girls' hearts and now a father wants Devin to pay."

Willie was tired of the doctor's Eddie bashing. "I am going to ask you one more time. How do we reverse Devin's memory loss without causing him any harm?"

The doctor smiled in a sinister way, "They are going to kill her," and he laughed and cried at the same time. "If you had not come that night, then I would be dead," he stared at the wall. "Do you think that Devin really loves her? Willie, do you believe in fairytales? "You seal it with a kiss."

Willie was tired, and his patience was getting thin. He grabbed the doctor and dragged him into the bathroom. "I am going to blow your drunken ass to hell if you don't start talking, okay?" He said.

"I had to buy myself some time; they want Devin to suffer. If he really loves her, then he will do right by her and if she loves him, she will forgive him for Eddie indiscretion. He turned away, "Those boys have never had to take responsibility for their actions, they don't know the words 'I am sorry' and neither does their father. But Willie, they had better learn before it is too late. Eddie wanted his son's memory erased," he then stood up, and Willie thought the doctor was sober, because he stood straight up. "If they get a girl pregnant, Eddie will take care of it for them." Now he had a life and he would have to become humble to get it back. "There are different players in this game," he said, "and I just want to get away." He began to cry again, "They are going to kill her, Willie, and it will be all my fault. When you see Jason, tell him to start with the bar fight, and if Devin has not regained his memory, then I will call you in a few days if I am still alive. In forty-eight hours he will feel her pain."

He stopped and then started again, "I thought Eddie was a psycho, but he has competition for first place. He asked me to come back and program Devin to marry someone named

Darlene. Willie, I have destroyed one life, and if I stay, I will be forced to destroy many others."

Willie put Dr. Bryant on the plane. The doctor had paid his dues to Eddie and now he had to wait forty-eight hours until Devin regained his memory. Eddie had put Devin's fate in the hands of a man that hated him with a passion. Even if Eddie had a change of heart, the doctor would only make things worse and not better. Devin would pay for what Eddie had done.

Chapter 11

Mother pulled out her special oatmeal doodle cookies from the oven. She stopped and checked herself to make sure when father came down for lunch, she would take his breath away. She had been listening to his conversation with his associate and it was time for her to make her move. She had asked for a child and found out that it had been killed. She had sobbed all night long, only to find out that there was another one that would change her life forever. She needed the baby and she knew just how to get it.

"Hello Mother, you look beautiful as ever," Father said, as he sat down and mother began to serve him.

"I made your favorite today," Mother stopped and grabbed her back. "I don't know how much longer I can stay on my feet for such a long time. I have been up since five this morning baking for your guest."

Father did not know what to say. Mother would no longer have a child in a few months; the family had decided that they would not allow a child to be born to Carla Coleman, a woman who would have carried the child that Mother would raise as her own. Mother, about your child . . ." She looked at him, and he was mesmerized by her beauty. He was getting hot just looking at her. "Mother, your child died."

She wanted to pass out. She grabbed her head. "How did you let this happen, Father. You promised me a child. You promised me years ago that I would become a mother."

"I kept my word to you," he said. "I have given you everything you have asked of me. You wanted a family and I delivered."

She raised her voice in disgust. "I want my own child, a newborn. I need to hold and cuddle my baby. I want to breast feed." Mother could say no more. She ran to her room.

Father made a phone call. There would be a child for mother after all. "Mother, can I come in?"

She lay with her back to him. Her eyes were stained with tears. She needed a distraction, she need to be with her loved ones. She was competing with her own daughter for a family and if her daughter got the child, then her life was over and Father, the leader of the family, had deceived her.

"Mother, you are going to be a mother soon and guess what?"

She turned and looked at him, she was so happy. "Father, please tell me, Father that it is a girl."

He smiled, "Yes, it's a girl," and she hugged him, which is what he liked. "Look at what you did," he said in his pouting voice, "Daddy's got a hard on." He walked out of the room to get prepared before the others arrived. He entered the lovemaking room, as he called it, and dropped his robe, revealing his naked body.

"We have a problem," Father said. He turned to Simon, his first-born son. "Devin Jones is still alive. James and Al wanted to prove that they could be as ruthless as Simon, but they fell short." He assigned the death of Devin to James. James ran away, but Simon showed no mercy and he made sure the jobs were complete. He always burns his prey after he guts it.

"Carla, she too is still alive. He watched from a distance as Devin cradled her in his arms. Now we can let her and her father watch each other die." Simon said Father gave praise to a job well done, "Carla was punished for her actions, a fornicating slut, and now Carolyn has been added to the hat; the hat is used to pull the name of the one that will die next. She, too, must die.

She is a she-devil bitch," he said. "And now she will fear what the others already do.

Lisa has to die. She has not quite done her job, but she is close. But Mother still wants a child and I know just where to get one. Lisa Washington is now pregnant with the child of Devin Jones. The family thought they had killed him. He has escaped death once, but he will not do it again.

The cop, Susan Milo, has also served her purpose. She has been looking into matters that do not concern her. She can die. Both she and Lisa together," he said, "because I want to be fair. They have made our presence known to the Jones family and it is time for their departure." He laughed deeply, "One day, Devin will remember and he will mourn the loss of the bastard that she carried and took to the grave with her."

❧ ❧

"Lisa, I know you are being released from the hospital and I know I am probable the last person you want to see, however, I need to see you. I am sending you a fax. I think you are on the right track, but this is much bigger than both of us. I have to call in the big dogs." Susan walked through the parking lot. She hated talking to a recorder. She started to fumble with her keys as she approached her car. "There was no Lenny Samos, but we found a Lenny S."

"Detective."

"Yes," Susan turned to find someone very tall standing there, wearing a long black gown. It almost looked like a black wedding dress and the face was covered with a long black veil.

"He is here, Lisa. Oh my God!" Susan tried to reach for her gun, but he was too fast. She screamed and he placed a towel over her nose, he wanted to cut her throat but father said that it was forbidden, so he cut both wrists gently. His signature. She could not die yet; she and Lisa had to die together.

Lisa looked at her phone. Susan had left her a message she knew she should answer. She didn't want to answer questions about Devin and Chris, though. Besides, Jason would be at the house soon and she needed a shower. She looked at her fax machine and noticed a picture of a man. She did not have time to study it, so she placed it in her briefcase.

Jason was having coffee with Ellen, "Good morning, Lisa."

Ellen poured her a cup of coffee and said, "You only get one cup." Ida pulled out homemade biscuits and jelly and bacon. "Just how you like it," Ellen said, "over hard."

Carolyn walked in and said, "Jason," and he noticed a little disappointment in Ida and Ellen when she walked in. Carolyn could rub people the wrong way, but he hoped that they would still feel comfortable talking with him.

Ida was shaking; everything Lady Clem had said was now coming true. She wondered if she should say something to Jason about their visit.

Carolyn grabbed her head. "Are you alright, baby?" She wrapped her arms around him and said, "We found the body of a patient. Apparently, she had been dead for a while. She had her identification on her. Apparently, she had fallen down the elevator shaft."

Lisa gasped. She remembered when Carolyn had almost fallen.

"Her name was Maxine Turner."

Lisa grabbed her stomach and ran to her bedroom and closed her door. She had remembered her . . . Dr. Samuels had killed Maxine Turner.

Before Devin arrived, Jason wanted to talk to everyone about what was happening. "Eddie had a hypnotist erase Chris Weber from Devin's memory."

"What does that mean?" Ida asked.

"It means, Momma, the last five-and-a-half months of his life are gone and that means all of us. He went back to a day before the accident and he does not remember the accident or being in the hospital. He spent the night with Jason and me last night," Carolyn said.

"I had to fill him in again with all that we have worked on and we can take it from there." Jason looked at Lisa. He and Ellen and Willie were the only people who knew she was carrying his child. He could only imagine how she must feel to look at him, and he would not remember her.

Lisa excused herself from the table. She needed a minute to catch her breath as she lay across the bed they shared. Tomorrow she would go to work and return home to a memory. Devin knocked on the front door. Jason opened the door, and Devin walked inside. They walked to the kitchen, where Ellen was preparing breakfast.

"Devin, would you like some coffee?" Ellen poured him a cup, and she prepared his breakfast just as he liked it. She cut his biscuit and buttered it, and placed it on a hot skillet to get crispy. "Eggs over easy and bacon crispy. Just the way you like it," she said.

He looked at Ellen. He did not recall ever meeting her and yet, she knew exactly how he liked his breakfast. He looked at Jason, "How did you meet these people? They are amazing." He smiled and remembered him and his brother saying they needed women in their lives, and now Jason has found women that were doting on him.

Jason smiled, "They were yours first, baby brother."

Devin looked at him strangely because he had no idea what Jason was saying.

Lisa screamed. She had listened to her messages and could hear Susan being attacked. Devin and Jason ran to her aid, she was sitting on the floor crying. Devin picked her up and placed her on the bed. She played her message from Susan for them, her hands shaking.

"Why would they kill a cop?"

"A few reasons, Jason. First, she was going to call in the FBI. And second, they felt that her job was done with you. You did a lot; but you have not finished, yet."

"This is a game to them, a puzzle," Jason said.

"You and Devin put some pieces together, but Eddie interfered and we are behind again; but first, we have to figure out who the players are, and second, we have to find out where Dr. Samuels fits in with all of this. He killed her and I know it." Devin had no idea what she was talking about. "He killed Maxine Turner," Lisa said.

ᔆ ᔆ

"Susan, wake up," Father slapped her face. "Good you are up."

"Who are you?" She looked at her wrist; it had been stitched up. She could talk, but only at a whisper. "Why are you doing this to me?" she asked. "Because you had fraternized with the enemy?"

"Your job is now done, Susan. But don't worry, you will not die alone," Father said with pride. "Lisa will die with you."

"You're probably wondering what is going on." He began to preach. "Lisa has become a traitor. She had the opportunity to marry a prominent doctor," he pointed his finger as he walked back and forth. "We removed every obstacle. We gave her the chance to make an honest woman of herself. Instead, she slept with the enemy." He turned a computer screen to show Susan why Lisa would die. "Look at her," it was a recording of her and Devin making love. "That slut, she is a whore and she will die like one. I will take the baby and gut her like a fish. How do I expect to pull this off, you ask." While she lay silently, he showed her a video of Eddie Jones having his son's memory erased. "There will be no one to protect her and that gives me the chance to get her as soon as tonight."

Father was angry. "And do you know what that bitch did?" he asked Susan. "She got herself pregnant. She was given a chance to become a noble woman. She was given a position at the hospital and a man that loved her, and she spit in his face. I will cut her tongue out and the bastard she carries inside of her." He stood over Susan and continued, "The two of you can hold hands and sing a sad song before dying."

Susan looked at the incubator in the room of the old house, when a tear rolled down her face. She was with the monster that had taken the lives of so many innocent women and the police never had him on their radar. "Mother wants a baby. She and daughter have not been blessed to have children, detective." Father started yelling. "And neither was I. I had brains and charm, but I could never father a child. I had what it took to get what I wanted and that was money." He walked around her, as her eyes followed his every move. "You know what gets my goat, detective? Someone as beautiful as Mother and Daughter cannot have children and God blesses sluts like Lisa." He smiled. "Mother will have a child. Tonight she will become a mother."

Father did his dance of glory, and he sang *Oh Happy Day* when he suddenly felt a revelation. "I will play my Barry White songs for you, detective." (*Just the Way You Are*) His phone rang, and father nodded his head in agreement before saying, "Tonight, I will have her tonight."

✍ ✍

Ellen and Judy cleared the dinner table. "It seems that nothing has changed," Judy said. "Do you think Devin remembers anything?"

Ellen looked at him, "Something is not right, we have to say something."

Judy remembered what Lady Clem said. "Lisa could be in trouble. So far everything she said has come true."

Ellen stopped and looked out the window. She could see someone standing there. "Judy, come here." Judy walked to Ellen and they stood side-by-side. "Do you see it?"

Judy looked, "Oh my God, Ellen. Who is that and what are they wearing?"

❧ ❧

James Sr. Was shot in the chest and Jimmy was shot in the head. Devin looked at the drawing where each man was shot. There was no blood outside of the car, which means they were shot inside the car. So, who was the third person? Tomorrow I will ask Eddie if his father said anything about someone catching a ride with him and Jimmy.

"Devin, are you okay?" Lisa asked.

"I have a headache; it feels like my head is on fire."

Lisa gave him a painkiller she had been given at the hospital. She knew it was not a good idea to give prescribed medicine to anyone, but if someone in her condition could take it, she thought it would not hurt. She laid him back and placed a blanket over him. He looked at her and said her name before falling to sleep.

"Can we hypnotize him again?" Carolyn asked.

"No, you cannot, honey. His pain is psychological; there is no telling what this doctor has done to him."

She watched his breathing, as he slept. "Your father has gone too far."

Willie and Kandy had returned from their trip down memory lane. Looking at Kandy made Lisa forget about her problems. After all she had been through, she had a glow about her now.

Willie looked at Devin sleeping on the sofa. He pulled Jason to the side. "I caught up with Dr. Bryant at the airport. He said he took away being Chris Weber from Devin's memory only long enough for him to get away from your father. He also said that he knew that Eddie knew Lisa was pregnant, so he wanted Devin to feel the pain that Eddie has caused her. He wanted Devin to hate Eddie as much as he does. If Devin wants his life back, he has to become humble; he has never apologized for anything." Willie left out the part about him reprogramming Devin to marry Darlene as of tonight, that would not be a problem. "Also, he said start with the bar fight, what does that mean? Jason, I have seen people frightened, but the doctor was out of his mind with fear. He said they came to kill him. First, they paid him to erase your brother's memory, and then the older man sent the one you had a fight with in the bar to kill him."

Devin opened his eyes and looked around the room. He looked next to him and there was Claire, wearing a red nightgown. He smiled at her when Jason walked into the room.

"How is your head? You gave all of us a scare last night."

Devin looked at Jason. "Thanks for your concern, but I have felt worse than that."

"I have arranged for Uncle Willie to take Lisa and Carolyn to the hospital this morning. Claire also has an appointment," Jason said. "I will go with you to Eddie's house; we need to ask him some questions."

Lisa walked in to get Claire. "Why were you barking last night, Claire?" Devin asked her as he rubbed her belly. "Claire barked at the window," he said. "We need to get someone to stay here with the women. Lisa, remember, do not go anywhere by yourself."

She thought Devin would kiss her. Instead, he walked away. She had hoped that by this morning he would have recovered his memory. His concern for her was not love, he was only being a cop. "Sure," she said and walked out of the house disappointed.

๑ ๑

"Eddie, we need to talk to you."

Eddie looked at his sons over his glasses. "The two of you walk into the house and I don't even get a 'Good morning, Father'? What did I do? Because when the two of you call me Eddie that means you are upset with me about something."

"Do not be comical, Eddie, this is serious." His father was trying to manipulate him and Devin. They were, however, running out of time. In a few weeks, it would be another year's anniversary since James and Jimmy died, and every year someone dies.

"Good morning, Dad," Jason said. Devin said nothing. His head was starting to hurt. It was now ten a.m. And in twenty minutes, Devin would feel the wrath of the doctor.

"Devin, are you alright, son? Did you get any sleep last night?"

Devin looked at Eddie; he could not say a word as his head was getting worse. "I am going to lay down a minute," he said. "Jason, do not leave without me."

"Dad, did your father say anything about someone catching a ride with him and Jimmy the night they were killed?"

Eddie looked up. Darlene had walked in and said, "Where is my man?"

Eddie laughed, "He just went upstairs. Jason. You remember Darlene. He will be happy to see you, Darlene," Eddie said.

"I know what he will be happy to see," Darlene said. "I know what will make him happy and I am here to give it to him."

Devin's eyes were closed. His head was getting hot. It felt like it was on fire. It actually felt like he had run into a brick wall head-first. He could feel something pressed against his chest. Someone was rubbing his body.

"Hey, baby," she said as she started kissing him.

"Lisa, baby, my head is hurting," he said. He opened his eyes. It was not Lisa so he pushed her aside. He realized she did not have on any clothes, so he stood up, but she lay down, swirling her hips.

"Make love to me, Devin."

A pain shot through his head so hard, he yelled out-loud, and went down on his knees. Eddie and Jason ran into the room; Darlene was lying in bed and Devin was on the floor, screaming in pain. "Call 911," Jason said.

Jason rode in the ambulance with Devin, while Eddie and Darlene followed. Jason waited in the waiting room while Eddie went to the coffee shop for coffee with Darlene.

"Has he suffered with migraine headaches before?" Dr. Winn asked. "We have run several tests and found nothing wrong." Jason knew Devin was healthy and that his problem was psychological, not physical. The doctor had got his revenge on Eddie, and he watched as Devin suffered. Jason could see the fear in Eddie's eyes. He only hoped that he had learned his lesson.

Jason walked past Dr. Klein. He could see Lisa running toward him, when suddenly she dropped Claire; he thought someone in her condition should not be running.

Claire ran past him, right into Devin's room. Lisa was far behind. He could hear her barks, as she entered the room. The guard turned to look and Claire attacked a doctor.

Jason and Lisa ran into the room and Claire was not letting the doctor touch Devin. The doctor had what looked like a pen in his hand. Claire snapped at his hand and the doctor jumped, dropping his pen to the floor.

"I am sorry, Dr. Klein, she is a little overprotective of him." As Lisa grabbed Claire, the door opened. It was Eddie Jones. Lisa had never seen him in person, only the pictures Ida had of him. He was with a young woman she thought was much too young for him.

"What in the hell is going on in here?" Darlene said. "Who is in charge here, and why is there a dog in my fiancé's room?" Lisa felt sick.

Dr. Samuels walked into the room, "What is the problem?"

"Ms. Richardson is my name. Who is taking care of my fiancé? We were making love and he got this headache?" Darlene looked at Dr. Samuels. "I have contacted my attorneys."

Lisa could listen no more. She bent down to pick up Claire and noticed a syringe. It was what Dr. Klein dropped, and not a pen. She picked it up and placed it in her pocket before she walked out the door. She had wondered why when Eddie Jones had walked into the room. He was so focused on her that he did not notice the doctor had suddenly turned and walked out. Dr. Klein did not want Eddie to see him.

Jason watched as Lisa walked out; he wanted to go behind her. He knew she should not be alone. But he could not leave Devin. He needed to see him open his eyes.

Dr. Winn walked in and brushed something under Devin's nose; he opened his eyes.

"How do you feel, son?" Eddie pushed past Dr. Winn as Carolyn walked into the room. "How do you feel, Devin, because you are here for the night," Carolyn said.

"No, I'm out of here," Devin tried to get out of bed and he went down.

"Devin, you have to stay," Carolyn said. "I will call Lisa, if you would like."

"Who in the hell is Lisa?" Darlene asked. "You were about to make love to me and she wants to call Lisa, you son of a bitch."

Carolyn's mouth opened, she gasped.

"And, who in the hell is this?" Darlene asked, while pointing at Carolyn.

"Why is she here?" Devin asked. "You are a son of a . . ." Then he could say no more. "I am not one of your work projects; I am not going to marry anyone for you."

"Lisa just left," Jason said.

"She was here?" Carolyn asked.

"When Darlene said she and Devin were about to make love, she and Claire left."

Darlene was not happy, she had never lost a man before. She had been the one to end relationships. "You mean the girl with the vicious dog that attacked the doctor?"

Devin looked at her then at Jason. "Claire attacked a doctor?"

"Who is Dr. Klein?" Jason asked.

Dr. Winn replied, "I don't know, he could be visiting from another hospital. He's not a doctor on this staff. Devin, if all goes well, I will have you out of here first thing in the morning." Dr. Winn and Carolyn walked out with armed security.

"Lisa took a video of the doctor when he was not looking. He is a person of interest," Jason said to Devin.

"How does Lisa fit into all of this?" Devin asked Jason. "She is just a girl I saw at the mall where does she fit into all of this?"

Jason poured himself a drink. He thought Devin would remember, but he still did not, his head was spinning. Devin knows of Lisa, but he does not remember one single person that he has lived with for several months.

He wondered if all of this was his fault. If he had told Eddie that Devin was alive, would he have handled things differently? And now his brother was in the hospital, feeling the pain of the woman he's forgotten. He would never forget the pain on Lisa's face when Darlene said she and Devin were making love when he got sick.

Jason sat up. He needed to call Lisa and tell her the truth. He knew they were being distracted, but now he was too tired to think; he took a sip of his drink when he had a revelation. Eddie was young when all of the murders started. Dr. Bryant wanted Eddie to pay for all the pain he had caused others. Maybe whoever was hunting them wanted Eddie to pay for the pain his father had caused. It was not Eddie's sins he was paying for, but the sins of his father. Jason was lying down again when his phone began to ring.

"Jason, I see it! Oh my God, he is here."

Room 212. Mr. Johnson, was playing in his head. He could see he and Lisa going into the hotel and making love. She placed whipped cream on her breast and he laid her back with her head hanging from the bed as he enjoyed the desserts from her body,

and he made love to her again. "I will see you at home, baby," she said as he walked her to her black Suburban and watched as she drove away.

Devin opened his eyes and looked around. Where in the hell did that come from? He remembered telling Jason that he would drive down and find her. He pulled out an address that she had given him at the fashion show, and thought that part of his life was missing. He did not remember finding her, but she was here, he thought. He wondered if he had been with her because of the look on her face as she ran from the hospital. He pulled out his phone and it was not the same. He lay back and he could see himself wearing a wig as she did a dance for him and again, he made love to her. He did not want to think because his head was beginning to hurt again. *I want to get out of here.* He sat in the chair and watched television while Skeet walked in with a pizza.

"You cannot sleep, either," he said.

"Skeet, I do not need a babysitter," he said.

Skeet smiled, "I know, but your father insisted, so we are stuck with each other."

He had never felt so lost in his life. How did I get here, Skeet; it's as if the last few months of my life are missing."

Skeet opened the box and handed him a plate, "That is because it is, Devin. I need my job, so you should talk to Jason and maybe he will be able to fill you in."

He looked at Skeet. "Talk to me, man, I'm lost here."

Skeet sighed. "You had a life, a beautiful life that most men could only dream about and one day soon, you will get it back. That is all that I can say."

Chapter 12

Lisa cried all the way to her car. He slept with her and now she remembered her, Darlene Richardson was the woman that she had put on a fashion show for a week before she met Chris, who turned out to be Devin. Darlene wanted to see the wedding dresses on models, so she put on a fashion show that her rich father had paid for. She was a spoiled brat who always got what she wanted, so if her rich father could not say no to her, then she would overcharge Darlene. If he could not control her then he should pay, she thought.

She opened her car door and placed Claire and her briefcase on the backseat. She started walking to the driver's side, crying. Devin was with her three nights ago, and he could go back to his old life so fast and not ask any questions. He allowed Darlene into his bed and thought of nothing. Now she knew why he did not come for her, his life was with Darlene and she and her baby would be left alone. Eddie would not let Devin accept his child with her.

She pulled out her keys when someone stepped in front of her wearing its black veil. He grabbed her and she wasted no time. She swung first and she even kicked it in the groin. She turned running and screaming back toward the hospital, when another one came out of nowhere and grabbed her, placing something over her nose. Her eyes widened with fear, she was so close and, yet, so far away before she saw darkness.

Carolyn looked out of the window in the office. There were two security guards awaiting her command, she felt like a queen on a throne. *Should I request lunch or dinner later* she thought. *This is what it feels like to be Jason's woman. She would be served.* She thought of Lisa today. *She learned that she would not be with Devin anymore, which served her right,* she thought. Devin is a Jones, and that means they would have been in-laws.

Lisa is a goody two-shoes and sometimes makes her look bad in other's eyes. She could deal with Darlene because she could be a bitch herself and Jason would appreciate it more.

She walked to the other side and looked out the window. I need to make love tonight, and Jason has been so focused on that crap with Lisa and Devin that we have not made love in a week. Lionel was out of town and she needed her man. She looked toward the street. She thought she was seeing things, so she closed her eyes and opened them again. It was still there; someone was there wearing an old black dress and a long black veil over its face. Her eyes widened in horror, her heart started to pound: it was there again!

She turned to run to her security but could say nothing. She just pointed at the window, "Call Jason, hurry! There is someone watching me!" She screamed at the men as one ran outside to have a look. Christian looked and there was no one. He walked back into the building and by then, a crowd had begun to gather. The doctor was trying to get Carolyn to calm down and she was not hearing it. He turned back to the door when he saw a dark-colored van exiting the parking lot.

Carolyn was hysterical when Jason reached her. Dr. Winn tried to calm her down also. "He was outside my window and he pointed at me." Carolyn walked back to her office with Jason and the security officers.

Jason was angry, "Where in the hell were you two?" he asked Carolyn's guards.

One of them said, "We were here all the time, sir. When we heard her scream, we ran in immediately."

"What did you see?" he asked.

"No one was there. Ben stayed with her, while I checked the perimeter and there was nothing but a dark-colored van pulling away from the parking lot."

Carolyn began to yell at the man, "Are you saying that I am crazy you son of a bitch?"

"No," Ben said, "I am just saying that they were gone before we got there."

Carolyn thought she would take advantage of the situation. She had been given a sedative to calm her down. Now she lay in Jason's arms, wearing his pajama shirt. He would not leave her side, even if she had two armed guards in the other room. She would not share him with anyone tonight. She remembered when Lisa said she wanted to make love to Devin and wear his pajama shirt afterwards, she thought it was silly and childish, but now she knew why; she could smell his scent. She reached up and kissed him, she pushed her body into his.

"What do you know about Ellen?" he asked her.

"Nothing much. She is Lisa's favorite. Lisa loves her to death, I only know she went crazy and I think she wants my man. Seriously, Jason, she looks at you funny. First Devin and now you." She kissed him. She wanted to feel him inside of her. Instead, she saw darkness.

He looked at the phone to call Ellen, but he thought it could wait. He wanted to talk to him, but he had to stay focused. It had now shown itself to Carolyn and pointed at her, just as Lisa said it had done to Susan Milo before it took her.

🌀 🌀

"Sit down, Ellen; you are getting on my nerves." Judy said.

" Lisa should be home by now; she would have walked in or called." Ellen said

"I am warning you," Judy said.

"Ellen is right," Ida said. "Lisa should have been home hours ago."

"Christian, one of Eddie's bodyguards, said that she was upset when she left the hospital. It is happening just as Lady Clem said." Ellen started to cry. "She is pregnant, and Devin does not remember her."

Judy and Ida both cried, "It is nearly midnight and she is not home." Ellen said.

Ellen picked up the phone but Judy stopped her, "If you call and she is with Devin, then Carolyn will be pissed. Let's wait, and if she does not come home in the morning, then we will call Jason."

ᗡ ᗡ

Susan had been cut open twice. She had become a human lab rat. She wondered if she died now would Lisa be spared.

The door opened and the large one was carrying a limp body. "Get my tools ready," one yelled.

She had counted and there were seven that wore the black veil. They laid it on the table as she closed her eyes. "Look, detective. I told you that you would not die alone." She looked over and it was Lisa. A tear rolled down her face as she watched her friend be slapped several times.

Someone else walked in to revive her and now he yelled, "Father, put something to her nose," and she started to cough. "You're carrying his bastard!" He yelled at her. He began to slap her over and over again.

Lisa was in shock. She began to fight back, she swung her hand and she kicked him with her high-heeled boot several times before the man called Father grabbed her. She was getting nauseated, so she lay back. She had no idea where she was or what was happening to her.

"Calm down, girl," Father said, while the other one raised her shirt and looked at the one called Father, "Take it out now."

Lisa grabbed her stomach and turned in a fetal position. When the one called Mother walked in, she wore no veil; she was a glamorous woman. Susan noticed she, too, was pregnant. But quickly realized that she was pretending to be pregnant because she would have to explain where the child she planned to take from Lisa came from.

"Is she the one?" Mother asked. She walked up to Lisa, "May I see the baby. I will not hurt it; I only want to touch it."

Lisa looked at her. There was something familiar about her.

"I just want to touch my baby," she said.

Lisa gently turned around. She knew if she was going to save her baby she would need help. Lisa watched the expression on Mother's face, she was happy. Lisa said, "If they take it out now, it will die, and you will lose your baby."

The angry one went to strike her again and Mother grabbed his hand. "You will not hurt my baby. He said I could have this baby and you will not hurt it. If you hurt my baby, so help me . . . " Mother said to them both. "You promised me a baby five years ago and you failed to deliver. You also promised Daughter one, and you killed it. You said it was tainted. I will not lose another child."

Mother walked out of the room into the evil stare of Daughter. "How do you get a child, it should be mine." She started to yell for Father. "You killed my baby and you will give her a child first. How could you do this to me?"

🌀 🌀

Carolyn opened her eyes and reached for Jason, but he was not there. He was in the bathroom shaving. She walked in and placed her arms around him.

"How do you feel?" he asked. "You gave me a scare."

She sighed. "I had a panic attack, that's all. One moment I was thinking about you and the next . . . " She did not want to repeat what she had seen. She had him all to herself for the day. She did not want Devin or Lisa to come around. She just wanted the two of them to be alone.

Jason jumped into the shower and Carolyn joined him. She wanted to feel him, she wanted his attention. She started kissing his chest and pressing her body against his. He lifted her and carried her to the bed where he gently laid her down. She opened her legs and he entered her. She was in ecstasy as he moved in and out. She moaned, "This is what I need." They were locked in passion when Jason's phone rang. "Don't answer it, Jason."

"Baby, I am sorry, it could be important."

She became angry.

"It will only take a second," he said as he gave her a soft kiss. "This better be important," he said to the person on the other end of the line.

"Jason, this is Ellen."

"What can I do for you, Ellen?"

"Ellen, you've got to be fucking kidding me!" Carolyn yelled. "Is she fucking crazy? Oh yeah, that's right, she is," she said sarcastically. "Didn't the loony hospital teach her anything?" She stormed out of bed, went into the bathroom, and slammed the door. Jason tried to stop her, but she was outraged at Ellen for interrupting them.

Ellen listened to Carolyn's outburst. She knew neither of them was pleased with her at this moment. She knew something was wrong when she went to bring Lisa coffee this morning to find that she had not come home. Lisa was in trouble just as Lady Clem said, and Ida was having a fit. "I am so sorry to disturb you, but Lisa did not come home yesterday."

Jason's eyes widened. Lisa was missing. "Goddamnit," he said. He jumped from the bed and grabbed his clothes.

Carolyn walked from the bathroom. "How dare Ellen call you? She has overstepped her boundaries and she will hear from me. Where are you going, Jason?"

"Lisa is missing," he said.

It started to flash in her mind. "What do you mean?"

"I do not know," Jason said.

"No one has seen her since she left the hospital yesterday."

The guards noticed as soon as Carolyn's moaning started, it stopped. She began to scream at Jason about his phone.

The guards listened as Carolyn started to scream. Christian jumped and went toward the door. He had worked on Eddie's security team for years and never had anyone accused him of being incompetent as Carolyn did. They were on pins and needles when Christian received a text from J.T., asking if Lisa was there with them.

Christian looked up when Jason opened the bedroom door and said, "Lisa is missing."

Jason called Devin. "Are you still at the hospital?"

"No," he said. "Me and Uncle Willie are at Eddie's." Devin knew something was wrong. He kept getting a strange feeling all night, which is why he did not sleep a wink.

"Meet me at the hospital. Lisa is missing, she did not make it home yesterday." Devin felt light-headed. Eddie and Willie could see fear in his eyes.

"Devin, what's wrong?" Willie asked.

"They got her, Uncle Willie, they got Lisa."

"Goddamn!" Willie yelled. "Bob said they were going to come for her. I thought he was drunk and we let our guards down again." He looked at Eddie, "They said they would kill her."

Carolyn wanted it to be a misunderstanding. "Maybe, Lisa is upset about Devin and Darlene, and decided to take a break from things. Maybe, she wants attention," Carolyn said, "to break up Devin and Darlene."

The two guards looked at each other. Jason looked at Carolyn. "Okay, let's say that is the case, where would she go?" Carolyn said nothing, she knew Lisa was a creature of habit; she had been in Atlanta for years, however, she would not leave her comfort zone. Something was wrong. The four of them drove back to the hospital.

The car did not stop, but Devin jumped out when he saw Lisa's black Suburban, the one he dreamed of. When Jason and Carolyn and the guards arrived, there was no sign of Lisa. They were about to leave when Devin could hear a scratching sound. He opened the back car door, and there was Lisa's briefcase and Claire's dog bag, Claire began to cry when Devin unzipped her bag, her body trembled as Devin placed her under his jacket.

Carolyn and two security guards took Claire to the vet, while the others went inside Lisa's office to check her security cameras. "Go to ten thirty," Jason said. He would never forget the time. That was the time Devin's forty-eight hours of torture was over.

All three men watched as Lisa carried Claire to the car, and she put Claire inside. Devin closed his eyes because he could see that she was crying. Then they saw it—the man in black. They watched as Lisa fought one to get away, then they saw why she never made it back into the hospital—there was more than one of them.

Willie called his security team to bring the women to the big house, they needed answers and they needed them now. Security officer J.T. walked in; he was assigned to Lisa. J.T. stood about five-six" and Devin is six-three. "Why did you leave her?" Devin yelled at him.

"She did not come back; we thought she was with you. When she heard you were in the hospital, she and Claire took off. We watched as she approached Jason and we thought she would stay with you." J.T. said.

Devin turned to Eddie; you could see the contempt in his eyes for his father. "We know where she is," J.T. said. "At least we can find her." He started to walk toward Eddie's computer. "May I, sir?"

Eddie waved his hand, inviting him to sit. "Lisa has a tracking device on her body. J.T. is an electronic geek; if you name it he can make it."

He started typing in things on the computer and suddenly picture slides started to appear. Devin was getting frustrated; he knew if they did not move soon, Lisa would die. "Nice slide show, J.T., but that does not tell us where she is."

"There," J.T. shouted, "she is in there."

He started to explain how the house keeps appearing on the boss's screen. "Someone has wired the system incorrectly. They wanted the boss to see what was happening at Lisa's house, but all of the systems are now connected. They can see this house and now we can see theirs. The boss was having trouble with the gates. When he keyed in his security code, nothing would happen. he asked Eddie to key in his code, and he placed the screen on full view. Eddie put in his code and a door opened at the house. Whoever wired the house code would open the boss's gate.

"There she is," J.T. said. "Lisa is the red dot."

"Why is it blinking?" Jason asked.

"It is her heartbeat, which means she is still alive." There was another red light flashing and Devin asked what it was.

J.T. looked at him and Eddie stepped in, "You all have to be careful. Let there be no distractions." Everyone left the house when Eddie asked, "J.T., what was the second red light?"

"Her unborn child, sir. When I was hooking her up, I told her she had two heartbeats She rubbed her belly and turned away from me." J.T. looked up at Eddie.

"He doesn't know and he won't find out," Eddie said, turning back to the screen.

Jason handed Devin a .44 Magnum. "It's dark. We have the element of surprise." He put on all of his gear, including night vision glasses. Jason noticed that Devin said nothing. "Devin, are you alright?"

"Yeah, I am fine. It is just that everything is happening so fast. Two days ago, I was having breakfast at her table and then she was taken so fast.

Jason would not lie to Devin. That was the agreement they had with each other. He had failed. While he was drowning his sorrows, he had left Lisa out there alone.

"I should have kept an eye on her. I knew better. They showed themselves to Carolyn yesterday and she panicked because she had never seen them before and I forgot about Lisa."

"I should have known that Claire was barking because they came for Lisa that night. They could not get her because we were there, and she should not have been left alone."

"Lisa was the target and we were distracted with you being in the hospital."

"They got her and we will get her back," Devin said as he prepared to do battle.

Everyone was in place. "J.T., have Eddie put in his code now."

Devin and Jason came through the front entrance, Willie and Mark covered the back, and Skeet and Thaddeus Walker covered the side of the house.

Jason had requested a background check of all of Eddie's security personal. Thaddeus stopped by Eddie's house to drop off the paperwork to Jason when J.T. got a reading on the tracking device he placed on Lisa. He offered to follow alone and wait for backup.

"Susan, are you okay?"

"Lisa, you have to get out of here," she said.

"I can't," Lisa began to cry.

"Listen to me," Susan said. "I am running out of time; you have to make a run for it. The mother wants your child. She will let you out to move around, find a way out. There are seven total, including Father and Mother; I have not seen Sister, I have only heard her voice. Don't let them burn me," she said with a tear rolling from her eye. "Amos, not Samos. Lenny Amos."

Then Susan's eyes stared at the ceiling. Lisa grabbed her and held her. She was gone and now Lisa was alone. Lisa stuck her hand in her pocket. She felt a pen and pulled it out. It was the syringe that the doctor was going to inject into Devin. It was her only weapon and she needed to use it.

She was trying to remember how many there were, seven, and the leader was the one that promised the mother her child. She noticed his hood was longer than the others, and when he thought she was unconscious, he lifted his skirt and she could see his shoes; he wore brown loafers, she remembered because one loafer had a penny in it and the other had a dime. Lisa was trying to think. Lenny Amos. What did Susan mean? But it did not matter. If she got away she would leave Atlanta to save her unborn child. "Help me, please," she yelled. The door opened, she hoped it would be Mother; she could handle a woman. However, it was not, it was one of the big angry ones, the one who wanted to kill her child; she needed to get out, it would be hard, but she had to do her best; she needed to get out and get help before they noticed Susan was dead.

"I have to use the bathroom," she said. "Please, I am pregnant and I need to use the bathroom."

He looked at her with anger, "Do not throw that bastard in my face, bitch," he said. He walked her out of the room. She could see the door and suddenly it opened all by itself. Lisa pulled the syringe from her pocket and shoved it into the neck of her captor. Before he had fallen to the ground, she ran out the door and down the stairs. She was confused; she did not know if she was in front or the back of the house, she just started running.

"Jason, Devin, she is out of the house!" J.T. yelled on the walkie-talkie. "Willie, she is coming your way. Willie go to your right," J.T. directed.

He ran to his right, then he could see something was moving. He stopped and waited in position. It was Lisa and she ran right into his arms, "I got you, baby," he said kissing her head, "I got you." She looked into his face and held on to him for dear life before her body went limp

"Devin, Jason, where are you?" Devin turned down his radio so the person chasing Lisa would not hear.

The man in black stopped and listened. He turned slowly and started doing a dance, "You will all die," he said.

Eddie watched the monitor. "What's going on J.T.?" he asked, as Ellen and Judy and Ida listened. "Why aren't they answering?" He began to panic. "Pull them out! Jason! Devin!" He began to yell. "Who is that?" He could see three people wearing black robes coming from the house. "Jason, Devin, all of you get the hell out of there!"

Suddenly, there was gunfire, and it sounded like the shootout at the O.K. Corral.

"Willie, are you there? Mark, somebody answer me." Eddie was in fear for his sons and his best friend. Suddenly, everything was silent . . . Dead silent.

"Sir, look!"

Eddie turned to see one of the men in black running back into the house; he looked in disbelief as something stood at least eight-feet tall wrapped its arm around the smaller one and, in the blink of an eye, the screen went dark and they were gone.

"Devin, Jason, answer me, please," he pleaded. It was silent for a few seconds. He did not say it, but he could not live without his boys and, if his sons had died, it would be all his fault.

Suddenly, the radio came on and he could hear what was going on. He could hear Jason ask if everyone was okay and Willie answered, "I got her; I have Lisa."

The police went into the house, Jason and Devin followed. They found the body of Susan Milo. Thaddeus checked the pulse of an unidentified man lying face down by the stairs near the front entrance. They checked every room in the house and there was no one.

"How could they have gotten out without us seeing them?" Skeet asked. "I watched as one ran back into the house," but he could not say all that he had seen because he could not explain.

They entered a room where they found life-sized pictures of themselves on electronic mannequins, which Jason recognized right away. They appeared to be the mannequins that he had seen on the road when he was searching for Devin. They had erect vibrators strapped around their waists. Jason's likeness stood tall, while Devin's lay in bed, wearing his pajamas and also Lisa's red lingerie, which had been taken from her house the day Kandy was attacked.

"How could they get out of the house without anyone seeing them?"

Jason looked at Devin, "They knew we were coming. There is a traitor on Eddie's team and I think I know who it is."

Lisa refused medical treatment. She hung onto Willie as if her life depended on it. She was confused. She did not know who she could trust. She only had her instinct and it told her he was the one. She felt safe with him, as she drifted off in silence. Devin was with Darlene, and now she was alone.

When Devin and Jason entered the room, Lisa said nothing. She did not look at either of them, she watched the floor as another man entered the room. "Ms. Washington, I would like to ask you a few question," he said. She did not look at him. She kept her face turned and her eyes to the floor. She could only see his shoes, and they put fear in her body they were the loafers, with one penny and one dime inside.

Her body began to shake and she screamed, she jumped out of bed and began to run, right into Devin's arms. She looked at him, "Please," she cried, "don't leave me. Please don't leave me here alone. I don't want to be alone." She turned to see who was the man wearing the loafers and her body went to the floor. Her body and brains were both tired, as she will soon have to accept her fate because she could run no more. She thought of the mother who wanted her to look at her, but she could not think, so she just closed her eyes and laid in silence.

"Where are you taking her?" The man in the loafers asked.

"We will be at Eddie's house."

"I will stop by tomorrow. I need to know what happened in that house while it is still fresh in her mind."

Jason looked at him, "I don't think she will ever forget."

The man started to walk away. "Why do you think she reacted that way?"

Jason wondered the same thing. He and Devin stayed in the room, and people were in and out, but she did not respond. Lisa knew something and they needed to get her out of the hospital and somewhere she would be safe.

"She was surrounded by people in hoods with a dead woman next to her." Jason looked at him. "Do I need to say more?"

"You have always been a smart ass, Jason," the man said. "Let's get drinks, guys, soon, and you can let me know what it is the two of you are up to."

"Lisa, wake up." She opened her eyes to see Momma Ida. "You have been sleeping for a while now." Ida smiled, she was so happy to see her. "Devin brought you home."

Lisa looked around the room, "This is not my home, Momma."

"I know, baby, this is my old home. It is a lot bigger now than it was when I lived here. You remember, the big house that you said you would never be in because there was big money living here?" Lisa smiled. "Well, you are in it now," she said. Ida looked around again. "This is a big ass bed," she said. "Six people could sleep in it and not touch each other." Lisa's smile faded. If this was Devin's bed, it was the bed he shared with Darlene the day she was taken.

"What's wrong, honey?" Ida asked. "You are supposed to be on bed rest."

Lisa rubbed her face, she had to get her mind right. She could not afford to be weak, she needed to get away. She talked to Ida about what had happened at the hospital. How she was left alone, while Devin was in the room with Darlene.

Her mind was racing. She remembered the man in black, carrying what she thought was a mannequin. It was wearing similar clothing to what Darlene was wearing.

Ida put her back into bed. "You are not going anywhere, honey. It is not just you that you have to worry about. I know," Ida said, "the first day of conception, I knew. Devin loves you very much." She went on to say, "Eddie made a terrible mistake this time, and he will pay."

Lisa cried, "He doesn't remember me, Momma."

Ida stroked her hair. "He will remember, we will make him remember; hell, he doesn't remember me, either, but you don't see me making bad decisions because of it. I gave that boy the best days of my life," she said, and they both laughed. "Pull yourself together, baby, and help him. When he finds out about this baby, he will be so happy," Lisa and Ida said simultaneously, "mark my words."

"I was so lonely, Momma, all I could think about was being home with you guys."

"I know about being lonely, honey. I sat in a house for months before you came along." Momma started to reminisce about her childhood. "When I was a little girl, Momma worked in the fields, and I was alone all day," she looked at Lisa with tears in her eyes. "I was an only child and Momma and Daddy worked all day long. I was allowed to help on weekends. It was hard work, my hands were blistered and I swore if I had children, they would never have to work like that."

Lisa looked at her, "You were an only child?"

"Yep," she said. She and Lisa lay in each other's arms.

"Momma, there was a picture with a man with glasses, and he was in a family photo. Who was he?" That picture was haunting her. She needed answers before she could make her get away.

"Jeffrey Thomas," she said, "he was a sweet boy and always helpful."

When Devin and Jason walked in, Lisa needed to know that they had not abandoned her. They needed to regain her trust.

"How do you feel?" Devin asked.

Ida thought she would lighten the tension in the room. "I feel fine," she said, "just this damn arthritis acting up." Momma tried to get off the bed, "I am going kill my damn self, trying to get off this bed. Where is everyone?" she asked, "We are going to have a family meeting in a minute."

Jason said, "Ooh, that sounds serious."

"I better go and change because shit might start to fly." Ida said and she walked out.

Lisa laughed. She did not want to get emotional, but she could not help herself. "Claire, I forgot about Claire. I left her in the car."

Devin sat next to her. "Claire is fine; we found her and she is at the vet." He was at a loss for words. "I know you think we abandoned you, that we did not care and, if that is what you think, you are wrong. As soon as we realized that you were out there, we went looking for you. Can you tell us what happened?"

"Susan was alive when they brought me in," she said. "There were seven and that included the mother and father, but I think that there were more. The mother said that she was promised a baby years ago." She looked at Jason. "She was promised Lionel, which is why they shot you. They wanted Lionel."

"I did not see the sister, but I did see the mother briefly; she wanted me to see her. I think she is there against her will."

They did not understand, "What makes you think that?"

"Because I was given a choice." Lisa did not know what to say, but she knew what the meeting was about—confronting the past, no more secrets.

"What choice?" Jason asked.

"I could join their family. The first chance I got, I ran for the door. I killed him," she mumbled. The two of them looked at her, "I think I killed one of them," she cried. She reached for her jacket and pulled out the syringe.

"The Dr. Klein dropped this when Claire attacked him. He was about to inject this into you," she looked at Devin. There was so much going on inside of her head, so much she was trying to remember. "I think the leader wears a different hood. He stood over me and I pretended to be sleeping, but I saw his shoes. They were loafers–brown, and one had a penny and there was a dime in the other."

❧ ❧

"She got away. That bitch got away," Father was outraged, "the incompetence." He turned to his prize possession. "Simon, if you would have been here, none of this would have happened. Your brothers are dead and that whore is out there.

"I will revenge my family, Father, but there could be a leak. We did not receive any warning that they were coming. How will they know where to find her?"

Father paced the floor. "Mother and I barely escaped," he said. "They were on us like a fly on poop. We have to narrow the field. We will get the others and work out our strategy." Father handed Simon an envelope filled with money. "Your brother's girlfriend will be here soon to wait with Mother. She was shaken by this all and you and I will drive by the Jones Estate and see what is happening."

Simon looked at the envelope. Father did not know it, but he would buy himself a good woman tonight and drink until he passed out. Tomorrow, he would work on avenging his brother's death.

He went to Big Mac, where he is well known. "Your usual, Simon?" The bar tender asked.

He looked around to see if there was any taker of his money. "Can I buy you a drink?" He walked up to a young woman, who was sitting and crying.

"No," she said, "I just want to be left alone, if you don't mind."

"I could be a shoulder to cry on," he said. He pulled out his roll of money and said, "Give the woman what she wants," he said to the bartender.

"Just a cola, please," she said.

"My name is Simon."

"Hello, Simon, my name is Jessica."

Simon listened to Jessica's problems, but when he noticed a few of his friends had entered the bar, he walked over to say hello.

"A little young for you," the man said to him.

"She is pregnant," he smiled.

❧ ❧

"Devin, do you remember me?" Ida asked.

Jason sat and listened as Devin was being interrogated by the women. Ellen jumped in, "Do you remember Lisa?" She pulled out pictures of the party and all the times they had dinner.

Devin went through the pictures. He stared at the one with Lisa wearing a red dress with the sheer side. He watched as he kissed her, and the way he held her in his arms. Ida told him about the hospital, how Lisa brought him home and took care of him, how his knee was injured, and how she massaged it every day. She started to laugh, "We teased her, saying she was getting a free feel, but she should go for more than the knee." Ida's eyes pleaded for him to remember. "Lisa and I used to park outside of the gate. One day she was squatting down and that is when I saw you first. You were driving a red sports car and you looked at her. That was before you thought your name was Chris Weber. Do you at least remember that?"

Ida was shocked at his response to her question, "Yes," he said.

"You and Lisa were so good together."

Jason thought Ellen would let the news of the baby come out. Instead, she kept it in. Judy told him about Kandy being attacked by someone wearing a black gown and veil, and pulled out pictures of her and him.

Devin sat and listened. "So, you are saying I was in an accident, Lisa brought me from the hospital and took care of me."

"Devin, the two of you were so good together. She loved you so much and I believe that you loved her. You didn't let her go," Ellen said. "You were taken from her."

Devin looked at Jason. "Tell him, Jason; tell him what your father did," Carolyn demanded. Everyone was so focused on Devin that they did not hear Willie and Carolyn walk in.

"Eddie had Mark and J.T. with Skeet as the driver, to come and drug you and in the process, Lisa ended up in the hospital. Eddie had your memory erased of Chris Weber, which is who you lived as when you met Lisa."

"We have lost him," Ellen said. Ida and Judy would be fine. She and Lisa, however, were on their own.

"Her eyes are so sad," Devin said to Jason. "I have to talk to her." He wrapped his arms around her and said, "You are wrong; you have not lost me." "I remember some of the things you are saying. I remember her from the mall and from outside of the gate . . . " Something started to happen to him. He suddenly remembered kissing her at her home. Devin went upstairs, he wanted to talk to Lisa. Something was drawing him to her, and if he loved her before, he would love her again.

Jason pulled Willie aside, "He should remember by now; the forty-eight hours are up, Uncle Willie. What did that doctor do to him? I thought seeing Lisa in danger would have done it, but it didn't."

"Dr. Bryant is a drunken quack," Willie said, and then he remembered what the doctor had said: *Seal it with a kiss.* "Devin has to kiss Lisa."

"You are fucking kidding me, right? And where did Eddie get that asshole from?"

"I remember now," Willie said. "he asked me if I believed in fairytales, you have to seal it with a kiss. If they kiss, I think it means forgiveness and he has to become humble. He thought you boys were spoiled brats and said you never apologized for anything. And if Devin wants his life back, he has to become humble."

Lisa went through the many files in her briefcase. She looked briefly at the last files she had received from Susan Milo. She watched the computer screen of her house, everything was as she left it. All of the gifts she had received from her birthday party were still there. She started looking at the slide show and the entertainment.

"Everyone is downstairs," Devin said to her.

She was so focused on her pictures that she did not notice him there. "Okay, I will be there in a minute." Lisa lay on her side when he lay next to her. She explained to him what she was watching.

"Is that me?" he asked as he watched the video of himself and Momma being Ike and Tina Turner. They laughed at Ida shaking her hips.

Devin placed his hand on Lisa's hips. He was so close to her, she turned to look at him when he kissed her. She wanted to push away, but she could not. She still loved him, and she needed him more now than ever. If they were given a second chance, she was willing to take it.

She could not tell him that she was carrying his baby and the woman called Mother wanted their unborn child to raise as her own. If, by any chance, she was captured again, she knew she was a dead woman. She was given a choice and she chose Devin. But now she had a bull's eye on her back.

Devin closed his eyes, "Are you okay? That night in the hospital my head was spinning because I felt something was missing. I felt like I had been there before, and if what everyone says is true about you and me . . ." He pulled her into his arms. "It was you. You are what I was missing that day." He kissed her passionately.

They both heard someone talking. Devin looked at her computer. "Who is that?" He pointed to the screen at the man sitting in her office. He watched as Lisa looked at the camera, as if she wanted someone to pay attention to him. She did a head gesture to the camera in the direction of Lenny; she hoped that Jason and Devin were watching. She wanted Devin to look at him because his face looked familiar. There was something about Lenny Samos. He had brown eyes and a low cut hair but there was something about him, as if she had seen his twin.

"That is Lenny Samos." She remembered what Susan said—Lenny S. Amos. It was important because they were Susan's last words, but why?

Devin kissed her again, when there was a knock on the door. Devin sat next to Lisa when Ellen walked into the room carrying a pot of coffee. "Devin, I am so sorry. Lisa, I thought you were alone.

Devin watched Ellen. He did not know if she was embarrassed and blushing.

"Someone wants to see you, Lisa." It was Claire. She ran across the bed and jumped up and licked Lisa's face.

Jason knocked on the door. "Carl Miller called. He found out who owned the house in the woods." Devin got off the bed and grabbed his .44 Magnum. "The guy's name is Kevin Klein."

"The doctor?" Lisa asked, worried. "Be careful."

Jason explained that Kevin Klein was a patient at the same mental hospital as Ida and Ellen.

Devin stood and opened the nightstand next to his bed and retrieved his .44 magnum. He and Jason walked out of the room to go visit with Kevin Klein.

Lisa looked at her files. She picked up a picture of a dark-skinned man and looked at it. She wondered where it had come from. She looked at the fine print and saw 'Lenny S. Amos' and her eyes widened. He was reported missing the same day James and Jimmy died. Susan had attached a note and a phone number; she grabbed her phone and dialed the number.

They arrived at the home of Kevin Klein. Jason noticed Devin was quieter than normal.

"Well, how do you feel, Jason asked?"

"My headache is gone, I feel good."

"What about Lisa, do you remember anything?"

"Yes," he said when he stuck his hand in his jacket pocket and pulled out some pictures, "And I find it very hard to believe that I would not remember being with her. " However, if what everyone is telling me is true, then I am willing to try again."

Devin pointed to his head, "Jason, I have tried everything to remember her."

Jason sighed. He did not understand what kind of fairytales the doctor read, but he had messed Devin's life up. Jason hoped that Lisa would not run away, because Devin would at least be there for her to keep her safe.

Devin still did not know Lisa was pregnant. He would not steal their glory. When Devin got his memory back, she would tell him about the baby, if there is a baby. These people were after her and the next time, she might not be able to escape; they would kill her first. She had outsmarted them, and now they would want revenge for it.

He needed answers from Devin. Uncle Willie said something about a girl at the doctor's office, begging her father not to kill Devin, which is why Lisa had become the target. Willie believed that the doctor had erased Devin's memory so he could get away from this man and his daughter.

"Who is she, Devin?"

"Who is who," he asked? He looked at Jason with a puzzled looked on his face.

"The night of your accident you said you were coming so that you could meet Lisa. But there was a woman in the doctor's office, begging her father not to hurt you."

"I have no idea what you are talking about and if there was another woman, that would be in the direction I would have started the investigation the jilted lover is always a suspect , but there was no one." Devin closed his eyes as pictures flashed in front of him.

"Are you alright?" Jason asked; he looked at the picture of Jimmy Jones and another of a smaller man wearing glasses, and then he remembered where he had gotten them. "Remember the fight I had with the guy at the bar?"

Devin laughed. "That was no fight. You hit him, and he hit the floor."

Jason smiled. "The guy's name was Simon Thomas. I had Carl find an address on him through the Department of Motor Vehicle. Apparently he is one of them. His address is the same as the old house. It appears that he went to threaten Dr. Bryant to make sure that he kept his word in erasing your memory."

"I don't think we have to find him," Devin said, "because he will find us, since we have eliminated half of his family. Lisa said that they were like a cult.

Jason sighed. "I sent Christian and Ben to Big Mac's and guess who has been hanging out there?" Devin turned and looked with curiosity. "Skeet," Jason said, "and he is the only one of Eddie's security team that did not check out."

"I get a good vibe from Skeet," said Devin.

"So do I," Jason said, "however, we have to be sure."

"Something is not right," Devin said. "It could be a setup because Christian said that Mark had been acting strange."

Jason smiled when he told Devin what Ida said about Mark's dislike for him.

"Then I will make it a priority to pay Mark a visit," Devin said. "I owe him an ass whipping."

Chapter 13

"What took you so long?" Kevin said to Devin and
Jason. "I see now that the two of you are taking this
seriously," the man said to them, "because God knows
your father hasn't. You can put your guns down, boys. You can't
kill me, I am already dead." He looked up at the wall then he
raised his shirt. "They have cut me open so many times, I lost
count."

"They called themselves the Brotherhood. They consist
of law enforcement, doctors, and lawyers; they are people
affected by your grandfather, James Sr.," he chuckled. "He had
a wandering eye, if you know what I mean. He sired a child
with another woman. He left town and came back with a new
wife. He disowned his other child and left the mother living in
poverty, which drove the mother to suicide. Each of the children
was raised by separate people who then joined together as adults
with one common goal: to get revenge on the Jones family.

"The mother was supposed to die in the hospital that night,
as they felt her time was up. But we all know that she did not.
The girl saved her and kept them from getting a second chance
at her. They have people in high places," Kevin Klein said. "The
girl was given a choice: them or you." He looked at Devin. "And
when she made a run for it, they knew she had chosen you. She
is a dead woman the next time they get their hands on her, and
they will try again. She and the child she carries will both die."

Devin looked at Jason. "James Sr. had a heart of stone.
My mother was one of his conquests," he said. "No, I am not a
Jones," he said. "My mother had trouble holding things together.
She could barely keep food on the table. When she met him, he
was charming. She said he knew how to get what he wanted.
He preyed on single, struggling women. We lived in a home he

owned and when Mother found out he was married and had no intentions on leaving his family, she ended things with him. He got angry with my mother and threw us out on the street. We lived in the woods for a long time. I took it with a grain of salt, but the woman who said she had his son did not. It was said around town that he had sired a child that he would not accept because the child had dark skin, while he kept his fancy yellow wife and kids living the high life."

"Who is he?" Devin asked.

"I do not know," Kevin said. "They wore black robes when they tried to recruit me. I said no because they were no better than James Sr. Was. They were killing everything associated with the Jones family, innocent people, and one day I woke up in a mental hospital being cut to pieces. I do not know who the leader is, but I can tell you that his mother committed suicide. She slashed her wrists and somehow she managed to set her house on fire. She had become a drunk and she had knocked over a lantern while her boys played in the yard. She had two boys and one she carried to its grave with her. She was with child when she died, which is why they will show the girl no mercy." Devin and Jason were walking out. "Oh, there is one more thing . . ." Kevin said, "the younger brother fell in love with one of the Jones kids."

Jason repeated, "one of the brothers fell in love with one of the Jones kids, Ida's daughter, which is why they were killed. How could their death be ruled a suicide? We have to find out who wrote the police reports. That could be the missing link. It could be James Sr.'s supposed son."

Devin said nothing about what Kevin Klein had said, he wondered if all of the hypnosis had affected his short-term memory. "How did I let Eddie get control of me? They say you have to be weak-minded to be able to be brainwashed."

"You were drugged, man, that's how."

Devin looked out of the window. "I thought that I could make it work with her. I have been thinking that if I cared about her before, then I can care for her again. But she is pregnant."

"Devin has no memory of ever meeting Lisa at all, Uncle Willie. He now knows she is pregnant, but refuses to think that the child is his." Jason was done with it. He could not focus on Devin's problems and the case at hand. He has been told repeatedly about himself and Lisa, but he could not remember, so he would not accept Lisa's unborn child. There was nothing he could do about it.

❧ ❧

Eddie was at his desk. He needed to fix the problem with Devin. He had received a call from Darlene's father. She had been missing for over twenty-four hours now, and he had not heard from her. Eddie watched as Lisa walked to the kitchen, "Lisa, I need a word with you." She looked at him. She had left one madman's house and ended up in another's.

Lisa walked in and looked at him. Suddenly, she knew what Carolyn had felt years ago when she was confronted by this man. "What can I do for you, Mr. Jones?" He looked at her. *You can get the fuck out of my life* he thought, however, he decided to keep that to himself.

"You are a psychotherapist, right?" Lisa looked at him as he opened his wallet and threw a one hundred dollar bill at her. "I need a session." She sat down; this was her opportunity to see why he is such an angry man. "I buried my son a few months ago. One day, I was sitting in this very spot when I received a phone call from one of my sons telling me that he thinks my son may be in a canal, and one day I stood there as they dredged the canal and pulled out his car. Ms. Washington, I had hoped that he had gotten out until they pulled out a body, burned beyond recognition, and I died that day, too. I was going to have to bury my son. As a father, I was torn apart; I began to drink and sleep did not come easily and one day, Ms. Washington, I turned on my computer in order to see him alive and well, fucking you."

Now she knew why he resented her. "And to make things worse, my first-born child knew this and he said nothing at all to me. He let me grieve while you opened your legs and got yourself pregnant." Lisa lowered her eyes, ashamed. Mr. Jones was a cruel man. "You call yourself a professional woman," Eddie looked at her with contempt. "How did that happen?"

"Mr. Jones, I will take responsibility for what I have done. However, you need to do the same. You played God with your son's life, you went inside his head and implanted what you wanted and removed what you needed."

"Devin did not remember you, Ms. Washington, because he was done with you; it is his way of telling you he has no interest in you or the child you carry. Do you know what was taken from his mind?" Lisa shook her head no. "Chris Weber . . . Being called Chris Weber and, Ms. Washington," He got in her face, "I watched the video, Ms. Washington, and I can tell you this. When you were moaning with your legs open for him, you were calling him names and none of them were Chris Weber. If he was so into you as everyone thinks, wouldn't he remember that?"

Lisa wanted to cry but did not. "I just want to keep my baby."

"I don't give a damn about your baby." He then stopped, "Now you know what I felt. I just wanted to see my son."

"I did not know, Mr. Jones," she said to him.

"Maybe, the next time you spread your legs to a man, you will know who he is first. Do what you came to do, and then leave. If you care about him, you will do your job first. You're supposed to have all the answers; get your fucking mind right and start thinking with you head and not with what is between your legs, or you will not have to worry about having a baby."

Lisa gathered her notes. Her hands were shaking. She knew if she left now they would find her and kill her and her child. She walked to the door. She could hear screaming downstairs, however, she could not stand being in the house any longer. She would go back to New Orleans and be with her family, and try to put all of this behind her.

"How dare you talk to her like that," the ladies were in Eddie's face, Carolyn leading the pack.

"You have gone too far, Eddie," Ellen said.

Eddie clapped his hands. "Now she speaks. Ellen, you have kept your goddamn mouth shut all this time; I suggest you do the same thing now or I will throw your sorry ass out in the street. The only problem with that is no one will care if they kill you."

"You are a cruel bastard," Carolyn said, and I will not stand for it."

Eddie looked at Carolyn. "Okay, Ms. Young, let me tell you what you are. You are a wannabe. You spread your legs and got yourself pregnant and out of pity, Jason took you back." He got in Carolyn's face. "If you did not have Lionel, Jason would have been with someone else."

"Stop, everybody. Stop!" Ida yelled. "She has failed as a mother, but she will not fail again." She walked up to Eddie and she slapped his face. "Who are you?" she asked him. "You want everything, Eddie, but you will end up with nothing. " You are so damn stupid, you do not see how much beauty there is in front of you. You would rather see your sons with whores than see them with women that make them happy. You will lose, Eddie, your sons and your grandkids, and you will be in this fucking hell-hole all by yourself. Lisa will forgive you, but Devin was raised by you and he will not forgive you as easily.

We have lived with him for months, and we all noticed some of your characteristics in him. You need to be helping your sons. Instead, you are here tearing apart what they have built.

"Let me put this in plain fucking English for you. Devin will protect Lisa and that baby, and Jason will protect Carolyn and Lionel. If you want to keep your sons, instead of being part of the problem, you better become part of the solution."

Lisa walked into the room with her files in hand. She also had her suitcase and Claire in a carrying case. "Carolyn, will you deliver these files to Devin and Jason?"

"Where are you going?" Ellen asked, "Because I am coming with you."

Lisa agreed she had never heard such cruel words before and she has been stuck in a house of horror for what seemed like eternity. Ellen went up to pack her bags when Kandy decided she would also leave. "We can watch each other's back," Kandy said when Willie protested and appealed to Lisa's sense of reasoning.

"Baby girl, none of you are safe out there."

Lisa laughed sarcastically. "We are not safe here, either. Out there, we have one madman to worry about. In this house, we have one, also. And I rather take my chances out there."

Lisa sat and waited for Ellen and Kandy to pack. She pulled out her computer because they would be a while. The name Lenny Amos was important to Susan.

Jason and Devin walked and everyone was sitting downstairs. The men could tell something was wrong the moment they entered the room. Lisa was working on her computer, she could see everything more clearly; she needed to find out who Lenny Amos was. They looked and they could see that there was luggage packed and ready to go.

"Since the two of you are here, I can give these to you myself," they turned to find Ellen coming down with her luggage.

"What in the hell is going on? Ellen, you cannot leave." Devin said

"Lisa and I are leaving, and Kandy is, too."

Devin turned to Lisa, "What's going on?" he asked her.

"That is not a question you should ask me. I am not welcome here and your father has made that perfectly clear." She looked at her watch, "We should be in New Orleans in eight hours."

"We, who is 'we'?"

"Me, Ellen and Kandy."

Judy and Ida intervened. "Ellen, you know what Lady Clem said about them getting Lisa's baby . . . "

Ellen closed her eyes. She would not accomplish her goal, but now it did not seem to matter; they were coming and even in the house had alarms and cameras for security. They were not safe. She could see the disappointment on his face. He was now feeling anger toward his father. He had watched the videos of him and her and knew she has suffered. Never were there any consequences to Eddie's actions, and now she would leave and take her chances.

"I am sorry for the pain that my father has caused." Devin closed his eyes as if his head was starting to hurt. He kept going. "Every woman's file on that table is a woman that Jason or I have dated, and they were all killed by these people. I couldn't take it if what happened to them happened to you."

Lisa smiled, walked over and stood in front of him. She gently kissed his lips. "You better get started on the files." She turned to collect her bags when Devin closed his eyes again. Then Devin started talking. This time she listened.

Devin walked up to Lisa and looked her in the eyes and said, "I was coming for you that night," he opened his eyes. "When

I exited the interstate he was there, standing in the middle of the street and waiting. When Chris Weber ran to flag me down, he threw his fire-bomb as soon as he got to my car and I bailed out. I saw you standing at the admissions desk and later at my bedside. I knew there was a higher power at work and later you said that you saw my mother," he sighed, "with the dress we buried her in and the pin I placed on her the last time I saw her." He went on to say, "I knew that I was not Chris Weber, but after seeing the figure in the hall staring at you, I became him in order to protect you. After my memory was erased, I had flashbacks of you, Ms. Johnson." He laughed and so did she. "You see, babe, try is as he may, Eddie could not take me away from you; it is hard to put your life back together when people are trying to take it away." Devin pulled the photos out of his pocket of the short man with the family.

"His name is Jeffrey Thomas," she said, "I had asked Ida. Here is where we will start."

Eddie had a puzzled look on his face. One day he had drunk so much he thought he had a conversation with his late wife asking him to help Lisa and save Ellen. But he did not know who Lisa was at the time.

Lisa dropped her bags. "Do you remember me?" she asked and closed her eyes until he answered. "Yes, and I cannot let you go now, but later, if that is what you want," he turned to Ellen and Kandy and pulled them close to him, "we will all leave together. Now, though, we have to stop this before anyone else gets hurt."

"We are all going to die in this house," he said in anger. "There is another family of killers that wants revenge on this family and we are all fair game. Do you understand, Eddie, a family? They are sick and twisted, but they lookout for each another and they respect one another. We better become a family if we want to survive, because they know how to get inside of this house without us noticing them. This house is one big casket, and we need to put our heads together and find them before they come to us. They want our baby for a reason. They could have any child, but they want this one and we have to find out why."

We were all here in the same room the night mother was killed but none of us saw anything whomever killed my mother knows this house inside and out, there is another way to get inside of this house without being noticed and they know because they have been here they walked in and no one saw anything.

"Dad, do you remember that guy at the bar that night you and Betty were there? He accused me of looking at his girlfriend?"

Eddie smiled, "How could I forget that night. You dropped that son-of-a-bitch with one punch. Willie, you'd have been proud that night; this guy was big and one hit and he went down."

"Dad, he could be one of them. We took out three of them, but there are more. And he will want revenge."

Eddie smiled. "And we will be waiting for his ass."

Jason and Devin were being put in a bad position, having to open up a can of worms. They both loved Ida and neither of them wanted to hurt her, however, they needed answers.

"We talked to a man by the name of Kevin Klein; does that name ring a bell for anyone?"

"Was it the doctor?" Lisa asked. She remembered his nametag said K. Klein.

"No," Jason said. "But, they used his name."

Lisa told them about the nurse that also had a nametag that read R. KLEIN when Momma went into the hospital. "She served her food, which I thought was odd because the kitchen was closed."

"That is because she was sent there to kill Ida; Momma Ida, you were the target that night and the dance of death was for you."

Lisa became dizzy. But she did not want Eddie to think she wanted attention.

"She poisoned the food, which is why she got upset when Momma did not eat it," Devin said, "and if you had not been on your game that night . . . " he did not say anymore, he just looked at Eddie.

"I poured it in the toilet," Lisa said, then she reached over and held Ida.

They told everyone about the Brotherhood against James and it was they who killed James and Jimmy.

"Are you sure that this man wasn't crazy?"

"No, Dad." Jason said. He knew everything, including what happened to Lisa. He said, "She was given a choice."

Eddie looked at them. "A choice to do what, Jason? This does not make any sense."

"A choice to become a part of their organization or be with Devin and die, and when she ran away, they knew what her decision was."

"He talked about a woman who said she had a child with your father."

Devin's head began to hurt; the last thing he wanted to do was hurt Ida, however, he lost the coin toss and it had to be said.

"My father did not have any other kids," Eddie said. "That's crazy."

"Your father was no saint, Eddie," Ida said. "I know he doted on you and you worshiped him, but he was no saint."

"I loved him, and I wanted to believe everything," he said.

"There was a woman," Ida said. "I know, because she knocked on my door. You were about four and Jimmy was two. Your father was watering the flowers while you and Jimmy played in the yard. I looked outside when I saw a woman stop and talk to your father. I didn't think much of it at first, until I saw your father start spraying them with the hose. I ran outside with towels because she had two children with her and she carried one in the belly.

"She had told him that the oldest child was his and that he should take on his responsibility. He sprayed them again and told her to get her and her black ass children away from his house. Her name was Gloria Jean Milton; I will never forget it. I dried the children off while your father stormed inside. I was scared to death. I thought he was going for his gun.

"I dried the child off that she said was his, while I apologized to him for James's actions. He never looked at me. He stared at Judy with a look that made me shake. Before I ran outside, I had grabbed the money I had in my purse and put forty-two dollars in his hand. The smaller one was crying, so I tried to console him. When the mother asked if Judy was his child, I told her no. "She had this cold look on her face and she said that a girl child would be punished to have James for a father.

"Judy walked up to the boys and gave them her cookies. It was probably the only thing they'd had to eat in days. When James returned, he grabbed her and started whipping her with his belt. He said she had fraternized with his enemy. I tried to stop him, but I ended up with a black eye. The children watched as I covered her body with mine. I threatened to leave him," Ida said. "He looked at me and said if I did, he would send Judy back to my sister."

Jeffrey Thomas was her son. Ida went upstairs to get pictures because Lisa had asked her about him. "Your father felt guilty about his father dying on one of his jobs. He started to mentor him, but he did not like him. I did because he was the sweetest little thing and very smart, but your father thought there was something weird about him," Ida smiled. He and I would cook and he would help me do everything; he was like another son," she said.

Devin held Ida in his arms and thanked her, because that child had become a man and he could be the one who killed her husband. They had made progress, but it was not over. Ida had a daughter who could be a hostage of this man.

Judy cried, she remembered it as if it was yesterday. "I am sorry, Judy. But we needed to know. I did not mean to open up old wounds."

"Old, Devin," she said. "They don't seem so old when you remember them like it was yesterday. I hated that man with a passion," she cried. "I was made a live-in babysitter for his badass children and I was only a child myself.

"Everything they did wrong, I was beaten or punished for it. 'I will send you back to your drunk ass mother,'" he would always say. Judy looked at Lisa. "What is that you always say? You never forget pain that is caused by another. You will forget a toy or a party, but you will not forget the pain.

"I remember when I was nine, Jimmy spilled water on the sofa." Judy looked as if she were in a trance. "I had to wash dishes and Jimmy got a glass of water. I did not see him," she said, and he spilled it. James beat me so badly, it traumatized Jimmy. He tried to help me. He put bandages on my bruises and after that, Jimmy would do no wrong. He would help me with my chores and everything, but your father was a monster," she laughed. "He never thought of anyone but himself."

Carolyn had had enough—Judy was in pain and Eddie still looked as if he was gloating. She yelled at Eddie, "You are a son of a bitch. I cannot take this, Jason, I want to go home." She needed to show Eddie that she was Jason's woman, and Eddie would respect her. She was in control and she knew just what to do.

Jason was stung with Carolyn's outburst. "Your father insulted me today and I will not stay here one minute longer." She looked at Eddie, "You are the devil!" Carolyn started to cry. "Your father brags about how many women you have screwed, and that I meant nothing to you." She then turned to Lisa and said, "I lied when I told you that he was active in Lionel's life. The truth is, I walked in on him fucking someone when I went to tell him about Lionel."

Jason looked at Devin, who hunched his shoulders. Carolyn decided to throw in a curve ball. "You only got to hear Darlene tell you how she and Devin were screwing. But I watched Jason with another woman. I searched all over town for him." She looked at Eddie and yelled, "I even parked outside this goddamn place and one day I hit pay dirt. I saw him driving and I followed him to his home. I sat outside for an hour and twenty minutes, trying to find the words to say. I was so distracted, I did not see her walk past me. Finally, I walked to the door. It was unlocked, so I walked in and there they were in his bed."

Carolyn was venting; she had held this in for a long time. "I was paralyzed. I just stood there like a freak and then, finally, I could move again. I ran in and beat the hell out of her, so you should thank your stars that you only heard about how Devin screwed Darlene."

Jason remembered that day Carolyn walked in on him and Stephanie, but he could not allow her to leave, so he tried of stop Carolyn from walking out.

She looked at Eddie. "You think you are so fucking high and mighty. Fuck you, Eddie! And fuck you, too, Jason!" Jason grabbed her and held her, he tried to calm her, but he could not. She started yelling at him, telling him how much she hated him. Carolyn was out of control. Everyone watched as he tried to hold her, then suddenly it happened, he slapped her. She placed her hand on her face. "You are just like your father!" She cried and then ran upstairs screaming. "You said you would never hit me," and she yelled, "I hate you!" He grabbed her, but she broke away. "You are just like your father!"

Eddie lifted his glass. "If he had not slapped the shit out of her, then I would have."

Lisa walked to the kitchen while Jason went to see about Carolyn. Lisa had prepared lunch; she needed to talk to Jason and Devin about the files. Carolyn wanted to control the situation. Once again, they were distracted. It was no secret as to what was happening, and yet she felt the need to draw attention to herself and take Jason away from the matter at hand.

Eddie's words began to haunt her. *I just wanted my son.* Although she had never held her child and would do whatever it took to protect it, she could only imagine what he must to have felt to think his son had died in the manner in which Chris Weber did.

Jason ran down the stairs, yelling at Eddie, "What in the hell did you say to her, Eddie?"

"Carolyn wanted attention and she is getting it," Eddie said. "She is a goddamn drama queen!" Eddie yelled as Devin intervened.

"Does she understand the importance of us staying together?" he asked. "What did you say to her, Eddie?"

Lisa walked out of the kitchen carrying a plate of food. The other women watched in horror as Jason looked as if he would strike Eddie, while Devin held him back. "Your father had a meltdown today," Lisa said. "A few months ago, Eddie buried his son, and while he grieved the loss someone decided to play a cruel joke on him. They sent him a video, letting him know his son was alive, while the one person he thought he could trust knew and did not tell him.

"I know your father is a hard man to deal with. But he deserved better from the people he loved so much than he had received, and he got angry." Lisa placed a plate of food down on the table in front of Eddie. She reached over and picked up his drink and took it away. She had been in the home with him for days and had not seen him eat as much as a cracker.

"We wronged you," Lisa said with tears in her eyes, "and I am sorry for my role in everything. You were right. I had every client checked out, and I knew about the amnesia. I did nothing; I should have known that there was someone that loved him besides me. Instead, I was selfish. I did not want to lose him, so I did nothing. I wanted to hate you, but I feel your pain and, maybe, if we would have handled things differently, then maybe you would have also." She placed a spoon of food in his mouth. "Please forgive me. No one thought of your feelings, and I am sorry; no one thought that a hard man like yourself could feel pain and get lonely, too."

Ida's eyes watered. She was so proud of Lisa, especially after Carolyn tried to provoke Jason into striking his father. Carolyn was a drama queen and today she put on a performance that she should receive an Oscar for. Ida placed her hand over her mouth as she was witnessing the revelation. Both Jason and Devin were making up with Eddie.

Jason and Devin watched Lisa and decided that they had misjudged their father. After Asia's death, they both had turned their backs on him and they wronged him. Jason walked up to Eddie, "Dad, I am sorry, Lisa is right; I should have trusted you, forgive me." Devin followed; when he realized someone was stalking him and Lisa, he should have talked to his father. He knew his father loved him and would grieve over him. He should have shown him respect.

While Devin and Jason embraced their father, Lisa noticed her screen; someone was in her office. "Devin, look at this," she said. All three men watched as a man in a black robe did a dance in Lisa's office.

"What in the hell is he doing?" Eddie asked.

"It's the dance of death, according to Kevin Klein."

"Someone is going to die," Devin said.

Eddie called in extra security and had the house perimeter checked.

Jason went in the bedroom to talk to Carolyn, while Lisa put everything together. She did not need any more drama; someone was going to die, and they needed to be sharp to stay alive.

Ellen walked into Devin's room, "Wow, this is a big bed," she said. Lisa looked at Ellen, remembering what Eddie had said to her and how she looked afterwards. Suddenly, they heard Carolyn moaning. She wanted Eddie and all of them to know she was in control.

Devin watched Lenny Amos video over and over again. He studied him. There was something about this guy, he kept saying out-loud as he rubbed his face. "Who are you?" he asked the screen.

"He is not Lenny S. Amos," Lisa said. "I talked to his sister today. Lenny Steven Amos went missing the same night that Jimmy and James died." Devin looked at her. "According to his sister, he was a student at the same school that Jimmy attended and, get this: he told his sister he would be catching a ride with his friend J.J. and his father. James and Jimmy gave Lenny a ride home, only Lenny never made it home," Lisa said. "But there were only two bodies found in James's car. Someone got away," she said.

"Or one of them were taken," Devin said. "Jeffrey Thomas fell in love with one of Ida's children, but it wasn't Judy."

Eddie tried to sit up on the sofa. He had drunk so much the last few days, his head hurt. The doorbell rang, but he could not sit up.

"Sir, there is a detective here to see Lisa."

Eddie did not open his eyes. He just lay there when the detective walked in. "Mr. Jones, I am Detective Walker and this is my partner Detective Johnson." Eddie tried to sit up. He rolled over and when he looked down, his head hurt less. Eddie looked and he remembered what Lisa had said about the penny loafers, a dime in one and a penny in the other. He looked at Detective Walker when that voice started again, *Help Lisa.*

Eddie stood and went to his desk. "Ms. Washington is resting," he said. "She was traumatized, detective. Eddie had hit the speaker button in Jason and Devin's rooms. He had sent a signal to his security team. "I will have my driver drive her to your office later today, if that is okay with you."

Detective Johnson agreed, but Detective Walker declined. "We need to talk to her now, Mr. Jones."

Eddie needed to warn the others. "Then I will go and wake her."

"Detective Walker is here for Lisa," Eddie said, walking into Devin's room. "Son, look at his shoes; I will get Jason and Willie."

Jason and Eddie came down for upstairs while Lisa was being interrogated by the police. They stopped when they reached Willie, who said, "We can kill him now and save ourselves a lot of trouble." Jason stopped him from reaching into his pocket, saying, "And leave a witness, when accidents happen all of the time," Willie said.

Detective Johnson said nothing. He looked around while Detective Walker asked all the questions. "We know that you have been through a traumatic experience. However, we are here to help," he said as she stared at him. "We need to know, Ms. Washington. What did you see?"

"Just a room, like a hospital room," Lisa was careful not to say too much. "Detective, I was drugged, I was out cold."

"At what point did you see Detective Milo?" he asked. "Did she say anything?"

"No," she said, "Susan was dead already."

His next question jerked Devin's head around. "Who allowed you to escape?" And then the detective rephrased his question, "How did you escape?"

Lisa looked into the face of Detective Walker because she recognized his voice. He was the person standing over her at the old house. She tried not to stare at him and answered his questions. "Someone left the door open and I ran."

Detective Johnson then joined in, "Did you recognize anyone?"

"No," Lisa said, "they wore something over their faces."

Eddie then stepped in, "That is enough, detectives. Ms. Washington has been through enough and she needs her rest."

The detective got angry. "I am not done with her, yet."

Eddie then got angry, "Yes the fuck you are!" When Detective Johnson started to talk, "I don't want to hear what the fuck you have to say. Now the both of you, get the fuck out of my house."

Lisa walked out of the family room from where she was being interrogated. She was careful not to let the detectives see her shake. She went back to the bedroom, as she needed to catch her breath. "That is him," she said.

"We'll have someone follow him. That way, we can find out where the main headquarters is." He looked at her. "You did well," he said.

"Look at me, I am shaking. And your father, I have never been so proud of him."

He pulled her into his arms, stroked her hair and said, "We are getting close to ending this nightmare, and we'll be able to live a normal life." For the first time, he touched her stomach. He smiled when, for the first time, he felt his baby move. "There is something else we have to take care of before we can go any further."

Lisa went to rest as Devin and Jason called for Skeet. "There is a leak in the security here," Jason said. He then walked behind Skeet as Devin stood in front, and both aimed their guns at Skeet.

"Who in the fuck are you, Skeet?" Devin asked. "And you better have a good answer."

Skeet held up his hands, "Please don't shoot. Please. I have a picture in my pocket."

Devin allowed Skeet to retrieve the picture. "Move slowly," Devin said.

Skeet pulled out a picture of his mother Betty and handed it to Devin. "Betty Jackson was my mother," he said, he then showed his driver's license to Jason before they lowered their guns.

"My name is Trevor Jackson and I am not a snitch or a traitor, I'm a man looking for answers. You remember when I said we have something in common? We both lost our mother in almost the same fashion." Skeet pulled out another picture of his mother, and handed it to Devin. "That is my motivation," he said. Her face was not recognizable, and you could see that she had met the same fate as Elmira Coleman and the others.

"My mother called me, she was hysterical. She said that someone wearing a black robe and veil was following her, and when it saw her, it pointed at her and did some kind of dance. I was in the police academy when I received the call," Skeet's eyes began to water as he remembered his mother. "I tried to get as much information from her as I could because she truly feared for her life." Skeet passed a copy of his mother's death certificate to Devin. "She was beaten before her death and then they cut her open."

Devin looked at Eddie. He remembered when he and Jason stopped Eddie from beating her that night. Eddie had thrown her out of the house and they never saw her again.

He pointed out the window, "Do you know how hard it is to keep your sanity when you can look out and see the exact spot where your mother was tortured to death? They tied her to a pole, killed her, and burned her because they wanted you to see Mr. Jones," Skeet said

"What does Jeffrey have to do with this?" Eddie asked. When he thought of him, he could not forget that day and then he thought that maybe they were on the right track. If anyone would want to kill him, it would be Jeffrey.

Devin stepped in front of Skeet. "I know what you are going through, Skeet. We all do, and the most important thing is that you are not alone. We will get them all. They showed these women no mercy, and we will show them none." He extended his hand and Skeet did the same.

"We have lost three members of our family," the boss said. "While they live in luxury and eat their fancy meals. Lisa is a traitor, and if she will not come to us, we will go to her." The boss had hoped that she would be returned today. She had planned to leave and they were prepared to receive her, however she allowed the Jones family to influence her again.

"Are you ready, Father?" The boss asked. "Are you ready to give Mother her child?"

Father stood and cleared his throat. He had his special voice ready, it was deep and it commanded respect from the others—it was his Barry White specialty. "Yes, magistrate, I have had all of the equipment delivered from the house, and I am ready."

"Lisa is a back-stabbing whore, who will die like one."

"Yes," the boss said, "she has allowed Devin Jones to bed her again."

Father covered his mouth, "Sister would be devastated to hear such talk." He could not tell the others that Sister had fallen for the Jones boys and they had corrupted her, so he excused himself from the meeting because women were not allowed. She sometimes eavesdropped, however.

"What is he saying, Father? Why would he say such cruel things about my love?"

"Shut your mouth, girl," Father yelled at Sister. "They are trouble!" Father got Sister under control before he went back to the meeting.

"Tonight, we will deliver a package to the Jones home with a note for Lisa. She will see the fate that will await her. Father, if you will do the honors . . . " he was pleased that no one held him responsible for Sister's actions. They knew once a girl became thirty, they get out of hand and he could no longer control her. Father pulled a name out of the hat; the hat of fate, which contained the name of the one who would die next. There were only four names in it at the time—Ellen and Lisa, or Carolyn and Kandy—we should kill two birds with one stone," Father said and thought they were punished for their action. They would kill them all when the time was right. "Carolyn is a slut," he said, as he remembered punishing her. She carried a demon and he had removed it.

Father was happy, he had grown tired of the wait. He had to step down because he had to focus on Sister as she had been up to no good. "Boss, I have a suggestion," he said, "why don't we kill one and bring the other back for punishment. We have not punished anyone lately and I think it is a sign of us getting soft." Father had begun to preach, "If we allow them to get comfortable, they will become complacent. They do not deserve to be happy," he said. His sons cheered him on. "They are dirty and they stink of sin," father said.

After the meeting, Father was exhausted. Mother had fallen asleep, and he needed pleasing. After his shower, he wore only his robe as he walked to Daughter's room and opened her door. She went out to the bar and would be out late. He walked inside and looked around. "What in the Sodom and Gomorrah is going on in here?" Father watched as a mannequin with Jason's picture attached stood there with an erect penis and one of Devin lay in bed with one. Father was appalled at what the men said to him, "What did you say to me?" he asked. "You want to fuck me," Father gasped. "I am a God-fearing man and I will not fraternize with your kind."

Suddenly, Father found himself bent over and naked, as Jason shoved his erection into him, while Devin made him take him in his mouth. "I am not this kind of man," Father said, as he pushed the button to go faster. "The two of you are nothing but a bunch of savages," Father said, "and you should die like one." His body jerked. Father lit a cigarette and lay next to Devin, but he quickly jumped up when he heard Sister come into the house.

"What are you doing in my room?" she asked Father.

"I came to see what you were up to in here, and I must say I am appalled at you! How dare you bring these beasts into my house?"

"I love them, Father, and I am going to have their baby," she said. "I have been at the hospital waiting for one, but there were none. But soon, Father, I will become a mother very soon."

Father was disappointed in Daughter, having a baby has clouded her judgment. She used to be so respectful and now she lay with the devils. Everyone would tell him how beautiful she was and now he has lost control of her. "Daughter, these boys are trouble; first, there was one and now they are both in my home doing these things to you."

She began to cry and beg, "Father, don't hurt them because I love them."

Mother listened at the door; things were getting out of control. They were planning to kill Lisa and she got away. Now they would go to the house and kill her and Ellen right under the Jones family's noses. They were outnumbered. There were nine more of father's children. She had gone to see the psychic, Clem and smiled when he told her to make an appointment to see the psychotherapist, Lisa Washington. She would spread the news, but she was not allowed to leave the house to keep her appointment. She recalled when she had left the house without Father's knowledge and when she returned he and Simon were waiting for her. Simon held her, as Father slapped and kicked her. She had appealed to Simon as his mother, but his loyalty was to his father. But now Sister was in trouble as she had fallen in love with the Jones boys, she smiled because that love had taken the attention away from the Jones boy. And placed it on the ones that they loved. Sister would kill the women just as she had killed all the other women that the Devin and Jason had cared for.

Mother looked at her cell phone, which she had purchased without anyone's knowledge. She looked and read her messages with a smile. "I love you, too," she said, "and we will be together soon." She smiled and grabbed her heart because it was breaking. How much longer will I have to live like this and not be sure what her future held for her? *I hope that you all are as smart as I hope and will end this all soon,* she thought as she looked at her knife and thought about killing herself. She removed her wig and sat on the bed, *I have to find a way to warn them,* but she was not allowed out since Lisa's escape. Now Simon was keeping a close eye on her. She smiled, if she could get him to go to the Jones home alone, then Jason and Devin would kill him and that would be the distraction she would need. She would be able to warn Lisa that there were others and she would be able to return home.

Chapter 14

❝ According to Klein, he said one of them fell in love with one of the Jones kids. It could be Ida's daughter. We have to talk to her now and find out what happened to her daughter, she could be the one called Mother."

Christian, J.T. and Skeet sat in another room while the family sat down to dinner. Lisa walked in, "Gentlemen, come to dinner."

They looked at each other. They had never been invited to sit at the table. Devin smiled and mumbled for Skeet to watch out because she seated him next to Kandy. "Christian and J.T., you can sit here."

Everyone listened as Eddie and Judy shared their mischievous childhood, how they used to TP the neighbors' homes. Everyone waited for the other shoe to fall; it was dead silent. They had enjoyed a special dinner prepared by Lisa and Ellen, and now they knew something was wrong. Devin was the bad guy before, and now it was Jason's turn to ask the questions. He thought he should take a different approach. If his sister had been disowned by her family for falling in love with the wrong man, they needed to know.

"Dad, where is your sister?"

Eddie looked at Jason like he was crazy. "Son, I do not have a sister and that man is not my brother. My mother had two boys, me and Jimmy, and that is it. No girls." Eddie started to laugh. "Remember the curse?"

Momma Ida did recall James talking about a family curse. "Son, there has not been a girl child born to this family in a hundred years, only boys."

Devin laughed.

"You're kidding," Jason said.

"No," Eddie said, "I am serious. My father said it and since I have been born, there has not been a girl child born to the Jones family, and supposedly the curse was lifted about five or six months ago."

"Jason, I said that. I am not lying to you, son; I want to be part of the solution. I do not have a sister."

Christian, J.T. and Skeet stood to leave and give the family time to work through their problems. "Do not leave," Devin said. "The reason you are all here is because you are now a part of the family and its secrets, and that has been used against us all in the past. Uncle Christian, you have been around since day one. And if you can help to shed some light on the situation, then it would be appreciated."

"Uncle Willie was right," Jason said. "Maybe this is about stopping the Jones bloodline, maybe they do not want us to procreate." Devin gave Jason his undivided attention.

"Jenny gave the ladies a pregnancy test, and shortly after that Kandy was attacked," Jason said. "Someone was watching Devin and Lisa. And Lisa was kidnapped and they wanted to take the baby," Jason said. "Maybe they want a girl child."

"Dr. Samuels," Devin said. "He told Lisa he could protect her, and when he found out she was pregnant, he gave the order to abort the baby. And he killed Maxine Turner."

Tears welled in Skeet's eyes. His mother was pregnant at the time of her death. "My mother said she started being stalked right after she met a woman in a bar downtown called Big Mac. She would sometimes go there to relax and listen to old music when a woman approached her. Mother said the woman was tall and had a shoulder-length haircut, and she was pregnant. After her death, I went to Big Mac. The first day nothing happened, but the next day she came in," he said. "I was alone, so she sat next to me, and she had no problem unloading her problems on me. 'I lost a child,' she said. 'Father said I could not have it,' and then she began to cry on my shoulder. I offered her a drink," Skeet said, "because I knew she was the one I was looking for. She began to tell me how her father had taken her child from her because he said it was too soon. She started to tell me how her great, great, grandfather and two of his friends made a pact with the devil, and then she said something about a girl child, before she realized she was saying too much. My mother was only fifteen when she had me," Skeet said. "She tried to be a good mother. She sometimes fell short. She was kind to people and she did not deserve to be treated as she was.

"I am sorry," Skeet said, "for not being honest in the beginning. I thought if I said I was Betty's son, you would never have hired me. I know about you, Mr. Jones, and my mother, she thought very highly of you. She said you were kind to her. I asked her to come here that night before she died so she would be safe, but she never made it."

Judy was furious at all the abuse she suffered at the hand of James Jones, and for someone to receive kindness from Eddie, kindness that he had never shown her. Judy looked at Ida as she said nothing. "You're going to say nothing, Ida?" Judy looked at Jason, "If she won't say anything, then I will. But first, why are you asking?"

Devin stuck his hand in his jacket pocket, and pulled out a picture. At first glance, he thought it was a woman, and then he looked again.

"When we talked to Klein, he said that one of them had fallen in love with one of the Jones kids. We think it's Ida's daughter. She may be being held against her will."

"Tell him, Mother!" Judy yelled at Ida. "At least she gave birth to me, but a mother she has never been."

Eddie and his sons each shared a look. They realized he really did not know that Judy was his sister. "I do not know what to call you two—nephew, cousin—I am confused," she said with contempt. "Close your mouth, Eddie, you do not have to share the wealth with me, baby brother; I am not your problem, you have always been mine.

"I was Ida's firstborn; she gave birth to me, then she left me and went on her merry way. Then when I was . . . How old?" Judy looked at Ida, "Well, help me out, Ida, I can't remember it all." Judy was being sarcastic. " Let's say four or five, I had to return to live with Ida, who had married and had two other children, and that was the beginning of my life of hell."

"James did not know Ida had a child before they married, so when I went to live with them, he was told that I was Ida's sister's child, which was funny," Judy said in a whisper, "as she does not have a sister.

"I believe what you said about the curse," she said to Eddie, "because your father hated me. He said he could not explain my presence and he made my life hell for it." Judy started to share her pain. She thought if she finally was able to talk about it, she could move on. "One time, Eddie dropped ketchup on his shirt and I got sent to bed with no dinner. I could have forgiven it all, and I did until I was twenty-two years old and I fell in love with the man of my dreams. James found out I had gotten pregnant and I told Ida; she promised she would not tell, but he found out. I was so happy. For the first time in my miserable fucking life I was happy. I had a man who cared for me and I was carrying his baby.

"He made me have an abortion. He made me kill my baby. So, if your question is if someone fell in love with Ida's daughter, the answer is no. Jason, no one loved her, not even her own fucking mother." Judy got up and walked away.

Lisa knew Ida was an only child, but thought it would be better if they found out this way. But she was happy that Devin had allowed it to be said by Judy, as opposed to him telling his father that he and Judy were brother and sister, he had come to the conclusion that Judy was Ida's daughter when he and Lisa went through Ida's pictures. It was same day he was taken by Eddie's men but Eddie had his memory erased, and now it had opened up deep wounds for Judy but it explained why Judy hated Ida so badly.

Lisa cried in the shower. After Judy's story, she decided to use Jenny's pregnancy test—blue for boy and pink for girl—and the stick was pink. She was having a girl child that would be disowned by her grandfather.

Devin was restless; he could not think. Now everyone knew that Judy was Ida's daughter, which he had an idea of and wanted the family to come clean, which worked just as he expected. However, they were running out of time. He went through Eddie's computer. First, he checked the perimeter of the house: the coast was clear. He watched as Ida comforted Judy and thought they needed their privacy.

He went through the video file and he saw himself with a woman, he sat up straight. It was Lisa, she did a dance for him, and then he carried her to bed. He watched as he made love to Lisa. He went back for days, and saw unopened videos. He watched as Lisa brought him breakfast in bed, and then more of them making love. He looked closer and he could see someone watching them through the bedroom window, wearing a black hood over his face. Klein said Lisa was given a choice and she had chosen him. He watched her in the shower from the door in his bedroom and could see how much pain she was in because of him to wonder if she could trust that he would not let anyone take their child. She was trying to be brave, but she was falling apart. He had never told her about Darlene, that they were not a couple. She had shown Eddie compassion and she had received none from his father. Devin watched their video again and then clicked to others, where he looked at the person in the veil standing in Lisa's bedroom and pointing his finger at the camera, with a picture of Devin in his hand. Devin was furious because Eddie had been watching Lisa all along and knew that

Lisa was being stalked, and when someone held up his picture for Eddie to see, Eddie had him kidnapped and left Lisa alone. He left her to die alone.

Devin went upstairs as Eddie was coming down. "Have a drink with me, son," and Devin walked with Eddie into the kitchen and poured a glass of tea. "I'm a man of my word," he said. "I agreed not to drink alcohol for a few days and I will keep my word. Lisa is an amazing woman," Eddie said. "I thought she was the other one."

Devin laughed, "Do not let Jason hear you say that."

"All I am saying is I owe her an apology."

Devin and Eddie clicked their glasses together before Devin asked, "Did you know she was pregnant?"

Eddie lowered his head, "No, son, I did not. I found out when she was kidnapped that the extra red dot was the heartbeat of the child she is carrying. I have seen her also," as Devin placed the glass in the sink, Eddie words came from left field, "your mother; and after I had your memory erased, I realized I had made a big mistake. Two days after your accident, I lost it and I drank so much I saw a light and it was Asia. She told me to get up, pull myself together, and help Lisa. She kept repeating, *help Lisa*, and when Willie said he was seeing a therapist named Lisa, I knew she was the one."

Eddie viewed Lisa as a woman that would keep her word. Soon she will leave and now Devin will be with her. When Lisa leaves, they will follow her and Devin will be in danger. Melissa Thomas had at least nine children and if Jeffrey Thomas raised them all, they are all natural-born killers and his son will die. Eddie remembered Melissa from over forty years ago, only her name back then was Melissa Johnson. She dated Jeffrey Thomas, only she considered their relationship as open. They both dated other people, which was how he met her. She attended a summer party and they started a sexual relationship.

Lisa pulled out a paper. "I found this among my files."

Devin looked; it was a picture of a dark-skinned man and at the bottom of the photo read LENNY STEVEN AMOS. Devin said, "You know that saying, don't give up your day job," he looked at Lisa. "It does not apply to you." She smiled and he walked away. "I am going to take a bath," he said, "my body is aching all over."

She was concerned about him ever since they had been in the house, he had barely slept and now she was worried. "I have some lube," she said. He looked at her and laughed. "I mean I have some muscle relaxer I can rub on you when you finish your bath."

Devin lay on his stomach while Lisa straddled him. She rubbed his muscles for as long as she could take it. He did not move, so she thought he had fallen to sleep. She climbed off him and laid on her side of the bed in silence.

Eddie stayed up late watching the security monitor and went room to room to make sure his home was secure. He watched as Carolyn lay on top of Jason in their room and Ellen lay with her eyes pointed to the ceiling. in her room. He sat up because she had not moved; finally she turned and looked in the direction of Jason's room and then turned back to focus on the ceiling again. If what Devin said was true, someone would be able to walk inside of their home and without anyone knowing they were there; no one was safe.

Eddie entered the kitchen, walked up to Judy, and opened his arms; she climbed in. "We are going to be alright, Judy," he said. He looked at his liquor cabinet then walked back to his computer.

Eddie checked the hall and he checked Lisa and Devin's room. He saw little Claire sit up at attention, looking at the door. She started to bark as Devin lay on his stomach, yelling for her to stop. He watched as Lisa hurried out of bed to take

Claire into the bathroom so that Devin would stop yelling at her. He then went back to the hall; he could still see Jason's door open while Carolyn lay on his chest. He went back to Ellen's room and she was lying in bed with tears in her eyes, staring at the ceiling.

Willie handed Eddie a drink; he looked at the glass, "You know I made a promise today."

Willie laughed, "Have you ever kept a promise?"

"No," Eddie said before he took a sip of its contents.

Willie looked at the monitor. He could see that she was tired and wanted affection. She lay on her side with her back away from Devin as he lay on his stomach. He watched as she cried and placed her hand on her stomach. He wondered what would happen to Devin if he could feel the pain Lisa felt as she lay next to him. All of this was taking its toll on her. They had a beautiful thing going and now they were both exhausted.

"Dr. Bryant wanted to punish you by hurting Devin. Devin suffered with migraines and he felt the pain that you caused others. But Devin got over his pain. The only person who really suffered was Lisa. You made a big mistake, Eddie; you say you love Devin and yet, you put his faith in the hands of a madman. You knew she was pregnant, didn't you?"

Eddie sipped his drink. "Okay, Willie, you want to know the truth? I have been watching Devin for days. I watched him eat, sleep, and fuck for days and then, one day, the person stood there in Lisa's bedroom. He had a picture of my son and I watched him set it on fire as he pointed his finger at me." Eddie looked at the screen. "That is when I knew I had to get him out of there. I got my child out of harm's way; here I could protect him."

"What about Lisa?" Willie asked.

"She was not my responsibility!" Eddie yelled.

Willie yelled at Eddie, "She was his responsibility! You think that you are winning, Eddie? You are not." Willie paced the floor, "Do you know what Carolyn did today? Why she caused such a scene? She wanted to let you and everybody know that she was a force to be reckoned with. She plans to be in Jason's life, and if you do not like it, then you will lose Jason. She is willing to use any weapon necessary, and that includes Lionel."

"I know, Willie, I made a big mistake. I should have listened to the voices, but I did it my way and I hope that when all of this is over, both of my sons will forgive me."

Jason rushed out of the bedroom; Claire was barking. "Lisa, make her stop!" Devin yelled when they heard the doorbell ring. Jason rushed back to his bedroom to grab his gun; he was careful not to wake Carolyn. He looked in the room where the women were sleeping before he and Devin walked down the stairs and stood in position.

Willie opened the door quickly and pulled out his gun. There was no one at the door, but there was something hanging on it. Willie thought it was a test dummy, but it was not. He turned away. It was Darlene. She had been tortured, her long black hair had been shaved, and her face was blue. He could see that she had been cut open and her stomach was pinned to reveal her insides.

"Cut her down!" Eddie yelled, which Skeet did. He laid her down on the floor while Devin and Jason looked around outside. Eddie poured another drink, "Why Darlene? She has nothing to do with this. How did they know about Darlene?" Eddie yelled.

Skeet handed Eddie a letter, which read, I did not burn the bitch because I wanted to let you see what is going to happen to Lisa.

Skeet and Jason checked the left side of the house while Devin and Christian checked the right. They found tire tracks.

They walked back inside of the house and J.T was checking the security camera. One minute there was nothing at the door, then suddenly Darlene appeared.

"How could she just appear like that?" Skeet asked.

J.T. hit the keys on the computer. "Someone placed a time delay on the camera." J.T pointed at the clock and there was a five-minute delay. He rewound the camera and said, "There he is. J.T. looked at the man's walk and his build. "Is that Mark?" he asked.

"What do you know about Mark?" Skeet asked. "There is something strange about him; he has these outbursts and he hates you guys. I have been keeping an eye on him and I think he has been giving out information to someone. I follow him to Big Mac all of the time and he would meet a tall man that talked funny. When he saw Ben and Christian, he went for the back door. I tried to follow him home one night, but he checked into a hotel instead."

"Find Mark," Eddie said, "and bring him to me. And I want two men around each corner of the house, and in the security tower I want a sniper waiting on duty."

Devin ran a background check on Robert Samuel and found that he died twenty years ago. He ran a background on James Johnson, the name that Maxine Turner called Robert Samuels at the hospital before she died. He also checked James Thomas since he was the son of Melissa Thomas. He received the file on James Thomas, but they were still searching the Department of Motor Vehicles for James Johnson. He handed Lisa the envelope. "This is James Thomas." And she looked, however, it was not Dr. Samuels or Janitor Al.

Melissa Thomas had nine children; we have to find out who the others were. Are you busy tomorrow?" she asked. "Maybe there are high school yearbook pictures of the others."

"Stay away from Mark. If I am not around, get Skeet or J.T. to run your errands."

He briefed her on Skeet, and his mother was one of the files on her desk. "He has been looking into his mother's death and he knows some of the others. He thinks that Mark is one of the Brotherhood."

Chapter 15

J.T. and Ben waited at a distance as the police officer examined Darlene's body. They were asked to take her away from the house and put her somewhere she would be found. J.T made an anonymous phone call, saying there was something suspicious lying in the road.

"Darlene did not deserve that," Eddie said.

Willie said, "Neither does Lisa, you read the note. They are coming for her and her unborn child."

"So, what I thought was a myth must be true. My father told me stories, but I thought he was drunk, so I paid it no mind. If it is true, they do not want to kill Lisa's baby, they want to raise it."

Willie was puzzled. "That makes no sense, Eddie." He ignored Devin and Jason standing there. Lisa's baby is a Jones. Wouldn't you have to be a Jones to claim anything?"

"I am not sure because I had never given it any thought, but now Jeffrey is taking it seriously."

Devin looked at Jason, "One of the Jones kids," he said. Devin pulled out a picture and asked Jason to glance at it and tell him what he saw. A light-skinned woman: Devin smiled. "Now look again," it was a picture of Jimmy, his father's brother. "Did Jimmy have any children?" Devin asked. He was trying to make sure he covered all the bases before he said what he thought. Did he have any women in his life?"

Eddie was fired up. Devin and Jason thought he missed the comment they had just made or he would not allow them to get away with it. "Go fuck yourselves," he said to them both. "I know what you are implying and you are wrong. Jimmy did have a woman in his life and he was quite taken with her."

"Who?" asked Jason.

Eddie looked at him. "Ellen. Jimmy liked Ellen a lot. Every day he would go to her house and when she had studies with Judy on weekends at our house, he was always in her face."

"Was Ellen's baby from Jimmy?" Jason asked. Eddie said nothing.

"Or, did your father kill Ellen's baby also," Devin joined in. Devin knew the only way to get answers from Eddie was the make him angry. He would curse him for everything but the child of God, but he would answer. But Eddie did not answer. Now, it was Devin's turn to get angry. He tried to appeal to his father's soft spot and if that did not work, he would have to go hard-core.

"Dad, that letter is directed at Lisa. They will find a way to get to her. Earlier, you said she was kind and gentle and now you will keep something from us that might help save my child." Eddie still said nothing.

Devin looked him in the eyes. "You said you owed her an apology, not to count the fact that these people have targeted Ellen. Lisa was given a choice and she chose us." Devin stopped. His father had made her life a living hell on his behalf, and he had done nothing to make things better. "I am going upstairs and apologize to her for yelling at Claire. When these people come around, she always barks and I should have remembered. Yet again, I have upset her. When I return, I want some fucking answers from you."

❧ ❧

"Is everything okay downstairs?" Lisa asked Devin.

He did not tell her what had happened to Darlene. She has had to deal with more than she should have and if he told her that she is what they want, then she would panic. He could only hope that all of this stress was not hurting his baby.

"Lisa, let me get to the point; I am losing it, baby, I cannot think straight. I have you and the baby to worry about and there are so many secrets in my family that they would rather let someone walk in and slaughter us all than to come clean. I should have remembered when Claire barked what was happening. Instead, I yelled at her and she was trying to communicate with me." He picked up Claire.

"I am sorry, you're tired," she said and placed her arms around him. "Remember what I said about being happy as long as we are together. I meant every word. The baby and I are happy now that we are a part of your life again."

"I did not touch Darlene. My head was spinning before she came and even if it wasn't, Darlene was not my type," he laughed. "She was a daddy's girl and ran to him for everything. If I am to be with a woman, then I wear the pants, not her daddy."

He kissed her, and she knew she should make him stop. But she did not. She wanted to feel his touch again and he would connect with his child. Then she would welcome the shame she would feel as his father's eyes watched the computer screen.

⌒ ⌒

"Devin is going to be a while," Willie said with a smile. "That should give you enough time to think about how you can tell Jason that Ellen is his mother."

"Ellen and I had some good times also because I did care for her, but I fell into peer pressure and I started to treat her like crap. She was good to me and for me, and when father said that I had to marry her, I was willing to do that and be a good husband, but I hurt her too bad and then I received the phone call from Asia."

"Don't you think it is time you tell Jason that Ellen is his mother?" Willie asked.

Eddie was in deep thought. "I have wanted to since the first day she walked into the house. All I see is pain on her face. However, I will not have my sons going at each other. I do not want Jason to feel that I favored Devin's mother over his. Willie, I was young and destructive, I made nothing but mistakes. I can take Jason being mad at me, but for him to think that I favor Devin in any way, I can't take it."

Lisa did not want to look up, as she knew that Eddie would be watching the monitor and that she was breaking her word to him. He told her to keep her legs closed and she did not. She moaned softly as Devin moved in and out of her.

"Your body is amazing, baby," he said to her. She wanted to respond, but she found it hard to focus knowing that the next day she would feel the wrath of Eddie Jones. He defended her with the police only because he needed to let them know that he was in control, not because he felt something for her.

"Eddie, the doctor was playing on both teams. They knew when to strike. J.T. said that they had your computer hacked, not your house, so they should not have been able to know what you were doing, instead they knew everything. The doctor ran because he was caught in the middle of two madmen. He did what you asked and what they wanted, he took Devin's memory just long enough for him to get away from you both. But Devin now remembers."

Willie looked at the screen, "The doctor wasn't a bad guy. He knew that Lisa was pregnant and I do not think he wanted to cause her pain. But something went wrong. He said something about a father and daughter coming to his office and the daughter begging her father not to hurt Devin. But Devin said there was no one. They are still out there." Willie frowned,

"Something is still wrong." Willie and Eddie looked up when they heard Lisa scream.

🌀 🌀

Lisa rolled over, she was basking in the glow when she looked up; one of them was in the bedroom with her. "We want her," he said. "We want the baby." She screamed when Carolyn came into the room and closed the door.

"Let him take the baby," she said. "I will not lose Jason and Lionel because of a child that no one wants." She started to attempt to reason with Lisa as he held her down. "Devin is in love with Darlene and he will never love you or the child the way he loves her."

Lisa started screaming and kicking uncontrollably; she could not stop herself, her legs went high. She was not only fighting him, she was fighting her best friend.

"Lisa, wake up." She could not; she had kicked so much and had fallen to the floor from the bed. She could not open her eyes, she was done and could fight no more. She had lost the battle in her mind. She and her child would die.

Devin picked Lisa up. "She is having a nightmare," Devin said. He tried to wake her, but she would not wake up. "Something is wrong," Devin said. He moved his foot and kicked something. There was a towel on the floor.

"I am calling a doctor," Eddie said. He called his friend Leonard Pendergrass.

"Have J.T. check the security camera," Jason said.

Lisa opened her eyes to find Devin, Jason and Willie standing over her. There was a scent of lavender and something chlorine. The towel had a chlorinated smell. "Don't touch it," Devin said. "It smells like chloroform."

Jason noticed a red dot on Lisa's pajama shirt that she was wearing; Devin unbuttoned her shirt to find that she had a small cut on her stomach. "How did they get in here? Someone got in here right under our fucking noses." Devin was pissed. It was déjà vu, the same thing that happened to his mother.

Christian stood guard in the hall with Lisa's bedroom door open while Devin and Jason looked over the security video.

"There he is," Jason said. Lisa was having a nightmare and started screaming and kicking before he could do anything, which is why he dropped his cloth next to her; she must have inhaled it, which is why they had trouble waking her. "The video does not show how they are getting inside the house," Jason said. "Maybe they never left the house. Maybe they are still in the building."

The house was checked up and down; they could find no one. Willie talked to the gardeners and they could only say that someone walked in the house through the side door. Whoever walked into the house was gone.

Eddie looked at the computer monitor, and a car was at the gate. It was Leonard Pendergrass, the family physician. Eddie smiled because things had changed since he last saw Leonard. Eddie recalled the last time he talked to Leonard. They both drove to the lake when Devin's car was found. When they pulled out a body, Eddie could not look at the body, but Leonard did and said, "That is not Devin, it can't be." He thought Leonard was talking out of grief, only Leonard was right.

Eddie opened the door and Leonard walked inside. "Hello, old friend," Leonard said.

"Come in," Eddie said. "Did you bring the ultrasound equipment?" Eddie asked. Eddie thought that the girl child was a myth; only Jeffrey was taking it seriously and now he would do the same.

"Why all the security?" Leonard asked.

Eddie explained the myth and someone trying to kill Devin.

Leonard was in disbelief because he had heard of the Florida cage myth and that of the Brotherhood who killed girl babies. "Surely you do not believe in all of this hocus pocus," Leonard said.

"I didn't," Eddie said, "until I saw these people with my own eyes. And they have killed friends." Eddie stopped and thought of Asia. How could he tell his friend that someone had walked into his house and killed his wife without him knowing? Leonard said that Asia could not have committed suicide because there was no way she could cut both wrists so deeply.

Eddie called Devin and Skeet to retrieve the equipment from Leonard's car. Eddie and Leonard walked upstairs to Lisa's room. Lisa was lying in bed. She looked at Eddie and wondered if she could trust him. Eddie had taken an interest in knowing the sex of the baby and called his friend. "Lisa, this is Leonard Pendergrass." Lisa smiled slightly and looked at the door when Devin and Skeet walked in with the electronic devices.

Leonard took Lisa's blood pressure and lifted her shirt, revealing her belly. He placed gel on her belly and moved the ultrasound device up and down and then in a circular motion on her stomach. Lisa listened and watched. The only sound there was was the humming sound of the equipment. She looked over and the family was standing in the room, looking at the monitor. Lisa grew panicked because she could not hear the baby's heartbeat.

Lisa looked at Carolyn with tears in her eyes. "Carolyn, the baby does not have a heartbeat," Lisa said.

Devin held Lisa' hand and asked the doctor if something was wrong.

Leonard did not speak; he moved the equipment around and suddenly there was a beep and a thump. Leonard smiled and pointed to the screen on the television monitor and said to Lisa and Devin, "There is your daughter."

Devin smiled and said, "Look at her." Devin kissed Lisa and smiled and said, "We have a little girl."

"I will fix you something to eat," Ellen said.

"Everyone, let Lisa get some rest," Eddie said. Eddie walked out of the room and asked Christian to stay by Lisa's door.

Devin and Skeet placed the equipment back into the car and walked around the house again.

Lisa walked into the movie room, where Ida was watching a large screen television. "Hey, honey," Ida said. "Come and watch some pay per view with me; they have all of the channels."

Lisa looked at the screen; it was so big it nearly covered the whole wall. She thought of how vain Eddie was. "No, Momma, I have to go and face the music," she said. She knew he had watched her and Devin, and today he would ask her to leave his house.

❤ ❤

Detective Walker looked at the picture of a girl that was found on the side of the road. His partner walked in, "Her name is Darlene Richardson," he said. "I asked her father to come down to the station. He said that she had gone missing a few days ago. First, he thought nothing of her being gone because she would sometimes take some of her friends away for the weekend on their private plane. But when she did not call, he began to worry.

"You are not going to guess who she was dating," Detective Walker said.

"Who?" asked Detective Johnson.

"Devin Jones," Detective Walker answered.

Detective Walker pulled out the pictures of Darlene Richardson. With a sinister look on his face, he had asked the Brotherhood to be careful not to get other law enforcement officers involved. But they got lucky because the case landed on his desk. Giving the Richardson girl back so quickly could cause problems, especially now that Susan Milo's office was involved.

"Darlene's father Cecil Dubois said she was at the hospital with Devin and that was the last time he had seen his daughter. I am going over to have a talk with Devin now; don't you find it strange that his fiancée is missing and he did not report it?"

☙ ☙

"What's up?" Devin said. Detective Scotty Johnson and Devin were good friends. They worked murder cases together and Devin was in Scotty's wedding. Devin knew why he was there, and he knew it was about Darlene. "Where is your partner?" Devin asked. He wondered if Scotty knew what his partner was doing in his spare time, if they had recruited him to join the Brotherhood. He had known Scotty for a long time and thought he was on the up and up. But he also thought that about Thaddeus Walker, only to find out that he had been setting his family up.

"He is at the office going over case files. We found your fiancée's body last night on the side of the road."

Devin looked at Lisa; he knew she was listening. "Okay, Scotty, let's not play games; I do not have a fiancée."

Scotty sat down. "Okay then, we found the body of a woman by the name of Darlene Richardson, and do you know her?"

"Let's not play games, Scotty, we both know that you know I know Darlene; her father and my father have done business together in the past and they both wanted me and Darlene to get together. However, it did not happen. She was not my type."

"What's going on, Devin? First, Lisa and then Darlene? Susan Milo was associated with Lisa and she was gutted like a fish, as was Darlene, and if Lisa had not escaped, she would have died the same way. You and I have worked together. We have partied together, and I even got kicked out of my house by my wife Glenda and slept on your sofa. Devin, talk to me, help me out here."

"There is nothing I can say, Scotty. I'm a lost," said Devin when Scotty decided to give his own information.

"There is something strange about Thaddeus. I have been assigned to work with him a little over three weeks, and he has me concerned with some of the things he says." When he did not get a response, he went a little farther, "He said that Susan Milo was cut open and sewed back up several times." He looked at Jason, "How would he have known that? And, he also bragged about coming into a lot of money real soon, he bragged about getting some girl pregnant," Scotty paced the floor, "but he had a vasectomy."

"Does he talk about his mother?" Jason asked when Scotty eyes went to the ceiling.

"Only that she died when he was young."

Scotty walked out and offered to send over files on Melissa Thomas and Jeffrey Thomas that he thought would help. He walked out of the house with a sense of accomplishment. He smiled. It was show time.

As Ida walked through the house, Simon opened the door slightly. He wondered if he did a bonus killing, would Father reward him? She was so close to him that he could touch her. She turned and looked around, feeling watched. She walked to look at what was in the closet, her hands reached out. *That's it, old lady*, he smiled. *I will give father a bonus killing.* He pulled out his blade and was ready to strike.

"Momma, come to lunch." Lisa touched her shoulder and Ida jumped, "What's the matter, Momma?"

"You scared me," Ida said as she took one last look at the closet before she walked into the kitchen with Lisa.

～ ～

Detective Johnson had a package delivered to the house. It was information on Melissa Samuels. He also wanted to dig deeper into the life of his partner before he went to a higher authority about his partner of three weeks.

Skeet pulled out the file on Melissa Thomas. "She had a total of seven children, all boys."

Devin looked at the file on Jeffrey Thomas. "He was a cosmetic surgeon and a fertility doctor. He was fired from the hospital because he was said to be unfit; he impregnated a woman with his sperm and not that of her husband. The woman aborted the children." Devin looked at Skeet, "There was more than one. It looks like the doctor needed a doctor of his own," Devin said. "A fertility doctor and Melissa was his incubator. He was impregnating her so she could have more than one child at a time. Melissa first gave birth to twins and then triplets and twins again." He read the death report on one of her children. "Ross Thomas died when he crashed his car into a building, killing himself and his wife."

"Devin, look at this," Skeet said. He removed the label and they both smiled because their suspicion was confirmed, when suddenly they turned their attention to the television. The woman's face that flashed across the screen was familiar to him. "Officer Glenda Johnson was said to be responding to an emergency call when she was shot and fell into the water off the pier."

"Skeet, hang around. Something is going to happen because tonight is the anniversary of Jimmy and James's death and someone has died every year. I suspect that they will keep up the tradition."

"Okay, Dad, no more fucking around, it is time for answers; I think you know more than you are saying. You are a cold-hearted son of a bitch and I know hearing that gives you a sense of pride, so let me lay it out for you. Someone is walking into this house. They know the layout of this place, so it is someone that has been here before. They are coming for Lisa's baby, Dad, my baby, and I will do everything in my power to prevent that from happening. They are going to have to kill me to get their hands on my daughter, so if you love me as you say you do, then you will stop bullshitting around and come clean. You said that Jimmy was seeing Ellen and we know that Ellen had a child. What happened to Ellen's baby, did your father kill it the way that he killed Judy's?"

"Okay, son, you are right," Eddie said, "no more secrets. All I ask is that you and your brother forgive me. After all of this is over, we could be like this—all together as we are now. I held back the truth because it has been so good having you boys home, eating good food every day, and sitting in the family room, talking about the past—the good past—so promise me both of you that you will keep things as they are."

Both fell silent and so did Eddie. He would not talk until they agreed to his terms, "Okay, Dad, start talking."

"I lied when I said I did not know Melissa Thomas, only when I knew her she was Melissa Johnson; both she and Jeffrey Thomas have been here on several occasions." He pulled out an envelope with pictures of Melissa and Thomas and there was one of Ellen.

"Dad, who is this?" Jason pulled out a picture of a woman with long black hair in a ponytail. She was covered in clothing, but you could tell she was attractive.

"That is Ellen."

Jason pointed out that the doctor at the hospital when Devin was admitted was Thomas. He could not tell by Ida's pictures because it was a profile of him. He was older, however, they are the same and now he knew why the doctor departed the room when Eddie walked in. He did not want him to see who he was. Eddie was so focused on torturing Lisa. He had walked right past a murderer.

Eddie looked at Willie and smiled at the thought of her. "Melissa was a freak, she was a woman that aimed to please, you asked and she delivered. Yes, I had her many times and so did Willie, hell Dad might have had her also that was the type of woman she was." Eddie looked at Willie. "She had about four or five kids at that time and a total of nine at the end. She would come over with Thomas, a man who, at the time, was a medical student. We partied and screwed when Mom and Dad were not around. We wondered what the connection was with Jeffrey and Melissa because he would be in one room and she would be in bed with whomever.

"My father loathed him, he said that he was a sneaky son of a bitch. But for some reason, he tolerated him. He would say that he was a son of the man that died at one of his construction sites. I did not care, I wanted to get my rocks off and Melissa would do just that. Ellen was a student at the community college and she was an honor student, so Mother asked her father if she could tutor Judy on weekends; she would spend the weekends at the house and study with Judy."

Willie listened, he wanted Eddie to get to the point, but he was beating around the bush. If Eddie did not tell Jason soon that Ellen is his mother then he would lose the guts.

"Ellen had been coming for months when Mom notice how Jimmy was when she was around. He would laugh and talk to her and at night, they would hear him and her laughing and talking. Jimmy was dating a woman by the name of Arleen. He was a little old fashioned and took his time to get to know her.

Before things happened with the two of them, though, she died when her car hit a pole. He was hurt by that so he took a liking to Ellen. He said that she reminded him of Arleen.

"All good things must come to an end. At least that's what I thought. One day I was in bed with . . ." Eddie was trying to recall, "and I never heard my father walk in my door. I thought if he knew what Willie and I were doing on the weekends, he would have a fit. He said something to the effect that they were girls, so they were their families' problem and not his, and if they opened their legs, I should climb between them, and that is what I did.

"He sat on my bed after I finished with . . . " Eddie still could not recall her name, there had been so many. "He told me that Jimmy needed to get laid, he had grieved Arleen long enough. He knew Ellen and Jimmy were close and he wanted Ellen to sleep with Jimmy."

Devin shook his head, "Your father was a sicko," he said.

Eddie sipped his drink, "No, son, my father was a man who did not give a shit."

"What role did you play in getting Ellen to sleep with Jimmy?" Jason asked.

"I was to offer her money and get both her and Jimmy drunk, but there was a problem."

"Did she tell you to go fuck yourself?" Jason asked.

Eddie knew Devin and Jason did not share his values; and they both cared for Ellen. They were raised to respect women and how to be a gentleman in one's presence, which is why he was not successful with them. When he would hire women to come over and pleasure them, they would ask him if he was out of his fucking mind, just as Jimmy had years earlier.

"She probably would have, but it never came to that. I recruited Judy to find out things about her. Judy acted as if she was Ellen's friend, in order to find out personal things about her."

Now they understood why Judy felt guilty. She had used Ellen. "Instead, she found out that Ellen came from a very strict family, Ellen was pure—she was a virgin, and she had never even kissed a boy before. So, instead of Ellen, I got Melissa; if anyone could pleasure him, she would be the one. It was easy access and he could go as rough as he wanted, hell I once broke my bed screwing her, it fell right to the floor and she still delivered."

Jason and Devin shared a look. "I know what the two of you are thinking and you are wrong, she repulsed him. Even full of alcohol, he would not touch her; he called me every name including bastard, and he accused me of trying to get him a disease. He said she was a whore and he had his own girl and to cheat on her with a slut was an insult. That is when I found out that he was just helping Ellen; he would give her extra money so she could buy things for herself. Momma had taught her and Judy how to sew and he would buy material for her lessons because if Ellen did not bring home the money she worked for, her father would beat the hell out of her."

"How did you know that her father was hitting her?" Jason asked.

"Because it all made sense." There was a lot more to the story, so he listened.

"One night, Mom and Dad went to dinner. Ellen's father had called for her before they got back, so she did not get her pay. She returned an hour later black and blue for it. She apologized for having to come back, however, her father was not happy that she had come home with no money. Jimmy held a towel on her black eye, and when Mom came home, she paid her and made Jimmy and I take her home."

Devin asked Eddie a question that no one expected him to; one minute they were talking about Ellen, and they had no idea where it came from. "Dad, you talked of how you got your rocks off with Melissa, is there any possibility that her last children are yours? Melissa's last pregnancy, she had boys, twin boys. Melissa Thomas was first Melissa Klein, and then Melissa Samuels, and then Melissa Thomas; this woman really got around. What I don't understand is why waited so long to kill her? She was allowed to have her babies and she died a year and a half later, why wait?"

Eddie had dodged another bullet; instead of Devin asking about Ellen's baby, they were more concerned about Melissa.

"You should have told them everything, Eddie."

"No, Willie, I said all that I could at the time. I told them what they needed to know and as soon as all of this is over, then Ellen is out of here." Eddie sat and stared at Ellen, "She stares at the ceiling every night," he said to Willie. "I know she is in pain, but I can't lose my boys."

Eddie performed his nightly routine; he searched through every room. He could see Ida and Judy watching the big television; he also noticed what they were watching. Eddie laughed. He searched through Carolyn and Jason's room and Lisa and Devin's; he watched as Lisa lay in Devin's arms, and he had his hands on her belly. Little Claire was looking at the door. Devin seemed to have gotten his memory back fully. *Yes*, Eddie laughed, *she has the peace of understanding any time she could fuck him and get his mind right at the same time; I was thrown a curve ball.* He smiled, *my son was not only Chris Weber, he was also Mr. Johnson. Their love is clouding their judgment. Melissa Thomas had nine kids, and I know that and she was never married, not that I recall, not even to Jeffrey.*

Willie realized his friend had no understanding about relationships. He was married to Asia, but he had not grown from the process.

"Willie, I hope when all of this is over, I can still have my family. It has been good, being a family. I messed up and I hope that I will be forgiven for it." Eddie watched the screen. He admired his sons for wanting a normal life. Now he sat and watched his sons in the arms of the women that the loved, while he sat up at night and drank himself into a stupor. He viewed the hall and all of the doors were open. He wondered if he should talk to Ellen and make amends with her. He filled the screen to find that she was asleep. He checked on Judy and Ida; they were eating cheese and crackers, and watching porn. Jason lay with his eyes closed and Carolyn was asleep. Lisa and Devin were talking, while Claire sat up in bed. She looked as if she were trying to get their attention.

"It was your baby Judy aborted, wasn't it?" Eddie asked Willie. "When I was with God knows who, you were with Judy."

Willie put down his glass. "I cared a lot for Judy and, yes, if she was pregnant, it was mine. She called me and told me she had something to tell me, but when I got home, she was gone and that messed me up."

Eddie looked into his glass.

"He made her leave; he threw her out on the street and there was nothing we could do about it," Willie continued. "I was in Michigan with your father, wrapping up a business deal. Your father came back, and I stayed a few extra days. He knew about us, he said Judy was trouble and I should disassociate myself with her. I was upset, so I told him that whomever I decided to be with was none of his business. He left before me and now I know why, he wanted to come home and make her have an abortion before I got back and when I returned she was in the hospital and a few days later she was gone."

Eddie didn't say a word, he just watched the screen. He watched from the hall, and when he noticed that Ellen's room door was closed, he tried to get the camera in the bedroom to work, however, it was stuck. He lifted his eyes to the stairs. Claire was going crazy, and he could hear her running down the hall.

He looked at the screen and that is when he saw it, someone was in the bedroom with Ellen; he could see it do the dance as she watched. She did not move, but he could see the fear in her eyes. Eddie grabbed his gun, "He is with Ellen."

Ellen was sleeping when she felt something pierce her skin; she opened her eyes, which was all she could move. He stood over her. He was looking at her and she wanted to scream, but she had no voice. She was paralyzed; her body would not move as it danced.

"Hello, Ellen," he said in his demonic voice, a voice that he had perfected. He was so proud of it because it put more fear into the women he had killed than his size. He was the biggest and the eldest of all the boys, and he had to set an example for the others—he would show no mercy. He was a natural born leader.

Ellen's eyes pleaded with his. "No, Ellen, your time is up," he said. "Father was disappointed with me earlier, but tonight I will make him proud." He wondered what gift he would receive for his work tonight. When he killed Betty Jackson and all the others, Father praised him and bought him anything his heart desired. "I get no pleasure in killing you, which is why I have allowed you to live much longer than you should." He fixed her clothing. He wanted her to look perfect while her body burned. He stood over her as a tear rolled down her face. "Killing you, I will get no pleasure, but I will be praised by my family and God." He walked to the other side of the bed and looked down at her, "You see, Ellen, I get no pleasure in killing you because no one will care if you die."

He drew back his scalpel, when he heard a man's voice say, "Think again, motherfucker."

His body felt hot in a certain area. He tried to run, but he had lost his footing. His body was on fire as it fell to the floor. Suddenly, his eyes were focused on the ceiling.

Devin met Eddie and Willie in the hall. He picked up Claire and handed her to Lisa. Jason asked Carolyn to go into the room with Lisa and close the door. Eddie got all other security to check around the side of the house. There was a truck there that should not be. All of the men walked to Ellen's room. They slowly opened the door. They had listened as the man tortured her with his words. They watched a tear roll down her face and she suddenly closed her eyes.

Devin and Jason all opened fire on the man, who fell to the floor next to where Ellen was lying. Jason grabbed Ellen from the bed and took her downstairs where Carolyn and Lisa followed. On their way down, they could hear gunfire from the side of the house.

Eddie and Willie opened the door to find Skeet and J.T. coming back to the house. "We got one of them," Skeet said to Eddie.

"And so did we," Eddie said with a smile as he shook their hands. "Take the truck and park it down the road, and get back here fast."

J.T. drove the van and Skeet looked in the back. Skeet wondered if the van was where his mother met her fate. It carried a bed and straps to restrain their prey while they used their scalpel to cut them open.

"Are you alright?" J.T. asked Skeet, as he sat in silence.

"Yes, J.T., I am alright."

Lisa held towels on Ellen's face while they waited for the drug to wear off. "We are here, Ellen," Lisa said as she held her in her arms.

Judy and Ida entered the room with Christian. "What is wrong with Ellen?" They asked as Lisa was tapping her face calling her name.

"They came for her tonight," Lisa said.

Judy laughed and cried at the same time, "You mean all these years she has been telling me the truth. I mean that night at your house, I thought that I was seeing things when I saw him standing across the street."

"I told you, Lisa, he was sitting in a truck watching your house at night," Carolyn said.

"When you told Jason about the truck parked across the street, Jason and I waited for it." Devin said. "We found out that it was Old Man Duncan from across the street." He said that his wife thought that he had quit smoking, and every night when she went to bed, he would sneak inside of his truck and smoke a cigarette, and afterwards he would drive around the block to get rid of the scent.

"He stopped after a few days because he was seeing the man in black watching the house. He said that the devil watched the house at night, and it put the fear of God in him, so he no longer left his house."

Ellen still lay with her eyes to the ceiling. "Is she going to be okay? Should we take her to the hospital, Jason?" asked Carolyn.

"We have to wait for the drug to wear off. It is some kind of anesthesia and there would be nothing they could do except what we are doing. He tortured her mind," he said. "I only hope she comes out of it soon."

Devin looked at Ellen again and he got angry and threw the files to the ground. As J.T. bent down to retrieve them, Devin said, "Don't bother, J.T. I remember them all by heart. Reese died in a car crash, the one that held Lisa captive was Rodger, and the one that chased her was Richard. The one J.T. hit was Ricky, the one who attacked Ellen was the oldest called Roland, and you have Rodney and Robert Samuels, who we know is a doctor at the hospital."

"Lisa said that there is one called Sister."

"Rodney Samuels is the one called Sister. It's more than likely that his father had performed a sex change operation on him to make him a woman, which is what is in the files, but he wanted a normal life . . . A family . . . Which is why he wants a baby so badly. He kills women to take theirs."

"First, my mother," Skeet said. He did not want to say anything, because he knew that she had had a physical relationship with Eddie Jones and he knew that it was more than likely the baby was his. "My mother was pregnant, the baby was removed from her, and it was less than three months old, which means it had no chance of survival." Skeet was still confused. "Why would he inseminate her and not do it the normal way?" Skeet asked, "They were married, right?"

"Because," Devin said, "he was gay. Melissa was a carrier for his children and the reason your father despised him so much is that he knew it. Jeffrey Thomas was not interested in Melissa. She was only for show. A big and prominent doctor had to keep up appearances when he was with his colleagues. Klein said that one of the Milton woman's children fell in love with one of the Jones children. It was not Judy, Dad, it was your brother Jimmy."

"All of that is a bunch of bullshit, the files that Scotty delivered were to throw us off. Those are not the real Melissa Thomas files." Devin said Eddie clapped his hands, "I see, son, that 'juicy' has not made you crazy," he said as he turned and looked at Lisa. However he would not let his son insinuate anything about his brother. "Jeffrey might have fallen in love with Jimmy, but there could be a reason why."

Eddie hit the roof, he thought his son's words were revenge for what he had done to him, but if Devin wanted a war of words, then he would give him a fight of his life. Eddie stood and Willie grabbed him, "I am okay, Willie," he said. He looked at both Jason and Devin. "You and your brother think that you are so fucking high and mighty because now you are fucking one woman instead of the revolving door you used to have. Your brother fathers a son with Carolyn and suddenly decides it is time for him to become a man, which you and I both know he would not have done otherwise. And you, Devin, you meet a woman and get her pregnant and she don't know who the fuck you are. She screwed you last night, you didn't know who the fuck she was, and you stand here and start judging my family. We were not perfect, but neither are you two." Eddie was proud of himself. He would have to find a way to get to Lisa, but he knew he had hit pay dirt with Carolyn.

"Thank you, Mr. Jones, for that performance," Carolyn said. You are such an asshole, but I have been so selfish. I listened to my best friend tell me that I was in her nightmare. I have been so insecure that I have done nothing but make mistakes. For years, I have let your words make me a bad person. It hardened me, and I am sorry for that." Carolyn looked at Devin and she only hoped that Eddie was paying attention. He needed to pay for what he has done. "Do you believe in fairytales?" she asked him. "I found it hard to understand how you could suddenly remember Lisa, and then she explained to me about the fairytale thing, and then it made sense what the doctor did. I do not condone it, but I understand."

She took a deep breath when Lisa said that in fairytales, the bad guy never owns up to what they have done, they never apologize for the pain that they have caused, and when you did, it broke the spell. It showed that you cared and she was not just a piece of ass to you. She had been carrying around the guilt of Stephanie's death because she felt responsible for it.

"Jason, I hope you do not hate me for what I have done." Carolyn checked Ellen before she began. "When I saw you with Stephanie that night I was devastated. I could not get that picture out of my mind and instead of talking to my understanding friend," she looked at Lisa, "I turned to Dr. Samuels. I cried on his shoulder. It was me that told him that I saw the two of you together. I had no idea about any of this, and I could have gotten you killed and my own son taken from me."

Jason held Carolyn as she cried. "It was not your fault," he told her, and everyone agreed that Stephanie would have been a target sooner or later without her.

"Your brother is alive, Dad, he was not the one that died with your father." Both men tried to reason with Eddie, but he could not get past the point that they thought his brother was gay. Jason wanted to show compassion to his father, although he had not shown him or Devin any. He knew things were coming to an end, and he did not want to be left alone. Eddie had a heart after all.

"Dad, I know you thought that Jimmy was in love with Ellen, but something else was happening. I think that James Sr. Knew, which is why he wanted Jimmy to prove his manhood." Ellen listened, her eyes wide in shock. Eddie wanted to make Jason think that she was with Jimmy and not him.

She sat up, and then stood to face him. She only hoped that Lisa would keep her word and not leave her alone.

"You are a liar!" Ellen shouted. Eddie stood up. He wanted to intimidate her, and it was working until Ellen looked at Devin, who gave her a nod. It was time to finish the puzzle and Ellen was a big piece. "If you will not tell the truth, Eddie, then I will." Her hands began to shake.

"I was a student at the community college when Judy started her attendance. She was rebelling, so she did nothing, she did not even try. I was an honors student, which is how I got to attend school. My family was poor," she said with a smile, "we had nothing. One day Judy missed a class. I decided to share my notes with her. I explained to her how everything was done and she passed the test. Ida was so proud that she asked my family if I could tutor her with pay, of course, and Daddy said yes.

"On Fridays, Ida would pick us up from school so she could give us both sewing lessons, and one Friday she couldn't, so Jimmy and Eddie did. That is when I became somewhat of a celebrity," she said. "Girls that made fun of me wanted to talk to me because they saw me with the Jones boys. Jimmy knew I was being bullied, so he would always look for me at lunch. He said I had become a member of the family. Jimmy was so kind. He would always talk to me. He would come into the room that Judy and I shared and talk to me. He and Eddie were so different. Eddie never said a word to me. He would talk at me, but not to me."

Ellen looked at Judy; now she knew Judy was setting her up to get extra money from Eddie. Judy had only pretended to be her friend.

"One day Judy shared some of her secrets about her boyfriend and said we were friends, and that we could talk about anything. So, I told her I had a crush on someone and I told her that I had never kissed or dated anyone. It was supposed to be our secret.

"Eddie was dating a girl name Yolanda," she said when she looked at him. "They had broken up because she was a real snob, which is what he liked about her. Finally, Eddie started talking to me. I was walking down the hall and he cornered me. 'Judy said you have never kissed a boy,' he said to me, and then to my surprise, he kissed me. I was shocked because I had a big crush on him. I went to my room and lay there when he came in and told me that he was looking for a girlfriend and he had chosen me. He then took me to Ida's sewing room and picked out several dresses that Ida used to sell from the house. I told him I could not take them because Ida would be angry. She wasn't, though. He brought me fancy perfumes and got my hair done." Ellen smiled when she said Eddie told her she had a hot little body. "Everything seemed to be going along nicely until I started making mistakes. One day he asked me to make him a sandwich, which I did." She said. "But I forgot to cut the crust off and he went crazy on me. He started slapping me, six times. I counted. I apologized," she said, "but he did not speak to me for days."

Devin looked at Jason. He had no expression. He knew that the only reason Eddie wanted to be with Ellen was that no one else had. He wanted to break her in. He thought Jimmy was interested in her, so he decided to get her first. Her father was beating Ellen and she was looking for a knight in shining armor, someone to rescue her from her unhappy home. Instead, he abused her, too.

Ellen knew she had to finish. If she didn't, then Jason would never know. She looked at Lisa with tears in her eyes, "Please don't leave me," she begged. "Without you I have no one." She turned to face Jason and Devin again. "Eddie did not talk to me, so I went to talk to him. This time, I fixed his sandwich just the way he liked it and I brought it to his room. Eddie took the sandwich, and he looked at me. He asked me if I wanted to be his girlfriend. I was happy because he was giving me a choice." She looked at Jason, "No one had ever given me a choice. I said yes, and that is when he told me that he had needs and if I was not going to fill them, then he would get someone else. I did not know what to do," she said. "But I did not want to lose him. That is when he kissed me," she said, "really kissed me. A kiss that put fear in me because I knew what was next. He asked me to take off my clothes and my hands started to shake because I was scared, but I did and he did the same, and that is when he lay on top me and tried to . . . " she stopped. She knew she was giving too much information. Nevertheless, her pain could be a lesson to others. "When he could not enter me, he became angry.

He said he thought that Judy was lying when she said that I had never done anything. He got up and poured himself a drink, and then another, before he tried again. When he finally got in, he showed me no mercy. He was so rough that I bled a lot and when he was done, he was angry.

"One Friday, Ida made the boys take me and Judy to the picture show. She said we needed to get out of the house. On our way back, we ran into Tyrone Walker, one of Eddie's enemies from school. Tyrone said Eddie slept with his girlfriend and they did not like each other. Tyrone looked at me. Eddie got mad and started beating me on the street. I did not know what I had done. He said I disrespected him because I looked at Tyrone, but I hadn't," she said. "He said he needed to show Tyrone who was the boss."

Ellen sighed. Everyone knew she still felt the pain of her past. Now they knew why Ellen did not look people in the eyes.

"After a month, Eddie said he had no more use for me. I begged him to take me back and he did, and he was nice to me because I promised him that I would try to do better. I cooked and cleaned for him and I even tried to please him, until I got sick one day, and then he was done with me. I tried for months to get him to take me back, but he wouldn't. He was back with Yolanda and he made sure I knew it. I saw him and Yolanda in bed when I came to tell him that I did not have a period. I never got to say anything because he'd put me out."

Ellen kept her eyes to the ground. "I was three and a half months pregnant when I found out. Unfortunately, Daddy found out, too. I had to write on the calendar every month when I had my period and there was nothing marked, so Daddy knew something was wrong. At first Daddy said nothing, but then said, 'Is that boy going to do right by you?' he asked. I said nothing, so he demanded that I say something, and that is when I told him that Eddie wanted nothing to do with me and that infuriated Daddy. He started beating me and kicking me. He said

I was a goddamn whore and after he was done, he demanded that I go and tell Eddie, which I did," she said.

"I went to the house, but I did not tell Eddie because he was not there. He had gone to Hawaii with James on business, and I was in no condition to feel Eddie's wrath. Ida looked at me and said that my father was a monster and that I should stay with the family and Judy and I would share a room. Jimmy held towels on my eyes. I could not see for days," she said. "That is what Jimmy was to me," she said, "a shoulder to cry on."

Jason and Devin both looked at Eddie because they both knew that Hawaii is where Eddie met Asia, and he had only visited once when he was a boy. He said she had called six weeks after his return to inform him that she was pregnant, and arrived in Atlanta three weeks later.

"I was four and a half months pregnant when he found out. I got the last laugh," she said, "I was too far gone for him to take me to the baby doctor." Ellen then explained to everyone what the baby doctor was. "It was a place you went to if you did not want your baby, but I wanted mine. Eddie and I were in the house alone. He came to my room, he wanted to . . ." Ellen stopped, "and I said no. He grabbed me. He said that there was something different about me. I tried to pull down my shirt when he noticed the small bump in my stomach. I ran to the front and he caught me. He hit me and I flew into Ida's sofa," she said. "I flipped the thing right over. I got up and ran out the house. I tried to go home and Daddy said I did not live there anymore." Ellen went on to say how she slept under the house and she then went to a shelter when she was eight months pregnant, and how when she could no longer afford the shelter, she lived under a bridge for a few days.

Eddie said nothing. He could tell by the looks on his sons' faces, Ellen's story was getting to them. He had lost their respect. He had had only a little ammunition to work with and now it was gone.

Ellen did not stop. She was getting to the good part. If she played any part in the destruction of her life, she would own up to it, but they needed to hear everything. If Jason was going to hate her, she would accept that, but at least he would know.

Ellen looked at Willie. "There are some angels in this world," she said. "I had to sleep under a bridge inside of a box, when I picked the wrong spot to sleep across the street from the coffee shop. One day I saw Eddie and his new bride, they were walking with other people. He looked through me as he always did, but like I said, there are some angels in this world. It was cold outside, he walked up to me and gave me his coat, and he put money in my hand—five hundred dollars," she said. "I looked at him, he smelled really good," she said and everyone knew that Willie was the man she was talking about. "He told me to go across the street to Dave's bar and tell Dave that he sent me, which I did," she said. "And Dave gave me a room upstairs from the bar and a job. I was over eight-and-a-half months pregnant then.

"Every morning I would clean the bar and some evenings I would work the room and bus tables," she said. "Then finally he was born," she said. "I was so excited, I was not alone anymore. I saved all of my money and my little boy wore the best clothing. I was doing it; I finally had peace. One day I was cleaning the bar while my baby slept. Dave decided to have Karaoke night, and I did not know what that meant, so I pushed a button, and there was music to a song that I knew." Ellen smiled, "So, I started to sing to it. I thought I was the only one there, but Dave listened and he offered me a job singing there. He said that a talent agent would be coming through and that I had some pipes," Ellen smiled, "and it happened. It took a year and a half, but it happened," she said, "a talent agent came through, and I was offered a recording contract. My little boy and I were going to California. I called Judy and told her about the good news, and she said she was happy for me."

Ellen began to cry. "I thought that finally I would be able to afford a home for my child and we could be happy. When one night I was taking my baby across the street to get a hamburger," she cried, "he really liked hamburgers . . ." Jason stood and faced her. "When he was ripped from my arms, I was hit so hard by one of Eddie's men it burst my eardrum, but I kept fighting for you, Jason," she said, "until I could fight no longer. I could not see for a few days."

Jason looked at Eddie, and then charged at him when Devin and Willie grabbed him. Eddie pleaded for him to understand, but Jason was out of control. "You told me she left me by a dumpster. You said I was abandoned, you motherfucker."

Jason looked at Ellen. Her eyes were pleading for him not to hate her, but to love her as she loved him. "Please don't hate me," she begged him.

"Jason is your child," Carolyn said, "Why didn't you fight for him, Ellen? You said you loved him. You allowed Eddie just to take him. What kind of a mother were you?"

Ellen knew Carolyn would not understand. She knew she had to finish. "I did, Carolyn. After I was released from the hospital, I came straight here, the guards were ordered to keep me away, and they did. I was arrested and told that if I went back to the estate, I would be placed in jail. I cried myself to sleep that night, and the next morning I woke up in a mental hospital, I stayed there for years, and I would still be there. They were telling me that I did not have a child and until I admitted it, I would be there. I did not know how to say those words, until Judy visited and she told me that she would take me home if I just said to them that I did not have a child. That I could not get him back into a place like that. Therefore, I did. It took me almost ten years, but I did."

Ellen told Devin that it was Asia who would give her pictures of Jason every year. She would stand outside the side gate and Asia would sneak out and give her a picture of Jason.

She told him that a week before his mother's death was the first time she had seem the man in black. "I was squatting by the gate. He didn't see me, but I saw him walk by and then he turned and disappeared." She told him that Asia had given her a box, and she asked Skeet to get it from under the bed that she slept in. "She said that the devil was coming for her. She told me that she had taken care of mine and I should do the same." Ellen laughed. "She even told me how you two like your eggs and bacon."

Jason stormed out of the room, but before he exited, he punched a hole in the wall. Carolyn gave Eddie a nasty stare before going after Jason. He returned. He wanted to hurt Eddie. Words could not express the pain his father had caused him. "You had her put in a mental hospital?" he asked. "You had what you wanted, why did you have to do that to her?"

Eddie was at a loss for words. "I didn't, son. I never knew until she was home, about a month after she was released, when I saw Judy and she told me. If Ellen was put in a mental hospital, it had nothing to do with me.

"Jason, I do not apologize for taking you," Eddie said, "you were my first-born son and the fact that she was going to leave the state with you, I could not allow that to happen."

Jason had enough of Eddie's bullshit. "Your first-born son, Eddie. But you thought nothing of me when you were beating the hell out of her," Jason said.

Eddie tried to reason with Jason, "I searched for Ellen because my father demanded that I do right by her, but I couldn't find her."

Jason went after him again. "No you didn't, you son of a bitch, you had another woman pregnant. You did not check under the fucking bridge, you rolled over her every day. Who took me from her?" Jason asked, "Which one of your people took me?"

Eddie did not answer. What he thought would happen had come. Jason thinks that he favors Devin because of Ellen's words.

"Who hit her, Eddie?" he asked.

"Cordell Johnson. He is dead. He died of a heart attack, so you cannot get revenge on him. Jason, I cared about Ellen. I was only twenty years old at the time and I panicked when I found out."

"She was afraid of you!" Devin yelled.

"And so was Mother," Jason chimed in. "You think we do not remember?"

Eddie had had enough of this holier-than-thou crap from the two of them. "Was Lisa afraid of you?" he asked. "Ask her when she thought that she was pregnant, and I will guarantee you she had an idea long before she found out and she said nothing to you because she was afraid, so do not come to me with that shit you are talking." Eddie threw his head back, "I was raised different from the two of you. I was told that a woman should stay in her place and she should be trained to respect you as a man. I am not saying I was right, but now I know better. The pain I caused Ellen kept me from caring about your mother because of guilt."

Devin looked at Lisa and remembered the day he had watched as Dr. Samuels kissed her. He had found the pregnancy test and threw it on the bed where she was lying, which made her hold her tongue with him. He had given her the impression that he did not want a child with her, and she kept the secret from him.

Ellen handed Devin the box that his mother had given her. "She wanted you boys to have this."

He looked at her. She had been at Lisa's house several times and she always carried the box with her. Ellen was a woman of her word, he admired her, and she would always have a place in his heart.

It was quiet, no one said a word. Eddie watched Jason as he stared into space and Ellen stared at him. He hoped for forgiveness for them both because Ellen did nothing wrong; it was entirely his fault.

"How did Ida end up in the mental hospital?" Devin asked. "Did you put her there?" he asked Eddie. Ida lowered her head. "Yes, he did," she said. Now that everything was being laid on the table, it was time to tell it all, so that they could heal and move on.

"When I lost my husband and my son, I lost everything. Because of your father's treatment of Ellen, he did not trust anyone, so he kicked Judy and me to the curb and took the money with him so we had nothing, either. I asked him for money for food and he gave it to me, and that is when I saw him. After all of those years, I saw my first boyfriend, Henry Stanford, and he had not changed. He was making a good living for himself as a musician. He asked me out, and I went. When I called to tell my son how lonely I was, he told me to get a pet. I wanted so badly to see you two and be a part of your lives, but he would not allow it, so I married Henry and we were happy until . . . " Ida lowered her head, "we were sitting in the backyard and there it stood, big and tall and wearing all black. Henry thought nothing of it, but it scared the hell out of me. He came for Henry, because I was happy and I had to suffer. Henry had a doctor's appointment and suddenly a healthy man began to fall apart. He began to get ill and it kept coming around and told me that I had to pay for what I had done, and I did," she said. "I had three beautiful years with him, and then he was gone and I was all alone.

"After the funeral, Judy came back, but she was still miserable. She said that she had married the wrong man and she could not take it, so she stayed with me. It came every night to tell me why it took my husband from me, so I called my son and begged him for help. I told him what was happening to me and he had me committed and when I got there, I was not alone because Ellen was there and we made the best of a bad situation."

Devin opened the box. Inside of the large box were two individual boxes, one with his name and the other with Jason's. Inside his box were letters, jewelry, pictures and a brown envelope. Devin read one of his mother letters.

Letter 5

Son, today the devil came for me. I was walking in the garden and I did not notice the black van parked on the side of the house. I walked because I wanted to see if she was there, the woman with the sad eyes. I walked out the gate when she pulled me to the side. She said, "Look, there are two of them," and we hid and waited in the bushes for them to leave, but they did not. I talked to her and as we waited, I learned that her name was Ellen and she was Jason's mother. She told me of how he was taken from her and all the other terrible things that had happened to her. Your father's guards came for me, but Ellen was left to protect herself, I do not know if she got away safely, because I would not be here if she wasn't there that day.

Devin realized that he was reading the letters out of order. He put them in order by number and started from the beginning. He noticed that Jason's letter read the same. Devin looked in the box again and noticed that there was a *Letter 8* addressed to the both of them.

Letter 1

Son, there is a woman who has been coming for years now. First, she used to stand across the street. She watches Jason and you as you play. I noticed her because she has sad eyes. The next time I see her, I will ask her name and hope to find out who she is. When she walked away, there was something standing there. I had seen it before, but I thought it was only my imagination. It stands and stares at me. It wears all black and it is evil.

Letter 2

Son, today I told your father about the devil and he asked me if I was on drugs. He thought I was making up things to get attention because he refused me another child. It gets so lonely without you and your brother. I then asked him if he had noticed the lady with the sad eyes and he became angry with me, he slapped me, and forbade me to go to the gate again.

Letter 3

Son, the devil was standing there at the side gate. It danced the dance of death. It stood there and then it pointed at me. Its voice was demonic. It told me it would come for me soon. It will come for me when the time is right. It called me a filthy whore and said I would die as one. I wondered if the lady with the sad eyes had seen it. And if she has, does she fear it as much as I do.

Letter 4

Son, this house has become a living hell. Your father keeps me locked in my room and I am surrounded by guards, and he yells at me all of the time. Now we have a new housekeeper. Her name is Betty Jackson and your father said she would be a live in. I could swear I hear moaning coming from her room at night. He said that I am a disgrace to him now, and if I say anything else about the devil, he will have me put away. So, I lied and told him that I only wanted attention from him, that he was spending more time with the help than he was spending with me. I have been in my room for days and I need to get out. I am not sure, but I think that I saw the devil in the house. It walked the hall as if it belonged here and I hid in my closet in fear. The reason I am writing this is that it said that it will come for the both of you one day and I need you to be aware of the devil in black.

Letter 6

Son, today I followed Ellen to her home, she also has a shop. If your father knew this, then I would have hell to pay. I know my time is getting short because the devil has found its way into the house. It danced over me and told me that I will burn in the pit of fire. I was happy to see Ellen today at the gate. She said that she was so worried about me that I had so much to live for. I gave her pictures of Jason growing up, and she smiled and cried at the same time. I had never seen anyone do that before. She and I talked and we ate a dinner she prepared. I only wish I had more time because I have found a friend. I was so happy to find that she had made it home safety. She offered me to stay with her. I think that she has seen the devil also. Your father hired an off-duty police officer John Simon. He has been coming off and on for a month. I do not like him, he looks at me funny and when I said something to your father, he said that he would not return. He was the one who threw Ellen in the street and I found it funny that his job was to protect and serve and, yet, he was so brutal.

Letter 7

Son, your father is out of control. He was angry with me because Jason questioned him about his treatment of me. He hit me again. Said I'd brought another man into his home. It is his home, and I was only a guest. I am happy because I will see my boys. I want to tell you about my friend. One day you will find her and she will take care of you both, just as I would have. I shared both of your lives with her and I know she loved you both, as she watched the both of you grow together. She said things about you both as if she was a proud parent of the two of you. She attended both of your graduations in the shadow. Find her and take care of her because I know she will love you both as I do. And, show her compassion and understanding for she has been through hell. I hope the both of you will show her love for she has never known what it feels like, and I know she will protect you with her life and if it comes to it, I know she would die for you both.

Chapter 16

E llen sat in the kitchen. She had no idea as to the contents of the box. Jason has said nothing to her. He has not even looked at her. She knew that Carolyn would not come to her defense because she, too, has not spoken to her. She only hoped that Jason believed her and would not ask her to leave. Ellen jumped when Jason and Devin walked into the kitchen. "Ellen, can you take us to where you used to stand at the gate. You said you saw one of them and suddenly they disappeared, that could be where they are getting in."

Ellen showed them where she was when she saw the man disappear. She showed Devin and suddenly they hit pay dirt—there were stairs that led down under the house. The contractor had planted shrubs to cover the area and hide them. Ellen went back to the house as the men walked down the stairs. Before she walked away, she yelled for them to be careful. Devin turned and smiled as Jason tried to get a flashlight to work.

"Two men were found dead in a truck," is how the news reporter started. "They were found with multiple gunshot wounds." Father was happy, he was so proud of his sons' handy work. He watched the news in anticipation. He thought he would hear the names Jason Jones and Devin Jones. Instead, the picture sent chills through his body. It was a picture of his truck. He ran to his sons' rooms and they were not there. He screamed and cursed when Sister came in.

"Father, what has happened? Will brothers be coming home? Please, Father, do something."

Mother stayed in her room. She looked in the mirror. *It is almost over*, she smiled, *Father will go for revenge and it will all be over.* She watched as a man came into the house to talk to him. He was one that she had never seen before. She placed the knife under her pillow. She only wondered if she would become a victim of his rage and smiled. Now that Simon was dead, she could become who she really was. She had endured his pain and his torture for years, and there was nothing she could do about it. She watched as people lived normal lives, which inspired her to make a pact with the devil to become something that she was not in order to survive, and now she had to end it all and she knew how. She would send him and Sister to get revenge for Simon and that would seal his fate and she would be free once and for all.

⌒ ⌒

The men walked under the house. They found old boxes filled with pictures and old movies. They even found letters. They carried the boxes with them as they walked to a dead end. When they noticed a door, they turned the knob, went upstairs and found themselves in the house in a room to the back that was used for storage. They walked through and came up to steps that led to the upstairs.

Eddie denied knowing that the opening was there. "My father had this place built," he said, "I was away when he and I would come by sometimes and check on the progress, but the place was not complete until after his death."

Their attention was drawn to the news report about two men found dead. It also had a picture of the truck. Devin looked at Jason. "They will be coming for revenge soon."

Eddie had his sniper in place, just in case something happened. "Take a look at this," Skeet said, "I went down to the department of records. The detective gave us a file on Melissa, but not enough on Jeffrey, so I wondered about him. Apparently, the doctor had his medical license taken away because one of his patients died on the operation table. The article reads that he was preaching a sermon while he was performing surgery, and the patient died." Skeet looked at them both. "Rodney Samuels is not Sister," he handed Jason the article. "Rodney was the patient that died at the hands of Jeffrey Thomas."

Devin pulled out another paper. "It seems that the doctor is a basket case himself. Dr. Thomas suffers from bi-polar disorder and he has paranoid schizophrenia, and it is says he suffers from multiple personalities."

"He was more than that," Eddie said. "Jeffrey was more than that, Jeffrey was different." He thought he would give the apology thing a shot and then try to help to end the problem.

Ellen brought lunch to the men while they went through the files. She had prepared hamburgers for lunch, and she had received a response from Jason that she did not expect. He laughed and gave her a kiss on the cheek. Skeet was impressed. Ellen had cooked it to perfection, "This is good, Ms. Ellen, it has been a long time since I have eaten anything homemade." Ellen walked back into the kitchen, when suddenly you could hear the men screaming at each other.

"Everything was fine, Ellen, just fine until you had to tell Jason the truth." Judy was angry, "Listen to them attack their father because you could not leave well enough alone." They could hear Devin call Eddie a liar, and then Jason started yelling at him also about his baby picture.

Lisa walked in. "Judy," she scolded, "you should be ashamed of yourself. We listened to you share your story about the child that you were forced to give up, and how much you hated the man that had taken it from you. It is hypocritical of you to think that Ellen would feel any different. Jason was going to find out that Ellen is his mother." Lisa said. "And if Ellen had died, then Jason would not have forgiven Eddie for what he had done to her."

"You said that I was brought here when I was a newborn!" Jason yelled. "Where are my baby pictures, Eddie?" There were pictures of Devin from birth and you made Asia take them away. You were abusive to Ellen and when Mom called you out on it, you started abusing her."

Eddie turned to Devin, "Son, your mother had overstepped her boundary. She brought another man into my house and that was unacceptable, even if it was your brother."

Ellen handed Jason a box. It was filled with baby pictures. He and Devin sat and looked. There were hundreds of them. Jason noticed that Ellen had a gleam in her eyes, as she smiled and doted on him. He looked at Christmas pictures. There were at least four of them. Ellen explained to him that he kept attacking the Santa—he had snatched off his beard, taken Santa's hat, pulled off his glasses, and he even tried to bite him. "And the final shot was when Santa decided he had lost the battle and let you wear the hat and beard.

Devin laughed at how fat Jason's legs were.

"Those are muscle," Jason said. "And don't forget that."

Eddie called everyone into the family room. He had a guest coming and he wanted to explain to everyone why she was coming. "First . . ." he said. He stopped and noticed that Ellen was sitting between Devin and Jason. They were looking at baby pictures, when she placed them aside. "I owe everyone in this room an apology. I have caused nothing but misery for you all. I first saw the person wearing the black robe at your house, Lisa. He mocked me and spoke to me in actions, when he showed me a picture of Devin and then he burned it. That is why I took Devin from you." He walked to her, "I had no idea about your condition, and I thought if I could get him away then I could save him. I had lost him once, and I did not want to lose him again."

He then turned to Carolyn. Eddie was pouring his heart out. He needed his boys to know that he was not a monster. "Years ago, when you came and talked to me, the woman that is coming today, she is a psychic and she told me that every woman that my sons touch will burn in the pit of fire, and so will the children they carry until the time comes. I had no idea what that meant, but two of the women that my son dated were killed and burned."

Carolyn sat up straight. Had Eddie saved her from a fiery death?

"I thought it was a coincidence until I talked to her. That is why I sent them away and you also. I went into denial after Asia's death. I had to take my sons memory because he was becoming me. He was out of control," he said when he looked at Devin. He turned to Ida and Judy, "I abandoned the both of you because of the wrong that I had done to Ellen, but I loved you both and it made me a worse person, because I hated myself so badly." Eddie asked them both for forgiveness. "I could not be a husband because of the guilt. I was living in luxury while the two of you were out in the cold and it made me resent Asia and I started making her life a living hell." He turned to Ellen. "I was only a boy when I met you. I was taught that a woman should be trained and now I know better. Words cannot express how sorry I am. What I did to you was wrong and I have suffered dearly for it," he reached for Ellen's hand. She turned and looked at Jason. She knew if she did not make peace with her past, she would keep living in it. She paused before she extended her hand. "Ellen, please forgive me," he asked.

"I hope that what you said is true, that Jimmy is alive, but I thought about what you said about Jeffrey and you could be right. Jeffrey was obsessed with both Jimmy and me. He would watch us all of the time, which is what my father thought was weird about him, but I thought that he was alright," he said, "but eager to fit in and he seemed to care for Melissa a lot. He wanted to be her. . ."

Lisa mumbled and Devin asked what she said. "I looked at some of your father's pictures of Melissa Thomas and it seemed that he was creating a perfect family. He wanted to be Melissa and have Jimmy to be the doting father, but something had gone wrong and the roles were reversed."

"I am so proud of the both of you and you, too, Lisa, because you allow the two of them to think," Eddie continued. "Melissa was seeing Tyrone Walker," he laughed, "but he was not enough for her, so she turned to me and he said that they were over, but she had several children with him. So, he moved on. She would have whomever. And he had his other women who would come over when Mom and Dad were out of town, along with Jeffrey.

"One evening when Willie was with his girl and Tyrone and a few of his friends came over, they asked me if I knew about Jeffrey and I said no. They said that he was a girl and a boy. I had no idea what that meant, so I ignored it." He laughed, "I was only interested in one thing at the time. I had no idea that Jeffrey had come to the house and what they had done to him until we found him later. Jimmy was with Arleen and he came home late and he saw something in the yard. He called me and Willie and we went to investigate: it was Jeffrey."

"What did they do?" Jason asked, while shaking his head in shame.

"They'd tied him to a pole in the backyard and taken off all of his clothes, revealing his female parts and his male parts—he had them both—and they put a corn cob inside of his female part. Jeffrey Thomas was born a hermaphrodite, even though his mother thought it better for him to be a boy, and Melissa went along with everything. She told them Jeffrey's secret and they were curious.

"We cut him down and gave him food and Jimmy found him clothing and helped him. Jeffrey was calm, but Jimmy hit the roof. He cursed me for being such an ass and allowing our home to be a bar on weekends, and after that, there were no more Friday parties or dates. But apparently it was not enough and I thought nothing of it when Tyrone and all of his friends died. They were shot and then burned inside of their cars, and you all were right, that night started the chain of events because dad found out, and instead of him showing sympathy to Jeffrey, he thought only of what he was and asked him not to come around anymore.

"Lady Singleton will be here in a minute. She is a woman that used to talk to Asia and warned her," Eddie said. "I do not believe in all of this psychic stuff, but she has been on the money so far." Eddie told the family that she told Asia why Ellen was there and she told her to beware of the devil in black. Eddie paused, "She also said something about a tunnel that led to the house," he said. He warned them that they had to be quiet and listen, "Only speak when you are being spoken to."

"Lady Singleton is here, Mr. Jones," Skeet announced.

Eddie stood, "Mrs. Singleton, it is good to see you," he said.

Lady Singleton looked up. She did not acknowledge Eddie but said, "There has been a lot of death in this house and also there are the walking dead." Eddie said nothing, he knew she was in what she called a trance and if it was broken, then it would take days before she could re-enter. "I was here," Lady Singleton said is what the woman is telling her. "I was here and when I drove to the gate, I was taken.

Skeet wondered if she was talking about his mother because she was taken from the front gate.

"Make the claim, people," she said, "they want the child. They will have to rethink everything. They want the child because she is valuable, not for love, and after they receive it, she will die," as she looked at Lisa. "Hello, Ida," she said. Eddie gave Ida a look. He put his finger to his lips, asking her to keep quiet. "Accept what you have here," she said to Ida. "Everything else means death to you, and the other . . . He has become a two-face. He is not as you remembered and you have carried the guilt of your actions for too long and allowed the devil into your home and your heart. I want my family," she mumbled, "I need to be with my family and be normal again. I need to put my family together."

Eddie watched Lisa's lips when she said Jimmy's name after Lady Singleton's last comment.

Lady Singleton began to shiver. "There is so much pain in this house," she said as she turned to Ellen. She looked at her. She then asked Jason and Devin to get letter seven from the woman that is named after the continent and read the last six words. *She will die for you both* is what the letter read. They both looked at Ellen. They did not say a word, as they did not want to break the trance. They did not know what to believe because so far, she was on the mark.

"United you stand strong together as a family, forgiveness is the key. Divided you will all fall, for when you think it is over, the devil will still be out there."

She looked at Devin and Jason, as they still looked at the letter, "Love will be the key to survival, you must not be distracted. Act fast.

"Listen, Eddie, you must listen. Put aside your prejudice and accept what you cannot change," she scolded. "All is not as it seems and your mind is all over the place." She looked at a picture of Jason. "The two of you are on the right path, but you must hurry." She looked at Lisa, "You have not opened your gifts. Get them, because you have lost focus. The devil you killed in the house is here. He will haunt you in death as he has in life. He is the cloud that keeps the sun from shining over this house." She looked at Eddie, "It is time for a change. What you started, you should finish very soon. There will be more bloodshed in this place.

"Open the door," she said to Skeet. He looked at Eddie and he gave a nod. Kandy and Willie walked in and Lady Singleton looked at the wall. "One at a time," she said to the air. "Hello, Nibble," she said. Kandy was warned not to speak. "Her vision was of a woman standing there with two boys, both adult, and she carried a child. I found him," Lady Singleton said when she turned her attention to Judy, "William Joseph." Judy gasped. She had never told anyone that when she was pregnant, if she had a boy child, she would have given it that name. "I will guide yours here," she said, "and you will guide mine there." Judy looked at Kandy, who was still in shock that the lady called her Nibble. Lady Singleton laughed as she talked to someone that no one else could see. "She will love again," she said. She looked at Kandy and then to Skeet.

"I will stay the night," she said, "and I will stay for the party." Lady Singleton's trance was broken. "They will come when they think you have let your guards down. Be prepared," she said. "Plan the party, get the gifts," she then turned to Ida. "I would love to watch a movie with you," she said, "and, Eddie, I will not refuse a drink, and none of that cheap shit either."

Lady Singleton walked upstairs with Ida. She knew that Ida was living in the past and in denial. She could see the deception in her vision and she knew that Ida's love would end in death for her and her family.

Jason held the letter in his hand. He read it to Skeet, "Ms. Ellen?" he asked. Jason shook his head, called every man on their security team and ordered that Ellen not be left alone. "She is to be guarded with your life!" He yelled. "Nothing is to happen to her," he said adamantly. Skeet and every man agreed, when Ellen walked in.

"There has been a cooking challenge in the kitchen, old school against new school," she said, and we could use something from the store." Jason arranged everything and he asked two of the men to retrieve Lisa's gifts from her house. "Lady Singleton had a vision about them," he said to Devin, "she said that we had lost focus. It is time to end this madness."

❧ ❧

Father prepared for battle. He had watched the Jones house for days and knew that soon they would get comfortable and let down their guards. Today he watched as Eddie's security guards carried in gifts. He knew that Lisa's party had been crashed when Kandy felt his wrath. He also watched as the guards carried in several bags of food. "Oh, you want to invite me to your party, Eddie," he said. *Yes, I will attend*, he thought with a sinister laugh.

He looked at Sister in the back of the car. "May I go with you, Father?" She laughed. "I want to dance and sing."

He rubbed her face and smiled. "That is not why we will attend. You and Mother are all that is left of the soldiers. The others have betrayed us."

A tear rolled down his cheek. He could not get his mind off his son Simon Jacobs, his pride and joy, the one son he had created that he was proud of. He could not count the holes that were in his son's body, as he lay there with his eyes still open. He listened as the coroner said he had tried to close them, but they would not stay.

When he was left alone with his son, Simon spoke to Father. Take me home, Father, I do not want to be here. It is cold and lonely here. And he did, he brought his son home.

I know I can fix this he thought. *I will bring my son back.* He laid Simon Jacob on the operating table and worked his miracle. "You look great, son," he said. "I thought that I lost you for a while." Simon sat at the table as Father prepared his dinner, "Eat up, son, you need to get your strength back. Soon we have to avenge your brother's death," he said. Father listened as Simon said that he wanted to take care of the Jones family on this own, but father knew that he would have to rest and let him handle it on his own.

"Mother, come in," father said as he gleamed with happiness, "Simon is back." She closed her eyes and chose her words carefully. "They hurt him," she said, "and you as the head of this household, must make them pay for what they have done." She turned away at the sight of Simon because it repulsed her to look into his dead eyes. "Remember what they did to you?" She continued. "How they allowed the others to humiliate you? That is when Sister was born. You created a beautiful daughter that they have desired and could not resist."

Father smiled. Just as every woman did, Sister had been lying about her age. "Not in front of the children, Mother." He frowned and thought of that evening. He had wanted to talk to Jimmy, but when he had gotten to the Jones home he was not there, but there were others and Melissa. "She was a slut," he said to Mother, "and I asked her why she had to be with so many men. She said that she got so much pleasure, that her body craved it. Then she mocked me and said that I was a freak, while the others laughed and asked me to let them see. I listened to the music coming from Eddie's bedroom. Eddie did not hear my cries for help. He was screwing some whore in his bedroom." Father closed his eyes, "Which is why I had so many beautiful children, so that I could train them never to show mercy to anyone, especially the Jones family, and never allow anyone to hurt them as I had been."

He looked at Mother, "I tried to run and they grabbed me and held me down and began to remove my clothing. They watched me and laughed. 'He has a pussy,' one of them said and started to touch me, while Melissa lifted my penis with a corn cob." He thought of Melissa, a woman that he desired to be like. She did not allow anyone to hurt her because she had disassociated herself with her body and was not capable of true love. She had fallen in love with Eddie Jones, but he rejected her and she moved on to the next man. Melissa wanted someone to take care of her and that is what he did. He offered her money to have his children and she said yes. And Simon was born."

Eddie walked into the kitchen and asked Devin and Jason to ride with him. Eddie wanted to show his sons his project. He asked his driver to take them to the place. Jason and Devin had no idea as to what Eddie was saying, however, they did what they were asked. As they pulled from the driveway, they both noticed that what Lady Singleton said was true. There seemed to be a veil over the house, there was no sunshine there. It almost looked like a haunted house and it was no longer a home. Eddie was quiet for a while. He wanted to express the words correctly to his boys. He was never at a loss. Still, he knew that they were both unhappy with him at this time, so he had to be careful.

"I had never taken to heart anything Lady Singleton had said," he started. "First, I thought that she was crazy even if some of the things she said were true, and it cannot be a coincidence that she knows some of the things, because I had never told anyone about the project."

The driver slowed down as he was asked, "That is the project," he said to them. He ordered the driver to keep going. If they were being followed, he did not want anyone to get suspicious. "I had this house before Asia died. Lady Singleton was right, I ignored the signs and now I am paying for it. Asia always talked about seeing someone and I thought she was seeking attention," Eddie said. "But I hired more security workers anyway, only it did not change anything. She was still killed."

Eddie ordered the driver to keep moving. They arrived back at the house. Christian walked out of the kitchen. "Man, do not go into the kitchen, the women are at war in there," Christian said, "and you don't want to go in there." Jason looked; he noticed that the guards were like shields on Ellen. Every time she turned, she would say excuse me to one of them. He was proud to see that they were taking what Lady Singleton said seriously because he was getting a feeling that something was going to happen soon.

Jason walked into the kitchen, when Ellen picked up a plate of battered fried chicken and offered him a piece, "Foul!" Yelled Lady Singleton, "she is trying to prejudice the judge," as she shoved a piece of her famous meat loaf in his mouth. When Devin walked in, Jason signaled him to run. He was being attacked with food, but Devin moved too late. Judy sat him down and the battle began, which tasted better, the women asked. Which do you prefer, they asked as they shoved food in his mouth. Devin did not answer. He was happy because, finally, the house was full of joy, but he was glad when Christian bailed him out.

"Devin, I think you better have a look in here," he said. "They had a bake off first," he said.

Devin counted, there were thirty-six cakes and pies and cobblers. "We are in trouble," he said when Eddie walked in, "What in the hell is all of this?" he asked. Eddie asked Christian to discard all of the desserts. "Do not touch a thing." Devin got in Eddie's face, he remembered when he was younger when he and Jason had returned home from college and they had stopped and picked up some candies and pastries for their mother and Eddie would not allow her to eat them. He later found out that he had thrown the candy and pastries away because Eddie he did not want her to gain weight.

"Turn around and look, Eddie." Devin asked just as Jason walked in. "Look at their faces." Eddie watched as each woman laughed and talked as they prepared the special dish for dinner. "This is the first day since they have been in this fucking house that they feel some normalcy, and if you think you are going to take it away from them, you're crazy."

Just then, Jason stepped in, "Eddie, you always talk about family. Take a good look," he said in a low tone, as he did not want the women to hear him. "This is what family is all about.

They are not a fucking business deal or a negotiating tool you use to profit from. They will cook and if you do not want to eat, then do not come to the table, but some of us want to enjoy life as it should be enjoyed." He did not want to be hard on his father. "Dad, this is all that they have for now, so let them enjoy it."

Eddie walked into the kitchen when he was bombarded. Judy and Ida had snatched him. "Eddie taste this and tell us which is better," they asked when all the others joined in. Eddie realized that his sons were trying to get him to understand family, and now he got it. He turned to his boys and smiled. They knew that they had won the battle, but the war was yet to come.

Skeet set up the karaoke machine, "What is all this?" Eddie asked.

"The women want to do a sing-off," Skeet said. He showed Eddie how to operate the machine. "It only plays the music," Skeet said. "You have to use your own voice to sing."

Eddie thought it was too much, but he had to deal with it, and he at least had to pretend to be a team player.

❧ ❧

"Simon, do you like my new dress?" Sister asked. "I nearly got caught," she said. "There were men at Lisa's house as I tried on her clothing." Sister was thrilled. She had barely escaped the Joneses again. "Wait until I tell Father that in two days they are planning a party so that Lisa can open her birthday gifts." She jumped for joy. She would finally do her part and help to protect her family. She had fallen in love, which is something she had not allowed. She only hoped that she could control herself when she laid eyes on the Jones boys and not feel the passion that she had with the both of them.

Father came in, "Son, I think you should get some rest. You look a little blue," he said. Father loved Simon so much.

He listened as his son, who had been shot multiple times, argue with him. He wanted to assist him in the killing of the Jones boys and bring Mother her baby. A tear rolled down his cheek as he and Simon played chess. In two days, Father said this would all come to an end. Mother will have her baby and I will have my revenge.

"Finish your story, Father." Simon asked, "What did they do to you and why did Mother allow it?"

Father sighed, "I knew about the baby. My mother would always ask me and my brother to have lots of children, because her father had left a pot of gold for the first girl born, so that is why I became close to the Jones family." He laughed because the Klein family was all dead, except for one, he smiled. And he would not be having any babies. "However, there was Eddie Jones and he was a monster with women. So I thought that we would eliminate the competition. But he was slick. He sent his boys away and we could not find them, so I took away his wife and everyone that they touched."

Father placed his hand over his mouth to hold in the scream that he wanted to let out. "I was not born normal and I'd shared my secret with Melissa, but I did not worry about her because I had already sealed her fate. But she had talked when she began to drink too much and told her first child's father. She wanted him to know that we were not together."

"Jeffery and I are just friends," Melissa told Tyrone. "He is a freak of nature. They undressed me and touched me as a woman, and I liked it at first, because for the first time, I felt a sensation and that is when I knew what Melissa was saying about the passion she felt." He turned away, "Then things got out of hand and they started to penetrate me with things, before one of them suggested that they tie me up, and let the world see what a freak looked like. I was not there for long, when Jimmy came home and I could hear him call out to Eddie, and they came and cut me down. The sincere look on his face as he scolded Eddie for allowing someone to get hurt, I knew then he was the one for me, and I showed them all. I had my revenge on them all."

❁ ❁

"Jason and Devin, get in here," Eddie called as he listened to the news of a missing body. "That son of a bitch stole his son's body," Eddie said. They all watched as the coroner spoke to the reporter. He said that the body of Simon Jacob Thomas was stolen from the coroner's office two nights ago after his father had come to identify the body.

Before dinner, the women gathered in the family room. Lisa wanted to see if the karaoke machine worked. It had been long since she listened to music and she thought it would be fun to have a talent show. It would also be nice if Eddie would join in with everything. She had noticed the tension between him and the other men, and thought if they could take their minds off things for a minute, they would work better together.

Lisa pressed a button on the machine and the music started. She requested older music since today's music was mostly rap. Ida would have a field day. Yet, she thought it needed to be toned down. She looked through the selection when she noticed a song she had performed at a talent show. "Ellen, you have to sing this one," she said. "This is an old classic, *Misty Blue*. She pressed the button and the music started, and she handed Ellen the mic. First, she protested, when everyone started cheering her on. Ellen started to sing and everyone stopped doing what they were doing to watch. Jason and Devin watched from the other room, but no one noticed Eddie as he watched her, also.

"Oh, it's been such a long, long time. / Looks like I'd get you off of my mind, but I can't. Just the thought of you, / turns my whole world misty blue." She sang the entire song and everyone was praising it, even Carolyn.

Lady Singleton's eyes were still closed, "Little Eleanor, I thought I was listening to the original singer. You have my utmost respect," she said, as she and Ida clinked their glasses together.

Lisa laughed when Kandy held up her hands and said, "Girl, Eddie heard you." Ellen looked shocked. "You know you were singing to him," she said as she gave Lisa a high five. "Girl, old boy is still cute and don't act like you haven't noticed."

Ellen had an expression on her face. You could not tell if she was blushing or angry. "I hadn't noticed," Ellen said. The tension was released when she started to laugh.

"He does still have it going on," Lisa said and held her hand up, "I am just saying."

"Maybe you can make an honest man out of him," Kandy said, "and I bet he knows what he is doing in the bedroom, too." She high-fived Carolyn. "Girl, do not let some woman come in here and take your man. Then you'll be all up in here fighting, and I know about that, right, Cal?"

While Jason shook his head in the other room he said, "Please do not open up that can of worms again."

Carolyn stood preaching to the choir, "Girl, because you think that you can do without them until you see them with someone else, and then all hell breaks loose, am I right, Lisa? Tell the truth, if you were not pregnant, then you would have beat the shit out of Darlene in the hospital."

Lisa laughed, "Oh yeah, I was going to snatch her ass, but Jason was so concerned and Claire was having a fit, and all that I could do was cry because I wanted to grab her so badly."

No one noticed when Eddie smiled as the women complimented him. He watched Ellen as she sang. There was a glow about her and a voice to match. He walked from the room, "Excuse me, ladies," he said.

"You know you were listening with your good-looking self," Kandy said.

Eddie smiled and walked away blushing.

"Is he blushing? See, Ellen, he is a changed man."

Judy looked up to see Willie coming inside. She turned away when Lisa elbowed Kandy. "Hello, Poppy, Judy said that you are sexy and cute."

He laughed, "And Judy is sexy and cute, too."

Judy looked like a little girl blushing. She put both of her hands over her mouth and laughed, kicking out her feet, "And she said that she would love to cook you a romantic dinner," when he turned around and looked at Judy.

"And I would love to have one anytime, anywhere," before walking away.

"Oh my God," Lisa said. "Is he not the most perfect man you have ever met? Have you ever had someone that would kick your ass with class?

Judy laughed, but she wanted to cry. Lady Clem said this would happen—Lisa would put Willie back in her life, but someone would take her baby.

"Judy, you can use some loving, huh? For the first time since she has known Lisa, she embraced her because all that has been predicted has happened, and the only thing left is that someone would take Lisa's child. "Seriously, I think you and Poppy would make a good match, and Ellen and Eddie."

"Kandy is a little fireball," he said to Jason and Devin. They looked at Eddie and they could swear that he was blushing. Eddie said nothing else. Listening to Ellen sassing, he knew even if he complimented her voice, he would open up a floodgate of emotions from Jason. They had set the trap for two days and they must stay focused.

After dinner, everyone watched Lisa's birthday video. No one knew why it was so important, but Lady Singleton had an interest in it. She and Ida danced to her rolling-on-the-river video. "Oh, Ida, you are one sassy momma," Lady Singleton said. Eddie was worried that the two older women would throw their hips out, shaking the way they were, but the video stopped and they were still standing. "Stop the video," Lady Singleton said, "it is time to open gifts."

Lisa started opening her birthday gifts. "Open this one," Lady Singleton said as she reached Lisa a box that was all pink with a pink bow on top. Lisa knew that this gift had some meaning, but she had no idea. It was a breast pump. She looked at the name on the card and it was from Jenny.

"What is that?" Devin asked. He looked at the card when he saw Jenny's name. "Nobody knew then," he said, "no one knew that you were pregnant. How did Jenny know?"

"Because, honey, she was there when the wires were hooked to the house." Lisa pulled out the picture of Jenny as Marilyn Monroe. She handed it to Devin.

"Son of a bitch," he said. "Dad, look at this picture. Eddie had no idea what he was supposed to see, so he handed it to Jason, who then pulled out a picture of Jimmy.

Eddie watched the video of Lenny Amos. "Dad, is that your brother?

Eddie looked and answered, "It can't be."

Willie watched also, "Eddie, that's Jimmy. Look at his hand," he said. One day while we were playing basketball Jimmy's finger got caught in the net and it pulled off the tip."

Eddie watched in silence and listened to the man's voice. Lisa said, "Jimmy was being held against his will. Maybe we can help him and bring him back home."

"He stopped them from taking her baby, right? Maybe, he wants us to find him and save him."

Willie handed Eddie a drink. "When he came to see Lisa, Eddie, if he wanted to be here, he would have come."

Eddie looked at Lisa, "You said that Jimmy was being held against his will."

Lisa was at a loss for words. She knew that Eddie would resent her.

Lady Singleton knew that her work was not done. She also knew that Eddie would be in denial and it was going to cost lives. "Eddie!" She yelled, "I stayed because I fell in love with this family," she said. "I knew that there was so much love and compassion, and I wanted to guide you. I cannot give the answers, but I can point you in the right direction," she said. "I can read your thoughts. I knew that your mother would make a decision of the heart and not the head, which would end the lives of the people she loved, the people in this house."

Lisa passed Eddie a picture of the real Lenny Amos. "This is the man that died with your father that night. Did Jimmy pull the trigger? I do not know," she said. Ida stopped and began to listen. "I love you, Momma," she said, "and I would give anything for you not to hear these words, but they have to be said." She dropped her head in her hands. She needed to think. Lately, though, it had not come easily. Lisa rubbed her face. She had become dizzy.

Devin went to her side, "Are you alright?"

"She tried to tell me." Everyone turned to her. "Jenny tried to tell me something, but she didn't get the chance. She said I was the only person she trusted and she had to talk to me, but I was not feeling well that day and I never saw her again. She set the camera up for you, Eddie, so you would put the family together under one roof, but you did not. You took Devin only. She knew we were outnumbered and she set the code to get in and out of the house. When she saw Jason that day, she knew then you were Devin. She was trying to help us get us out of harm's way."

"I am not buying that," Carolyn said.

Lady Singleton said to Momma, "He wears two faces, and now you sit here and praise Jenny for trying to find out if one of us was pregnant, and letting them take our children to torture."

Ida lowered her head. She had hoped that she would see Jimmy and have her son back before she left this earth and now Carolyn was putting a nail in Jimmy's coffin.

Jason went through the files again. These were files of three different Melissa's. He was a good detective and would not make a mistake like that. "We are close and he is trying to throw us off of their trail."

Jason walked to his father's bookshelf and looked for his high school yearbooks. "Maybe these will help us." He called in Skeet: "We are going to Big Mac tonight."

Lady Singleton went into a trance. She began to mumble, "I had my appendix taken out. He saved my life. He ripped the child from the core."

Carolyn gasped and ran from the room.

"Momma, I will go home and get dinner for the two of us. How about a nice warm bowl of gumbo? If they bring up food, just leave it. I do not want you to spoil your appetite. It's time for the old bitch to die," she mimicked a voice that no one knew. "Put the poison in the food and she will eat it. "Hello, Mrs. Stanford, I have a light dinner for you. It is what the doctor ordered."

Ida remembered it like it was yesterday, when she only has gas and the doctor told her she had a virus and later offered Lisa a job. They were going to kill her, but fate threw a curve ball and Lisa met Chris, who was Devin. Ida stood up. She was the oldest of the group and it was time for her voice to be heard. "I love you all so much," she said with a smile full of tears. "You are my family and a family sticks together." She looked at Jason and Devin, "You have saved us once, do whatever you need to do to save us again. United we stand strong. Divided we will fall." She looked at Eddie, "Boy, get that stick out of your ass and accept what you cannot change. We lost Jimmy forty-two years ago, and if he has been brainwashed, then there is nothing we can do about it."

Eddie nodded, then he turned to his boys, "Let's enjoy today because tomorrow will be hell on us all."

Lady Singleton threw up her hands, because the family was not still as one. She yelled out, "Everyone sit and listen. Your thoughts are all over the place, so let one voice be heard because, Lisa, they talked and you listened. So, it is now time for you to speak and for everyone to listen, because you are the only one that can read the thoughts just as I can. You pay attention because you have to, no more distractions because an innocent life will be lost if you keep your silence. Start from the beginning and address Eddie first, because you both are right," she looked at Jason and Devin. "However, there is more to it."

Lisa closed her eyes.

"Take your time, baby," Devin said.

"Eddie," Lisa began, "you want to rescue Jimmy so that you can be the one to kill him because you think that he killed your father. But as you said, you partied all of the time, which allowed Jeffrey to have taken your father's gun. We have been all over the place because of secrets and lies. However, I went through the files and the men that hung Jeffrey were all killed with your father's gun. Jimmy was away at college when one of the men died, so he could not have killed him. Jeffrey killed him to get revenge for what they did to him with your father's gun."

Eddie's legs went limp and Jason helped him to sit, "Dad, are you alright?

"When you said that Jimmy was alive and I started to hate him because Dad had to trust someone to let them get close to him, so she is right. I wanted to look him in the eye before I killed him."

"Keep going, child," Lady Singleton said.

"Jeffrey had the house wired," Lisa continued, "and Jimmy knew. He watched you also and knew that if he came here, you would have hurt him because you were so cold and distant. Your life was one big secret and he knew you would not believe him. Plus, there were so many of Jeffery Thomas' children. We know that Melissa had nine but there could be more, which left us outnumbered," Lisa said. "So Jimmy is sending them here one by one because he knows now that we have become a family.

"Momma Ida described Thomas 'like a son,'" Devin said. "He was smart and he probably kept up with family history, but he miscalculated the time the curse should have been lifted and when he found out that Lisa was pregnant, he got Dr. Samuels to propose to her because no one in his family was carrying a girl."

"Hold up," Eddie said, "that son of a bitch proposed to you? Oh no," he said, "that is a snake in the grass and he needs to be taught a lesson," said the man that slept with every woman he could.

Carolyn said, "You are no saint and all of the wrong you have done, you have the nerve to talk about what is right."

Eddie gave her a look. He knows that he and Carolyn will never get along and will never see eye to eye on anything, but he knew how to get to her and that was all that mattered. "I did not go to them, they came to me and you were more than happy to accommodate."

"Right," she said with disgust.

Something was not adding up to him and now he would pull Carolyn's string. "You talked to the doctor about Stephanie. Did you talk to him about Lisa?

Carolyn jumped up, "You son of a bitch!" She yelled. "Your brother is the back-stabber, not me."

"We had a random drug testing at the hospital and that is when they found out that I was pregnant."

"That might be true, but something had to point them in your direction," he said. "You were already pregnant when the cameras were placed in your home."

"Dad, they watched us when we were together," Devin said. They had come so close and if he kept throwing water in Carolyn's face, then they would all fall in and drown.

Carolyn stood. The guilt was getting to her. She had talked to Dr. Samuels after the Friday dinner and told him that she had deceived Lisa and asked for his opinion, because she was worried that Lisa had become pregnant when she and Devin started sleeping together. "It was Jenny, or should I say Jimmy. She asked us all to take a pregnancy test and she reported back to them. She is the traitor and now Lisa sits here and calls her a victim. . . If I am being held against my will, the first chance I get, I am out of there and she had many.

Eddie looked at her as they both stared at each other. "Ms. Young, your guilt is showing."

Her eyes widened, "Fuck you, Eddie!" She yelled and stormed out.

They wear two faces. Willie asked Lisa what it meant. He needed to change the subject and get things back on track.

"It's the Jekyll and Hyde syndrome. Dr. Jekyll was a prominent man well respected and a pillar of the community, but he and Hyde were the same person and Hyde was a killer. If you put it in street language, you tell one person one thing and tell someone else something different." Lisa looked at the picture of Jeffrey Thomas, boy or girl. Devin looked at her as she said, "This looks like the nurse that brought Momma food. I think she means that whatever happens tomorrow, not to let our guards down."

The music started and Ellen began to sing, *These arms of mine . . .* Willie thought of Elmira, how that was their song. He wondered if she knew how much he really did care for her, and if it were in his power, he would never have left her that day. "Ellen's voice is outstanding," he said. There wasn't a sound made until she had finished.

Jason shook his head, "Wow, she is better than when she did Tammy Terrell and I thought that was magnificent. However, I could listen to her all day."

He looked at the letter, "Stop," Devin said, we will protect her, we will not lose her."

"You have shown her nothing but love and affection," Jason said to Devin. "However, I have been distant and cold."

Neither of the men noticed that the music had stopped and the women listened as they talked. "Jason, you have had a lot on your plate, it was a lot to digest at one time. First finding out Ellen was your mother and the letters, and to find out she was treated so badly, and most of all, how much she suffered for loving you so much."

Jason yelled, "No one will treat her like that again! I want the twinkle in her eyes again, as I saw on the pictures," he said.

Devin agreed. "After all of this, maybe we will take her on a trip to the Bahamas."

"I will take her on a trip to the Bahamas," Jason said.

The men began to argue about which one loved Ellen more, when they heard Lady Singleton yell, "You both can take her and you both love her, okay?"

Ellen laughed as the two of them went at each other. She rolled as Lady Singleton and Momma Ida performed *Back That Thang Up*. Everyone was on the floor. "You are a real fine woman. Back that thang up." Momma Ida asked Skeet if he had any Dr. Dre and Snoop Doggy.

Skeet laughed, "I'll see what I can do, Momma."

Kandy performed *Family Affair* by Mary J. Blige.

"Where in the hell did Momma learn all of this?" Eddie asked. "She and Lady Singleton had been watching porn?" Eddie hit the button on the television and it went to the shows Momma Ida had watched since she had been in the house. He looked for a while when he became angry. "This is going too far with Momma," he said.

He listened as his boys attacked him again, "What is it hurting?" They asked. "It is only entertainment, Eddie, let it be. Stop trying to control every goddamn thing. She is not living it," they said, "she is just watching." Devin knew that Eddie would start in on Lisa because she had taken care of Ida and he would feel that she should have never let her watch such programs.

"Eddie, we are living in a new era where people are individuals and each of us is different. You or Lisa cannot control Momma Ida and, if this takes her mind off her problems, then who is it hurting? There are much more important things to worry about."

The house wore a shadow over it. Even from the inside, it felt like a morgue and had the oppression of death inside. There was little laughter, mostly sorrow, as they waited for the inevitable to happen. The day before they enjoyed the entertainment of karaoke, but today they were waiting to see what their fate held. It was silent, and Eddie made sure the security was in place.

Skeet waited in the sniper tower for Eddie's command while the others hid behind bushes.

Eddie looked at the pictures, trying to remember the face of the woman called Jenny. "Lisa, I want to talk to you," Eddie commanded. He had become consumed with anger. "I do not want to talk to you, Devin, or you, Jason!" He yelled, as Jason held up both hands as if Eddie had pulled out a weapon on him. "And especially not you," he said pointing at Carolyn, who gasped. "I do not trust many people," he said, "and lately, the number has decreased, but I have come to trust you. If you look me in the eye and tell me something, then I will believe it. You have my word on that. I need to know what you think of my brother and if you think he is a part of the Brotherhood."

Lisa looked at Devin and he gave his approval to express her opinion to his father because he needed answers. "You were with these people for a while, what do you think?" he asked.

Lisa stood because all eyes were on her and there was so much pain, that the walls rained blood and tears in the house. "When Lady Singleton talked of two faces, I do not believe she was talking about Jimmy. Momma Ida described Jeffrey Thomas as a good person, but he was getting close to the family that he had planned to destroy one by one," she started. "Jeffrey Thomas was a malevolent man, who from day one was breeding a family of murderers to kill this family. I believe," she said as she looked Eddie in the eyes, "he killed your father so that he could keep your brother against his will. Now that he is attacking Jimmy's family, he is coming out because he wants his family to rescue him, which is why he came out as Jenny." Lisa smiled, "I don't think that they know he is Jenny or who Jimmy is."

Carolyn had heard enough, "I will not sit here and let you defend Jimmy, and I will not let my family get killed by these people, not Lionel and not Jason." She then stood and faced Lisa, "How could they not know and live in the same house? It does not make any sense," she said. "Lisa, you need more schooling. If he is still there, then he made his choice and his choice is to be with them and not us."

No one understood where she was going with her statement, and then it hit them that Jimmy was in trouble. Lisa turned to everyone, "This is only my opinion. The family was very close; they refer to each other as Brother or Sister. They were trained to love and respect their family." She recalled two of them meeting in the hall and how they embraced each other and shared their money, "Whatever is mine, is yours," one brother said to the other, and they each shared the same enemy and that was the Jones family. "If they knew that Jimmy was a Jones, one of them would have killed him a long time ago, because that is what they were born for and Jeffrey would have lost all of their respect. What choice do you have when you are being held prisoner and your own family is the target, where do you turn? The people that were trying to kill his family were working for his brother."

Ellen was still confused, "Is Jenny Sister?" she asked.

Lisa smiled at her. "I thought that at first, but the voices were different. When Jimmy is in the house he is Mother and Mother is Melissa. That is why the makeup is different and almost everything else. She is transformed into Melissa, a woman that he admired because she accepted him as he was." Lisa then thought of the picture that Jenny had given her and she needed time to think before she shared her other thoughts with the family.

"Jeffrey Thomas is keeping a secret from his family," Devin said to Eddie, who has now breathe a sigh of relief that his brother is not trying to kill him, instead warn him, through Lisa that he was out there and still alive being held against his will.

"When they kidnapped me, Mother came in and removed her gloves, so that I would know that she and Jenny were the same person. Inside the house, she is Mother, but outside she became Jenny, someone the family did not know, someone who was protecting the three of us. Mother and Jenny looked different, but there is one thing that they both share and that is the missing nail. Jimmy wanted Kandy to see it because they were about to strike and he set up the video for Eddie."

Carolyn still was not convinced, "So that he could watch you and his son screw because that is what he saw," she said, "and if Jimmy knows his brother," and she gave Eddie a look, "then he knew that he would take his son and leave you to be killed."

Lady Singleton turned to Ida, whose eyes looked down. Lisa's mind shut off. She kept thinking of the picture and what Lady Singleton said. She would show the picture to Devin and tell him what she thinks. She turned to Eddie and Willie and hoped that she was reaching them. She did not want to bring up the past to be relived, however, it had to be done. She addressed Carolyn, but she was talking to the men because they were in denial that the devil existed, and they needed to see it for themselves. He was warned by Kevin Klein, a man that ended up cut to pieces and left to suffer and watch as it all unfolded. "Momma saw it and she was placed in a mental hospital, Ellen saw it and Judy did not believe her, and Elmira saw it and she still was taken, but no one addressed it. Asia saw it and she was not believed. It was not taken seriously by any of us until Kandy got hurt and when it burned Devin's picture, Jimmy hoped that Eddie would want to protect us all out of anger, if not of love.

"Melissa Thomas was killed two years after her last child's birth, which we know now she gave birth to these children and turned them over to Thomas for training. We are not talking about one, we are talking about nine."

Devin pointed out to Jason that he had trouble with just one when Lionel was two years old and Carolyn had to go to a convention. He had to hire babysitters and, besides, who would allow a man to constantly get other women pregnant and then bring the children home to tie you down, unless you had no choice.

Eddie was listening; he did not blink. "Mother is Jimmy," Devin said, "and now that they want his family dead, he is fighting back, which is why he wanted Lisa to see him. He knew we would put two and two together."

Eddie and Willie checked their weapons. "We have to get Jimmy out of there and then we will take care of Mark and Scotty and all the other motherfuckers!" Eddie yelled, while Jason protested, "Dad, Jimmy is sending them to us. Besides, we do not know where they are and once we get rid of Thomas, we will have taken out of the leader and Jimmy will find a way to us through Lisa because he trusts her only."

"Okay, now I am confused again," Eddie said, "because first you said that Jeffrey wanted to be Melissa, so how did Jimmy become Mother?"

Lisa looked around; all eyes were on her. She grabbed Devin's hand for support, "Jump in when you are ready." She smiled at him. "Okay, Dad," she said and then she realized that she was talking to Eddie. "I am sorry," she said, "I did not mean to call you that."

"It's fine," he said. "If there is any woman that I would like to call me Dad, it would be you," and they both shared a smile.

"Jeffrey was probably more a woman than a man, which was his attraction to Jimmy. He was warm and kind. However, he was attracted to you also, which is why he started killing the women that both of you dated, because neither of you shared his feelings," she looked at Willie, "and you too, Poppy. Melissa had that I-do-not-gave-a-damn attitude and that is what he liked about her—she did things and did not care what people thought of her. So, he started to build a family from her and took Jimmy because he wanted the perfect children and the perfect husband. However, Melissa's children were older and they would know that he was not she. Jeffrey Thomas was mentally ill. He was not attractive to Melissa. He needed her. When Jeffrey killed Melissa, he thought that he could replace her. Jeffrey had the family he wanted, but his children needed a mother. Jimmy started living as Melissa. Jeffrey's plan backfired because he could not present Jimmy to his children because Jimmy was a Jones and he was training his children to kill the Jones family. Jimmy became a woman because Jeffrey hated women. They would not find him attractive, which is where the mannequin came into play. And most important, there is no real death certificate on Melissa, and how would he explain to his colleagues the disappearance of his wife?"

Ellen sat next to Jason and Devin. They were looking at more of Jason's baby pictures, every picture had a story, and they had time to hear them all while Judy and Ida played a card game with Kandy. Carolyn and Lisa sat at a table, looking at baby clothes, and Eddie and Willie sat and waited.

"It's time," Father said. Tonight he and Simon agreed that it was time. Sister came along to prove her loyalty to the family and to meet the brother of the man that created her. After that night at the Jones house, Sister was born. The men would not be able to take their eyes off her, which is how he would be able to take out Jason and Devin. While her beauty was mesmerizing them, he would be able to kill them both, and then turn to Eddie and claim his victory before cutting the baby from Lisa's belly. "Mother is smart, don't you think?" he asked Sister.

"She is great, Father. She understands me and I love Mother so much."

He thought to wear his platform shoes to scare them all because they made him stand tall, but he needed to be on his game. He had distracted the family, but tonight the only distraction he needed was Sister. "May I make love to them?" she asked.

"No, girl, you can only dance."

⟋⟋ ⟋⟋

"Sir, there is a black van that just pulled up on the north side of the house, and there is what looks to be someone getting out of it." Eddie's security team was in place.

"Let them enter," he said. Eddie looked at Jason and Devin, "The time has come." They were careful not to tell anyone what was going to happen tonight, they wanted everyone in one area of the house and that was the family room. That way, no one would be caught by surprise and the snipers could have a clear shot.

Everyone looked up when the door opened. It was Jeffrey Thomas. "Hello, Eddie, it has been a long time since we last meet." He looked at Ida, "Hello, Momma," he said, "You look lovely, as usual," and went to place a kiss on her cheek.

"Thomas, what a surprise," Eddie said. "Can I get you a drink?" Eddie offered. "How long has it been?"

Thomas's eyes looked around. He had lost focus. "Can I dance now, Father?" Sister said.

Thomas snapped back, "No, not yet, child. Eddie, I do not indulge in the devil's juice for I am a God-fearing man."

"I will have one," Sister said, "and you can fuck me."

"Stop it, girl!" Father yelled.

Skeet listened from the outhouse, as he remembered the voice of Sister, but he only had a view of one person in the house and he was waiting for the command to take the shot.

"I came to discuss a little matter at hand. Your sons, those two beasts over there," he waved his gun in the direction of Devin and Jason, while Ellen was overwhelmed with fear and gripped their arms as if her life depended on it. "They hurt my son Simon, while they killed Matthew," he said and turned in their direction again.

"No, Father, don't hurt them. I love them," Sister said.

"And do you know what these boys have been doing with Sister?" Thomas asked. "They have been turning her into their sex whore!" He yelled.

"I love them, Father," Sister said again and, suddenly, in front of everyone's eyes, Sister removed her coat to reveal her sexy lingerie that she had taken from Lisa's house. She pulled out a chair and started doing her seductive dance, while she taunted them with words. "Make love to me, baby," she looked at Jason and said as she swirled her body.

"That will be enough for now, Sister," father said. "She is a beauty, isn't she?" Everyone watched, as Father became Sister right in front of their eyes.

Jason mumbled, "So that is the two faces Lady Singleton talked about.

"Thomas, why don't we talk about this?" Eddie said. "Put your coat back on and let's talk."

"She is beautiful," Father said, as he turned to Willie, "do not get any ideas," he said, "I know your type."

Eddie had no idea how to handle this situation Thomas was Sister also and he felt pity for him.

"Your boys are monsters, Eddie, but my Simon was the perfect son. My boys were the apostles and I was God," he said. "I remember the pictures he showed me of that, what was her name . . . Betty, I think. He carved her open to precision." Father placed his hand on his chest. He was truly proud. "But the younger woman that was Sister, she watched all of the foul things these boys were doing with those women, and the vulgar things," he said with disgust. "The moaning and the touching, it nearly drove her crazy."

Father tried, but he could not control Sister. She looked at Lisa, who sat by Christian as he wrapped his arms around her and she squeezed his hand.

"I want to touch the baby, Father. You promised Mother a baby before me. You killed my baby, Father," she said.

Father asked, "Eddie, do you see what these boys have done? Just the sight of them and she is being disrespectful. She is thirty years old and now she thinks she knows everything. Sister was older," he whispered. "She was born forty-two years ago Two days before the death of James Sr."

"He loves me and not her, and that is my baby!" She yelled, as Christian grabbed his gun, ready to fire.

Everyone watched as Father talked to himself. He would become Sister in the blink of an eye. He argued with himself back and forth. He was truly a mad scientist. Thomas was out of it. He was truly mad. "Eddie, let's get down to business," he said.

Thomas pulled off his coat again, revealing his sexy red lingerie. He put on his long, black wig and began to swirl again. "Do you like this, baby?" She said, while looking at Devin.

"Thomas, what in the hell are you doing?" Eddie yelled. He could take no more of this freak show. "Where is Jimmy?" he asked.

Thomas looked at Eddie, "I killed Jimmy the same night I killed your father," he said. That son of a bitch called me a freak," he said, "he mocked me and told me that no son of his would ever be with the likes of me. So, I introduced Jimmy to his daughter—Sister—and he just stared at her because of her beauty. He wanted me to take her and go home, and I would have, but your father disowned her and called me names. Where are my manners? I have raised good respectful children and they would be upset with me if I did not start from the beginning.

"I followed them from the school. I pulled in front of the car and I jumped out. I asked Jimmy to come with me and he asked me what I was doing. So, that is when I told him that we had a daughter and he was confused, but when those men touched me that night, his face was all that I could see and I knew that if he were there, he would not have allowed it to happen. Did you see the look on his face when I was tied to the pole? It was love and his words," he looked at Lisa, 'They should not have done this to you,' was all that I needed. That is why I killed Arlene, because I saw the two of them together in bed and he loved me and not her. I called Sister from the car, and he could not believe his eyes, he just stared at her. Momma, this beautiful creature is your granddaughter."

"Hello, Momma," Sister struck a pose and gave a wave of the fingers. James jumped out of the car, and Jimmy tried to hold him back, but he went to look for the gun and there I was, looking him in the face, and I shot him."

Eddie wanted closure; he needed answers no matter how hard it was to hear. He needed to know, and what about Asia?

Thomas moved closer to Judy. He pulled her out of the chair, "I am no fool, Eddie, you want to know about Asia," he said. "Then I will tell you. I wanted to kill the both of them together, both Ellen and Asia, however, Simon said no one would care if we killed Ellen, so we made her suffer. We wanted her to watch as she learned that we had killed her precious son." Father had regained control, "When she was in the hospital," he started to yell, "all she had to say was that she did not have a son and she wouldn't," he said, "so I punished her daily." Father looked sincere, "My Simon was brilliant, Eddie, do you know what he said to me? 'Father, then let her watch him die,' which is why he granted her time to get close to him, so she could watch him kill Jason and burn the demons out of him." Father looked at them both, "The two of you are just thugs," he said, "you touch Sister and the both of you would have her performing sex acts on you both at the same time."

"Please don't hurt them, Father," she said again.

He looked at Eddie, "They are out of control. Sister is a God-fearing girl. She would attend church and she always listened to me. I would tell her that they only wanted one thing and I put a stop to it, but Sister would not listen. She allowed them to come into my home, the both of them, and started touching her, and making her do these foul things with them again. I tried to tell her that they meant her no good, however, she had become their sex whore and I could not stop it."

Sister looked at Lisa, "They will come for the baby," she said. "She wants the baby."

"Who wants the baby?" Eddie asked.

"Is it Mother?" Eddie asked.

"No," Sister said, "Brother and Chloe. Father would not let Mother or I come to the meeting, but we listened at the door. She wants the baby, but it is mine," Sister yelled. "And I will not let her have it. I asked Father if I could kill her, but he said no, she was family. She came to visit with Brother; the brother father said was a traitor."

Now Father knew it was time. Sister began to do her dance while everyone looked.

Eddie looked at his phone. He could see the message, YOU ARE BLOCKING THE SHOT.

"You know what, Eddie?" Father came back in. "You took my sons, and now I am going to take yours."

Jeffrey raised his gun in the direction of Jason and Devin. Devin and Jason both jumped up and aimed their guns at Jeffrey, and Ellen pushed Devin out of harm's way and threw her body in front of Jason. "Take the shot!" Eddie yelled, while he moved clear. Jeffrey was hit twice, once in the head and once in the chest, killing him. Before the fatal shots were fired, Jeffrey

Thomas was able to deliver one of his own. Jeffrey laid on the floor with his eyes staring in the ceiling.

"Is everyone alright?" Eddie asked.

Carolyn checked Jeffrey's pulse and confirmed that he was dead.

Eddie called Skeet. "It's over, and Jeffrey is gone."

Eddie dialed the police and turned when he heard Jason yell out, "Oh God! No!"

Ellen laid her head on Jason's chest, "I was so scared. For a minute, I thought he hit you," she said when her legs buckled from under her.

"Oh God, no," Jason repeated. Jason looked down to see a hole in Ellen's chest with blood coming from it. Devin turned in Jason's direction with his heart pounding. "Call an ambulance!" Jason yelled. Everyone looked. The shots were too late. "Help me!" Jason yelled.

Eddie asked a dispatcher to send over an ambulance. The dispatcher asked what the emergency was. Eddie informed the dispatcher that there had been a shooting and there was one person dead and another person injured. Eddie informed the dispatcher that there was a doctor on the scene.

Carolyn ran to Ellen's side. "Get me some towels."

Lisa ran and got towels and applied pressure to her wound, as her body shook in pain. "I love you both," Ellen said. "We're going to the Bahamas."

Devin said, "Hold on! Please!"

Ellen was drifting off, "I love you both," she said.

Devin applied pressure to her wound, begging her not to close her eyes, while telling her how much she meant to him. "You were my miracle," she said, "you gave me hope. I felt special with you," she said to Devin. "You are a mother's dream come true." She tried to smile when she looked at Jason and her hand reached for him. "I just wanted to hold you again, my baby," she said with tears rolling down her face.

Jason grabbed her hand, "Momma, please," Jason cried, "please, don't leave me. She smiled and closed her eyes.

Carolyn and Lisa performed CPR. Carolyn pumped her chest while Lisa blew life back into her body. Minutes passed and Lisa looked at Carolyn while she checked Ellen's pulse. "We have a pulse," Carolyn said.

They could hear the siren from the front gate. Eddie pressed the button to allow the ambulance to enter and drive to the front door. Skeet ran outside and guided to paramedic to Ellen.

"We have a female victim with a gunshot wound to the chest," Carolyn said. "We administered CPR and now we have a pulse."

The paramedic placed an oxygen mask over Ellen's face and took her blood pressure. "Two hundred over one twenty," the paramedic said. "Let's get her out of here." They lifted her on the gurney and rolled her out of the house and placed her in the back of the ambulance. Jason jumped into the ambulance with her and Devin and the family followed her to the hospital.

❧ ❧

Jimmy sat and listened, and just as he thought, Jeffrey could not live without Simon. He listened as Jeffrey entered his family home. He tapped his finger because it was his last chance to leave Jeffrey's home and never return. Jeffrey could not control himself. Sister kept interrupting. Without Jeffrey's knowledge, she had planted a listening device so that she could hear it all. He thought it was a brilliant idea as Mother suggested for Father to take Sister along for his final battle. "Father, you cannot go alone," Mother said, "take Sister with you. She will be able to distract the others while you kill them all."

Father was proud of his work with Sister, she was sheer beauty and the boys would fight to be with her. She always watched, as Sister would brag about the women that she had taken away from the Jones boys, and she knew that Sister would pleasure herself with them first. It was Devin and then later it would be Jason. They would go and watch through the windows at night and then Sister would come and throw a tantrum in the house.

Jimmy listened and jumped when he heard Jason's screams for help. "Someone got hurt," he cried. Jimmy prayed that it was not a member of his family. He only wanted freedom to be with his son Cody and Coretta without having to look over his shoulder. He listened and it was a female victim. Jimmy closed his eyes and prayed. "Please God, grant me this one favor and let her be alright." Although he did not know which female was hurt, only that there had been too many innocent lives lost already.

☙ ☙

"Where is your boyfriend?" Detective Thaddeus Walker asked from the doorway, when his radio went off. It said that there had been a double shooting and gave the address of James Eddie Jones. He smiled at her. "It's over," he said.

"I know," Chloe said, "Scotty called to inform me." Chloe is Scotty's girlfriend.

Chloe did not ask because she did not want it to seem as if she cared. However, she wondered if the second person shot was Eddie. He looked at her and walked in her direction, "You are a beautiful woman," he said. "From the first time I saw you, I knew I had to have you at any cost."

She then stood and removed her robe, as he started to undress. He lay on the bed fully naked, as she took his handcuffs and cuffed his hand to the bed. She looked at him. "I have been your slave for years," Chloe said, "but no more." She reached under the pillow and pulled out her knife. His eyes widened as she began to stab him, jabbing the knife into him so many times she lost count, as he gurgled blood from his mouth and took his last breath.

Chloe stood and walked into the shower. She cried. She had never taken another life like that. She had done many things and this was her first hands-on kill. But if she was going to get her life back, it had to be done. She dressed, packed a suitcase and walked away without looking back. She made a phone call, "My job is done for now, you do yours and get the rest of them out of the picture." Scotty agreed. He knew just how to get it done without getting his hands dirty. "I will be at my new home," she said, "and maybe I will have a margarita or something," she smiled before hanging up the phone. She touched her belly. *I will be a mother soon.*

🌀 🌀

The ambulance pulled into the emergency entrance at the hospital, where Dr. Davis and his surgical team waited. They rolled Ellen into surgery. The family paced the floor in the waiting room. "No distractions, right?" Devin said. "We let our fucking guards down. We should have not allowed that freak show to go on."

Eddie did not say that he was blocking the shot. Nonetheless, he did blame himself for what had happened to Ellen. "We should have sent her away when Lady Singleton said she would get hurt, we should not have allowed her to stay."

Jason shook his head. "She would not have left and we all know it. She wanted to protect us and that is what she did. We got distracted and we could lose her for it."

Dr. Davis walked into the waiting room. "We removed the bullet and she is going to be fine." Everyone exhaled. Dr. Davis looked at everyone, "She has a lot to live for. She came through like a champ," he smiled. "We will be putting her in a room soon." Jason and Devin waited for Ellen to be taken out of surgery. They were taking no chances.

Ellen opened her eyes. The room was silenced of voices, only beeps came from the heart monitor. She tried to look around, but she could not move. She was in the hospital. She started to cry. She had been placed in the mental hospital again, and she was being restrained. She lifted her head and turned. She heard a voice from the side of the room. "I told them that you would not be comfortable," Eddie said. But they wanted to be close to you. She looked at Devin who was lying on one side of her and Jason was lying on the other. Jason had his arms around her like a shield. Ellen smiled gently. "I love it," she said. The nurse walked in with a food tray, and Eddie ordered it away. Skeet and J.T. walked in with food and coffee for everyone.

Dr. Davis walked into the room. He checked Ellen's heart and her blood pressure. "Everything seems to be good."

"If I take my medicine, doctor, can I go home?" she asked.

Eddie had a way of getting what he wanted, but not this time.

"We lost her, and we resuscitated her. She will be extremely weak for a while." He looked at them all. "It was touch-and-go for a while, and she will need all of you, but she needs us now. Let us do our job and we will send her home with you in good shape."

Lisa wrapped her arms around Ellen. We are not moving," she said. "We have been taking turns going to the hotel to shower and change, so all you need to do is focus on getting your strength back."

Chapter 17

Days had passed since the shooting. Eddie had someone come to clean the house. But it was still haunting. He looked out his window and he could now see it. Lady Singleton was right; there was no sunshine around the house. The manor was no longer a home, when he walked through the hall, he could swear that he saw shadows moving across the walls. He had never feared anyone or anything, but he knew that there would be no peace if they stayed.

"I went to the pharmacy to get Ms. Ellen her prescriptions," Skeet said when he walked into the house. Eddie turned and watched the expression on Skeet's face as he looked at Jeffrey Thomas's final resting place.

Skeet said nothing, while Eddie turned and looked out of the window. Skeet looked at Eddie and said, "The new place is ready, sir, whenever you are." Eddie could not take his eyes off someone outside. Skeet walked to stand side-by-side with him. He looked also and he saw her, a woman was standing at the gate.

"Do you have your piece?" Eddie asked.

"Yes," he said before asking how long she had been standing there.

Eddie turned his head to face Skeet. "She has been there for a while now, and it is time to put an end to this."

Skeet grabbed Eddie, "No, sir, we are going to get out of here and go to the hospital with the others to wait." Skeet had listened to Lady Singleton's words. "Remember, sir, united we stand, divided we fall. This could be a trap."

On the way out the door, Eddie turned to his desk to pick up the letter that Asia had written to Jason and Devin. Eddie read the last six words, SHE WILL DIE FOR YOU BOTH, and he, too, realized what she was saying. He had been stubborn in the past, but now he would no longer question things. "This is not over, Skeet," he said, as he handed him the letter, "both Jason and Devin will blame themselves for what happened to Ellen because we all became distracted by the show that Thomas was putting on, and we allowed him to strike first.

"Your mother came here that night before she was killed," Eddie said. "She'd had had a few drinks and I thought that she was drunk." Eddie looked at Skeet, he knew that his mother was a heavy drinker and knew that one day it would get her into trouble. "She told me that there was someone after her," he said. "When I asked her who, she began to tell me about some cult where they take your child." Eddie stopped talking. He knew that Skeet would hate him if he found out that he sent Betty away that night and she was kidnapped while she was leaving, not when she was arriving.

Eddie remembered the night Betty died as if it was yesterday. Betty had been missing for a day, and after a night of drinking with Willie he walked up to his bedroom to find Betty stealing his jewelry. "What are you doing?" Eddie asked.

Betty turned around when she heard his voice. She grabbed the knife that she had used to unlock his jewelry box and placed on the nightstand next to his bed. She held the knife in his direction and said, "I am sorry, but I have to kill you."

Betty lifted the knife in her hand and moved towards him, and that was when he grabbed her. Betty was not herself. Normally she was in a good mood, she was always making jokes, and she loved to dance and listen to old music. But that night she said he had to die. Eddie grabbed her, but she was strong and she attacked him with her bare hands after he managed to get the knife out of her hand.

Eddie and Skeet noticed that the limousine was at the gate. Eddie pressed the button to open the gate. He and Skeet looked around one last time and they walked out of the house and climbed into the back of the limousine. "We will continue this conversation when the others are around," he said. "However, I want you to know that this is your family now. I know that both Jason and Devin trust you and they will agree to this. Our home is your home, now I have three boys," he said.

🌀 🌀 ▩

Skeet and Eddie arrived the hospital and took the elevator to the second floor to Ellen's room. Ellen was being discharged after weeks in the hospital. Judy and Ida sat with Ellen and waited for the rest of the family to arrive. Lisa and Carolyn went to the coffee shop across the street with Jason and Devin while Willie and Kandy drove back to the house so that Kandy could pack some clothing.

"Eddie, I think that your driver is off track or drunk," Judy said, while she and Eddie had a laugh at the driver's expense. Judy had met with a real estate agent about the sale of the shop. She knew that from this day on, Ellen and she would not be able to handle it. They kept the shop open and had hired employees to work, but they worked a week and did not return. And there were the shoplifters. But now that Lisa was no longer sewing, it would be overwhelming to hold on to.

"I have a surprise for everyone," Eddie said. Ellen looked out the window. A week ago, she thought she had breathed her last breath and now the sun was bright and shiny. She inhaled and closed her eyes. She could smell the flowers. The driver pulled into the circular driveway. Skeet and J.T. followed in Lisa's Suburban with everyone's suitcases.

Eddie opened the door while Judy and Ida followed. Jason and Devin looked. They wondered how he could have pulled off getting the house ready in such a short period of time, which was not the problem. They did not know if the women would want to sell their homes and live under one roof with Eddie.

Carolyn was in, "Ah, wow," she said. "This place in a palace. Is this a hotel?" she asked.

Eddie smiled. He knew that Carolyn would be a hard sell. She would want to take Jason and move away. However, he was set on keeping his family together. "If you look through this window, Carolyn, there is a park for the kids and I know that Lionel would enjoy it," he said.

"Lionel," she said, "I want to ride the train now. I have never been to an amusement park, let alone have one in my own backyard."

Eddie was winning when he gave his final pitch. These rooms downstairs are the family rooms, however there are condos upstairs, each with three bedrooms, so if you need additional rooms, they are available.

"This place is going to cost a fortune to run," Judy said. "It is like living in a hotel with an amusement park in the backyard."

The women walked outside in the back of the house. The grass was cut and there were large picnic tables with a large barbeque grill. Eddie looked at the joy on their faces. "It almost seems normal," Eddie said. "Just a few days ago, it was touch-and-go." He looked at Ellen and watched as she laughed at Ida and Judy trying to jump on the carousel. They tried to jump on it while it was still moving. Although Ellen could not participate, she looked so peaceful.

Jason smiled as J.T. tried to pick Ellen up and put her on the train. He watched as the electronics geek struggled and Skeet stepped in to give him a hand. Thank God for Skeet. He watched to see if there was any chemistry between Skeet and Kandy. Lady Singleton said that Kandy and Skeet would have a connection. Eddie smiled, "He is a good kid and he would be good to have for backup for you boys. Maybe you could take him under your wing and direct him," he looked at Devin and

Jason. "We are all that he has left in the world. I know what it feels like to be alone, and I don't wish it on anyone."

The ladies walked into the house. Jason knew Carolyn would be upset when she would have to return to work and face Dr. Samuels. Knowing what he had done to her, would she be able to keep her cool around him?

Devin placed his arms around Lisa. "I will not let you out of my sight," he said. "Still, we have to find out where Dr. Samuels fits into all of this, and see if Jenny will return." He placed a soft kiss on her lips and walked into the next room.

Carolyn walked into Lisa's room, "Girl, this place is amazing," she said. Lisa looked at Carolyn. She knew that Carolyn did not want to discuss the decor of the house. "He took my child," she said, "I was so angry with you when you suggested that he had done something to me and it turns out that you were right. We will get that motherfucker, right?"

Lisa smiled, "Yes, we will, but we have to keep our heads on straight." Lisa went back to the moment when she was being held captive. The older brother said, "He said kill the baby," she looked at Carolyn, "and I knew that they were talking about him. Both Jason and Devin know what he is capable of and they will stop him."

Devin's cell phone rang. "Hey, Dee, this is Scotty Johnson." Devin was not surprised to hear from him, considering that he was the detective on duty when the shooting took place. "If you and Jason are not busy, I could use your assistance with something," he said to Devin, who found it strange that the detective would call him and Jason for a business call instead of asking any questions about the shooting, Devin wrote down the address. "Okay, Scotty, we will see you in a few."

Jason looked at the address. It was close to where the old house stood where Lisa had been held captive. Skeet watched Devin's expression as he pulled out his gun to check it. "Do you guys need backup? You could be walking into a trap," Skeet said.

"No," Devin said, "let's see what is going on first."

"Well," J.T. said, "if you guys are going to go out there alone, then you are going to need this." J.T. was an electronics genius. He handed each of the men a pair of glasses.

They put them on. "What in the hell is this, J.T.?" They said, while laughing. "I can't see a damn thing," when they realized that they could see what was behind them.

J.T. pointed out the reverse button on the glasses. "Press this button," J.T. said, "and if someone is behind you, then you will see them. If you are looking in front of you, turn the reverse button off."

Jason and Devin went to meet Scotty, and they reminded Skeet not to let Mark know that he suspected that he was a part of the Brotherhood. They hoped that if Mark or Scotty were a part of the Brotherhood then they would lead them to the other brothers.

Jason asked Skeet to be careful. Skeet nodded and checked his gun.

"Man, what do you think about all of this freaky shit happening with the Jones family?" Mark asked Skeet while they drove to the airport to pick up Kandy. The family was careful not to let any others know about the new house. J.T. was busy, so he asked Mark to follow. Skeet put on his camera glasses. He knew that Mark was also a part of the Brotherhood and they needed to know where he came from and who the others were. "Man, you must be freakin' out to know that Eddie let someone kill your mother right under his nose," Mark said.

Skeet's temper began to flare. He realized that Mark was up to something. He pulled into the parking spot when he saw Kandy, but he could see that Mark seemed to be reaching for his weapon. Skeet jumped out of the car and called for Kandy. He walked to the back of the car and placed he arms around her as if he were going to kiss her, pulled out his weapon, and gave it to Kandy. "If he moves," he said, "shoot him." Skeet kissed her. He did not know why he did it, but he did. He found her attractive, but he did not know if her father would approve of him. He smiled because, to his surprise, she kissed him back.

❧ ❧

You could smell the scent of death in the air. Detective Johnson briefed Devin and Jason in the car. "This is the home of Jeffrey Thomas. I thought that we could go through the house before the FBI starts their investigation." The men drew their weapons upon walking through the door. It was dead silent and the smell was unbearable. They placed a towel over their faces and proceeded inside. They walked into each room. The first bedroom was where they found the mannequins of Jason and Devin. They found Simon Thomas in the second bedroom. The men gagged and walked out of the third bedroom, which contained the body of Thaddeus Walker. He had been stabbed so many times that his body looked like leeches were attached. He lay on the bed naked and he was handcuffed to the headboard. He had been caught totally off guard. They went through every room and found no evidence of a woman ever living in the home at all. The closet only carried men's clothing.

❧ ❧

Kandy was so excited, "Skeet gave me a gun," she said to her father and Uncle Eddie.

"What?" Willie said. He was upset. "Why in the hell would Skeet give you a gun?"

Eddie tried to calm Willie down, however, it wasn't until Jason and Devin walked in that Willie really blew up. "Skeet gave Kandy a goddamn gun!" Willie was overprotective of the girls, but Eddie thought that he was blowing the whole thing out of proportion.

"Calm down, Uncle Willie," Jason said. "I know how you feel about your girls," he said with a smile, "but if Skeet gave Kandy a gun, then he did it for a good reason."

Skeet walked in carrying Kandy's luggage. He did not acknowledge the men, his eyes were focused on Kandy. "I am sorry for what I put you through today, but I would have done anything to make sure I got you home safely."

Eddie smiled, while Willie looked at Skeet. He liked Skeet, and now he had a newfound respect for him. Skeet turned to Jason and Devin. "Mark was going to kill me today. I watched with J.T.'s glasses and when I saw Kandy, I gave her a piece to protect herself just in case he got me." Skeet played the recording for everyone, and they could see Mark reaching into his jacket. When Skeet jumped out of the car, he released it and sat back. They could clearly hear him say, "Next time, motherfucker."

Chapter 18

Lisa sat at her desk in the hospital. *Something is off* she thought, when Carolyn walked in. "Hey, girl," Lisa said to Carolyn, "how does it feel to be back at work again?"

Carolyn smiled, "That is why I am here. The last time you were here, you were being taken," she said.

Lisa exhaled, "I was shaking when I first walked in here. However . . ." She turned her computer screen around so that Carolyn could see the house and so that Jason and Devin were watching.

"Have you guys seen Dr. Samuels?" Jason asked.

"No," Carolyn said, "he is not in today, I checked. I wanted to poison that son of a bitch." Both women heads jerked up when a man walked into Lisa's office. She turned the screen around so that the man could not see Jason.

Lisa stepped from behind the desk. "Wow," Detective Peter Henderson said, "how did that happen?" Referring to Lisa's bulging belly.

She laughed. "It is funny, no matter how intelligent the man is, when they see a woman in my condition, they always want to know how did it happen?"

Detective Peter Henderson got straight to business. "I checked out what you asked me to and you were wrong," he said.

Jason and Devin looked at each other. They had no idea that Lisa had spoken to anyone about the case, but she wanted them to know, which was why she did not close the screen.

"When you said something to me about the apostles, Robert Samuels was not one of them," he said. "You had the wrong Melissa Thomas. You were looking at Melissa C. Thompson's file. She had seven children born a year apart. No twins, and none of them named Robert Samuels. And they were Caucasian," he said. The father had shot the mother after binge drinking, killing her, and then he shot all of the kids except for one, who was at a friend's for a sleep over. He died three years ago. Melissa Johnson Thomas, she once dated a Daniel Samuels, who had a son named Robert Samuels, but he is dead, too. He attended medical school, but they never married. She was the mother of nine children. . ."

Lisa looked at him. "Wow," she said, "I am having problems with one, let alone nine."

"And her sister had four total, one girl and three boys, and none of them named Robert."

Detective Henderson was a tall man, thin, with black hair. He looked like Al Pacino in *Scarface*. She would tease tell him that and he would blush and say to her, "You are my mother." She remembered one year for Christmas when Patricia, his wife, was carrying their second child. She and her sister prepared dinner for the family. They had set up their Christmas tree and brought gifts for Peter Jr.

"Talk to me, Lisa," Detective Henderson said. "I do not want to bury another family member. The same girl that was killed at the Jones house is responsible for Susan's death and your kidnapping. Susan told me you were in trouble," he said. "She did not get into details. But, I feel that someone in the department knew what you and she were working on."

He pulled out a picture of Thaddeus Walker. "This is the oldest son of Melissa Thomas. He was a cop."

Lisa looked at the screen and Devin gave her the okay to talk to Detective Henderson. They would need him because they had been running in circles. There were others and now he knew for sure Melissa had nine children. Where are they?"

Lisa explained everything to Peter. He was horrified. He had heard of the pack, but thought it was a myth and now he believed the urban legends. He put his cell phone number in Lisa's phone and he handed her the two files. "Go through these when you have time," Peter said to Lisa. "You work this end and I will find out what I can." He held her and noticed that her body was shaking. "Nothing is going to happen to you or the baby, okay?"

Lisa and Devin went through the file of Melissa Thomas. They found nothing of Dr. Samuels.

Carolyn and Jason brought in take out from the Chinese Restaurant. "Did you find anything?" Jason asked.

Devin kept looking, "His name is not on these papers, and not only that," he said, Melissa Thomas had a sister Clementine Johnson, but none of her kids is named Robert Samuels." Devin started to eat. "No distractions," he said, "we will not let our guards down. I know that he is involved some way. We just have to figure it out." Devin looked at his watch. It was time for Lisa 's surprise; the nurses at the hospital wanted to throw Lisa a surprise baby shower.

❧ ❧

"Surprise!" Lisa jumped when she entered the hospital lounge. Everyone was there, including Jenny and Dr. Samuels. Lisa wanted to be careful not to say anything that would let Jenny know that they knew who she was. "Jenny," Lisa said and held out her arms to her.

"Look at you. My God you are big, girl." Jenny was still Jenny. "Girl, this baby is killing me," she said.

Lisa smiled, "It is so good to see you and before you leave today, make sure I have a phone number on you so that we can go shopping." Lisa held Jenny again before Jenny asked her if she knew what she was carrying. Lisa pulled her to the side and tried to explain to her all that had happened. She knew that Jenny already knew the story, but she wanted to develop trust between the two of them. "I have not had time to get an ultrasound," Lisa said then turned to Jenny, "What are you carrying?"

"Oh, a girl, Lisa! It's a girl."

Lisa looked at her. She then turned to see if she could find Devin. He was standing and watching. She gave him a look and he came to talk to Jenny. "Jenny, how many are you carrying?" he asked. "You look amazing for a woman in your condition." Devin was at a loss for words.

"You are a smooth talker," she said, "and I like that," Jenny said in her flirting voice.

"He is right, Jenny, you have a glow about you."

She smiled, "I am a free person now," she said. "I'm free," she said with a smile.

"Come home with me, Jenny. We will talk and have a drink of juice," she laughed.

"Not yet," Jenny said, as she looked at them both, "it is not over, yet." As she looked around, Dr. Samuels was walking towards the hospital entrance. Jenny did not say any more, only, "I love you, guys, okay?"

Lisa held her as she looked up and saw Eddie and Willie watching. "Be careful, Jenny," she said, as Carolyn and Kandy walked up. It was like old times again.

Robert Samuels watched from a distance as Kandy embraced Jenny. Kandy and Jenny were close friends. When Kandy called out to her father, "Dad and Uncle Eddie, come and meet my friend," Jason watched as Dr. Samuels moved closer and stood where he could not be seen. Jenny looked at Eddie and gave a nod, and he did the same. She removed her gloves and stuck out her thumb to shake his hand. Lisa walked over and they started to tell stories about their friendship. "Jenny, remember when you pepper sprayed yourself?" Kandy asked and they laughed and breathed a sigh of relief when Dr. Samuels walked away, but noticed that the janitor Al was nearby.

❧ ❧ ✦

"How much do you know about Scotty?" Lisa asked. She was going through the files and noticed it was a different Melissa Thomas. Her maiden name was Johnson. Nevertheless, this was four different files in one. Melissa Johnson had nine children, not seven. Devin had remembered his father saying that. "So there are others, maybe," Lisa said. "There is a file on a fire that is supposed to have claimed three of the lives. The autopsy report said that the men were placed in the building and then someone burned the building down." Lisa said she was getting that feeling again. "If Thomas lost three sons, wouldn't he try to replace them?" she asked. "It seems he wanted to die since he had lost Simon. Could he have fathered children with other women?" Lisa asked.

Lisa pulled out a copy of the file on Maxine Turner and passed it to Devin. She was a ninety-year-old woman who had fallen down the elevator shaft. Melissa Thomas had a son named James who died, but Mrs. Turner was upset at the hospital when she was calling a man named James who did not answer her. Devin was trying to understand what she was saying.

"Babe, she was calling Dr. Samuels, although he ignored her." She had checked Eddie's yearbook and found a Robert Samuels, but he was much older than the Doctor Samuels that worked at the hospital. She even went through all of the files Susan sent her before her death and there was nothing. She placed the files and yearbooks aside and laid down to rest her eyes.

Devin left the room to pick up Chinese take-out and to stop at the library to pick up more yearbooks. He picked up the food and thought that if Lisa was right then she was looking in the wrong place. Doctor Samuels was about his age, not Eddie's. He walked into the room carrying other yearbooks he had retrieved from the library. "We are looking in the wrong years. We should be looking in the years that Jason and I were in high school, not my father."

She grabbed the yearbook and went straight for James Thomas, but he was not Dr. Samuels. However, she looked at the years before and saw Devin and Jason, the star football player. She smiled. Even then, he was cute, though his haircut was off. He wore a long tail in the back of his head that was braided, while Jason sported a large curly Afro. *We are missing something here*, she thought, as she looked through a yearbook with a class of nineteen hundred and ninety, and saw janitor Al, Alpheus Johnson. She smiled, "No wonder he said he would have to kill me if he told me his name," she had wondered what that meant.

She lay on the bed and stroked her belly, "My sons are the apostles," Jeffrey Thomas had said and, for some reason, it was echoing in her head. "It is not over, yet," is what Jenny said. "They will come for the baby," she wanted the baby is what Sister said.

Lisa drifted off to sleep, which had not come easily. Her mind drifted back to the old house, as she watched and listened, as two of the Brotherhood members talked. "She carries the golden seed," one of them shared with the other.

"Then we should take it out and destroy it now," he yelled, before someone in the shadow spoke, "Do not touch it because it belongs to us. You lived in luxury, while we lived like dogs, eating crap. That baby is our golden goose."

She tossed and turned as a voice said, "Name the apostles and you will know the name of your enemy."

Carolyn shook her, "Lisa, wake up before you hurt yourself."

She sat up and looked at Carolyn. "Do you know the names of the apostles?"

"What is this all about?" she asked.

"Jeffrey Thomas is dead and now we have a new life and a new home with the men that love us." Lisa smiled, last year at this time she was miserable, and now she was with the man of her dreams. "I know, Carolyn, but it is not over."

Carolyn stood, "I hope you are wrong because I have not seen my period and I will not go through what you have, I am not that strong. Lionel is coming home and I cannot live with the fact that someone wants to harm him and my unborn child."

She looked at the files and found that the other family involved was called the Klein family, of which there was only one member left alive, and it is Kevin Klein, the man tortured by the Thomas family. His wife and family died in a car accident when he refused the Brotherhood, but Jeffrey Thomas was a mad man.

The men watched the news and listened as Scotty Johnson talked after being in court as a young man was given life after shooting a female police officer. Devin turned off the television, when Lisa entered the room. "What do you know about the inheritance bounty?" She called it.

Eddie pulled out paper that his investigator had researched. "My great, great grandfather and two of his friends had entered a gold mine and became delusional. They could not find their way out and something appeared to them. That is when the pact began with the so-called devil, as I was told, which is why my father never accepted any of the money from the family. He started his own business, but since there was a pact, my grandfather and the other family worked and saved their money, and started their own bet, as we call it, that their family would give birth to the first girl child, which is how my father met Jeffrey Thomas. The Klein family were all dying . . ."

"No, Dad, they were being slaughtered by the Thomas family and left one to be punished, and watch as they eliminated the competition. We have to talk to Kevin Klein again. Maybe, he will say who the others are now that Jeffrey is dead."

ᗡ ᗡ

Robert rolled out of bed. "I have to get to the hospital," he said to her.

She sat up and kissed his shoulder. "I need you, baby. Stay with me tonight."

He laughed. "What about your husband?"

She smiled. "He is with her tonight and I will be with you."

Where did I go wrong? He thought, as he looked at her. He had his life all planned out. He would be with Lisa and they would have started a family now, but fate had shown itself to him and he would have crumbs instead of cake. Lisa rejected him because of fear, he thought. She needed protection from the crazy family that stalked her and she turned to Devin Jones instead of him. Now he found himself sleeping with a gold-digging whore instead of in his bed with Lisa. Chloe touched his shoulder. "Soon we will be together and Scotty will be dead and we will collect the money and leave with the baby."

"It will not be that easy," he said. "We killed Thaddeus and we have to kill Scotty, but we need another baby to make the switch."

ᗡ ᗡ

Kevin Klein rolled through the room. He pulled out a can of beans from his cabinet when someone knocked at his door, "Enter!" He yelled. "Good work, boys," he said as he turned and noticed Devin and Jason standing in front of him with a bag of food. Klein reached for the bag and sniffed. "I have not had food that hasn't come from a can in years," he smiled. "To what do I owe this pleasure?"

Devin wasted no time. "How many of them are left?"

Klein laughed. "Jeffrey Thomas wanted twelve children. Why, I do not know. You took out the big dogs, but there are seven more." He said, "Do not believe the hype that some died in a fire, or some had different mothers and wanted no part of the Brotherhood. Melissa Thomas had nine children, and now five are dead, but another woman had three, when Melissa's last child was killed. Thomas turned to another woman and she gave birth to one of his children, which means she has three more somewhere and the last four are right under your noses.

"My compliments to the chef," Klein said. There will be a war. Thomas was very wealthy and he had some children living the high life, while others were second in his eyes. They did not join the Brotherhood, however, they will want the money."

Devin paced the floor. "No riddles, Mr. Klein, what are their names."

Kevin got serious. "I do not know!" He yelled. "If I did, I would have told you from day one. They all use aliases. Look at me," he demanded, "I only wanted a normal life. I had a wife and two boys and they were ripped away from me in the snap of a finger. Thomas was evil. He even killed his own brother because he thought that he was a Jones and he wanted nothing to do with the Brotherhood. "Now he has these psycho children that he bred to kill. I tried to warn your father about your mother and he sicced his dogs on me. I begged him to listen. Which one of you killed Simon? You do not have to answer, I heard you both open fire on him at the same time," a tear rolled down his face. "Thank you both. Simon killed my wife and sons. They were eight and eleven. He killed my family and I tried to tell your father. That is when Simon gutted me like a fish. He was Thomas's favorite. He had the DNA of a serial killer."

Devin turned and sat down while Jason stood.

"All of the kids had different fathers. Thomas worked at the prison and he would smuggle things in and give them to the prisoners that he chose to father a child with Melissa. They had to be tall and have a bad criminal history, that is what he wanted and he did not stop until he had enough. He was caught and he paid his way out of everything. He was filthy rich and now the mother has it all and the others will want their piece of the pie. That's why they want the baby: they feel that they are owed it and they are willing to turn on each other to get what they want. Do not let them take the baby, because if it's a girl, they will collect the prize. They want to stop the Jones bloodline and they will kill the boy first because he carries the Jones name and the girl because she is the prize. More important, she is a Jones."

Chapter 19

The television played while Eddie looked out in the yard. He could see that the children were having a good time. He stopped when there was an announcement about a missing girl on the television. Nineteen-year-old Jessica Hayes was reported missing by her family. She had left her home on Monday morning for a doctor's appointment and she had not been seen since. Witnesses said that the young lady was last seen talking to a man in a black Chevy Tahoe. During the time of her disappearance, however, they could not get a good description of his face. A feeling came over him as he watched and his heart went out to the family, he thought that he would reach out to them because it was not long since his family had gone through the same situation. He made a note to call the station and get the address of the family, so that Jason and Devin would start an investigation as to who could have taken Jessica.

ॐ ॐ

"Mr. Jones, this is Amanda Heart of Palms Real Estate."

Eddie looked at his calendar. It had only been a few weeks since he had placed his home on the market. He talked Carolyn and Lisa into letting his agent handle the sales of their homes and Judy's store, but he thought it would take months before he received a call.

"I called to inform you that we have several interested buyers for the properties that you have listed." Amanda read her Rolodex. She was adding up the commission as they talked. She knew she had to move fast if she wanted to sell all of the properties at once, and now someone was interested in every home he placed on the market.

"If you are free today, I can stop by your home and bring the paperwork."

He declined her coming to the house. Ever since the last incident, he wanted to keep the house closed to outsiders and as stress free as possible. Besides, Lisa and Carolyn might come home for lunch and he would not take any chances on them changing their minds. "I can meet you at your office today around lunchtime, if that would work for you." He knew she was seeing dollars signs and if he wanted to meet her in the middle of the Mississippi River, it would be fine with her.

Amanda graciously agreed before hanging up the phone, she then turned to the woman and man sitting in her office. I will try and have you settled in your new home by the end of the month, if everything checks out. The woman stood up. She was very big pregnant. "Are you due soon?" Amanda asked, while the woman looked at her with contempt. It sent chills down her spine. She could swear that she had seen her picture somewhere, but tried not to stare.

"Very soon," she said. While her husband was a little friendlier, he explained that their child was due soon and they wanted to get the boutique started before his wife went into labor.

He handed her several envelopes with cashier's checks inside. "If you can make this sale happen, Ms. Heart, there would be an additional bonus for you. He looked away. He never looked directly at her. She wanted to make eye contact with him, but he never removed his sunglasses. She reached out her hand to him, but he ignored it and walked away. Amanda breathed a sigh of relief as he walked out of the building. She thought of how rich people had it made and how they looked at you with their noses in the air and treated working folks like trash, but there was something different about this couple that scared her. She would make the sale and she would not have to see them again. She looked out of her window and wondered if she should lock the door, and thought not, when she witnessed the two of them get into their black SUV and drive away.

"Skeet, have you seen Devin or Jason?" Eddie asked. He got a strange feeling about the Hayes girl and he did not know why, but he felt he had to do something, before it was too late.

"Jason is in the office and Devin is on his way to the hospital to have lunch with Lisa."

Eddie did not know why, but he thought of Lisa. The Hayes girl was also due in a few weeks, but Lisa was due in a month. Maybe, he was being paranoid, but he got a gut feeling that something was going to happen.

"Did you hear about the missing girl?" he asked Skeet. He wondered if it was not just a coincidence that a pregnant girl went missing right around the time that Lisa was due to have her baby?

"Yes, I was talking to Jason about it, which is why Devin went to the hospital for lunch. Are we losing it, or does someone really want to take the baby?"

Eddie picked up the phone and dialed his attorney. He wanted to meet with them and discuss the inheritance money, when the attorney informed him that Ms. Lisa Washington had just left the office and wanted to claim the Jones inheritance.

"Mrs. Jones, your husband is here to see you." A smile came over her face. She had not heard anyone call her Mrs. Jones before. She and Devin had decided to have a private ceremony at their new home before the baby was born. She hoped it did not offend her new husband that her desk plaque still read Washington, but she would order another one as soon as she could.

"Please send my husband in," she said, when she received a phone call from Eddie. He called her Ms. Lisa Washington and asked her if she had left her office that day. He still disliked her, but he tolerated her because of Devin. She thought that he was being sarcastic and there was a reason he was asking, but she did not ask, "Eddie, I am booked all day and Christian is here with me. We came straight to the office." She looked up a minute later to see that Christian, too, was being called and asked if they had left the office.

Devin walked in carrying Styrofoam plates of food, the look on his face said that something was wrong. Without saying a hello Lisa asked, "Does your expression have anything to do with why your father is calling me and asking if I had left the office today?" The look he gave her told her it did not.

"There is a missing pregnant girl." When he said those words, she knew that it was starting all over again, and lowered her eyes. "I wanted it all to be over, but it is just beginning, I stopped by Big Mac and I found out that she had been seen there with Simon."

"Someone out there still wants our baby," she started to cry. "I have been so happy the last few days and now it is all about to end."

He held her. "I will not let them take her away and I have men all over this place. We will not let you out of our sight."

Lisa jumped when her secretary came over the speaker, "Mrs. Jones, there is a Mr. Lenny Samos on line one." Lisa grabbed her stomach. She was getting a strange feeling and now she knew why. "He wants to know if you can give him all day on Friday. He said that it was important that he see you."

Lisa looked at Devin, as he nodded his head, "Yes, that would be fine, Donna," she said. "He is trying to get back with the family now and I know why."

Devin agreed, "That is why we have to get answers from him and get him somewhere safe. I felt his pain when I first saw him. The feeling that came over me is one that I could not explain, and now he is out there all alone with no one to talk to and he said that it is not over."

Donna Weber knocked on the door, as they finished their lunch. "I thought that you might want to know that your two and four o'clock appointments have cancelled and rescheduled for next week, and there are no more appointments scheduled for the day." Lisa smiled at her. Donna was a nice woman, who she knew from years ago when she lived in New Orleans. They worked cases together and ran into each other at the market. She told Lisa that she was having trouble getting settled in Atlanta because she could not find employment, when Lisa hired her on the spot and had not regretted it.

"That means that my wonderful husband can take me home and you can get home to your family also."

He looked at his phone and there was a text, asking him if he was still with Lisa, *what is going on* he thought and dialed his father.

Lisa scanned the files from her computer. She also sent a fax to Jason and Devin's office. It was the file of Clementine Johnson, the sister of Melissa Thomas. Devin helped with the files because he had heard the name Clementine, however, he could not recall where. They stopped at the secretary's desk. Lisa noticed that janitor Al was, as usual, cleaning the same exact area across from her office. "This should be the cleanest area in the entire hospital," she said to him, as he gave her a look that made the smile fade from her face instantly.

Devin walked past her to confront him. "Do you have a problem?" he asked janitor Al who smiled, revealing a missing tooth that once held his gold nugget. It had been lost during a bar fight days ago.

"No, I was just caught off guard," he said before he apologized to Lisa. "I lost my prized possession," he continued as he turned and walked away.

Before they exited the building, Devin looked at the man in the lobby, who was filling out papers to see the doctor. They walked Donna to her car and once she was inside safely, they were on their journey home.

Andrew pulled out of the real estate office. "Well, that went well," he said, his new wife sat next to him. She wanted to go inside of the house again. They pulled into the long driveway of what was once the home of Eddie Jones. She walked into the house again. It was the same as before, just as the family had left it. She turned suddenly. She thought that she had seen someone in the house. "Hello, is anyone there?" She yelled. She turned to look at the wall and there was something moving on it. She yelled for Andrew, "Did you see that?" she asked. "What do you think that it could be?"

He watched as a shadow moved across the walls, "There has been a lot of negative activity in this house and that is why I purchased it, because I need this house to serve its purpose.

"Where is she?" Chloe asked.

He looked at her, knowing that she was not happy with the way he thought that things should be done, but now she agreed with him. "She is in town, seeing a head doctor and before all of this is over, everyone will think that she is a fucking basket case and that will seal her fate." He backed her against the wall, "You are intoxicating to me and all I want to do is make you happy, and soon all of this will be ours together."

He kissed her and pushed his body into hers, he ripped off her underwear, and lifted her, "Careful, honey, you will hurt the baby." They both laughed. "This place gives me the creeps," she said, "however, that is why we purchased it. She would be adding the decor on the walls while we sip margaritas in the Bahamas, and after, we will start our new life together with our million dollar baby."

"James and I are brothers in faith and we have a different father, but we both agreed on one thing and that is we need Lisa's baby."

Chloe leaped in fear; she was upset the real estate agent said nothing of any activity in the house. Although she knew the history, she said nothing . . . That the dead did not leave. "I do not like her. That agent is a lying bitch, she is a gold digging whore that cares for no one but herself, and she should have her tongue cut out."

Chloe was unhappy. Her husband reached over and held her hands, "Now, honey, a woman in your condition should not be getting upset, it is not good for the baby." He reached over and rubbed her belly, "What are you going to call her?"

She stared out the window. She had not thought that far ahead, she had only had one thing on her mind and that was finding a suitable home for her unborn child. "What about Christina Michelle?"

He closed his eyes. "That sounds beautiful for our little girl." He held her hand, "I love you and we will leave and never return when this is over, because it would not be safe for you."

Chloe looked with curiosity, "Honey, what is wrong?"

He thought of James and the others and what he had witnessed was unreal. "Stay away from James. That is all that I ask of you, because he is not what he seems to be."

☙ ☙

The apostles, Lisa looked in the Bible, she knew that there were several of them. When Jeffrey Thomas said that his sons were the apostles, she knew that there were more than nine.

"Babe, did you pull the papers off the printer that we faxed today?"

Lisa looked up over her glasses, "No," she said, as she stood on the bed while he held her for balance. "Maybe Jason took them."

Devin rubbed her hips. It had been a few weeks since he had touched her. She rolled her fingers through his silky, black hair, looked down at him and planted a soft kiss on his lips, careful not to arouse him. She just wanted a little affection from the man that she loved so much.

Carolyn was still in the honeymoon stage. Jason was in the office, but only for a short period on time. He and Carolyn took Lionel out for the day because he had not been out since he had returned home. If Jason did not take the faxes, then who did? She picked up the file on Clementine Johnson, who had three children. She set down the file and picked up the file of Melissa Johnson, and noticed that she had a child die shortly after birth. She then looked again. Clementine Johnson had a daughter that was twelve before she started to have more children. Wow she thought, to stop changing diapers for twelve years and then find yourself having children again. She searched the file to see if she had married. Lisa handed Devin the original file to copy, when her phone rang.

"She is a psychic," the voice on the other end of the line said without a hello. A smile came over her face. It was Detective Henderson, someone that she could get legitimate information from. "Clementine Johnson is alive and well," he said, "and she goes by the name of Lady Clem. Her shop is a house on St. Ann Drive."

Devin looked at the note Lisa had just written, *Lady Clem*; he had heard Ellen say that name on several occasions. He made a mental note to visit her. He would like to see if she knows anything about the missing girl. He had never had any interest in fortune telling, however, Lady Singleton had made a believer out of him. He would see if she was as sharp as Lady Singleton, who would be coming in a few days to visit.

"Eddie, my friend."

"Leonard, it is good to see you." Eddie stood and shook his hand. "I will be collecting really soon," Leonard said, "When is she due?"

Eddie laughed, "Not so fast, Leonard, it is hard for me to believe that she is carrying a little girl."

Leonard was offended. "Eddie, I have been a doctor for over thirty-four years and delivering babies is one of the things I do very well. I have not been wrong, yet, and I have no intentions of starting now because of some 100-year-old curse. It is a goddamn girl, and I would place everything I have on it, even my reputation."

❧ ❧

"Help me, please!" She screamed, but her screams were in vain. Jessica looked around and there was no one, she wiggled her hands, trying to loosen her restraints, but she got nowhere.

The door opened and a woman walked in, "Are you in labor?" she asked. She began to get nervous as she was not prepared and began to bounce up and down. "Don't move," she said, "I will call for help."

Jessica looked at her and she did not recognize the woman, "May I please have some water?" she asked. "I am not in pain, it is not time, yet." The woman walked out of the room and returned with a tray of food and drinks. "Thank you," she said, as she lifted her eyes and thought twice before speaking, "Who are you and why am I here?"

"It does not matter who I am, but you are here because you are having my baby."

Jessica's eyes widened with fear, "Please, lady, do not take my baby."

"Do you know if it is a girl or a boy?" She looked at her with a sinister look on her face, "It does not matter, I will be a mother." She began to hum lullabies, while Jessica watched in horror.

This was a woman, she thought, that she could appeal to her feminine side, but it was in vain, she wanted a baby and that was all that mattered to her. She would die and her child would be raised by a madwoman. She remembered meeting the big man at the bar and he offered her help so that she could stay on campus. She had started college and when her grades began to fail because she was pregnant, she did not want her family to know because she did not want the third degree from her parents. He introduced her to his family, because they were in law enforcement and, if she needed help, she could call on them. But it was one of them that had taken her and his name was Luke.

๑ ๑

"Hey, babe, did you know that there were twelve apostles?"

Devin laughed, ever since he started bodybuilding, people think he does not have a brain. "Yes, I did," he said, "and I can pretty much name them all."

Lisa laughed, "Where were you when I was waiting for the computer to boot up?"

"Why the curiosity about the apostles?" he asked, but he was proud of her ability to remember every word that someone speaks.

"Thomas was a literal man when he was himself, he referred to his sons as the apostles." She passed him the file of Melissa Thomas. "She had nine kids, which means, at the time, he wanted to be God, in a sense. Wouldn't he have had twelve kids instead of nine?

Devin sighed, "Which is why he killed her. He looked at her medical file after the birth of her last child, she had a hysterectomy and she was no good to him anymore. He remembered that he had inseminated other women with his sperm donors, but the women terminated those pregnancies. He has four more children out there somewhere. Someone willingly carried his children for him."

Lisa called and asked Detective Henderson for the names of Clementine Johnson's children. Devin grabbed a pencil and paper and started to write down the names of the apostles. He looked at the names of Melissa Thomas's children. Simon and Judas died in the shooting. Thaddeus was stabbed to death. Alpheus, James and Philip died in a fire. And Thomas and Matthew were shot to death. Bartholomew died at birth and that leaves John, Andrew and James.

Devin smiled, "At least, we know the names of the men that we are looking for." Then he remembered what Klein had said the others did not die in a fire. It was made to look like that, which means they are more deadly than the others and when Melissa's child died at birth, he fathered a child by another woman."

Lisa pulled out the yearbook, and showed the picture of the janitor" Babe, this is janitor Al. He was at the hospital when Maxine talked about the Thomas family, she referred to them as bad boys." Devin read the name Alpheus Johnson. Then she remembered that Maxine called the name James Johnson, not

James Thomas. "Why would he need twelve children to kill?" He looked at her because he had wondered the same thing, "And why name them after the apostles?"

She smiled, "You would think that he was doing it for the greater good as opposed to the opposite." She made a file on the Thomas family and placed it on a USB drive, "Because we are missing something."

ﬄ ﬄ

"Ms. Heart, I am Eddie Jones."

Amanda stared at the well-dressed man that walked into her office. She breathed a sigh of relief that he was pleasant, more so than the others that had been in her office the day before. She was making a big mistake and she knew it. There was something wrong, however, she could not put her finger on it. He sat at the table, "I am sorry I had to cancel on you, however, let's get down to business."

Amanda started her presentation. She informed him that two of the women were soon to be mothers and the families were eager to be settled in. He was without any questions. He, too, was eager to get rid of the old properties and get on with life. With the properties gone, that meant that Lisa or Carolyn would not change their minds and separate the family.

He signed without so much as a glimpse at the papers, as he had allowed the real estate company to handle the transaction and the money was more than he had asked. His hand stopped, as if someone was holding it. *Am I jeopardizing my family for my own selfish need?* He had his partner in crime Judy, and he asked her how to get the women to sell their homes. "Lisa is easy. She loves Devin more than anything and if she takes him away, then she would be separating the family, and she is too good for that. Carolyn, she is the jealous type and if Lisa signed then so will she, because she will want to be the head of the house since Jason is the oldest."

"I just want to keep my family together and spend time with my grandchildren."

"Why would anyone pay more?" He looked at Amanda, who looked white as a sheet.

"I do not know, sir, all I can tell you is those people scared the hell out of me and the sooner we get this over the better, so I will not have to see them again. There is something strange about the families that purchased your houses." She looked from Eddie to Willie because she knew wealth and power and they had it. "Have you ever felt like you were selling your soul to the devil?" They listened and could see the fear on her face. "His eyes were empty, and so were hers. I have seen her somewhere." Her eyes looked past both men, she smiled, "maybe, I am just be silly, but I am frightened by them, that is all, and as soon as you sign the papers, then I will be able to move back home and be with my family."

"Let us take the women to lunch today." Eddie was in a good mood, he and Willie droved by the old house, where they saw a black Tahoe parked in the driveway and they could see a medium brown-skinned woman standing outside of the house. "Do you think that she is one of the new owners?" he asked Willie, who said nothing at all on the drive.

"Yes, I think that we should take Carolyn and Lisa out to lunch today."

Eddie watched Willie, "What is on your mind, Willie, you have been quiet ever since we left the real estate office?" Willie droved over to Lisa's old house, he and Eddie watched as a tall light-skinned woman walked from the side of the house. She was thin with long black hair. Willie looked at her she, too, was pregnant. "Something is not right, Eddie, did you see that agent's face? Momma's old house was purchased by a man named James G. Johnson," he said as he looked at the paperwork. They drove there before heading to the hospital.

"If it makes you feel any better, I will talk to everyone tonight at dinner," said Eddie. "Besides, it is better that we are together and not being picked off one by one."

"I agree," Willie said, "it is just that Lisa is such a good person and to think that someone wants to hurt her and her unborn child is upsetting to me, that's all."

Carolyn was sitting in Lisa's office. "Only a few more weeks before you will be out on maternity leave and I think I will take a few days off to spend with Lionel. He has been so happy to finally be home with his family and, to my surprise, Eddie has been a perfect grandfather." Lisa and Carolyn high-fived each other and yelled, "Girl power!"

"Thank you," Eddie said, as he walked into Lisa's office. "Your secretary was not at her desk and you had the shade up, so I took it that you were available." Eddie watched as Lisa walked from behind her desk and went into Willie's arms. She still did not trust him as she did Willie and that bothered him. He had made a mistake and she still had not fully forgiven him for it, when she walked into his arms also. "We have come to take the two of you to lunch," he said when he handed both Carolyn and Lisa envelopes.

Carolyn was excited, however, Lisa looked at it before she turned and looked at Willie. She was getting that feeling in her stomach again and she could tell by the look on Willie's face he shared her concerns, but she felt safe with the two of them and knew that she did the right thing. She would not put her husband and child in danger because she was being selfish. She said, "Lunch sounds good" and grabbed her purse. She wanted to sit outside and smell the fresh air again, just as they did before Jeffrey Thomas and his family began to stalk her.

✎ ✎

"Hello, Lady Clem, my name is Tiffany Johnson." Tiffany struggled with her cell phone as she tried to look at the navigational system, "I have an appointment with you today, however, I think that I am lost." She explained to her on the phone where she was. She was not familiar with Atlanta since she had lived in California all of her life. She came to Atlanta after she met her boyfriend and now husband, Andrew. This was his home and he talked of the growth of the city and all the things that they would accomplish together. They both became police officers and, after her accident, she no longer worked in law enforcement. Now she would start living her dream of becoming the mother of his child and opening up her own boutique. She pulled in front of Lady Clem's home. She took a deep breath before she exited the car.

Lisa picked up her new car from the dealer. She had decided to trade in her black Suburban for a tan-colored one. Why do you have to have such a big car?" Carolyn asked. But, ever since she began to travel with loads of clothing to Judy's store, she had learned to appreciate having more room and some old habits are hard to break. She would be the mother of two now and having to travel with a dog and a child, she could use the room.

She waved to Willie as he watched to make sure that she was in safely. He pulled next to her, "Can I follow you home?"

She felt depressed, she needed sometime alone; Lisa knew she was breaking Eddie's rules, and she did not want to go to Eddie's house. "No, Poppy, I will be in a little later" was all that she could say because being in the new house did not feel like home to her, although Eddie tried his best. She wanted to be alone with Devin, have a candlelit dinner and not have to deal with the family every day.

He followed her back to the hospital before leaving, and she stood by the door and watched until he was out of sight before running to her car. She looked up to see the janitor Al and Dr. Samuels talking. She exited fast before they could see her.

"What would your father say if he knew what we were doing?" Skeet asked Kandy.

"I do not know," she said, "but I am happier now than I have ever been. I hope you won't let anyone interfere with us, Skeet." Kandy turned her back on him, she needed to know that he was with her and would not let anyone tear them apart. She had cared for men before and they were only using her, however, she did not feel Skeet was that kind of man. He was warm and he cared for her and Justin and, if her father could not accept that, she would leave.

He reached over and touched her, "I should have had a man-to-man with him and now I feel like we are sneaking around."

Kandy turned to him with frustration, "He is my father, not my husband. Besides, we are adults, but if you feel the need to have a man-to-man then do that, but promise me that you will not let anything come between us." She was feeling insecure. She had lost men to other women, but she never thought that she would lose one to her father.

He rolled on top of her, "Can anything come between us now?" he asked before he entered her again.

"Lady Clem, my name is Tiffany."

"I know who you are," she said, her body began to shake. She did not look at Tiffany, "The boy did not shoot you," she said. Tiffany did not ask any questions. She listened and wondered how did she know that she had been shot? "You are being deceived. Your life is a lie. You carry a boy child, but a girl is required to get the job done." Lady Clem flipped a card, "The walls in the house you share are full of death and carry the souls of the dead and, in the end, you will be added to it." Lady Clem gave Tiffany a phone number. "Call this number and tell them everything, child, everything. If you do not, then the child you carry you will never see. It will die and so will you." She gave Tiffany a yearbook. "Give this to the one you talk to. You must hurry, and tell your husband nothing of coming here."

"What are you saying?" Tiffany asked. "Are you saying that my husband will kill me?"

Lady Clem looked into her eyes, which she had avoided in the beginning because they told of her death. She could see her eyes staring at the ceiling at the bottom of her staircase. "He has no soul, and he would think nothing of killing you and his own flesh and blood to get what he wants. When you became pregnant, he wanted a girl child. But he knows that it is not and he will kill it, as the others have killed theirs."

Lisa sat outside of the home she had once owned. She parked far enough away so that the new owner would not notice her. She watched as the woman, who looked to be due to have a baby any day now, carried boxes inside the house. She watched the tall, slender woman carry boxes two at a time and did not stop to catch her breath, not once. *I must really be out of shape she* thought. She put on J.T.'s glasses, as she watched in awe of the woman.

The woman walked and she swung her ponytail, wearing high-heeled shoes. Lisa thought that she looked so happy, as if she did not have a worry in the world. She began to cry and pulled out the cashier's check from the Palm Real Estate Company. She had not made a mistake selling the house because it was tainted, and it would no longer be a home that she and her child would feel safe in. She looked up again. This time she noticed a black Tahoe slow down to look at the woman. She stopped and turned. She did not look as if she was afraid; she even smiled and waved at the driver. She rubbed her belly like she used to do when she was a child, when she was hungry.

Lisa jumped when she heard someone knock at her window, "Oh my lord, Devin, you scared me." He opened the driver side door while Lisa slid over into the passenger side. "What are you doing here?" she asked him.

"Jason and I were driving through when I noticed you sitting here." He looked at the woman, "Wow, she must be in real good shape. You cannot carry a bag of potatoes chips without getting out of breath. I see old man Duncan is up to his old tricks," he said. They laughed at the smoke coming from his truck.

"I wonder how many cigarettes he smokes while he is out in his truck?" she asked and, "Why did he refer to the person that watched the house as the Devil?"

Devin looked at her. He knew when she was upset. He turned the key in the ignition, "Come with me, I want to show you something."

He drove to a house that his mother had given him the money to pay for and he and Jason had renovated themselves. She would tell them that they needed their own man cave and they never told anyone about their place. They pulled in front of a two-story house. It had a different look, almost like a cabin in the woods.

Lisa looked around, "Devin, this place is beautiful!"

Devin pointed three houses down, "That is Jason's place. When we needed a place for peace, we would come here."

Lisa Looked behind the house and there was a pond and chairs to sit and feed the birds. It was private and beautiful. She would love this. She could visualize herself and her daughter walking hand in hand along the pond.

Devin pulled plates out of the cabinet. He had picked up Chinese food on the drive down, and he now poured two glasses of iced tea, before sitting. "What is on your mind?" he asked her,

"I know you are unhappy and I cannot bear the thought that it could be because of me or my father."

She looked at him. He was the best thing that had ever happened to her and she did not want him to think that she was unhappy with him. "I am scared, baby," she started, "you are the best thing that has happened to me and our life before this was great. I enjoyed spoiling you." She lowered her head. "The thought that someone wants to profit from our child and take her is driving me crazy. And the thought that if they manage to get her, they will not love her. Our little girl is in trouble.

"Your great-great grandfather thought it would bring the family together, however, one family is dead and now there are others that want to hurt us all and, if we are not careful, we can end up hurting each other. Sometimes the tension gets so thick that I cannot stand to be inside of the house and I hope that we can get to an understanding with your father about Jimmy."

Devin turned red because he had thought the same thing. "Lady Singleton said that it would be brothers against brothers, and we would do battle with pure evil. I do not know what all of this means, but I will do anything it takes to protect you and Devinina."

They both laughed when she said, "Try again."

"I thought I would throw the name out there and see if you liked it."

Lisa walked into the yard and sat by the pond, her mind was free and for the first time in a long time, she felt safe and madly in love with her husband. Brothers against brothers, she said, "Thomas had children with different women, and he favored one set over the other."

Devin took a sip from his glass, "That is what I thought, because there were twelve and he worshipped Simon, so the others had to be happy when he died, and Thaddeus was the last of Melissa Thomas's sons, since we are to assume that three are dead. We know that a woman other than Mother killed him, so it has happened, brothers had turned against brothers.

She lay back in his arms as he placed his hand on her stomach and their baby started to move, "She is very active tonight." He closed his eyes and held her.

"Something else is bothering you," he said, when she pulled out a picture of a woman and teenage boy. "It was more than us he was protecting and we have to, first, let him know that we know that he is Jimmy, and then we have to find out all that he knows about Thomas's other sons and why he pretended to be Jenny."

Devin stroked her belly. "He pretended to be Jenny to get close to you all."

"Okay." She nodded, "then whose idea was it for him to be pregnant?"

"This is how I imagined us, but I almost missed it all." He thought of his father's action.

Lisa looked around as she turned and straddled him, wearing only his nightshirt. She kissed him passionately. "Now this is how I imagined us." He carried her inside.

Devin looked down when his phone began to ring. "Hello, Mr. Jones, my name is Tiffany Johnson."

Chloe danced in her kitchen. It was her first time cooking and it proved to be a challenge for her. Even with cookbooks and recipes that were left by the previous owner, she was not up for the challenge. She found a folder that contained menus from local restaurants that delivered, "Thank you, Lisa!" She yelled. She was good at many things, but she was not a chef.

She walked through her home and was proud of her decor and her specialty was her nursery. She rubbed her belly and talked to her unborn child, "Mommy will do better, I promise." She had never thought of becoming a mother, but now as she grew larger, she had become attached to the child that would soon be hers. After her doctor's appointment earlier today with Dr. Robert Samuels, she was convinced more now than ever that in four weeks, she would deliver a healthy baby girl.

"You will probably deliver early," he said to her. She first felt uncomfortable and uneasy, but he worked his charm with her and now she knew that she would keep her baby and live a normal life as a single mother. Her common law husband had taken care of her, but she has no desire to continue a life with him. He was a joke to her and she would end their relationship when the time was right.

She smiled and thought of her new life with James. He would be the perfect father to their child. She remembered as they made love and he told her what his plans were and she would become a mother, and now soon it would be true. She will have a child, a girl child. Her mind went to Andrew again and what he said about James, but it did not matter. James had cast a spell over her and she was his till death do them part.

❧ ❧

"Jason, may I have a word with you?" Ellen was concerned about Lisa. She had never said anything out loud about Lady Clem's prediction, and now the time was getting near and she started having nightmares of someone taking Lisa's baby. She needed to know that they were still keeping their eyes on her. "Where is your brother?"

Devin walked past the door when he was called into the room. Ellen handed Jason the check from the real estate company, "I want you boys to have this and make sure you are prepared for what is out there. I thought that I saw someone wearing all black again. They were across the street in the lot, but Eddie said that I was dreaming."

Jason handed the check to Devin, thinking he would return it to Ellen. Instead, he folded it and put it in his pocket. "Momma Ellen, we are on top of things, however, there is some unfinished business to take care of. We will have a meeting later when Lady Singleton visits and put everything into place. Both men kissed her, and she held them as if she would never let them go. "Be careful," she said and they walked out.

"Testing, testing." Skeet checked the equipment that he placed in Lisa's office. He hooked up special equipment to ensure that she had adequate protection. "If you feel any trouble is around." He pointed to a little button under her desk, "hit this and we are only two minutes away. Jason, Devin, and I will be at the office across the street."

Lisa hugged Skeet. She did not want him to know that she knew about him and Kandy, since they were keeping it a secret, so she just said, "Thank you" with a smirk that piqued his curiosity.

"Is something wrong?" he asked her.

She had a glow to her. "Nothing is wrong. As a matter of fact, things are finally getting right," she said. "At least they will be when all of this is over." She felt so much better after spending a quiet evening with Devin, "And it is good to have you in the family." She hoped that he would sit and talk, but he did not. He would not share his and Kandy's secret with her.

Devin opened an account for Ellen in her name. He left specific instructions for the bank teller, who had been a friend for a long time. "I will have someone bring her down to sign the paperwork this afternoon." He returned to the car where Jason waited for him and handed him Ellen's bank book. Jason looked at Ellen's check and bank book and laughed. "Eddie will not be happy. What are you up to?" he asked Devin, who looked at him with his I-do-not-give-a-damn expression.

"They used her, Judy, and all of the rest of them. Judy and Ida have a home and they have money to burn. Ellen's place is with us and God forbid if something was to happen to us, she would be left out in the cold or she would have to kiss ass for the rest of her life, and she is too good for that." He smiled. "Besides, Eddie owes her twenty years of child support. She is now paid in full." They both looked at each other, "There will be a war and we need to prepare for it. Something is going to happen. Last time, Ellen was caught in the cross fire. We cannot afford to let down our guards because we have to find out who Melissa's other children are and where we can find them and Jimmy has those answers."

❧ ❧

"Hey, baby boy." Lisa was happy to see J.T.. He had come to her office for lunch. "If I thought I could have this amazing lunch every day, I would get pregnant again in a heartbeat." She knew, though, that she was not getting the lunch date because she was pregnant. They were for her protection.

"What can I do for you, Mommy," J.T. asked, looking at her belly. She knew that he was calling her Mommy because they had become close and he once told her that she treated him like her son when she had given him advice on girls.

"Can you blow up some photos for me? The house has no photos of the family and I would like to have some framed to hang on the wall." Lisa pulled out the photo of Eddie and Jimmy. She picked up a photo of Asia, one that she especially liked, and also one of Ellen that she thought was beautiful. She wanted both pictures enlarged, when something caught her eye she looked from Jimmy and a photo of Melissa that was mixed with the others. *I was right* she thought *Jeffrey was trying to recreate Melissa and that is how Jimmy became Mother.*

❧ ❧

"Mother, are they dead, yet?" The woman begged her mother, "End this madness. Tell them so that it will end, or you will never see me or your normal family again."

"They will come soon and it will end," Lady Clem flipped a card and noticed it was the card of death. "There are too many distractions," she said to her daughter, "but it will end soon. It will be brothers against brothers. They will come for me," Lady Clem said to her daughter, "so I have sent you what you will need to get far away because they will come for you also."

"What have we done?" she asked her mother. "We created monsters."

Lady Clem sighed, "They were not born monsters. They were raised to become monsters and they will pay for it."

She flipped the cards again and the card of death appeared again. She stood and began to pace, thinking of where it had all gone wrong. She had lost the man that she had loved. The headlines read, "Man Died in a Car Crash." Carl Walker had left Big Mac bar around midnight. Witnesses said he was swerving on the road and lost control, hitting a tree and the car burst into flames, killing him instantly.

She had no money, only a young daughter that she could not support, when she was offered money for the use of her body by her sister that had everything, so she decided to take the offer and lived to regret it her entire life. She had given birth to the Devil's children, the spawn of Satan she called them. She tried to take the children and run, however, they had been corrupted too badly and swore if she interfered in their lives, she would pay with her own and now the cards tell the same story— she will die also.

She remembered when Melissa and her boyfriend came to her house. She was driving a new car and wearing the best of clothing, while she and her child had nothing. "How do you live like this?" She was asked by both, when Thomas stood and asked her if she would carry his child and he would pay her very well to do so.

Her sister had six children already and was carrying her seventh. "He wants a large family and I can use a little help," Melissa said. She should have known better but decided to accept the offer, and she had lived to regret it ever since.

He gave her money and asked her to be in his office to start the procedure and she did. After she had given birth to three, she could take no more. Then he turned to her child, who wanted to look good and smell of the finest perfumes and offered her own body, and she did nothing to stop it.

Melissa disappeared thirteen months after the death of her last child. She closed her eyes because she had never seen her again. She thought of their last meeting when she came to her and said that she had to get away from them because she had been with the Devil. Melissa was scared of Jeffrey, but she stood her ground with him. The last child she carried was not one of Jeffrey's and she said that he killed it because it was a girl and it was not one that he chose.

She turned the card because her fate was sealed, but she did not want her daughter to experience the death that was to come to her. She was all alone now and she would pay for what she had done.

Chapter 20

"Mr. Jones." Jason turned to find a woman standing in front of him. He offered her a seat when Devin and Skeet turned their attention to her. "I called you because . . ." She stopped. "First of all, my name is Tiffany Johnson."

Devin pulled up a chair while Skeet stood. He grabbed his recorder and a notepad. "Mrs. Johnson, please feel free to talk. We are not here to judge you or anything you have to say."

She took a deep breath before she started. "I went to see a psychic by the name of Lady Clem," she started. "She told me that both my unborn child and I would die." When she said those words, he thought of the missing girl Jessica Hayes. "She told me that the boy did not do it." Tiffany did not use her exact words, she knew she was told to say everything, but it was too painful. "She had also said that a girl child was required, however, I have no idea as to what that means. She gave me your phone number. Mr. Jones, my unborn child is a boy," she said with tears in her eyes. "There is a missing girl out there and someone is targeting pregnant women."

Jason made a note to talk to Lady Clem because of her involvement with Jeffrey, and she is the sister of Melissa Thomas. "Have you talked to your husband?" He noticed the look on her face.

"I was told by Lady Clem to say nothing to him, he would not understand and . . ." She stood. "There is something wrong with my new house."

They could see the fear on her face. Devin thought of Lisa, as he had watched the same fear in her eyes the night before. She wrote down her address and gave it to them. "Will you please come by? My husband will be out of town until Monday."

She went to walk out of the door before remembering the book, she handed it to Devin. "She said give this to you."

He looked at the book. It was a yearbook. "Mrs. Johnson, you said that the psychic said that the boy did not do it. What did that mean?" They knew that she was not telling everything and if they were to help her, they would need more information than she was giving. "I know that this is painful for you. My wife too is pregnant and I fear for her every day since the kidnapping. However, if we are going to help you, then you will have to trust us."

"Seven months ago, when I first found out that I was pregnant, I was responding to a call." She began to cry. "I was a law enforcement officer. I was shot in the shoulder," she said. There was an arrest. The man's name was Kelvin Hamilton. He said he was innocent and now Lady Clem says the same. He was sentenced to life and he is locked up in prison." She handed Jason a paper. "He had no priors up until that point."

❧ ❧

"Knock-knock, can I come in?" Kandy entered the office where Lisa and Carolyn were awaiting the entrance of Lenny Samos.

"Hey, baby girl." It had been a long time since they had been able to have time to spend together. "I was just thinking about the days when we used to walk around the park and afterwards stop at the coffee shop and have a cup of coffee and two donuts."

Kandy added, "And we would say that we would walk an extra block on the next day to burn up the calories."

Lisa knew that Devin and Jason were listening in. She thought that it was a good thing if Kandy was going to come clean about her and Skeet, there would be no second-hand information.

"I have been seeing Skeet," she started and finally she threw up her hands.

While Carolyn was in awe, Lisa said, "He is an amazing man, Kandy, and he is exactly what you need in your life and he can keep a secret." She laughed. "I tried to get him to talk, but he did not say a word. He is strong and confident, and he is most of all a loving man and stable minded. I was going to try and put the two of you together when Devin told me to mind my own business, but he started telling Skeet all about you." She laughed. "A double standard."

Kandy had her hands on her hips, "How did you know, because we have been so careful?"

Lisa stood. "Your bedroom is behind my bedroom wall and we can hear it all, girl."

"No," Carolyn said.

Jason and Devin looked at Skeet. They watched him smile when Lisa responded to Kandy words. Skeet was a good catch for Kandy and they, too, wanted them to get together.

"Strong and confidant, my eye," Carolyn said. "That is pure sexy chocolate, he is cute and sexy," Carolyn said with a smile that could win over a blind woman, "and if you were going to go through the virgin stage like this one here . . ." She pointed at Lisa. "Then I had many women that were asking questions about him. So, I approve also, Kandy. You and Justin need stability and now you have it."

Lisa looked at her watch. "Lenny Samos should be here any minute." Before Kandy left the room, she urged Lisa and Carolyn to be careful. "We are never going to see Jenny again." This saddened her, "I do not know Jimmy and I love Jenny."

Lisa sighed, "They are the same person. Honey, we just have to make sure that he is safe and that is why we are spending the day with him, to get information from him so that if he runs away, we will know where the others are."

Kandy walked across the street and waited with the men. While Carolyn waited to play her role in the act with Lisa, she was not convinced that Jimmy was Jenny and that she was trying to help. "It is time to bring Jimmy home to his family, but we have to do it this way because that janitor is watching our every move."

"Mr. Samos, this is Carolyn Young." Lisa did an introduction. "She will take your blood pressure to make sure that you are up to this and she will wait in the back in case you get into any distress and we have to pull you out of the hypnosis."

He sat down. "Are you sure that this is going to work?"

She looked up and jumped when she noticed a black shadow standing at the window. He watched her eyes, turned and looked.

Jason and Devin rushed to the computer to await the arrival of Lenny Samos. They watched his every move and were so focused that they did not notice Eddie pulling up in his car. "Guys . . ." Skeet pointed to the door as Eddie walked in. Kandy sat and read a magazine.

"What are you all up to?" No one said anything and he knew that something was wrong. He could hear Lisa's voice coming from the computer. He walked over and looked when he heard her say Mr. Samos. "That is Jimmy's voice. Then he looked at Lisa and Jimmy on the computer screen. "Lisa has Jimmy in her office and you son of a bitches knew he would be with her and none of you said anything." Eddie went to leave when they stopped him.

"Let her do her job, Eddie. We need to know what he knows about the others and if you go into a rage, then they will know who he is and he will be in danger."

"Something is happening," Devin said. "Where is Christian?" As he looked at Lisa staring at the window, he remembered that they had pulled him out of the lobby so that Jimmy would not be spooked by his presence.

✎ ✎

"Did you see that?" Carolyn asked. "It has to be the janitor."

Lisa snapped back and started to do her work. They had to move fast. "The subconscious is a powerful thing. Everything that has happen to you is locked inside of your mind. Sometimes, because of painful situations, we block things out and it is placed in the back of our mind, so to speak."

Lisa stood to pull his files, he watched her, and commented, "That was not there when I last spoke to you," she said, referring to her belly.

She sat and smiled. "Yes, it was, but it was not as noticeable."

She looked at the screen. She could see that everyone was paying attention. "I looked into the thing that you remembered from our last session and I have information and dates for you. My husband and his brother are both investigators." Lisa placed the file of James and Jimmy Jones on her desk. She wanted him to take the bait and hoped that he would start to talk and not have to waste time with a side show, as she had no idea how to hypnotize anyone, it was not her specialty. Then she placed the file of Lenny Samos with a picture of the real Lenny S. Amos on top, so that he could see it. She acted as if she was busy. She did not want him to know she was watching him. She then pulled out her trump card—the picture of Coretta and Cody—and placed it on her desk and watched as he looked at it with his eyes in tears.

"You are good," he said, "better than I had hoped."

She smiled, "We are family," she mumbled before she looked at the window and could only see something black.

$$\wp \quad \wp$$

"Lisa thinks that they do not know who he is so he has a reason to be in her office as a client, because that janitor watches and reports back to someone, and if you go storming over there, then you will ruin everything." Eddie sat and watched as his sons chastised him before filling him in on what was happening. "Dad, when you get your mind set on something, you go for it, but this time it can get us killed and Jimmy. There are seven more of the Brotherhood, but somehow Jimmy survived. We have to find out how and if he wants to be with his family or is setting us up." Jason stood angrily, "He pretended to be a woman and was diagnosed as being pregnant, so there are many questions. Did he make a pact with the others to survive and why did Jeffrey take him?"

Eddie said nothing. He just listened and agreed since Lady Singleton had warned him. His family was falling apart and he could see it. Jason was agreeing with Carolyn, while Devin was keeping an open mind and that could be trouble. He wasted no time. They needed answers and they needed them now. So, he stood and walked to the door, "I will get the answers from Jimmy one way or another." They protested him going and interrupting Lisa's session, but it was in vain. Eddie walked out. They turned to the screen and could see something black, a shadow in the window, but this one was tall.

$$\wp \quad \wp$$

Carolyn took Lenny's blood pressure and checked his heart rate, "You are a healthy man," she said. She looked at him again and now was getting the same feeling as Lisa did. There was something about him. Lisa said that she could feel his pain when he first entered her office. He smiled and it melted her, he was handsome and he had a beautiful disposition about him, but it was his eyes, they were the shape of Jenny's and the nose. She smiled back at him and gave the all clear to Lisa who could now see Eddie Jones sitting with his sons.

"Mr. Samos," she started, "do you want my help?"

He looked at her as if this was the first time seeing her. "Yes, that is why I am here."

Then remove the contacts from your eyes and, by the way, my name is Mrs. Jones."

He smiled. *She is sharp and she really did do her homework* he thought and finally he could talk to his family and bring his family together. He took out his contacts and, "Now I am going to need for you to relax. None of this is necessary." He said. "I know who you are and you know who I am, but we are running out of time." She reached for his hand and he held hers tight, "We have to move fast.

"Where are the others?" he asked. "Time is running out."

"Not so fast," Carolyn said. "Where is Jenny?" Lisa had been playing detective and now, so would she.

"I was Jenny." He looked at her.

"You used us for them or did you not know who you were?"

He looked at Lisa because Carolyn was not one of his favorite people. She thought that she was better than others. "I did not use anyone. It is not safe to talk here because James and the others are watching."

Before Lisa could say anything, she could hear a commotion in the waiting room, when suddenly her door opened. Both Jimmy and Carolyn looked at Eddie. Lisa's focus was on the computer screen. She was angry. She could lose her license if Jimmy wanted to hurt her.

Jimmy stood and faced his brother. After this session, she would need Carolyn to take her blood pressure. "Eddie, we are not done. Would you please wait outside?"

Eddie was outraged. "You are done," he said with gritted teeth. "I am taking you home," he said to Jimmy, "where you belong." He turned and gave Lisa a stare that sent chills thought her body and angered her. There were so many questions and now the others would know who Jimmy was and he would run away because Eddie had placed his life and the life of the family he had created in danger.

◈ ◈

The chimes on Lady Clem's door rang, but she did not look up. "What took you so long? The two of you ain't never on time." She laughed at them standing in front of her. "Sit," she said, "my time is running short."

Devin looked around her shop. He noticed a picture of five children, four boys and one girl, who seemed to be much older than the others.

"My daughter lives in California," Lady Clem said, "and she will never return here again. Her name is Connie, but I know that you are not here in reference to her." Lady Clem seemed sad. "Sometimes you sell your soul to the Devil, and you will pay later. Has your son ever said that he was hungry and there was nothing that you could do?" She did not look at Jason as she flipped her cards. "Please do not judge me, but I have seen it and it is worse than you could imagine. Jeffrey was no match. He is the worshiper of Satan and the lord of illusion. What you saw at the hospital, his dance and his levitation of his body, he knew that she would carry the girl child.

"He died so young. I was only fifteen when I became pregnant, but he did the right thing by me, he went to work and we had a little house, but we were happy and one day it was all over and I was all alone, raising a child all by myself." She closed her eyes. "I keep seeing Jeffrey's face everywhere I turn, because it was he who gave me the power of knowledge.

"After the birth of my last son, I said no more because the one before was a girl and she was taken and killed, just as my sister's last ones were girls. When James was born, he was my last and one day I felt ill and went to the hospital. I got worse, then I flat lined and I was revived by one of the doctor's after Jeffrey left the room, and from then on, I could see things before they would happen and I could read thoughts.

"They want the baby for different reasons. One for the money, however, one wants the power and is worth more than you would ever know. She wants the child and would do whatever it takes to get it, but her joy will be short lived. I cannot see Connie in the cards," she cried, "but I can see my future and it is dark.

"My time is short, so let me finish. Jeffrey was in over his head and thought that he was creating an army to fight the darkness, but their power was much stronger than anticipated. He thought that he would eliminate what they wanted, it would weaken them, but instead he got lost himself. They infiltrated his army and made it dark, turning brother against brother, and rendering him powerless."

"You sent a woman by the name of Tiffany Johnson to see us . . ." Jason said.

"And she did not tell you everything, right?"

Jason smiled. He had relied more on psychics lately than he had relied on his own common sense. "No, she did not."

"She will die," Lady Clem said, "they will take the baby too early and it will die also.

Devin studied her pictures. "Take it," she said, "if you think that it will help. A girl child is required." She flipped a card, "however, a boy will do. Her life is a lie and she will pay the consequence with her life. All that was yours is now theirs."

Devin was curious about the inheritance, and hoped that she would give him some information about it because it seemed to be the reason that they want his daughter. "You child is more important than the money. She is life and she is death to them. The money will come in the amount of $160 million, but it will be received in a job or a lottery because your family did not fall under its spell."

❧ ❧

The sun was shining beautifully. Lisa lifted her head. She stayed inside, but she longed to be out. She had not been out in a month, just hanging out, drinking coffee and having conversation with her friends. She wondered if her life would ever be normal again. Eddie crossed the line. He allowed his prejudice to put everyone in harm's way. He could not accept Jimmy's life and did not care what happened to him, and now Carolyn had made Jason think that Jimmy was the bad guy and was trying to hurt Lionel.

"A penny for your thoughts." Lisa turned to see Willie. He walked in carrying take out. She walked to him and shook her head, "I cannot go back to that house." Her eyes started to water. "He did not let me finish before he took Jimmy. He has placed my child in danger again and I will not forgive him for that."

Willie handed her a plate. "I understand how you feel, but I think that it is a good thing that he is where we can watch him." She looked puzzled, she thought that Willie would understand what she was feeling, but apparently he did not. She was alone. She only hoped that Devin would feel the same as she did and he would not betray her. "I want to have my men follow him around," he began to say. Willie reached over and grabbed her hand. "I will not let him out of my sight. Whatever he is up to, he will not get away with it."

She looked away because no one was listening to her. They think that Jimmy is the bad guy because of Carolyn. Jimmy was not the bad guy, but now they know that he is alive and they would try to kill him. Jimmy had a lot to lose also.

Tiffany unpacked the shipment of baby clothing, she did not know how to tell her husband that the baby was a boy. She had tried, but it angered him so she decided to let it be, when he saw their son, he would be happy. She looked at the entire boys' clothing line that was shipped to the boutique. She wanted to set up the baby room at the house, but Andrew would not allow it. "You will jinx the baby" is what he would tell her. When Lady Clem's words popped into her head, she had thought of packing her things and leaving until the baby was born, but she had no idea what to say to her husband. The door to her shop opened. She had only been open a few days and business was good. She had to do the grand opening herself and was grateful for the condition the place was in, she had little work to do and started with the merchandise that she had ordered before purchasing the building.

"Welcome to J's Boutique," she said to the woman that entered the building. She ignored her and went directly to the baby girls' selection of clothing. Tiffany smiled at the expression on her face. She seemed a little confused. She grabbed everything that was pink. She did not check the price tags or sizes, or any other color of clothing, just pink today, when yesterday her choice was blue.

Her eyes went to the door when she heard a car door slam. She breathed a sigh of relief to see the Jones brothers coming into her store. She was happy that they were taking her seriously and did not think that she was crazy for referring to a psychic.

Jason walked up to Tiffany while Devin stopped and noticed the woman that was shopping in her shop, he recognized her as the woman that now owned the house that he and Lisa once shared. "All that was yours is now theirs" is what Lady Clem said and, without hesitation, he called his father. "Dad, is Jimmy with you?" He watched and signaled for Jason to do the same.

"Hello, Mr. Jones." Tiffany looked at the two men and noticed that they were watching the pregnant woman.

"She is a regular," she said when Jason turned his attention to her.

"We have an appointment with Kelvin Hamilton and we also talked to Lady Clem." He reached over, touched her hand and looked into her eyes. They were sad. He wanted to comfort her, but he did not know where to start.

"Tiffany, is there anywhere that you could go alone without your husband? Someplace that he does not know about where you will be safe?"

She looked hard at him, "So you believe what she said." Her heart was pounding. "I cannot leave my husband. I am due in three weeks." She knew what was being insinuated. They believed that her husband was out to kill her and their child.

"We are going to need a picture of your husband." Before leaving the store, he advised that she talk to no one and he left a security guard with her. "We will call you when we have something for you."

❧ ❧

"Ms. Heart, my name is Lisa Jones. I am interested in meeting with you to discuss the property of Ida Jones." She was curious about the woman that had purchased her home. She still could not get the picture of her she carrying all of those boxes in high-heel shoes out of her mind. Eddie was being secretive about everything. The woman purchased her home for more than the asking price, which she had found strange. Why pay more if it was not asked? Devin called her and asked that she meet with the real estate agent to see what she could find out. There was no Johnson family lottery winner in California. "Hello, Ms. Heart, I was just about to hang up," Lisa said, "can you meet me at my office today, I have some questions about the family that purchased my family homes." Money talked, so she offered to pay her for her time.

Amanda grabbed all of the files on the Johnson family. There was something strange about them; however, she would be paid for her time and that is all that mattered. She walked out to her new car, which she had purchased two day ago. She grabbed a file for James Johnson, and noticed he had not signed one of the papers and thought that she would stop by his home after she left her appointment with Lisa Jones.

"Donna can you file these papers for me?" Lisa looked up when she saw a woman walking through the door and she looked hard as she heard the woman yell for a Mr. Johnson. The woman walked down the hall and handed Dr. Samuels a paper, which he signed and walked away. She stepped back so that he would not see her and she was in disbelief. Why would he sign a paper for a Mr. Johnson?

She walked back to her office when the same woman knocked on her door. "Mrs. Jones," she said. "I am Amanda Heart." Lisa noticed at how young Amanda looked. She was about 5'5" and 120 pounds, blonde hair, and blue eyes, but she would look better if she applied a little less makeup.

She wasted no time, "Ms. Heart, I noticed that you were yelling for a Mr. Johnson, however, you handed the paper to Dr. Samuels. Do they know each other? Amanda watched as Lisa began to count the money in her wallet. When she got to five hundred dollars, she stopped and placed it on her desk, "As I told you, I will pay you for your time."

Amanda placed the files on her desk. "The man that signed the paper for the purchase of Ida Stanford's home was Dr. James G. Johnson, not Dr. Samuels," she said. "He had wanted to purchase the home that you had put on the market, but Chloe and Scott Johnson had purchased it instead." Amanda had also divulged to Lisa that the man Scott Johnson looked the same as the man that came into her office with another pregnant woman named Tiffany Johnson, but he was called Andrew, and they purchased the home of Eddie Jones. She looked at the paper and notice that a John S. Johnson had purchased Carolyn's house with his brother Bartholomew as a co-owner of the property. Lisa mumbled under her breath, "The last of the men named after the apostles and now we will have faces." This was a revelation to her. Finally, they will be able to put an end to all of this madness.

Amanda left the building in a hurry. She planned to resign her position at the real estate company and leave town right away. Lisa Jones said that the men that purchased her home and that of the Jones family were murderers. And the man she called James Johnson used the alias Dr. Samuels and one of his patients was killed after she called him by his birth name. She now felt that her life was in danger. She had neglected to tell Lisa that Chloe Johnson did not exist. She was an alias of a woman whose real name was Chloe Winters and she was wanted for murder. Lisa had asked her to tell no one of their conversation because the people that sat in her office were murderers and they would do anything to keep their lives a secret. Amanda stopped to grab her cell phone from her purse, when she suddenly looked up to see a black truck coming toward her at full speed. She turned to run, but she was too late.

Lisa looked out the door to see Skeet, and ran to share with him what she had learned and to carry the pictures that she had delivered for the house. "These are beautiful," he said, "this will make them both happy, to know that you think so much of both of their mothers." Lisa was perceptive of many things, so he wondered where she was going with all of this. She has put a lot into making the house a home for everyone, but he sometime feel like an outsider. Sometimes the brothers would do things and not include him, and Lisa was very hush-hush about the Jimmy situation. He wanted to feel like part of the family. Yet, he knew that Kandy was strong minded and if he would leave the home, then so would she.

Lady Singleton said that brothers would go against brothers. The look on Jimmy's face when he looked at Eddie was unreadable. He was happy and he looked scared at the same time. She sighed, "There is a lot more to this than we know. There are still some secrets that have not come out, and if we do not stop it, then Eddie will end up taking the life of his innocent brother. If we do not make everyone talk tonight, then Eddie will end up hurting Jimmy because he thinks that Jimmy killed his father to be with Jeffrey and he is wrong, and I plan to bring joy into the house. Jason was upset about his baby pictures and now there are plenty of them and to make both him and Devin bond closer, I intend to show them both how special their mothers were and how much they were loved." She smiled. She planned to honor both mothers for being as asset to the Jones family.

"Ellen could have made Eddie and Asia's life hell, instead, she suffered in silence and Asia, who met Ellen and welcomed her with open arms and, although she deserved credit for raising exceptional men, she wanted to share it with Ellen.

"They are truly amazing," he said. "They thought of the children first and put aside their own selfish needs."

"Skeet, your mother was a victim also. She was a single parent doing the best that she could. She was looking for love, someone to love her because it could get very lonely." She smiled at him, "Because I know that feeling also. I used to become depressed when I would see a couple together because I would ask what did she have that I did not, so I fell in love with Devin when I first saw him and it may have a happy ending, however, it had a rocky start."

They both looked at the door when they heard screams from the parking lot. Lisa and Skeet ran to see what had happened. Lisa looked to see Amanda Heart had been dragged several feet under a car and lay dead in the parking lot. She tried to turn. Instead she fell into the arms of Skeet. The look on Amanda's face was of pure horror. She knew she was going to die. She looked at one of the offices to see that someone was looking through the window, when the janitor Al came outside to investigate. He looked at Amanda's mangled body, "That truck fucked her up," he said.

Al took a picture with his cell phone, "I will Instagram this," he said. "This is some freaky shit."

Lisa held on to Skeet. She had never thought that one man could raise such monsters. Each of the Thomas children was born without a heart because they showed no compassion for anyone.

Another miscarriage, Carolyn looked at all of the files of the women that lost their babies. *It was a damn epidemic* she thought, never in years had so many women come to the hospital with the same symptoms after receiving an ultrasound showing that their unborn child was a boy. She looked at the doctor's name and Robert Samuels was the doctor that treated them all. She looked through her door to see that Dr. Samuels was talking to the janitor and handed him an envelope. Before leaving, the janitor gave her a look that scared her and then he walked to her door when Christian stood and he turned and walked away. She called to see if Lisa had left for the day because she was afraid. She turned to Christian, "Let's get out of here." She stopped and sat when Lisa told her about the real estate agent's death and that she and Skeet were coming to her office, so that they could drive home together.

Chapter 21

" Kelvin Hamilton, there is someone here to see you."
Officer O'Keefe walked him through the doors and
pointed to Devin and Jason, who looked at him. He
was 5'10" and looked to be about 130 pounds. He was very
thin and could easily be taken for a 15-year-old boy.

"Did my mom send you?" he asked as a tear rolled down
his face. He looked around and wiped it away, and looked at
the two men standing in front of him. He had been locked up
for months and no one had come to see him. "Will you help me,
please?" He looked from one man to the other.

Jason thought of Lionel after looking at him, "Yes, we
will," Devin said to him, "but first you have to help us. Tell us
what happened that day." Devin looked him in the face, when
the door opened again.

O'Keefe walked in with a man holding a briefcase, he
patted Kevin on the shoulder, "Finally, son, help has arrived for
you."

"Kelvin my name is Walter Davis. I am a criminal attorney
and I have been hired by these two men to represent you."

He lifted his eyes to the sky and said, "Thank you, God."

"I was walking down the street," he started. "I had been
out of school for three days with the flu, so I stayed late to
catch up." He looked at them. All he needed was someone to
believe him. "You can ask Mrs. Williams, she was my tutor. I
was wearing earplugs and listening to music on my phone when
someone grabbed me. He was a cop." He looked at them again,
because he knew that cops stick together so he had to be clear,
"he was wearing plain clothes, so I had no idea.

"He called another cop, who was a woman in uniform. There was also another one with him." Jason and Devin looked at each other. "When the woman came around, she suddenly turned her head, and he pulled out a gun and aimed it at her. I panicked, so I lifted the gun, which hit her in the shoulder. Sir, he aimed it at her. He aimed for her stomach."

Devin pulled out several pictures of cops and Kelvin pointed to Thaddeus Walker. "He was with him," he said. He then pulled out six other pictures of cops and Kelvin pointed to the man they knew as Scotty Johnson. Devin leaned into Kevin,

"I believe you, but you have to stay clear here, and keep your head on straight until it is over." There was anger in his eyes. "We will try and get you put somewhere you can be safe, because if you leave here today, they will kill you."

Kelvin laughed and cried at the same time, he had not processed the last words that were spoken to him. "You believe me?" he asked. "You believe me." He hugged Devin like a frightened child, and repeated again, "You believe me."

Walter Davis looked at the men over his glasses. "I will go and see the judge, however, you men have to move quickly," he said before he walked out of the room. The highly acclaimed attorney had an epiphany, "This one is on the house," he said. "By the time I am finished with the state, I will own part of it."

Devin looked at his phone and read a 911 from Skeet.

Eddie walked the grounds of his home. He turned his eyes sideways, and he could see Willie standing there. "I did what I had to do, Willie. You might not understand now, however, you will later. I know that Lisa feels betrayed by me again." Eddie started walking. "It feels nice to feel the sunshine on your face," he said, "there are some things that you take for granted in life, some of the simple things that are pleasant, however, you think nothing of them until they are not there."

Willie wanted answers.

"Jimmy is not here, if that is what you are thinking. I dropped him off at a hotel." Eddie sighed, "He said he needed time to process everything, so I had Skeet follow the limo to the hotel in his car, so we sat and waited to see if he would come out as a woman." Eddie did not say any more, when he heard a voice behind him.

"This is nice, Eddie." Lady Singleton stroked his face, "Let's go back to the house," she said. "I will walk ahead. I want you to see how well my new hip works."

Eddie looked across the street into the vacant field. He and Willie noticed that Lady Singleton was walking with a twist, "Good, huh, Eddie." They both laughed.

🖎 🖎

"Everything has been taken care of. Sorry I did not get to cut out her tongue out," he said, "however, she is history."

James Johnson walked out of his office, he watched as Lisa collapsed into the arms of a man. *I should have been there for her* he thought, he had no idea as to why Amanda was here, however, she nearly gave him away. Why did she come to see Lisa? Could she have been here to discuss him? He smiled as the intercom began paging Dr. Samuels. This was better than he thought. He could end it all today if he pleased, and he would, but not today. He would rip the baby from Lisa's womb when the time was right. He laughed, not now, he had to let it live in order to reap the benefits and then he would take it away and destroy it. Dr. Samuels ran to the emergency entrance, where Amanda Heart was being wheeled in, and he almost smiled as her eyes looked at him. *Maybe, I will cut your tongue out, bitch.*

"The real estate agent is dead." Devin looked at Jason. "She was killed after she left Lisa's office." Devin dialed Lisa's phone, as he looked out of the window. How much more can she take? This is supposed to be one of the happier times in her life. Instead, she has seen nothing but bloodshed and pain. "Hey, honey, how are you holding up?" he asked. She assured him that she was fine and that he had to make sure Tiffany Johnson understood the importance of her leaving for a while. She needed him to take care of business, "And come home when you are done." She had some very important information to share.

⌒ ⌒

Jason drove through Lisa's old neighborhood and noticed a black Tahoe parked in the driveway. Devin wrote down the license plate number to find out who it belonged to.

"Your husband is trying to kill you, Tiffany, and if you do not listen, you and your unborn child will both die." Devin handed her a picture of Scott Johnson standing with the two of them at Scott's bachelor party. "We know him as Scott Johnson and he was married before to a woman by the name of Glenda Johnson."

Tiffany shook her head in disbelief. "He has never been married before, you have the wrong man." Tiffany looked at the picture.

"Kelvin Hamilton did not shoot you, your husband did." He looked hard at her. "He had seen women, hired them to do a job, and at the last minute, they'd allow their husbands to sweet talk them and it turned ugly in the end. Kelvin saved your unborn child. If he had not lifted the gun, he would have shot you in the stomach. He has no intention of letting you have this child."

"Andrew," she said, "that is his name."

Devin was stern with her. "The only reason they could not take a second shot at you is because people had started to gather around. When he realized that you and your baby were going to survive, he had to find something to do with you. Your husband is a part of the Brotherhood cult. Nine of the members are dead, including Thaddeus Walker, who was pointed out to be there at the time of your shooting." Tiffany cried. Devin was blunt and brutal, however, if it would save her life, he would say more. "They need a child and it is possible that Jessica Hayes is part of this. They need a baby because Jessica was seen talking with one of the Brotherhood members. That one." He pointed to the shadow on the wall, "and there is four members left, plus another woman, who we think wants your baby." Devin had no idea as to what her purpose was in all of this. He only knew that he needed her to leave before her husband got back into town.

"Jessica was taken in a black Tahoe." He looked at her, "Tiffany, what makes and model car does your husband drive?"

She lowered her head and cried out, "A black Chevy Tahoe."

He handed her a copy of the license plate number. Just the expression on her face said it all, "He is not out of town, Tiffany. You were not supposed to get pregnant and that could be why you and your child are in danger."

❧ ❧

"His name is James Johnson, not Robert Samuels."

Everyone turned and looked at her. Devin reached out his hand and pulled her into his arms. She looked as if she had worked all day with no sleep. Things were taking their toll on her, she was exhausted.

"Sit down, babe." Carolyn fixed her a cup of coffee. "That is why we could not find anything on any of them, they are using aliases."

"He purchased Momma Ida's house, all that was yours is now theirs," Jason repeated.

"Scott Johnson is Andrew Johnson." Lisa remembered that the real estate agent said that he purchased her house with his wife, Chloe. Lisa expressed to them that the real estate agent was terrified of the couple and with good reason. She walked into Devin's arms and described the look on Amanda's face at the time of her death. She knew that Andrew and Scott were the same person.

Jason grabbed the phone to call Tiffany Johnson, but he did not get an answer. Devin explained to Lisa about her, that she was pregnant and married to Andrew, and how the psychic said that she was in danger. She gave him the papers of the other brothers, who purchased Carolyn's old house.

"They are killing boy children," Carolyn said as she handed Jason the files of the women who lost their babies. She began to cry, "I cannot go back there." She walked into Jason's arms. "I am so scared, if Christian was not there today, then that janitor would have killed me," she cried.

"Lady Clem said that they will take the baby too early, and that it will die, but Jessica Hayes is due any day now, according to her hospital files. But, she is carrying a boy."

Jason called J.T. and Eddie was also present. Lisa walked up to him and reprimanded him, "How dare you barge into my office and interfere with a session!" They laughed at her sudden change. They had been so preoccupied with everything that they had forgotten about the Jimmy incident and the look on her face when Eddie walked into her office. "You should have let us finish, and now they know who Jimmy is and you have placed his life in danger."

"I was born on a day, however, it was not yesterday. I am sorry for the way that I handled everything. You are smart, Lisa, and I know it."

Suddenly, the whole family was gathering in the same room, which was at Lady Singleton's request. Before Eddie and Lisa would continue, she began to speak. She needed Kandy and Skeet to talk to Willie, "No distractions," she said. Skeet looked Willie in the eyes and told him about he and Kandy. Lady Singleton knew that the family approved of Skeet, however, Skeet did not know.

Willie smiled, "I love my girls," he said, "just as Eddie love his boys." Eddie walked behind Skeet and placed his hand on his shoulder, "Son, a blind man could see that the two of you care for each other." Skeet smiled, he never knew that Eddie thought of him as a son.

Lady Singleton walked up to J.T., who was raised an only child by his grandmother. "You have a pride in this family," she said to him. "You love them all, but you take a special pride in Lisa, making sure she is safe."

J.T.'s eyes watered, "She is very kind to, me ma'am. I never had a mother figure," he said. My grandmother was a hard worker and I was alone all of the time and Lisa is like a mother to me."

Lady Singleton's hands began to tremble, "But you call the men your brothers."

"Yes, ma'am," he said.

Lady Singleton sat and went into a trance, then she smiled at J.T. Devin looked at J. T.. He had studied Lady Singleton's pattern: J.T. was in trouble.

Jason had given him a task to do. He was to do an age enhancement on the pictures that he had been given from Lady Clem, he wanted to see what the other children would look like as adults and that included her daughter Connie.

Ellen had gone into the kitchen and prepared lunch for the men. Lady Singleton watched as she doted on them and how Jason and Devin did the same to her. She watched as Jason held her in his arms before she went into the kitchen, but she needed Eddie to receive the love of the women in the home. He felt alone, no one showed him any affection and that would be the distraction that would cost him his life. If Lisa led, then the others would follow.

"There will be bloodshed and life lost." She looked at Eddie. "Love and understanding is the key," she said before lowering her head. She looked at Lisa, "The two of you were into something before I interrupted." She waved Lisa in the direction of Eddie. She gripped her hand tightly, "Hurry, child," she said. "Brothers against brothers," she repeated and Lisa heard her that time.

She knew that was out of the question, Eddie would cut his own throat for his sons and his family. She knew from the start Eddie was the target because he was his father's favorite and a tough businessman. He was admired and envied by others. They wanted to build what he has, which is why she believed that Asia was killed. They wanted to punish him and now they would come for Eddie and his sons.

Lisa stood and walked up to Eddie. Devin and Jason thought that she would slap him, however, she did not. "You are planning to kill you brother, and that will be your downfall. You think that Jimmy killed your father because of the gun, but while I cannot tell you how Jeffrey got the gun, I do believe that he killed your father."

Lady Singleton looked at Ida as she just lowered her head, and Carolyn started to yell at Lisa. "He is dirty, Lisa, it all points to Jimmy . . . Him dressing as a woman . . . And the cameras, and I do believe he had the opportunity to come home, and he did not." Carolyn said with sincerity, "You loved Jenny and so did Kandy, and look at what happened to the both of you, and Jimmy could have said something, but he did not. He was at the party that night, both he and Coretta, and Jimmy said nothing. So stop trying to protect him because you regret getting pregnant, but Lionel is my pride and joy and both his father and I will not allow anyone to hurt him."

Carolyn was not done, as she planned to be the head of the household. "You have been depressed and you have had second thoughts about everything, including the baby and living here. I grant you that Eddie is like his father and there is no way that his father would have not said something about the gun, but Jimmy knew that he had it and when his father confronted him, he killed him and took off with Jeffrey and lived his life as a woman. However, you were right about something, if Eddie would not have sent me away, then I would have died." She turned to Eddie and gave her thanks to him.

Lisa sighed because Carolyn was playing on Eddie's weaknesses. He thinks that Jimmy is gay and that, in his mind, was a betrayal to the family. Eddie is like his father—he was a homophobic asshole that wanted to control everything and Carolyn was trying to cause trouble with Lisa and Devin.

"Answer her question," Devin demanded, his face turning red with anger. "If you want out, then just say so."

When he began to walk away, Eddie looked at the fear on Lisa's face. *Your prejudice will be your downfall* popped into his head. "Do not put another hole in the damn wall!" He yelled at Devin.

"Stop, please!" Ida yelled. "I did it." Her lips trembled. She had kept her silence way too long and it was time to open up. "I have been in fear ever since I have been here. I love you all so much." She stroked Devin's face. Devin helped her to sit, in fear that she would fall. "Now I know what you have felt for so long, Ellen, being left all alone. "All we had was you, my sweet baby," she said to Lisa. "When I saw you boys at the mall, I felt free to die because I just wanted to meet you and touch you. I gave Jeffrey the gun." Everyone stared at her. "When you asked me if I knew the Klein family, I told a lie because of fear." She looked at Lisa. "You're right again, but you are losing the war here. And I know that you love Devin more that life, so it is time that I came clean and take my punishment."

She turned to Eddie and pleaded with him to understand. "Your father came home with blood all over him. First, I thought that he got hurt on the job, but he did not. He said that he might have killed someone. I was shocked, he pulled the gun out of his pocket and placed it on the bed, and that scared me because he had a look on his face that I had never seen before. I thought that he might hurt me and you boys, so I grabbed it and hid it.

"Colbert Klein was the man's name and he had three sons and one of them name was Kevin. I found this out because one week later, the family house was set on fire and Colbert, his wife, and two of his sons were shot, and the house was torched, but his wife was cut open, and they all died. Kevin was away, visiting friends for the weekend and when he returned, he had no family and he was taken in by friends.

"James never said outright why he shot Colbert. He said something about the inheritance and he asked him had the devil visited him. Colbert was afraid because his wife was having another child, which is why your father allowed you to turn our home into a whorehouse. He did not want you out on the street. One day, Jeffrey came over and your father was talking and the look on his face . . . He was just so angry that I feared for me and Judy sometimes, so I asked Jeffrey to get rid of it. He said that they might come for me, but I did not understand what he was talking about.

She turned to Devin. "He was so hard to live with. He started hitting me and he would yell every day, and he treated Judy so badly. He even beat her all of the time. When he died, I had mixed emotions." She lowered her head. "The Klein family was burned to death." Then she looked at Eddie, "finally, karma is a bitch, son, because he burned also, but the pain and the loss I suffered was losing someone as kind as Jimmy." She held

Devin's hand, "Please, just hear him out, that is all that I ask and if you have your doubts, then do whatever you must do." She looked at Lisa, "There are no regrets with Lisa and you know that. You boys are used to this kind of action." She tried to smile. "The most excitement we had was going to the strip club and that was short lived. It is hard to be happy when someone is trying to take everything that you love away from you."

Ida stood to walk away, because now Eddie would hate her. "Momma, do not leave," Lisa asked. "No one came blame you for fearing for your life. There is a difference between us and them. We are bonded by love and respect and they are bonded by greed. They will stab each other in the back and we will stand together and fight to the end." Lisa looked at Eddie and wrapped her arms around him, "I love you and I want you to love me also. You resent Jimmy, but he went through hell and he had to find a way out. And Jenny was his outing, which is what I wanted to talk to him about. He could not return home to his family because there was no family to come home to, and the people that were trying to kill you . . . Some were in your home every day, but now we are all here working together and supporting each other." Lisa wanted to show Eddie the picture, but she did not know where his heart was and if she or Jimmy could trust him.

"Bravo!" Carolyn yelled. "How dare you put all of our lives in danger? I have waited for so long to finally be with the man that I love, to wake every morning next to him, and to have my son be with his father and play and build things. And most of all, the three of us are together." Carolyn was looking for a fight. Lisa was looking to be the family savior, but she was not having it. "Maybe, all you wanted was to get laid and, instead, got yourself pregnant. So, you feel trapped, however, Kandy and I will not do this with you." She turned to Kandy, "She is trying to ruin our lives and if you do not stand up for yourself, then you will go back to where you came from and that is a life of hell, getting your ass kicked by every man that you meet, while shaking your ass on stage for chump change."

Lady Singleton allowed a tear to drop from her eye, because she was losing. There is so much jealousy and envy under one roof. Carolyn resents Lisa for becoming a part of the family that she feels entitle to and living the life she should, and most of all, giving birth to the first girl child.

The men watched Lady Singleton and she was not crying tears of joy. No one had ever made her cry. She had once told them that in all of her ninety years of life that she had never cried, not even when her husband has passed away. She had time to prepare before it happened because she was born with her gift. Eddie could not recall what it meant when a tear rolled down her face, but he knew he had to do something. The men's heads turned from one woman to the other as they went at each other, while Judy and Ida cried, along with Ellen.

"You bitch!" Kandy yelled when Skeet walked from the room. "Do not worry because I have told him all about my past and he is still with me, so you can shut up. I agree with Lisa," she said as she gave Carolyn the *fuck-you* look. "If Jimmy wanted to hurt us, then he could have a long time ago, and no one would have known it was him."

Carolyn would not accept defeat, "Why would he hurt you himself, when he had twelve convict donors to do it for him?"

"That is enough," Eddie said. He enjoyed a good catfight, but things were getting out of control.

"I have not had my say," Lisa said, and she intended to get it. "You are the man that you hate. You are an inconsiderate, snobby bitch that sits behind your desk and judges people before you get to know them and, once you dislike someone, no matter what they do, you will not change your opinion.

You worshipped Dr. Samuels and he was no good, but you defended him. However, we all respected your opinion, although we did not agree. I am not asking anything of you, Carolyn, because even if you could help, you would not do it so shut the fuck up." Lisa charged at her, she had enough of her trying to ruin her marriage. Devin grabbed her, "You think you are the only one that is entitled to a family, a good man . . . Then bitch you are crazy because you are not the only woman on this earth, there are many. You are trying to put a gap in this family. All that I ask of everyone is that we hear Jimmy out. He was going to talk to us and you were listening, but Eddie came in and changed everything."

Lady Singleton smiled as Lisa continued to speak. "He asked where the others were, because they did not know who he was, but they do now." Lady Singleton gave her head a nod, as Lisa took out the picture, but she put it back. Jimmy needed to talk to Eddie, but if he does not, then she will.

"I love you all," Eddie said, and I would die for you if I have to." A tear rolled down his cheek. "You are what's important to me and nothing else. You women changed everything in this house, including me—the good cooking, the karaoke and the dance off with Momma and Judy after they both had a drink— it has been good, which is why I do not want it to end under any circumstances. I never want to see you all go at each other like that again." Eddie needed to clear his conscience with his family.

"I use to get so drunk." He talked to Lisa because he knew that she would understand, "and I would see Jimmy. He would stand over my bed and talk to me. He told me that they were going to kill my family if I did not pull myself together and, one night, I thought I saw someone standing over Jason, but when I turned on the light, no one was there and, once again, I blamed the alcohol. One night, Asia was sleeping and there was blood all over the bed. I woke her and she said that the good angel watched over her and he took away the Devil. I thought she was crazy, but I thought she might have started her period and that is where the blood came from.

"She wanted more children, but something was wrong, so when I took her to the clinic in New York. We found out that someone had removed her tubes, without our knowledge. But once again, I did nothing, not even tell her. Things were happening to my family and I did nothing, so Lisa, if you think that Jimmy is okay, then I will listen, but I want answers.

"Jimmy and I took a road trip." He showed a picture and Jimmy had cut his hair. "He had a new car that he had gotten for Christmas and he told me that he was going to go to school in another state, so we decided to spend a few days on the road." Eddie sighed, he was full of emotion, "His last words were, 'I love you, big brother,' and then one day he was suddenly gone."

"Your baby brother is alive and he is crying for your help. Jimmy needs you now more than ever, he needs you to understand." Lisa said

Eddie nodded his head, now he felt that his life had meaning. He had lost so much in his life, which made it hard for him to be attached to anyone or anything, and now he had a reason to go on. He would work side-by-side with his sons and do what he could to save his brother, who was in more danger now because of his actions. "But, if Jimmy is dirty, then I will kill him" were his last words to Lisa.

❧ ❧

J.T. started his assignment. He looked at the house while his computer did the work. He would make the family proud of him, as he knew that they were already. He wanted to thank Lady Singleton. He never had a real family before, especially after his grandmother passed away, and now he had brothers and a woman that was like a mother to him. He thought that strange, he always thought of Eddie as a father because he would call him son and they all gave him gifts for the holidays, and Jason and Devin taught him how to defend himself against bullies. They even gave him a gun and a bulletproof vest for his birthday, which he hoped that he would never have to use. He looked at the computer and he was in shock at two of the pictures. Skeet was right. He immediately faxed it to the house. He reached for the phone and dialed Jason, when the door opened, "Hello, J.T., it has been a long time."

꙰ ꙰

"You owe me," Lisa said to Eddie. She had watched Lady Singleton's expressions and they all knew what the term, 'brother against brother' now meant.

"You owe Lionel also," Jason said. "We want payment, Dad."

Eddie wondered what they were talking about, he had cleared the air and now they want more from him.

"You will have another grandchild soon, and you owe her," Lisa said, "and we want payment. We do not want money or anything," she said to him. "All we want is you, your love and guidance. Your grandchildren want you to bounce them on your knee, and play ball, and ride the train. You said that you were a man of your word." Lady Singleton was clenching her fist, "You promise us that." Eddie smiled and promised, when they heard the fax machine start to print and Jason's phone began to ring.

꙰ ꙰

"What are you up to, J.T.?" He stood and tried to lower the computer screen when Mark stopped him. Mark smiled, "You are really good," he said. "This picture is like looking in the mirror." J.T. began to step back when Mark hit the delete button on the computer.

"You going to kill me, Mark?" J.T. asked. "Before you do that, will you tell me why you want Lisa's baby?"

He laughed his cynical laugh. He had learned from Simon, who he always considered as a moron. "Okay, I will tell you.

Lisa has a pot of gold in her stomach . . ." He then stopped and pointed his finger. "Let's do first thing first. Thomas was my father, however, my mother knew that he was unfit. We went from luxury into poverty in a split second." He yelled, "We ate got-damn crumbs for breakfast and our dinner, we would go down by their restaurant and ask if they had extra food. They would say no. However, they would throw good food in the trash as opposed to letting hungry children eat it, while he and these assholes ate steak and eggs.

"Finally!" He shouted, "Mother Johnson had enough of us rebelling and allowed us to make a choice . . . Poverty or luxury." He looked at J.T. "You're a smart ass, you do the math. We went to live with Thomas and he opened our eyes as to who our enemy was, and it was the Jones family. He would tell us if we wanted to continue to have nice things then we all had a mission. He told us of the will left by our great-great-grandparents, that we should inherit it and not these motherfuckers. He had also told us how his great-grandfather had killed the third family by burning them to death. He also said they were working with the Devil, which was why we burn the bodies." He smiled, "to keep tradition alive and so their souls will not return. We were not going to allow anyone to take what is rightfully ours because we are many."

He pulled out his knife. "We missed it by that much," he said. "My donor carried a son he looked with such an evil that J.T. was shaking. Father called them donors because after we found out what sex of the child they were carrying we had no more use for them. It was a boy and so was the other, and come to find out that these no-good assholes hit it on the mark. Lisa's baby is a gold mine for the Joneses and Eddie knows it, which is why we tried to kill Jason and Devin. When time got close, however, we missed our target—this family." He smiled, "their nine lives will end soon and yours will end now."

He grabbed J.T. and lifted his knife. J.T. became distracted when he saw Skeet and Devin at the door. He tried not to look at them and keep Mark talking. "But how do you expect to pull this off? Devin will never let you get his baby."

Mark smiled, "We will get it with our real father's help. Too bad you will not be around to see it."

"How?" he asked, when Mark shoved the knife into him, and turned to find that he was surrounded.

☙ ☙

Jessica cried out in pain. "Please, help me!" She yelled, "I think the baby is coming." She began to cry when the door opened and a man walked in wearing a mask.

"We have to time your contractions," he said to her. She yelled again as he spread her legs. "We have time," he said as he untied her. "If you try anything, then I will kill you," he said. "I will give you an epidural for the pain." He walked out of the room.

Jessica tried to look around. She had no idea where she was. She lay on her side and cried, and said a prayer to God. She wondered if anyone knew she was missing. Was anyone looking for her? "Please, don't let me die like this," she prayed.

☙ ☙

Lisa lay in bed. She was tired. Her mind was racing about the old house that she was held prisoner in, all of the hospital equipment that was there and the fate that was sealed for her and her unborn child. She thought of Jessica, what she must be going through, when suddenly she heard firecrackers. She lay on her side and silently cried because Carolyn had made Devin yell at her. She only hoped that she did not ruin her marriage because she had gotten so angry that she was ready to strike her, and that would have proven Carolyn right.

She could hear yelling and screaming when Carolyn ran into her room and said that someone had hurt J.T. She tried to move, but her body suddenly started to ache, but she managed to get to her feet and walk out to find Devin and Jason asking her to stay in the house. They ran past her again carrying towels. She did not listen. She walked to the office where she saw Mark laying on the floor with several bullets in his body.

Carolyn walked into the office to find Mark dead and J.T. with a knife stuck in his stomach. She looked up to find Lisa standing there. "I need some help here," she said when Lisa rushed to her side. They both breathed a sigh of relief to find that J.T. was wearing a bulletproof vest, but the knife still went through and was stuck in his stomach. "This is going to hurt, J.T." When she removed the knife, he yelled, and she and Lisa started to cleanse the wound.

🍥 🍥

"Mark was the youngest. His real name is Bartholomew Johnson, however, he was not a child of Clementine Johnson, but her daughter," Devin said. "They sold their souls to the Devil and that was Thomas. It's funny how these women have the answers, but they talk in riddles. She had answers because she was involved and she knew exactly what Thomas's plan was from the beginning, but her conscience got the best of her and the fact that her own children would kill her and think nothing of it. In case you did not notice that she never mentioned Jimmy at all and, if she had the insight, then she would have said something."

They turned to find Lisa standing at the door, "J.T. is resting fine. The old house was full of hospital equipment, an incubator and monitor. They planned to take our baby there."

Devin and Jason jumped up and called Skeet before running out of the door. The house was supposed to be watched, however, there was another entrance that they did not know about. Somehow, the family got out right under their noses and cops had the house surrounded. This had to be how Jimmy was getting out without them noticing him.

Chapter 22

Chloe dabbed perfume behind each of her ears, and turned sideways to get a better view of what Andrew would see when he entered her home. She had made an emergency call to him and now she would set the trap. She had taken off her pregnant belly, which he hated her wearing, but she wanted to know what it would feel like to carry a child. After all, she would soon be a mother, but she had grown tired of the wait. She was ready now and Andrew could not resist her, he would give her what she wanted.

She would never forget when she first met Andrew. "Hello, Chloe," he said while he was dressed in his police uniform. "I know who you are." Her first instinct was to run because he was a cop, but he had other plans for the two of them. "I do not want to arrest you because I plan to be inside of you in a few minutes." And he was. She smiled and that is when he informed her of his plans to take the baby and she would claim the money and they would live happily ever after. He had fallen in love with her at first sight.

When he introduced her to his family, they were all weird and they looked funny. The only normal one was James. When she first met him, he was a prominent doctor and very good looking, and he was the one that she wanted, so she came up with her own plan so she and James would be the last ones standing. She hoped that he still trusted her because of the way she killed Thaddeus, who wanted her so badly. She would taunt him with her body until the time came that he had to die.

Chloe jumped into bed when she heard Andrew's car pull into the driveway. She struck a pose that he would not be able to resist. She had withheld sex from him, knowing that it would drive him mad. Nevertheless, it was necessary for her master plan. She smiled at the thought when she would pleasure him how he would look at her and call her a got-damn femme fatal.

She checked the wine to make sure it was chilled. She also placed a bowl of strawberries and whipped cream next to the bed, a dessert fit for a king. She had to pull out all of the stops, something that the bitch he had at home would not do, which was why she was his number one and got what her heart desired.

Andrew looked at Chloe. He did not speak a work, he was a man of action and he began to undress. "That's my girl," he said, "the beautiful woman that I fell madly in love with." He knew Chloe wanted something, but it did not matter. He would give her whatever she desired.

Chloe pulled out the whipped cream and started working her magic. Andrew's eyes rolled back as Chloe took him in her mouth. "I want the baby now, Andrew." He did not response to her as the pleasure was consuming him. "I want to become a mother today, Andrew," she said louder.

He looked at her this time. "You will soon, baby, I promise."

Chloe shouted, "I want it today!"

"Chloe, it is not that simple. If we take the baby too early, then it will die and we would be back to square one."

Chloe jumped out of bed and ran into to bathroom crying, "You promised me Andrew. He followed behind her, but she slammed the door in his face. Andrew tried to reason with Chloe, but she was not hearing it. She screamed from the bathroom, "I hate you and you do not want me to have a baby. I have grown tired of pretending to be pregnant and now you tell me that you will not give me my baby."

Andrew was having mixed emotions at the time. He needed to get inside of Chloe, but he knew that it would not happen if he did not try to give her what she wanted. "Baby, I will make a phone call and see what we can do, but first you have to talk to me and be reasonable." She watched herself in the mirror and listened as Andrew begged her to talk to him, she listened as he made a phone call, and she would become a mother as soon as tomorrow. She applied more lipstick and waited. She even dropped Visine into her eyes for tears. She waited before opening the door, her words and actions had to be perfect.

ℭ ℭ

J.T. waited for the command. As Lisa and Carolyn watched the screen, they could see their every move. Carolyn yelled for Jason to be careful, while Lisa's hands began to shake. She wished she had never said anything about the old house. Although they were not alone, they had backup from Peter Henderson and the police department.

Eddie walked in and started watching. "Why are they at that old house?" he asked in fear.

"Because Jessica Hayes could be there," Lisa said. She briefed Eddie on the house and its contents. "And the men think there is an entrance to the house that they are not aware of."

"Are you in place?" Jason asked. "They know that Mark is dead and they will come for her."

Everyone was in place when Devin gave J.T. the signal. The men entered the house and went directly to the basement, where they had seen the medical equipment. Jason slowly opened the door, as he could see movement. They entered the room while the other officers stood guard and checked the rest of the house. "Get an ambulance!" Devin yelled. He could see Jessica lying there and she was in and out of consciousness.

"Are you angels?" she asked. He untied her while Jason looked around for her child. "He took my baby," she said, before she passed out.

ℭ ℭ

"Can you read my fortune?"

Lady Clem looked at the man sitting at her desk and said, "That's not what you came for and you know it." She signaled the men to wait for her in a blind spot in her store. "Wait here and you will get what you've come for." She sat at the door and read the cards. She laughed aloud when she thought *soon it will be over.* She looked up to find a man standing there.

"You betrayed us," he said. "We allowed you to live the first time and this time your action has caused the death of our brother."

"You will not win," she said to Luke, "you will get the baby, but you will not keep it. Their bond is too strong. They are bonded by love, and you are bonded by greed. She will destroy you all. She will not share the money." Lady Clem turned the card, when Luke took out a scalpel. "Repent, Luke," she said, while the two men stood quietly behind him.

"Our father will protect us."

Lady Clem closed her eyes.

"You have lived by the sword, so you will die by the sword." He drew back the scalpel and Willie said, "That is no way to treat your mother." He shot Luke in the hand as he release the scalpel. He then slashed both of his wrists to the bone. "How does it feel?" he asked as blood dripped, before putting him out of his misery and shooting him in his chest.

Skeet dialed Peter Henderson to inform him that there was another shooting while Lady Clem held Willie's hand. "Judy still pains over losing you. She is still in love with you."

Jimmy took a sip from his drink and rewound the video again. He watched as Carolyn put him down and Lisa begged the others to listen to him, and that he was a good guy. But he was most proud of Kandy, a young woman that wanted to be loved so badly that she made bad decision in her life. He packed his bags with everything and called Coretta. He threw back his head because they had been in hiding for years with only an overnight visit once a year when Coretta would disguise herself and they would meet. However, it was Cody who concerned him. He was not able to be a part of his teenage life and he knew that he needed him now more than ever. He did not owe his brother anything, but he did owe Lisa the truth and vindicate her before the family. He listened to his messages and there were several from Lisa, asking him to come to the house.

❧ ❧

"I know what you have been up to, Andrew." Tiffany returned home and wanted to confront Andrew about his deception. "I know about her," she said, "you were never out of town and I know that her name is Chloe." Tiffany felt in her pocket to make sure the safety on her gun was off. "Did you promise her my baby? Well, she will not get it."

Andrew was on cloud nine, he had just had the best sex ever and he was in no mood for Tiffany's bullshit.

"What happened to your first wife?" she asked, "and I know that Kelvin Hamilton did not shoot me."

Andrew was angry because she had done her homework, he had sacrificed Glenda to the master, but Tiffany belonged to him. He loved Chloe and he would let nothing stand in the way of his happiness. He would get the child and they would disappear for good. He would not let any harm come to Chloe.

"Baby, it is not like that," he said. "I love you, Tiffany." He needed to get the upper hand, so he would appeal to her weakness. "I was being threatened by Thaddeus Walker," he begged her to listen to him. "Thaddeus shot you, baby, you looked right at him." Tiffany was getting confused. She did not know anything right now. She could only think of the dream she had of her sitting on a cloud, rocking her baby, and how she felt safe and at peace. "Baby let's go upstairs and lie down and talk about this. We are going to be parents soon and we need to be together. I will explain everything."

She began to let her guard down. "Do you remember the missing money from the bank heists? I was so deeply in love with you that I took the money and I used it to purchase your new car. You were all that I could think of." He looked to see if she was falling for his explanation and she was. He now had her undivided attention. "Thaddeus found out and started to blackmail me and he carried a lot of weight, so I did what he asked for a while. Then he wanted me to kill for him and that is where I drew the line. He said he would show me and one day Glenda was gone. I do not know what happened to Glenda, she just went missing, and with what Thaddeus had on me, I would have been blamed. The other woman, she is being used until you have the baby, and we can get away from here and start our lives as a family."

Tiffany lifted her hands from her pockets. "Let's go to bed and we will finish talking tomorrow."

Andrew started walking up the stairs while Tiffany followed and, when they got to the top, he turned, grabbed her, and shoved her down the stairs. She lay there unable to move as he straddled her. "You want the truth," he said, "Chloe is the woman I love and you are shit. When she and I are together, there is something special. We needed a baby and yours would have done the job, but someone has beaten you to the finish line, so your service is no longer needed. "And, as far as Glenda is concerned, that bitch is dead and buried, and you will be also." He took the scalpel and went across her neck.

꙰ ꙰

"We have to see Lady Clem tomorrow," Jason said, "she requested our presence."

Eddie looked around, "What the hell has happened in here?" There were pictures all over the house. He turned to look at the stairs and saw himself. The whole wall was covered with pictures. He looked at the one of Asia, which was his favorite, and the boys growing up.

"I hope you approve," Lisa said, as she pointed to the men where she wanted the other pictures hanged. He looked in awe at how the house now felt like a home.

Devin walked up the stairs. He looked around and smiled at his father when he saw all of the pictures. There was a wall with all of his and Jason's trophies and certificates and pictures of them playing sports. He turned to see his mother's picture on the wall.

Lisa looked at him and thought that she had gone too far too fast, when Jason walked up and looked also. "That is my favorite picture of Mom," Jason said. They both went up and down the wall with amazement that Eddie had the entire wall covered with everyone's pictures, including those of Jason and Ellen.

"Dad, this is great," they both said to Eddie, who was speechless. "You must have spent a fortune on frames alone." They laughed at the pictures of Jason playing football in college, how he had a large Afro and his helmet fitted funny on his head.

"Lisa and I thought that it was time to make this house a home. It is amazing how Lionel looks so much like both of you when you were babies," Eddie commented. "And, this is a wall for the baby over here," he said.

Lisa smiled because Eddie was taking credit for her work, which is why she gave him the bill for the frames.

"What will you name it, if it is a girl?" Eddie asked her.

Lisa had first wanted to name her after Ida, however, she thought that Asia should be honored because she believed that she led her to Devin that night and for that she was grateful. "Devin and I will come up with something soon," she said, "but Devinina is still out of the question."

⌒) ⌒)

"Skeet, did you pick up my Tupac CDs?" Ida asked. "Lady Singleton and I want to do karaoke tonight."

"Mom, what ever happened to the Temptations or the Supremes you used to listen to that all of the time," Eddie said.

Ida was getting mad, "I can't dance to that. We will let Ellen do her thing," she said, "and I will do mine." Ida looked at Lady Singleton, "These damn children think they know everything. Lisa and I would exercise to *Back That Thang Up* all of the time." Everyone turned to look at Lisa.

"Saved by the bell," Lisa said when she got up to open the door. She peeped through the hole and she saw Jimmy standing at the door. Lisa quickly turned and smiled, but she thought of the others, they would be angry that she had called him. So she ran back to the dining room with a look of mixed emotions on her face. She hoped that tonight would be the night that they all bonded and Jimmy and Eddie would talk. She had called his phone and left messages for him without the others knowing, and now he was standing at the door.

"What's wrong, baby?" Devin asked. When the doorbell rang again, he looked at her and said, "Stay here." He and Jason went to open the door.

"Dad, you have company." Eddie looked up to find Jimmy. Ellen placed her hand over her mouth, while Judy walked to Jimmy and touched him. Ida started to shake, she had heard that Jimmy was alive, but she had not seen him, so she did not believe it. Jimmy was still beautiful. He was tall and slim—but not too slim—he was perfect with the most beautiful grey eyes ever.

He held Judy, who kept touching him. "Is it really you?" she asked.

Jimmy smiled, "Yes, it is really me."

Judy started the interrogation. Whose house did we TP when Ida and James went to Macon for the weekend?"

Jimmy laughed, "I stood and watched while you and Eddie TP'd Mr. Anderson's house, though I did shave Mrs. Koodie's dog Trudy and gave her a Mohawk."

Ida pulled Judy back; she had to touch him for herself. She grabbed his cheeks as he gave her hand a gentle kiss, "My baby," she cried. "My baby is home."

Eddie gave Devin and Jason a look. It was not going to be easy to let Jimmy go, as Ida had attached herself to him already. Her lips had said one thing, but seeing Jimmy, her heart was now saying something else. Ellen sat quietly as Judy and Ida gave Jimmy a tour of the house. Jimmy looked at every picture on the wall, and Lisa watched as he looked at the picture of Asia. "You're the good angel," she mumbled and Devin looked at her.

Devin sat next to Lisa. Skeet and Willie told him that Lady Clem said that his enemy would get his child and he did not plan to let her out of his sight.

"Eddie, your house is magnificent," Jimmy said as Eddie handed him a drink. Willie walked in and you could cut the tension with a knife in the house.

Ida kept doting on Jimmy and Lady Singleton looked frustrated because time was of the essence.

"Jimmy, we need to talk," Lisa said. She could see that Devin was not happy with her and Jason was standing by Carolyn and Eddie was, also. She was alone on her quest for information.

Judy and Jimmy reminisced when Jimmy turned his attention to Ellen. "How long have you and Eddie been married?"

Ellen was stung. She did not know what to say. "We are not married," she said when Lisa stood.

"We are wasting time. When I get back, then we will talk." The comment put a smile on Lady Singleton's face. "I am going to cut the cake and make some coffee. We need answers and I will ask the questions."

Lisa tried to pull herself together. Everyone was looking at her and if something went wrong, then she would be to blame for it. Carolyn and she had not spoken and she knew that Carolyn was waiting to throw her under the bus.

Lisa rolled in a tray with cake and coffee. She thought of Jenny and the last time they had cake and she said, "Girl, Lisa, this cake is going right to my hips."

He smiled and it was glowing. "This will go right to your hips." She smiled also. Jimmy relaxed and so did everyone else, except Kandy. She was holding on to Eddie for dear life. He noticed the trembling of her body. It had not sunk in that Jenny was gone and she did not know who Jimmy was. She thought of what Carolyn said that Jimmy was a traitor and could have stopped the others from hurting her.

Ellen and the rest joined in to talk about their childhood pranks they would play on the neighbors. Jimmy remembered when they called Mr. Scott and told him that his refrigerator was running and it was coming their way and, to their amazement, Mr. Scott ran outside and started looking up and down the street.

Jimmy looked at his watch. "I must be going," he said. Ida was disappointed, she had wanted him to stay the night, but he had promised to return the next day for dinner and that was good enough for her.

Lisa backed Jimmy into a corner and gave him the smile that melted his heart. "Please, do not leave. You are now among the ones that love you and will not let you go."

He smiled with tears in his eyes, "You are the one that I trust," he said before looking at Eddie, because now he was alone without having Cody and Coretta to talk to since Eddie burst into Lisa's office. Now he had to watch his back.

"Tell him, Jimmy," she said. "Please stay and talk to us." She sat next to him. "I started to have little pain and I know that they want my baby."

"Let him go!" Eddie yelled. "He is a fucking traitor. He abandoned this family over forty years ago." Eddie stood tall with his men to back him and they would fire on his command.

Lisa looked at Devin for help, however, he was having mixed emotions, but he decided to back her up because she had been right so far. He stood next to Jimmy and looked him in the eyes. "I do not know why you became Jenny or why you never came home, but if Lisa is right, then you have something at stake here besides your own life. Lisa is the only one that believes in you, but I believe in her, so we stand alone here." He turned his head slightly in her direction, "She thinks with her heart, however, Carolyn thinks with her head. I cannot blame Lisa for that because that is what brought the two of us together, so talk to us."

Lisa then stood next to Devin. "Tell them and if you do not, then I will." She held his hand. "You said that you trusted me, then talk to me and Devin because we believe in you. "Please, Jimmy, because he needs your help."

Jimmy paused and that put doubt in Eddie's mind because, if he were innocent, then he would say so. Jimmy and Eddie stared at each other when Eddie gave a signal to Ben.

"You fucking asshole," he said to Eddie and stood. "Get your fucking hand out of your pocket!" He yelled at Ben, "and let him, for once, do his own dirty work." Jimmy wanted to look Eddie in the eye when Skeet stopped Ben from pulling his gun on Jimmy.

"How many ghosts do you have to see before you accept your responsibility in all of this, because it got bad that night and that is how we began to pay for the sins of our father. They knew how to get in the house and one night, I followed them and I watched as they looked at Jason because he was to be the first, but you got to him before they did. Thomas had six ex-cons that worked for him and they walked the hall of your home every night. I listened as Thomas ordered for your mother to be killed and I tried to wake Eddie, but he was too far gone. He was to kill her and bring Jason to him, so I came to the house and waited with your mother. We talked and she used to call them the Devil, so when he came into your mother's bedroom, I killed him with a scalpel and carried him to the road and left him, then and I came back to help her clean up, but I had to leave because, finally, someone was coming.

"I never returned home because there was no home to return to. I stood outside of the gate and looked and there was no family. I do not know how Jeffrey got a gun, however, he had one and he killed father, and then he, killed Lenny. Three of his bodyguards drugged and kidnapped me. He said that we had a child."

"Sister," Devin answered and he nodded yes.

I was taken to the old house and put inside the basement for years before he allowed Sister to talk to me. So one night, Sister would sneak out of the house and I watched, and that is how I found the way out through the basement and how I was able to get in and out of the house.

"Jeffrey made a mistake when he killed Melissa and that is when he finally talked to me. I had to build trust between us and I had to find out about his connection. He realized that Melissa's sister had reported her missing, so he had to recreate her and that is how I became Melissa or Mother. I was then allowed to be inside of the house with watching eyes.

"There were so many kids, twelve total, and the oldest are still alive. However, Jeffrey was not calling the shots. There is much more to this than we know."

"Lady Clem said the same thing. Who is the tall guy?" Jason asked.

"I don't know, but Jeffrey kept a trunk with everything, including his journals, and it is at the house in the basement. Women were not allowed in the house and none were allowed around. I was only allowed to be around a certain time of the day and some days not at all. Something was happening there. I could not see it, but I could hear it."

He handed Devin a picture of Coretta and Cody. She is the stepsister of Lenny Amos. I had decided to take my chances and find my way home when I met her and she said that the cops closed the case on Lenny because they were all in Jeffrey's pocket, this Brotherhood is large. Coretta was the only link I had to civilization and we became close. She was a makeup artist and she thought that if I wanted to be in the public and get information, then I should wear makeup and do it as a woman and it worked.

"I had access to all of his paperwork, which is how I found out that Willie had married." Judy turned away. "First, I thought it was Judy until they called the name Elmira. I tried to find her, but I could not, and later I found out that she had a daughter, so I tracked down Carla and she was hired at the hospital, until they decided what to do with her. That is why Jenny came to the hospital, it was to protect Kandy, and then she met her best friend and so did I. It was Lisa and it was perfect because everyone I needed to keep an eye on was under one roof for a while."

"What about Lionel? You asked them to take my son!" Carolyn screamed at him.

"I was only one man and I could not do it all. Matthew's job was to kill you and Lionel. They went to your apartment, but Lisa had taken Lionel from the babysitter." Carolyn placed her hand over her mouth because she had never talked to the babysitter again. Her mother had called for her, but she did not know what had happened to her.

"They killed Yolanda . . . "

"I do not know," he said, "but they wanted to take Lionel from Lisa, however she was a fighter."

Lisa sat and became dizzy, Devin rush to her side and so did Jason. "A man walked up to me and tried to push Lionel out in the shopping cart. He and I had stopped at the grocery store to get cookie dough and when I turned my back, he was pushing Lionel. I hit him with a bag of apples and he apologized, saying that he had the wrong cart."

Jimmy continued, "There is a trunk marked 'Sister' in the corner of the basement behind a wall. It contains pictures of all of their victims. It also has souvenirs or trophies, something that they had taken from each of their victims. Eddie ordered his men to retrieve the trunk, and they found out about Lionel because you talked to James.

Carolyn started to cry. "I did not know about this." She walked into his arms, "I did not know."

Jimmy held her, "No one knew. All of our lives we heard things, but we ignored it. We thought it was just an urban legend or something. No one took it seriously.

"Matthew followed you home one night when your son was running a fever." Carolyn turned because that was at the time Jason had left her. "I told him that you would be a good catch and he was hooked. He would not let any of the others come anywhere near you. However, it became a rivalry between Sister and Matthew and that is when Matthew shot Jason, which I did not see coming because he was not ordered to do so by Jeffrey."

Jimmy went on to tell why he thought that Jeffrey was just following orders. "Melissa's last two children were girls. Which means that James was not one of her children because if he were, he would not have been able to order Jeffrey to kill Lisa's baby.

"When the inheritance date got close, everything started to fall apart. Jeffrey was losing control because he could not control Sister and the men all wanted the money for themselves, and they were not taking any chances. Anyone that had any dealings with the Jones men would die, even their friends. After we left the strip club and I had taken Coretta home, I was attacked by Simon and I broke his jaw, which put him out of commission for a few weeks, but he got a punch in on me also. Lisa, remember the bruise on Jenny's face. The Brotherhood was big, you know James and Andrew and Alpheus and we all know what happened to Bartholomew. I was locked up and I never got to see the oldest children much."

Lisa smiled, she was right. "He would not know how to explain your presence and they would know that you were not Melissa . . . "

"Bingo," Jimmy said, "so he sent them to live with someone else. I do not know what they would look like as adults, however, I do have their pictures and I heard the name Dubois."

Devin turned to Jason, "Darlene's father . . . " when Jimmy looked at the expression on Eddie's face, "she was not his daughter, she was his lover, just as Chloe is Andrew's and will do whatever it takes to get what they want.

"She was to marry Devin and get Lisa's baby then kill him, but she was killed because she wanted to have a Jones child herself and that was betrayal, so someone ordered Simon to kill her."

"I am sorry that I doubted you, however, that still does not explain why you pretended to be pregnant."

"That was Coretta's idea. Every woman that got pregnant that month suddenly had a miscarriage because of their ultrasound that James ordered, and when you told him that Lisa and Chris were sleeping together . . . " Carolyn looked away.

"You told him that!" Jason yelled. "We told you how we felt about him and you still talked to him!"

Carolyn pleaded for him to understand, but she had totally misjudged him. "I am sorry, Lisa. I was so hurt because I deceived you and was at my desk and he asked what was wrong. I told him that I lied to you and now you were with Chris and, if you got pregnant and something went wrong, then I would feel so bad."

Lisa turned and looked at Lady Singleton, who did not look at her. "It is not your fault, Cal, they had all of this planned for years."

Jimmy agreed. "They would have given a drug test to make sure. Their interest was in Kay, you, and Lisa. They found out about Kay. Sister wanted a child, but Kay's test was blue. When they ran Lisa's it was pink, so I took the tube and changed the paperwork. Then Lisa got hurt and they found out that she was pregnant. They did another test, which was pink and that is when James ordered them to take the baby."

Lisa walked into his arms. He also reached for Carolyn. "You wanted to get an opinion, that's all. It was not betrayal. I sent Eddie the video so that he would protect the family, but I was wrong. You took Devin only and I was tired of trying to be a father and a protector because I failed Kay. I had no idea that they thought of her until it was over, and when they got Lisa, I prayed that you all would put the video together and realize that the houses were connected."

Jason was confused. He wanted to believe that Eddie did not have Ellen put in a mental hospital, however, he did not believe him. He wanted answers and he appealed to Jimmy, "Why didn't you help Ellen?"

Jimmy turned to her, "Because I could not find you and, one day, I heard Jeffrey talk to Simon and they talked about the mental hospital. I at least knew that you were still alive and that is when I found out that Mother was there also. Jeffrey took Ellen, but I do not know how Mother was put in a place like that. The mental hospital was their holding place, because Jeffrey ran the facilities and his sons all worked there. Many female patients went missing from that place and that is when I was going to get Ellen out of there, but Judy came along."

"How dare you come into my house and try to turn my sons against me. You could have knocked on my door anytime and you did not." His words angered Jimmy, "like Mom and Judy did. We were not in our graves, but you walked out and turned your back on your family and put them on the street."

"I wanted to knock on the door and tell you everything, and you and I and Willie would go and blow them the fuck up, but they were here, so I sent Kevin and he almost ended up dead. So, I was on my own and I thank God every day, fifteen years ago for Coretta, and now we have Cody. We are paying for the sins of our father, and your sons and mine will pay for ours." He handed Eddie Cody's picture. "He is why I stayed in that house, so that I would know what was going to happen. I do not want Cody or my nephew to burn as the others did and, Carolyn, if you thought that they would have shown Lionel sympathy, then you are wrong. They were not taught compassion, not even for a child."

Lisa smiled at Jimmy because finally they knew why he stayed at Jeffrey's house. She thought of him as brave, to stay under a madman's roof to protect his family. Lisa walked upstairs to her room while Jason and Devin went into the kitchen. Lisa went through Eddie's yearbooks and those of other schools, looking for the name Jeffrey Thomas, and noticed a man that she did not recognize. She looked again and saw a woman named Lou Ella Dubois. She turned another page, and there was Eddie Jones. She looked at Lou Ella Dubois again and stared at her, and looked at Jeffrey Thomas. It was not the Jeffrey Thomas that they knew. She read everything on Lou Ella that she could find, and she was a genius. She excelled in everything.

She looked up the pact and urban legend and she was shocked when it was written. Four men went missing in Florida. The hikers came across a cave and decided to rest for the night, when they came across buried treasure. The men said that they did not know how they got lost because the cave only had one path. As they continued, they met the Devil who offered them the gold, but only if they would give up their rights to any female child born to their wives and loved ones. Each man agreed and they had riches and power that was too much for each of them to bear and, instead of staying friends, they all became enemies, making a wager that the one family that give birth to a girl child first would inherit the pot of gold. She scrolled down and looked at the names—Omar Thomas, Joseph Jones, Ketchum Klein, and Dubois Farrow. There were four, and not three, and there was more to it than they knew. She looked for more information when she came across an article that read that one of the men took the gold and left the other men to die in a fire. She then pulled up the file on the executives of the hospital and the mental hospital, which are affiliated, and found that Cecil Dubois and Jeffrey Thomas were the heads of the hospitals.

"It is a lovely night don't you think?" Carolyn did not look at Lady Singleton. She just stared into the night. "Will he hate me?" she asked.

Lady Singleton sat and stared. "He does not hate, however, he is disappointed because there is a killer out there and you have been a part of the problem and not the solution. Work with Lisa and he will appreciate you and know that you are not the selfish person that everyone thinks that you are. And you should love what he loves, and that is his mother.

Lady Singleton turned Carolyn's face and looked her in the eyes. Lisa felt Devin's pain because of how he lost his mother and he was allowed to share that with her, but Jason was alone in his pain. "His mother was treated like an animal and you judge her harshly and you still do and if you think that having babies will make you happy then you are mistaken," Lady Singleton said.

Lady Singleton stood and walked back into the room where Judy and Eddie were talking about their past.

Jimmy looked at the older lady. He was not sure who she was, but he liked her. "Are you a psychic?" he asked.

Lady Singleton smiled. "It has been a long time since anyone has called me that, but that is what I do and when you return tomorrow, Ida and I will do karaoke for you."

Jimmy turned to Ellen. There was a gleam in his eyes when he looked at her. "Remember the school talent show?" He said. "You and I were Marvin and Tammy."

Ida placed her hand over her mouth, she had all but forgotten about that. "Stay tonight and tomorrow bring your pipes," she said, "we have competition in here." Ellen informed Jimmy that Dr. Dre and Tupac were in the house.

"Word up!" Lady Singleton said.

Devin walked up to Ellen and placed a kiss on her cheek, it was time for acknowledgement. "I have never thanked you for saving my mother's life." Devin handed her the letter that Asia had written about her.

"She was an amazing woman." Ellen thought she knew what was going to happen to her, so she found a way to put her in the life of Devin and Jason. Ellen prepared breakfast for the men and listened as they talked.

"Should we inform Lisa what Lady Clem said about them getting the baby?" Skeet asked.

"She would become paranoid and God knows that she has seen enough to drive her crazy. We will just keep a watch on her. "Devin said. The room got quiet when Lisa came down to breakfast while all of the men were at the table.

"Chloe Johnson is a real person," she said. "However, her real name is Chloe Winters. After Jimmy went to bed, I called Henderson and asked about her and she is real. She was a model for a small company and she met Andrew while he was doing an investigation. He fell for her head over heels. However, medical records say she had an abortion that led to her having an infection and she had to have a hysterectomy. She is not pregnant." Lisa gloated. "I knew she could not carry all of those boxes without getting winded.

"Andrew wanted to give her a child and, maybe, he promised her his wife's child. The baby would be his and she would be a mother. If you want to know more about her," Lisa said. "You can pull up her a mug shot. She was a con artist, she conned wealthy men out of their money, and one died of a mysterious death. There was a will left which his family contested and she went on the run. Henderson said that she was also wanted for questioning in an attempted kidnapping of a baby from the hospital."

"When can we have our son, Andrew?" Chloe was on cloud nine. She had stopped at the shop to pick up some boy clothing, however, the shop did not open today. The bitch gave birth to my son," Chloe said. She thought she should be rewarded for giving birth and although Andrew asked her to keep a low profile, she would do as she pleased. She could use a new car, a truck like that Lisa had, something big enough to drive her family around in comfort. Today she would receive her child, a boy child, and she would wait for her girl.

"You cannot get attached to him right away," he said to her, but then he changed his mind. She did not ask why because she did not care. She would be a mother of two children.

❧ ❧

"You boys ain't never on time," Lady Clem said. "Too many distractions will get you into trouble." They looked at each other. This was the first time that they had been chastised with a smile. "They will get the baby," she said to Devin, "and your father will pay a price to get her back. He is smart. He listens to everything. I cannot tell you how they will get her, only that they will not keep her. She will be returned to you in blood. She only wants a child. She betrays one brother with another, she does not care about the money because she already has more than she will ever spend. They are bonded by lust and greed." She looked at them. "You, too, are spoiled rotten. What did you two have for breakfast?" She asked while she laughed. "It is almost over. Tell Carolyn to get a bigger car. I see more children in her future."

Devin laughed.

"I do not know why you are so happy," she said to him. "Lisa will have more also." She looked at Jason, "He ain't laughing now. Thank you for my life," she said. "I know you sent Trevor and William to protect me, and tell Kandy that she is not taking birth control." She laughed. "I am forever grateful. He loves you all. He only wants to put his family together and get his revenge for what he has been through. He just wanted to be with his family," she said again, "and Lisa knows to trust her instincts because she is on the right path.

"Who is working with Thomas?" She lowered her head. "He is not of this world. He is pure evil. He levitates himself, and he is the lord of illusion. Trust your wives. They are on the right path. Do not stop them or allow anyone to stop them because all of your lives will depend on it. It is not over until he burns as the others have. Your father needs to see and he will. He is not a believer."

Jason dialed Detective Henderson. "Chloe came into money and we need to find out if it is Thaddeus's money. Lady Clem said she turned brother against brother, so she and Scotty set up Thaddeus. If Dr. Samuels plans to give Lisa's baby to Scotty and Chloe, then why kidnap Jessica?"

Devin sat outside and watched the house. He watched as Chloe with her pregnant belly drove up in a tan-colored Suburban. "You're going to need one of those." Devin laughed.

Carolyn missed her period. Jason said, "She has not said anything because of all of this, and I know she is tired of patching up holes. She just wants her family, and we will give it to them both. Devin said this is almost over and we will get our lives together." Jason looked at Chloe. She was preparing for the children as she had gotten a bigger SUV. He looked at his phone. He had not received a text from Tiffany lately.

Devin smiled at the revelation when Eddie embraced Jimmy. "I knew in my heart that you would never turn your back on your family." He even patted him on the back for getting Coretta pregnant. "Cody looks like you," he said, "he has your eyes. Go, and take Ben and Skeet with you and bring your family to be with us, and we will find the Thomas brothers and put them out of their misery."

Kandy walked up to Jimmy and gave him a container of pepper spray and they had a laugh on Jimmy. "Kay, you said that we would never talk about that day again." Kandy burst out in laughter. "I lied. When you get back, I'll tell everyone."

∽ ∽

"If Jessica was kidnapped for her baby and Tiffany is pregnant, then why take Jessica's baby, if he planned to kill Tiffany for her baby." Devin pulled from the curb. He drove to Tiffany's house as Jason called her phone, she did not answer. They pulled into her driveway to find that her car was there. They walked to her door and found it open. They both pulled out their weapons and entered the house. They did not get far when they spotted Tiffany's body at the bottom of the stairs. First, it looked as if she had fallen until they got closer and noticed that her neck was slashed so deep it almost decapitated her.

Both men turned their heads in sickness, when they looked to find that her stomach was ripped open and her unborn child was gone. "Where is the baby?" Devin asked. "How could he do this to her and his own child? That is why they took Jessica's baby, because they needed a back-up plan."

✿ ✿

Momma Ida and Lady Singleton were doing karaoke to *Rapper's Delight* while Coretta laid her head on Jimmy's shoulder and cheered them on.

Lisa yelled and suddenly the music stopped. Everyone looked at her. "I think I just had a contraction."

Skeet jumped up. "Boil some water," Jimmy said. Willie ran for towels, when Jason and Devin walked into the house.

Everyone was running around, when Eddie said, "It could be time."

Devin started asking Lisa to breathe, and Jimmy asked her to lie down, and then suddenly, it stopped. "Devin, if I stop breathing, then I am in trouble." She often wondered why that is always what a man say when a woman goes into labor. "Sorry, guys, false alarm."

Skeet came out of the kitchen with a pot of water. "Trevor, what are you planning to do, cook it?" Lady Singleton laughed. "Girl, you are in trouble."

The water ran down his body. He could not get his mind off what he had seen. The picture plagued his brain. He thought of his own child being cut from the womb, just as Tiffany's. He dried his body and dressed before going downstairs. He found Jason with his face in his hands. "We have to find Andrew. We can stake out his house and have someone do the same for Chloe. He has to turn up soon and we have only two weeks before Lisa is due."

"They are not there," Jimmy said. Eddie did not want the women to hear their conversation, but they all turned to the room when the Jackson 5 music came on, and Cody, Justin and Lionel started to sing. Jimmy smiled when Cody stood in the middle and Lionel and Justin danced as he sang. Jimmy looked at the smile on Coretta's face, something he had never seen. She and Lisa laughed and Carolyn and Kandy danced, yelling, "Sing it baby."

Eddie placed his hand on Jimmy's shoulder. "They are with family and so are you."

"I know where Alpheus is, he's at the hotel. He leaves every morning at 6:30 A.M. I followed him from the hospital and we can get him tonight. We can wait at the hospital and see if James is there. They will not return to the homes until they kill us and get the baby."

❧ ❧

"Andrew, he is beautiful." Chloe grabbed the baby. "We will name him Carter."

Andrew knew it was a big mistake to give Chloe the baby, however, she was a big part of his plan and keeping her happy was most important of all. "Baby, you cannot get attached to him."

Chloe took Carter and held him tight. "I will not lose him, Andrew. You promised me a family and now you are going back on your word. Look at him." She smiled and made faces at baby Carter. "We will be a perfect family, and you will have a sister soon," she said. "They could be twins," she said with excitement. Only baby Carter was dark skinned. She wondered if Lisa's baby would be also.

Andrew smiled at her, "Baby, Lisa's baby will be due soon and we have everything in place." He rubbed her silky hair, "The two babies will look so different that you will not be able to call them twins. Even fraternal twins have to have something in common and the two will not. Jessica looked more African than African-American. She had dark skin that was perfect—not a spot on her face—and so did baby Carter's father, who he met while he booked him for possession, while Lisa looked to be more Native American and Devin was light complexioned.

Lisa frowned and moaned. She grabbed her suitcase and started down the stairs. She looked around to find J.T. and Christian sitting in front of the computer. "Where is Devin?" They looked at her and then each other. "Please, guys, stay calm, call Devin and ask him to meet us at the hospital. Tell him I broke my water."

"Lisa broke her water," J.T. said to Devin when he answered the phone.

Skeet and Jason listened and laughed. "Pick it up with a cloth, you wimp. Why call me for that?" Devin laughed, "Lisa broke some water and he calls me for it."

Jason laughed. "Maybe he wants you to clean up behind her."

They sat and waited for minutes, when Skeet decided to Google what happened when a pregnant woman broke water. Skeet did not say a word, but cranked the car and burned rubber, pulling away from the curb.

"What in the hell is wrong with you, Skeet?" Devin asked. "We have to watch for Andrew," when Skeet handed him the phone.

"Lisa is in labor."

Lisa moaned, "Where is Devin?" While J.T. started to hyperventilate.

"I left a note for the family," Christian said.

Dr. Davis walked into the waiting room. "We are getting everything ready for you." He wheeled her into the examining room and asked the two men to wait outside.

J.T. wanted to document everything for the family. He had called and could not get through to Devin again. He decided to tap into the hospital computer system and he could see when Devin and the others came into the building. He went from floor to floor to get a clear view.

Dr. Davis examined Lisa. "Where is your husband? I thought he would be here with you."

She moaned. "He better get his ass here soon."

He turned and felt something pierce his skin before he fell to the ground. Lisa looked up to see Dr. Samuels standing there. Before she could scream, he placed his hand over her mouth.

You better get to the hospital, Eddie." Jimmy had picked up the letter, "Lisa is in labor." He smiled. "The bet is on, Leonard, I plan to collect today. Lisa is having the baby."

Leonard Pendergrass rubbed his hands together. "My hands have been itching all day and later I will be driving a new BMW. I told you, Eddie. I am a pro at babies."

Skeet sat at a traffic light when someone hit him from the rear. He looked to find a man getting out of his car. "Is everyone alright?" he asked. "I have insurance." Skeet looked at him, "Man, this is your lucky day," he said before getting back into the car and leaving.

Devin picked up his phone to find that it had powered off before turning it back on.

Christian watched as Lisa delivered the baby. He looked at the doctor. "That is not the same doctor," he said. He watched as he pulled out the baby and noticed a red mark on her leg. He looked at J.T., "Should she be out like that?"

J.T. called Devin's phone again and there was no answer. He called Eddie's phone, "What is going on J.T.?" asked Eddie.

"We can't reach Devin and something is wrong," he said. "Something is wrong with Lisa and we are not allowed in the delivery room."

The doctor walked from the room with the baby. "Wait here," he said to the men. "The nurse will bring her to the room in a minute."

"Where are you taking the baby?" Christian asked.

"To the ICU," he said. "Please feel free to follow."

J.T. looked at Christian. As he and the doctor walked away with the baby, the nurse ran from the room, yelling for the doctor, "Where is he taking the baby?" she asked.

J.T. looked at his computer to see where the doctor was taking the baby.

Eddie ran to J.T., "What's going on?"

"Lisa will not wake up," he said.

A nurse walked up and tried to wake her. J.T. was in shock. "Mr. Jones, he just took the baby." The men ran out of the room.

Dr. Davis looked for the baby. He walked out of the room to find Eddie Jones, who asked, "Where is my grandbaby?"

Dr. Davis was speechless. He did not know what had happened. "The baby is dead," he said. "He did not make it."

Leonard Pendergrass gasped. "What in the hell do you mean? He . . . We want to see the baby now!" He yelled.

Dr. Davis led them to the room where the baby lay. Eddie cried, "It is so small, are you sure, doctor? Lisa carried full term."

Dr. Davis could not explain what had gone wrong.

Devin and Jason walked in. "The baby did not make it," Eddie said. "It was a boy."

Devin looked at the small child lying on the table. He touched the child; it was cold as ice. "I have failed my family," he said. "I was so busy trying to avenge Tiffany's death till I failed my own wife and child." He rubbed his face. He looked at his brother with tears in his eyes, "How can I make this up to her? I yelled at her and now my baby is dead."

Dr. Davis said nothing while Dr. Pendergrass examined the child. "Sir, you are a son of a goddamn fish sandwich . . ." He grabbed Dr. Davis by the collar, "and if you think we are falling for this, then I will rip out your lily grey heart."

He questioned Dr. Davis. "Are you one of them?"

A curious look came over his face. "One of who?"

Leonard Pendergrass was appalled. Devin looked at the man that he had called Uncle all of his life. He had never heard him say a bad word in his life, let alone threaten anyone. "Where is my niece?" he asked.

Devin turned and looked at the baby again. He touched him.

"This is not our child. Lisa was carrying a girl child, and to think that you would be able to fool us, then you are wrong," Leonard said to Dr. Davis. He looked at Devin. "That is no more your child than it is mine."

Eddie looked at him. He knew Leonard was in financial trouble, but to carry on this way, he could not believe it.

"Lisa's baby is a girl." He pleaded with his eyes, as Devin stood in shock. It was time for tough love, "That baby over there has been dead for over a week." He could see that his words were haunting Devin. "Your baby is here somewhere. That is not your baby. It has been taken before its time and refrigerated."

Devin looked again. Then he turned to Jason, "That is why they needed a second child. They planned to switch the babies."

Dr. Davis grabbed his chest and agreed, and then started to tell all that had happened. He never saw the baby. Someone had attacked him from behind.

Eddie ran back to the room where J.T. was. "Rewind the video and tell me where the doctor took the baby." Eddie tried to call Christian, however, he did not answer.

J.T. rolled back the recording and watched as Christian and the nurse went into a room with the doctor, however, the doctor was the only one to exit and he then entered a different room, three doors down. He looked at Eddie. "They are on the second floor with the baby in Room 213."

Eddie ran down the stairs while J.T. watched.

"I am going with him," Jimmy said, he then called Devin and Jason to tell them where the baby was.

"She's eight pounds and two ounces," Dr. Samuels said. "I told you my way was the best way. If we had not replaced the child, the hospital would be on lock down by now and we would never be able to get her out of here."

Andrew wrapped the baby in a pink blanket and snapped a picture of her to send to Chloe. "Are you sure she's okay? She looked a little white to me," he said.

Dr. Samuels laughed. "Not all colored babies are born with brown skin, some of them have to grow into their complexion. She will tan, but not much."

Andrew looked at her again. "Come tomorrow, baby brother, we will be on a beach on an island somewhere, and will only return to collect our money." Chloe had made an appointment with the attorney. She even paid them a visit as Lisa Jones, and now this is money in the bank. "Hello, baby Christina," he called the child, your mother is waiting for you

Eddie slowly opened the door. He looked at the baby and smiled. *No distractions*, he told himself. He went for his gun, when he realized he did not have one. He grabbed the baby when the men turned and Andrew pulled out his gun. "Put her down!" He ordered.

Eddie knew he was in trouble, but he could not let them take her away. "You will have to kill me to get her," he said.

Andrew smiled, "Your sons are not the only perfect shots," he said. He pulled the trigger, hitting Eddie in the side, but he did not let the baby go. He clutched her tighter and ran into the hall before he fell to his knee. When Jimmy pulled him out of harm's way, he lifted the gun, fired and missed. Then he aimed and hit Andrew in the chest. Eddie ran forward and slid down a wall, when a nurse ran to his aid. He looked up to see Devin and Jason running toward him. He handed Devin the baby before he saw darkness. "You take her to get her help and I will stay with Dad."

Devin looked at his daughter. The pink blanket was covered with his father's blood. *She will be given to you in blood.*

Skeet and Willie ran to the men. "Dad has been shot." Willie went with Jason while Skeet brought the baby to be examined with Devin. They opened a door to find that Christian and a nurse had been drugged and were lying on the floor.

❧ ❧

Lisa opened her eyes and touched her stomach to find that the baby was not there. The nurse ran to her.

"Where is my baby?" she asked the nurse.

"Your baby is fine, Mrs. Jones. She is with your husband."

J.T. looked as if he had been crying when he and Devin walked into the room. "They are feeding her. You slept through the night and she needed to be fed." Devin looked as if he had not slept at all.

"What happened? Dr. Samuels was here," she started to panic. "Devin, I want to see her, please."

He looked at her. He did not want her to know all that had happened, so he called Carolyn into the room. "Lisa, she is perfect; a little pale, but perfect." Devin brought the baby to Lisa. She looked at her and smiled, and then looked at her leg to see if she still had the pink mark on it and it was there.

❧ ❧

"Where is everyone, Devin?"

He sighed. "They had taken her from you last night when Dad and J.T. tracked them to a room on the second floor and Dad got shot."

Lisa's eyes watered. "Is he okay, where is he?" she asked, when her door opened.

"He is fine," Eddie said. "He just wants to get the hell out of here. She laughed. "How is my granddaughter?" he asked as he walked in.

"It's over, sweetheart, now we can have a normal life and we can name her." Devin studied his daughter's face. "If we could call her Little Devin, that would be good."

Carolyn said, "She looks just like him."

"I have one," Lisa said, "however, I am flexible. How about Asia Elizabeth Jones?"

Devin kissed her. "That is beautiful. Mother would be proud and so will Momma Ida.

Lisa looked up to see Jimmy. "Come in, you come and hold your niece."

"Lisa, I would not be here if Jimmy was not there." Eddie patted Jimmy on the back. "He killed Andrew, which allowed me the chance to get away with Asia."

"Mr. Jones, what are you doing out of bed?" Nurse Cane patted the bed, "Get in here now. Your family is here and it is just as well that they only have one room to visit."

"Lisa, girl, did you have this baby or Devin?" Judy and Ida laughed.

"Girl, you know she is in love when the baby looks just like the father. She is whipped," Momma Ida said.

"No, Momma, only men get whipped, right?" Kandy asked Carolyn.

"And, she asked me like I know." Carolyn wanted to announce her pregnancy, but she did not want to take away baby Asia's glory. She would save the news until they were home.

Ø Ø

Lisa looked around her bedroom. She got out of bed to find Baby Asia gone. She slipped on her robe and walked to the stairs. She could hear someone talking as she walked into the family room to find Eddie holding Asia and Willie playing 'gaga goo-goo' with her while Leonard Pendergrass played with her with a stuffed animal.

"Good morning," she said, and then planted a kiss on Eddie's cheek and moved into Willie's arms. "You guys are going to spoil her."

Leonard played with the animal. "Sugar and spice," he said.

Lisa kissed Leonard also. "Devin told me what you did and we are so grateful to you," she smiled. "You called the doctor a fish sandwich!"

Leonard gloated. "I can get ugly when I have to."

"What in the hell is a fish sandwich?" Willie laughed, while Eddie took out an envelope, and walked up to Leonard.

"If you were not there, then I would have, again, buried the wrong child. Your persistence put my family back whole and for that I am grateful to you Leonard. You are a friend, indeed. You could have just walked away."

"And ruin my reputation?" Leonard gasped, and looked at Eddie. "I have made bad choices in my life and it has cost me my family, and now my reputation is all that I have, my friend. Leonard did not want to take the money, but his financial situation was bad.

"I called your wife, Veronica, and told her all that had happened and your role in it, and I also took care of the problem for you." Eddie lifted Leonard's hand and placed the envelope in of it. "When you need us, we are here for you. Meanwhile, Veronica will return home this weekend."

Henderson went over the house again with his men. "We cannot find her." He questioned if the men were not just seeing things when they called in the death of Tiffany Johnson.

"She was right here," Devin said. Both he and Jason stood at the bottom of the stairs, "And I bet you when you do a DNA on the baby, it will be her baby."

Henderson paced the floor, "We checked the backyard, there is no disturbed earth and we also went through the basement downstairs." Henderson suddenly remembered, "Congratulation to you both. Kelvin Hamilton has been released from jail and his family wants to meet you both. She asked me to give you this card."

"What happened to Glenda? She just disappeared just like Tiffany. They buried the bodies," Jason said and they both said simultaneously, "at the old house."

Henderson radioed his men to meet them at the old Thomas house. "I hope you guys are right," he said. "Maybe she just left town when she found out that her husband was a sicko."

Devin picked up baby Asia. "Hello, beautiful, Daddy's home." He sat in the rocking chair with her and thought of her birth, how he almost lost her. He thought of what Jessica Hayes must be going through. He hired a team of investigator to help her, and he was so distracted that he almost lost his own child, but now his family was together and he needed to be home.

"Time for a feeding." Lisa kissed Devin.

"How was your day, babe." He smiled and kissed her again. He watched her in amazement, how her body was almost the same as when he first met her. He could not tell that she had had a child a few weeks ago. The only difference was her breasts were a little bigger. He knew that some women go on a diet to get their shape back, but he thought that she had bounced back too fast.

He picked up his phone when it vibrated. "We found them," Henderson said. "Man, there are so many bodies buried out here, it will take us weeks to identify them all, but we have found the body of Tiffany Johnson and possibly Glenda Johnson."

Lisa placed Baby Asia in her bed, when there was a knock at the door. She smiled. "Come in, you." Jimmy walked in carrying a basket of pink things and a box of chocolate for Lisa. She kissed him and thanked him again."

"I missed with the first shot," he admitted. "I had no idea how to shoot the damn thing," he said, "and I fired and hit nothing."

Devin laughed, "You can take lessons."

"You look amazing," Jimmy said to Lisa. "How did you get your stomach so flat in such a short period of time?"

Lisa only smiled, she did not want to admit to a crash diet because she knew Devin would hit the roof, however, she would have dinner with the family and eat a normal meal now that she was back in her normal clothing.

Devin walked out of the room and left Jimmy with Lisa. Lisa paused at the television, when the reporter announced the death of a man, "He was found in his hotel room with both wrists slashed, and his throat was cut, before he was set on fire."

🕊 🕊

"Coretta and Ellen are having a cooking contest today. It is funny how the two of them bonded so fast, and Ida is so happy, and I hope that you will stay here with your family where you will be safe. Dr. Samuels is still out there somewhere and we have no idea who else they could have recruited for their mission. We love you and need you to be here with us."

Jimmy smiled her words were music to his ears, but he did not know if the rest of the family felt the same as she did. "Your husband and the others might know share your view, Lisa, and I would not want to impose on anyone."

Lisa picked up Asia and they walked down to dinner. "You have to talk to Kandy."

Jimmy sighed. "That is what I was dreading. She and Jenny were close and she sometimes gets confused."

Lisa handed Jimmy the baby. "She got hurt very badly and she does not understand your role in any of this, so when you talk to her, honesty is the best policy." Lisa laughed, "Besides, I know she will love you."

"It is good to see you eating normal food," Carolyn said, which made Devin turn to look at Lisa.

"What is going on, Lisa? I know you lost the weight fast. Have you been starving yourself?"

Lisa felt uncomfortable, everyone was looking at her and she had to tell the truth. "I went through a depression for a while," she admitted to the family. "There was so much going on in my head that I did not feel I could be happy. It was as if I was waiting for the next shoe to drop. I needed to know that all of this was over and I could not eat or sleep, but now it has been six weeks and we got back the DNA on Asia . . . " Lisa did not want to show weakness, she just needed to express what she was feeling to everyone.

"They took my baby. As hard as we tried to keep them away from her, they still touched and held my little girl, and I was having a hard time coping with it all." Lisa looked at Devin. "And now you are home more, and I now feel Asia and I are safe."

He held her hand. "I know that all of this was too much for you, that is why I took time off to be a good husband and father. I got caught up with it all and now the two of you have my attention."

Lisa took a bit of food, while giving Carolyn a dirty look, "And now we have to worry about Jimmy." He gave her a weak smile.

"I can take care of myself," he assured her.

Ida's eyes watered. She had counted on Lisa in the past to get her family together, knowing now that she was suffering in the process. And now Jimmy needed her to speak on his behalf to get the others to understand that he is not a bad person and he needed his family.

"So that is it? You come into our lives and now you will just leave me. I just got used to you being Jimmy Kandy said. Lisa and Jenny were all that I had, and I know that you tried to keep me safe while placing your own life in danger, but you cannot just leave us."

"Kay, I love you also. You were the daughter I never had and there is no way I can be without you in my life, however, it is not my decision. I have to make sure that my family is happy."

Kandy looked at Coretta, "She is happy," she asked with her eyes and Coretta looked at everyone and it was her time to speak.

"Cody is so happy and for the first time in years, we are not frightened at a knock on the door. His father is with him and he can be himself." She smiled. "So if you all will have us, then we will be happy to stay and our son will have role models here." She smiled at Jason and Devin. "Someone that can help his father guide him in the right direction." She lowered her head and then raised it to look at Eddie. "We feel safe here, not just for the two of us, but the three of us." Coretta closed her eyes. "Every day he walked out the door, we were so scared that would be the last time that we would see him, because he was all alone, and now he had the best to fight with him and we would love to be a part of this family."

"Who is going to open it?" Lady Singleton asked. The trunk from Jeffrey's house sat in the middle of the floor for days and no one dared to open it.

"It almost appears to be evil, because of the skull and crossbones and the red ruby eyes on the skull," Carolyn said as she turned to Lisa, who recognized it as the trunk from the picture that contained the gold.

"It is several hundred years old." She pulled out the picture and passed it around. "There is a lot more to this than we know and I am going to do some research."

"We," Carolyn said, "Since I will have a little time on my hands, Jason is going to teach me how to shoot a gun." Carolyn gloated.

Devin patted Jimmy on the back. "Maybe, you should have lessons also. You missed the first shot."

Eddie said, "He's got butter fingers." Willie laughed.

"I have never fired a gun before in my life," Jimmy said, "and I purchased one for protection."

"I want to learn also," Kandy said, and then she and Carolyn began to argue.

"If we put a gun in your hand, Kay, none of us will be safe," teased Carolyn, and Kandy thought the same of her. Carolyn turned and gave Kandy the finger, "Also, I will not argue with you Kay, because I do not want my baby to come out looking like you."

There was silence. No one said a word. "Like you all did not know," Carolyn scolded everyone, "I have gained ten pounds!" She yelled.

"I thought that you were getting fat," Kandy said, throwing up her hands.

"You're next, Kandy, and I will call you fat and see if you like it."

"While I have everyone here," Devin said, "I need to take my beautiful wife away for the weekend, and I could use a good set of babysitters."

Carolyn knocked Kandy over. "I will do it," she said. "I can use the practice with a girl."

Devin remembered, "Kandy, what pills are you taking?"

She looked at Lisa. "I borrowed your old birth control because I was afraid to go to the hospital and since you were not taking them and we took the same kind, I decided not to let them go to waste." Kandy pulled the pills out of her purse. "I will pay for your next prescription."

"Kandy, these are not birth control, I had my prenatal vitamins placed into this container so that I would not forget to take them." Devin and Jason looked at Skeet, who looked lost. "Sorry, Kandy, if you would have said something, I would have warned you."

✑ ✑

"This feels amazing," Lisa said, stepping down into the Jacuzzi with her tiny bikini. She was back and she wanted him to know it. I almost lost myself, I was breaking into pieces and, once again, you put me back together again."

Devin lifted her legs around his waist. "That is my job and now we can finally enjoy life as we should have from the beginning. Now everyone is happy and safe and you and I can bring our daughter here and be a family, without the family.

✑ ✑

"Hey, baby." Chloe smiled at her baby Carter, "it is just the two of us. She loaded the SUV with all that she could carry. Then she drove past her old house to find it surrounded with police.

She checked her rear view mirror and admired her new look. She was a beautiful blonde and she was a mother most of all. She pulled out one of her driver's licenses to see who she would now become with her baby Carter. *Melanie Williams and Carter Williams* she thought, repeating the name several times before driving by James's house, which was surrounded by police. She looked at her phone and read the code 3, 21, 9, 14, 2, 1, 8, 1, 13, 1, 19 and she smiled. "Come on, baby, it is time to take a trip." (C U N BAHAMAS)

☙ ☙

Eddie tapped the glass. "We need a vacation and I know that we deserve it, so I am taking the family to the Bahamas for a week and I also invited the Pendergrass family to come along. We can take the plane and return to celebrate the Thanksgiving holidays."

Ellen laughed, she had been promised the Bahamas and now she would get it, but the boys did not look happy that Eddie had taken their idea and Carolyn would probably complain the whole way, but she was happy because she would be with her family and friends.

She started cleaning the dishes.

"Momma, leave it," Jason said as he held her hand and they walked into the family room where she sat next to Lisa.

"Ellen, it is okay to fall in love," Lisa said to her. "It is time that you find happiness."

Ellen's eyes looked up and noticed Eddie staring at her. "Ellen, get your bikini ready," he said. "I am going to show you the time of your life."

She looked at her sons, would they approve of her letting Eddie show her a good time or would they think she was crazy for forgiving him. She only followed Lisa's lead because Eddie needed women to show him affection, but she did not know if she was ready to truly forgive him, when Devin kissed her cheek and asked her to enjoy herself.

Carolyn remembered what Lady Singleton had said, but she would not share her husband with anyone, not even his mother, so if Eddie wants Ellen, then he could have her. "Ellen, it has been over forty years and you have not had a 'good time,'" she said, doing the *quote-unquote* fingers.

Lisa wanted Ellen to go out into the world and broaden her horizons, but if she interjected then the others would be angry with her, mainly Eddie.

The family arrived in the Bahamas. Eddie had reserved a home for everyone. "Everyone, this is Sade. He will take us back and forth into town by boat."

The family sat for dinner at the Resort. Lisa walked to the beach with Jimmy. She smiled as she watched a woman and her son walking and looked as a man joined them. She stared at him. He had a full beard and mustache. When the woman gave her a nasty look, Lisa said, "I do not want your man." She and Jimmy laughed as they walked by. She could hear him call her "honey" and swore he said, "I love you, too, Lisa." Jimmy looked at her and then at the man because he had also heard it.

When Devin placed his hand on her shoulder and said, "Is everything okay?" She smiled and ran into the water, "Come on, Jimmy, everything is great!" The couple faded into the darkness.

"This is how the family is going to live, from here on out we are together and we are happy." Eddie tapped the champagne glass with a knife as everyone said happy birthday to Baby Asia. She wiggled in her mother's arms. "Put her down," Devin said. "Come on, baby, come to Daddy." It was silent as she walked into her father's arms. "That's my girl," he said, kissing her on the cheek. Lisa snapped pictures and laughed as she grabbed a big chunk of cake. Eddie turned to answer the phone, while the Asia opened birthday gifts.

"It's a boy," Jason said as he passed out cigars.

"That is what I am talking about." Eddie gloated. "Another Jones man to carry the name."

Carolyn laughed and looked at Lisa, "Well, maybe Asia will never marry and that way she can carry the name also, however, I do want a girl," she said, "but I am happy and so is Jason."

ᔆ ᔆ

Lisa tapped at the computer. She looked up 'Urban Legends,' and went through all write-ups about the lost men, but she found conflicting stories. First, she read that the four men went into the cave, and then one story said that only one man went into the cave and the others ran in after they heard the man yell out for help, but he was not found, and later joined his friends saying that he had gotten lost. She scrolled down and it talked about a tribe that lived in the cave for hundreds of years.

She smiled when Eddie and Ellen doted on baby Corbin Mason. Ellen had loved but one man and now Eddie had charmed his way back into her life and shares a bed with her. It was to her surprise when Eddie asked if Devin and Jason would mind if he worked on his relationship with Ellen, and Ellen asked her if she should give it a try.

"He is all that I know," she said to her, "and I am so lonely." Against her better judgment, she said yes, but Eddie had been great with the family and also with Ellen. No other man had touched her and Eddie was eager to find out if Ellen had shared her bed with another man.

She laughed when she could see Devin and Asia riding the carousal. She looked down again and there were pictures of the leader of the tribe. She looked at the ring on his finger. It was one of a lion's head with little skulls and crossbones. She stood and looked at the trunk and it had the same symbols. If it belonged to the tribe, then how did Jeffrey get it or his ancestors? She looked at the picture of the man again and his eyes were like fire. She read to find that the ring had power and that the tribe worshiped the Devil. She looked at the robe and veils. They were just as the ones that Jeffrey and his family wore. She wanted to read to find out why they were against women, when she heard footsteps and looked up.

"Take a break," Lady Singleton said, "and enjoy your family." She and Lisa walked out where Skeet and Kandy sat, and enjoyed lemonade, and Devin and Asia rode the train. Jason and Lionel played football with Jimmy and Cody, while Willie and Judy took Justin to the store to purchase Cody a birthday present.

"Family," Eddie started, "we are taking a trip to Miami next week." He looked at Kay, "I hope you are up for this, because we want to make a vacation out of the trip. Willie and I have a business deal to negotiate, but the water is beautiful there and we want everyone to come."

Lisa got a strange feeling in her stomach, but she did not say a word. She sat and watched Asia eat with her father doting on her. She was safe and so was their daughter. She looked toward the street and stared when she thought she saw someone there. "A trip sounds good," she said. When she looked again, and there was nothing there.

CPSIA information can be obtained at www.ICGtesting.com
Printed in the USA
BVOW05s1247240216

437884BV00009B/266/P